THE HORNED ONES
CORNUCOPIA

CHRISTINE M. MORGAN

THE HORNED ONES
CORNUCOPIA
by
Christine Morgan
2nd Edition 2018
1st Edition Trade Paperback 2012
All Rights Reserved

Dark Recesses Press
657 Craigen Road
Newburgh, Ontario
Canada K0K 2S0

Copyright © 2012 Christine M. Morgan

Edited by Jodi Lee
Cover art by Stephanie Lostimolo
Cover by Jodi Lee © 2012

Library & Archives Canada ISBN
978-1-988837-08-6

ALSO BY CHRISTINE M. MORGAN

ACKNOWLEDGMENTS

With special thanks to the cavers, divers, explorers, photographers, documentarians, National Geographic, The Discovery Channel, and everyone else who braved those deep places so I didn't have to.

And to the staff, guides, park rangers and others who look after the Oregon Caves, Vancouver Island, Carlsbad, cave-tubing excursions in Belize, and all the deep places I did get to brave.

DEDICATION

For Becca, my constant inspiration... however dark and twisted things may get, you know I'll be right there with you. Hiding behind you sometimes, maybe, but right there with you!

TABLE OF CONTENTS

Chapter 1

The Squeezes

Crushing pressure.

Choking dust.

Bob couldn't get a breath. Each heartbeat brought sharp little jabs of pain, as if the overworked blood-sack in the middle of his chest poked against splintered bone-ends with every throb. His lungs burned. They wouldn't expand. His throat pinched to a pinhole. Grit filled his dry mouth.

Why did he let Lindsey goad him into this? It was her fault, *all* her fault. Her idea in the first place! He and Danny would have been perfectly happy to spend their entire vacation at the resort.

But, no.

Lindsey had to make them get out and *do* something. "A nice change of pace," she'd said. "Something besides sitting around all day."

Hadn't he taken Danny to that Fun-O-Rama place? Arcade games and bumper boats and miniature golf and air hockey? But no, that didn't count. Hardly active. Especially when canceled out by pizza and root beer and cotton candy.

This dark, creepy cave, on the other hand... that'd be educational. And good exercise.

Educational? Exercise? They were on vacation, for God's sake! They were supposed to be relaxing and having fun.

But, no.

So here they were.

Paying through the nose for the privilege of a luxury resort with three pools, tennis courts, horseback riding, a full gym, a salon, a spa, a shopping arcade, a movie theater, live nightly stage shows, four restaurants, and everything... but Lindsey still said it wasn't good enough. Not when, as she must've pointed out five times a day so far, he and Danny didn't even use the pools or gym or tennis courts, and the very thought of them horseback riding made Lindsey laugh herself into nearly wetting her pants.

So they'd driven way up in the hills and paid even more money to descend creaking, slippery, rickety metal stairs into a dank, rocky, claustrophobic hole in the ground.

Bob didn't want to go. Danny didn't want to go. Logically, they had her outnumbered two-to-one.

Logically.

Right. Like that had ever made a difference.

To think he'd paid for this, that he had walked right into this! He could have gone around The Squeezes. The guide had even said so. There was an alternate route, a shortcut. He could have gone around and been waiting for them when they emerged on the other side.

But, no.

Lindsey gave him that *look* when they came to the cramped, narrow maze of crevices. They all gave him that *look*. Sneering. Amused. Mocking. Pitying.

The guide – Sylvia – hid it well. She probably always had people chicken out and take the shortcut. Feeble old folks, or parents with scared kids like the other dad who took his boy around.

Or people like Bob.

So, of course, like a moron, he did the big-bluff-hearty-laugh and said that he could handle The Squeezes. Sure, no problem.

For a moment, there in the white beam of Sylvia's headlamp, he saw Danny's grimace of dismay and almost changed his mind. But he also saw, and far more vividly, Lindsey's patented mouth-tuck. She stifled that little scoffing sound she liked to make, but he heard it anyway. He heard it often enough. He heard it in his dreams sometimes.

Now here he was. Stuck. Wedged like a cork in a bottle.

Damned if it didn't feel like the walls were closing in on him. Grinding him. Pressing down with unbearable, rib-crunching force.

He couldn't see. His eyes bulged. His pupils dilated so much they hurt, trying to drink in light like he might have tried to draw a super-thick milkshake through a straw.

His trapped, frantic pulse pounded in his ears. He couldn't hear anything else over the rush-thunder of coursing blood. Just as well. At least he couldn't hear them laughing. Couldn't hear the oh-so-helpful suggestions.

Not that it mattered. He didn't need to hear them. His own traitor mind more than readily supplied the voice-overs.

"Better get the Jaws of Life!"

"Maybe if we rubbed butter on him…"

"Suck it in, Bob! Suck it in!"

"Bob? Blob, more like it."

"Anybody got a crowbar and a towing chain?"

"Tell him there's donuts at the other end."

Voices. Voices from his past. His brother Walt. His dad. Neighborhood kids. High school tormentors. Lindsey.

Lindsey most of all.

As if it had never occurred to him before. As if he couldn't read the numbers on the bathroom scale or see himself in the mirror.

He knew, all right? He knew!

He knew, and yet he'd still gone and tried to get his gut through The Squeezes. And now he was stuck.

Forget squeezed, too. Squashed!

The walls *were* closing in on him. Heavy. Grinding. Unbearable.

Like some diabolical booby-trap in an Indiana Jones movie, and he, Bob Kemp, was the booby. Like a steamroller, slowly mashing him into a big blubbery pancake. Like the giant grape-presses they'd seen on the winery tour Lindsey dragged them on a couple of days ago.

What were they *doing* out there? Did they think he was joking around? Did they not realize he was legitimately stuck here?

They had to notice. It wasn't as if he'd been able to slink to the back of the pack. There were people behind him. Waiting for their chance to wriggle through and behold the wonders of Ribbon Falls and the Mermaid's Pool, wonders that couldn't be seen by anyone who chickened out and took the alternate route.

At least Lindsey went first. She wasn't back there staring at his fat butt, and trying to resist the urge to give it a good kick. Bad enough that the attractive brunette and her teenage daughter were at the rear of the pack.

A warm runnel dribbled down his forehead and into his eye. Sweating. Sweating like the proverbial pig. If he could breathe, he was sure, he'd be able to smell his own ripe and rising odor.

"Constant cool subterranean temperatures make caves a welcome reprieve from the summer heat." According to Sylvia, the guide, during her pep talk at the start of the tour.

And it had been cool. Almost uncomfortably so, even for Bob and Danny, who wore jeans and sweatshirts instead of tank tops and shorts like some of their fellow spelunkers.

Now, though, he was hot. Steaming.

Maybe, if he sweated enough, he'd get sufficiently oiled to slip right out of this vise like the proverbial greased pig instead.

The liquid ran a slow oozing course along the side of his nose and onto his upper lip. He reflexively licked at it. Salty and thick. More like blood than sweat. His head hurt.

Had he banged his head?

Though Sylvia wore a hardhat – part of the tour guide uniform, like the khaki cargo pants and low-topped hiking boots – she'd assured the rest of them that there was no need for similar gear. They could rent hardhats in the gift shop if they wanted, but as long as they paid attention and ducked under the overhangs whenever she warned them with, "low bridge," they'd be okay.

Until now.

He'd scraped his hands raw, the ends of his fingers ten abraded stubs from trying to force himself through the gap.

His jeans were shredded at the knees, his shirt shredded at the elbows.

Hell, for that matter, his knees and his elbows felt shredded. His chest and stomach felt like someone had taken a belt sander to them.

A rasping wheeze, intended to be a shout, escaped his lungs.

Did they really not know he was caught? How could they *not* know?

He couldn't remember thrashing around, but he must have been struggling like crazy to tear himself up this bad.

Why weren't they calling in to him, telling him to stay calm, help was on the way? Why hadn't Sylvia come back for him, the glare of her miner's lamp shining a reassuring yellow beam through this blackness? Why couldn't he feel hands on his feet and legs, trying either to pull him out or push him onward?

Why couldn't he hear them? He couldn't hear anything at all, except for his own gasping, strangling breaths and his pulse hammering on his eardrums.

They hadn't forgotten he was with the group, had they? Even if the brunette and her daughter had decided to go around by the shortcut instead, surely Lindsey and Danny would be wondering what was keeping him. Surely Sylvia paused now and then to count noses and make sure none of her charges had gone astray.

He tried the shout again, but he couldn't inhale. His ribs were too compressed to let his lungs expand. When he willed himself to take the deepest breath he possibly could, he both felt and heard a crackling in his chest. Like the sensation of twisting a double-handful of bubble-wrap, like chewing on gravel.

When I get out of here... when they get me unstuck...

No more caves. He didn't care about the rest of the fabulous underground wonders and spectacles that Sylvia had promised them. He'd go back up to the surface by the quickest available route – they had emergency exits, he remembered – and he'd take Danny with him.

Let Lindsey finish the tour, if she wanted. Bob and Danny would get themselves some hotdogs and soft-serve cones from the snack bar, and sit in the shade while they waited. Then, when she got out, they'd pile into the car and return to the resort.

She'd harangue him, blame him for ruining their vacation. Just like she harangued him and blamed him for everything else.

He didn't care. The Lindsey he'd loved and married was gone. That Lindsey, the sweet, cheerful, chubby Lindsey who had enjoyed sitting on the couch with him, watching a movie while each of them spooned their way through a pint of Ben & Jerry's, that Lindsey was a thing of the past. A distant memory.

"I swear, it won't change anything between us," she'd said. "I'll still be the same person I've always been."

"I know you love me the way I am," she'd said. "Just like I love you the way you are, my big cuddly-bobbums."

"I need to do this for *me*, for my health," she'd said. "I don't expect you to do it, too."

"I would never dream of forcing my new lifestyle and habits on you and Danny," she'd said. "I won't be one of those women who punishes her whole family by putting them on a diet."

Sure. Right.

To start with.

He had been supportive, damn it! Shelled out the cash for diet plans, gym memberships, the treadmill, the exercise bike… encouraged her and not sabotaged her efforts… even though he'd been sure all along that she would give up –

What was taking so long?

His chest ached. His lungs felt full of cactus spines. Blood flowed down his face and into his mouth, mixing with the dust to form a gritty paste.

A sudden, new and horrible thought struck Bob.

Had they *left* him down here?

Abandoned him?

No. They wouldn't do that. They wouldn't just leave him here, trapped and alone in the dark.

Unless they'd had to go for help to get him out?

Someone would have told him. Someone would have stayed with him.

Wildly, Bob cast his mind back, trying to remember exactly what had happened. He remembered the others on the tour... the boastful mom with kids a little older than Danny, the newlyweds, the brunette and her daughter. He remembered Sylvia in her khaki pants and white polo shirt with the Cornucopia Caverns logo on the pocket.

He remembered the spiral staircase, its little wedge-shaped slices of steps made from metal grids so that if you looked down to make sure you were putting your feet in the right place, you could see the plummeting cave-shaft below. Mincing his way down with the rail clenched in a death-grip, sure that he would slip and tumble all the way to the bottom, taking everyone ahead of him along until they ended up in a heap with the fat guy on top.

The formations... Sylvia beaming her flashlight around... the rippling sheen of wet limestone... the glint and sparkle of crystals in the gloom... names like Snowy Dome and Thunder Rock and Sleeping Angel...

And then, around the middle of the tour, The Squeezes.

Lindsey giving him the *look*. Danny's grimace.

After that...?

Only a blur.

He was stuck, sure enough. No denying that.

But he couldn't remember *getting* stuck.

God, his head! There seemed to be a guy with a power drill working on the inside of his skull. He still couldn't breathe, couldn't get any air.

Eerie green-orange lights flitted across his vision. Bizarre cavern-dwelling insects, flying, glowing?

That... or he was hallucinating as he suffocated.

He managed a shallow gulp of air, then coughed.

Mistake.

Oh, it hurt. It hurt way deep in his chest. Spit bubbled up and splattered out of his mouth, slimy-ropy-sticky on his lips.

Spit? Or blood?

No. No, he wasn't coughing up blood. Not blood.

He was hurt, okay. Banged up pretty good. Probably some cracked ribs. Maybe even a couple of broken fingers or toes… a sprung knee… a greenstick fracture of the lower arm or leg. A bump on the head, a split scalp.

But not internal injuries. Not punctured lungs or anything that horrible.

They were going to get him out of here. He just had to stay cool and not panic. All right, so suppose he was a little more than simply stuck. Suppose a boulder had shifted or something. It was even possible he'd dislodged it himself, trying to cram his bulk through the tight passage. But it wasn't like they would just *leave* him here.

Someone would get help. Sylvia'd been wearing a walkie-talkie or cell phone or some other communication gadget on her belt. They might just have to call into town for emergency rescue equipment.

Yeah. The more he considered it – thinking as well as he could while trying to ignore the flitting orange-green dazzles and a gurgling sensation whenever he took another of those increasingly difficult sips of air – the more convinced he was that he'd dislodged a boulder. It had come down on him, and they'd need hydraulic jacks or something to lever it up so that they could slide him out.

The nearest town wasn't that far away. There were probably park rangers or paramedics even closer. On the way already! He'd lost such track of time that for all he knew, they could be pulling into the parking lot right now. Or just approaching The Squeezes.

It wouldn't be long now. They'd have him out of here and into a bright, clean ambulance. He'd be able to breathe again. The cut on his head would get stitched up, the blood would get sponged away, any broken bones would be splinted or cast. A few hours from now, he'd be propped up in a hospital bed. Crisp white sheets, a carafe of ginger ale, his aches and pains medicated into oblivion, *Wheel of Fortune* on the wall-mounted television. And a cute little candy striper would be bringing him a dish of rainbow sherbet with a cookie stuck on top.

The blissful vision was calming, almost calming enough to let Bob forget the troubling fact that he seemed to have been left alone down here.

If Sylvia had gone for help, she would have taken most of the others with her. Sure. There were kids on the tour, and kids didn't need to see a guy trapped under a giant rock. But *someone* would have stayed. Someone should be there to give him a few words of encouragement and support.

"Just hang in there, buddy. Help is on the way."

That was all he wanted to hear.

"We'll get you out of there."

Just a few simple words.

"You're going to be fine."

Or a pat on the hand, or ankle, or whatever part of him was sticking out from under this damn thing! Was that so much to ask? Something, anything so that he would know he wasn't alone here!

And how come nobody could turn on a fucking light?!

He knew there were lights! Sylvia had her headlamp and a flashlight. Lindsey kept a penlight on her keychain. Even in this era of non-smokers, some people still carried lighters.

"Hey," he tried to call.

A clotted, croaking bullfrog noise burbled out of him. More fluid flooded his mouth, and this time there was no telling himself it was only spit.

Ambulance. Hospital bed. Medication. *Wheel of Fortune*. Candy striper. Rainbow sherbet with a cookie on top.

Bob clung to that image, tried to immerse himself in it. He concentrated. Focused his will. Tried to blot out the fear that made him want to flail and scream. Not that he *could* flail and scream. He couldn't move. Couldn't breathe.

Don't think about that.

Any second now, they'd have him out of here.

No more caves. Ever again.

From now on, he would vacation however he pleased, and if Lindsey didn't like it, fine. She could go hiking and camping and scuba-diving and hang-gliding. He would go on cruise ships and air-conditioned bus rides, and anyplace else that he never had to worry about wearing a swimsuit or taking off his shirt.

The vision of endless buffets and lavish restaurants calmed him even more. Bob almost smiled. His racing-rushing-roaring pulse slowed.

Then, finally, it dawned on him that he could hear. Only a little, but he could hear other people nearby.

He hadn't been abandoned alone in the dark after all!

"Hello?" he tried to say.

It also came out a burbling bullfrog croak.

He heard a low, pained moan. And sobs. Someone sobbing. Muffled. Sounding very far away. But sobs. Someone crying.

Crying?

A kid?

"Danny?"

A thick, viscous bubble burst on his lips as he mumbled his son's name.

The sobs went on, uninterrupted. He heard another moan, a gasping and terrible noise dredged up from the depths of someone's agony.

Fresh horror swarmed over Bob. God… what if he wasn't the only one who'd been hurt? What if he wasn't the only one trapped? What if he'd brought down a whole section of tunnel ceiling and buried everybody?

Danny had been just ahead of him, hadn't he? Following Lindsey?

The brunette woman and her daughter behind him… had it been one of them he heard moaning?

He groped blindly, as far as he could reach. His fingertips – the churned masses of hamburger that had replaced his fingertips – pawed and stumbled over loose rocks. He touched something curved and cool and plastic. It wobbled and sloshed. Liquid. Lindsey's water bottle?

A little further on, his searching hand found a shoe. A small shoe. The foot within it was motionless.

Danny's shoe? Danny's foot?

He couldn't tell.

A sneaker. Danny had been wearing sneakers. But so had the other kids, hadn't they?

"Dad?" came a distant, plaintive voice from somewhere in the blackness. "Daddy! Where are you?"

A young voice… Danny's voice? He couldn't tell that, either.

Had he actually been thinking it felt warm in here? Steaming and hot? It was freezing. Damp. Clammy. His sweat chilled on his body like a layer of slush. Shivers shuddered through him.

The foot still didn't move. He felt higher, found a bunched-up sock and then flesh. Cold, stiff, waxy-feeling flesh.

"Somebody? Anybody, please!" wailed the distant voice. "Help me!"

Orange-green flashes and flickers spun, whirled, danced behind Bob's eyes. He closed them. It didn't matter. He could still see the flashes, the flickers, the spinning-whirling-dancing.

Nearby, he heard another moan, and a fitful scratching as of fingernails weakly scrabbling. From further away, tearful, the voice called out again.

"Please! Isn't anybody there?"

Bob took a breath to answer. When he did, he felt a bursting pop from somewhere deep inside. Like an overfilled water balloon jabbed with a pin.

All at once, the orange-green flickers winked out.

So did the sounds.

There was only the blackness, and silence, and Bob sank into it like a rock dropped down a well.

CHAPTER 2
Goblintown

Didi knew right away that she still lived.

Just her luck.

She knew because of the pain. Because of the hopeless emptiness of soul.

And because, apropos as it might seem, she was pretty sure that the afterlife wouldn't actually feature the music of Evanescence.

The music was coming from her iPod, anyway, and not from any external, infernal speaker system. The earbuds plugged squarely into both ears filled her head with haunting chords.

Still the pain, the same old pain. Plus more pain. *New* pain.

Interesting.

Different.

A kind she hadn't felt before.

Not the clean, pure, steely-silver pain of a razor. That gave sweet release, like lancing an infected boil to let out the festering pus.

This new pain was big and blunt and gross and heavy. Uncouth pain. Rude pain. Imprecise, imperfect. Rough.

When she cut herself, when she made the neat and even slices in her skin, she felt as if she honed her concentration to a laser-fine point, centering it until nothing else mattered and she could to forget the greater melancholy ache that was her entire meaningless life. That pain cleared her mind.

This new pain, this crude other pain, wasn't like that at all. It blurred her concentration, diffused it. Muffled the melancholy, smothered it.

The razor was under her control.

This wasn't.

She had not done this to herself.

Other forces did it to her.

Like always. Like everything and everyone else, trying to dominate her and direct her and bend her to some other will. The petty, manipulative will of parents, teachers, schoolmates, society. The callous will of fate and circumstance and random chance.

So, with as much cool deliberation as she could muster, she rejected it.

The pain didn't vanish. But she overcame it, rose above it, and refused to let it rule her.

As Evanescence gave way to Rasputina, she opened her eyes.

Darkness.

Complete, enfolding, enclosing darkness.

Not the open star-specked vast blue-black forever of space. Not the storm-shrouded grey-black night sky of wind-tossed clouds.

Not the velvety-black shadows of her bedroom, which despite its blinds and drapes always had at least a little illumination. Ruby, amber, emerald and sapphire... the steady glowing jewels of her computer, her stereo, her phone charger, her electronic connections and escapes.

Not the vein-tinged darkness of closed eyelids, where galvanic nerve impulses sent jittering arcs of colors for which there were no names.

Total darkness.

Absolute black.

And pain. That crude-rude-intrusive pain. Pawing at her like a horny boy, groping and slobbering and telling her lies about how good it would be. When it was only ever tedious, uncomfortable and nasty, never worth the hassle.

Rocks?

Rocks under her. A lumpy, poky, uneven mound of them. They shifted and slid as she moved. Others covered her legs and feet. She sat up and shoved-kicked them off. She sensed them rolling, bouncing away.

Rocks.

Every inch of her body felt battered and bruised. Her palms, knees, hip and chin stung and smarted with scrapes. But nothing seemed broken. She wasn't badly hurt. She wasn't going to die.

Not right away, at least.

"Shit," she whispered.

Reaching up, she felt around carefully above her head to make sure she wasn't about to wham her face into anything. She pushed herself into a sitting position on her bed of rocks.

Her eyes had not adjusted, because there was nothing to adjust *to*. The darkness was total.

Didi plucked out the earbuds. Wails, groans and babbling voices replaced Rasputina.

The cave. The tour.

Dad and The Bitch and The Brat and Grumpy-Jack.

The whole drive up, she'd slouched in the back seat, music turned loud, arms crossed or hands busy texting her friends. Sullen. Surly. Silent. Ignoring every attempt to engage her in conversation, except to protest yet again that the last thing she wanted to do was visit some stupid, boring tourist attraction. She'd suffered in weary disdain. She'd rolled her eyes whenever Dad and The Bitch gushed about how *fun* this was, how *fascinating*, and how nice that they could all get out and do something so neat together, as a family.

Barf.

Double-barf.

And of course The Brat had started whining as soon as they got out of the car. He wanted a hotdog from the snack bar. He wanted to go to the gift shop. He wanted peanuts to feed the chipmunks. Like any chipmunk was going to let the little boogersnot get close.

Dad promised to buy him a souvenir after the tour. "If you're a good boy, Sam. You've got to be a good boy and walk the whole way, and then when we're done, we'll go over to the gift shop and you can pick something out."

A good boy. Walk.

Sure.

They hadn't even started their tour before he chased some little girl around with a bug on a stick, making her scream. They hadn't been on the tour five minutes when he pitched a tantrum about wanting to go to the gift shop. Ten minutes after that, he'd complained his way into Dad carrying him.

Yet, she knew, he'd still get a souvenir. *And* a hotdog. And anything else he wanted, because he was a spoiled-rotten boogersnot just like his mother, and Didi wished they would both be run over by a bus.

She could hear him howling in the dark.

Not hurt-howling. Scared, and indignant, and mad.

Unmistakably him. She'd heard him howl like that ever since the day he was born. Four solid years. You'd think by now someone would have swatted him. It might even have helped. It might even have shut him the hell up.

Though, really, she figured it'd just make him yell louder.

Didi fished her iPod out of her pocket. Its screen was normally a dim glow, but in this pitch-blackness, it cast a glare that made her squint.

"Hey. Hey, who's that?"

Someone crawled toward her over the rubble of rocks. Didi swung the iPod around until she got a glimpse of their tour guide, his face grimy and streaked with blood. Jason, or Justin, or something. Not that much older than Didi. Five or six years. A college guy. Cute in a rugged, outdoorsy sort of way. More Owen Wilson than Cameron Mack. But cute.

If you liked that sort of thing. Which the moms on the tour, The Bitch included, certainly seemed to. All fawning and flirty, embarrassing themselves. Twice his age at least. Cougar City, California.

Jason-or-Justin, not so cute now with the grime and the blood, with his eyes shocked. He peered at her, blinked, but recognized her as about the only other one on the tour between twelve and thirty. Plus the only one with facial piercings and a parody 'Hell Kitty' tee shirt.

"You okay?" he asked.

Didi nodded. "I think so. What happened?"

"Cave-in or something."

She looked at him. "But you just said–"

"Yeah." His lips twisted in a rueful grin that looked more like he was peeling off a sticky Band-Aid.

One of the moms – not a MILF by any stretch of the imagination, but one who sure seemed to think she was – had wondered out loud in an anxious tone what they'd do if there was an earthquake and the roof fell in on them. And Jason-or-Justin, with a warm laugh, told them all that the Cornucopia Caverns had been like this for thousands and thousands of years. If anything was going to collapse, he'd assured them, it would already have done it a long time ago.

"Famous last words, huh?" Didi said.

"You're not hurt?"

"Bumps and scrapes, no big."

"You've got a light." He nodded toward the iPod.

"So did you. Where's your helmet?"

"Lost it."

"Didn't you have a flashlight on your belt?"

"Broken. My walkie-talkie, too. Got a cell phone?"

Didi hoisted a scornful eyebrow at him. "Of *course*."

She'd slung the long black leather strap of her purse across her body from shoulder to hip. The pallid features of Jack Skellington caught the iPod's glow with a ghostly luminescence. She unclipped the silver clasp, opened the purse, and rummaged.

"Though it probably won't work," Justin-or-Jason said. "We never get reception down here." He raised his voice. "Everybody hold on. Stay where you are, okay?"

Replies clamored from the dark around them. And, of course, The Brat kept howling. Didi heard another kid crying too, one of the little girls, in great gasping watery sobs that sounded a lot more genuine than the noises The Brat made.

"We're screwed," Didi said, looking at her phone. No bars at all. Not even a sliver of one.

"Didi?" her dad called, his voice shaky. "Didi, is that you? Where's Sam? Do you see him?"

"Can't you *hear* him?"

"Sam! Sam, it's Daddy. Sam! Stop yelling, son. Daddy's coming."

If he heard Dad at all, The Brat just knew that he now had someone's attention, and *really* started hollering. Dad blundered off in that direction, calling The Brat's and The Bitch's names as he went.

"Dad!" she shouted after him. "Where's Grumpy-Jack? Is he okay?"

"Help me, okay?" Jason-or-Justin said to Didi. "Some people are hurt. You're here with your family, right? Your grandpa, your mom?"

"She's not my mom," Didi said.

"Just help me get everybody together. Didi, yeah?"

"And you're... Justin?"

"Yeah. Come on. Get up."

She let him help her to her feet on the mound of shifty-slidy rocks, thankful that her boots had thick waffle-soles of black rubber. She thought of The Bitch, who'd insisted on wearing those stupid high-heeled rattan-and-cork sandals with the thin straps, and almost smiled.

Flame flared in the black. A cigarette lighter. It threw yellow light and wavering shadow over the features of a forty-something man with an ugly, crusted cut on his cheekbone. He wore a Catalina Island sweatshirt, Dockers and running shoes. He knelt, with one arm gimped up and held close to his chest, making him look like an injured dog trying to hobble along on three legs.

The other dad. The one in charge of both other moms and a whole flock of little girls. Didi remembered them from the start of the tour, all standing around with their tickets in hand, everyone all happy and looking ready for some big exciting adventure. The two moms almost had to be sisters. The girls – there were really only four of them, but when they'd been scampering around and chattering, it had seemed like there were three times that many – looked like their moms and looked like each other. Cousins or something. Slim, tanned blondies. California beach girls in the making. Not dressed for the cool damp of a cave. They wore a lot of pink, a lot of floral print, a lot of tee shirts with pictures of Disney princesses. Flip-flops. Pigtails. Bright plastic barrettes. Their laughter like chimes of giggling gold.

And had they ever come to a quick halt when they'd gotten an eyeful of Didi?

The sudden appearance of a chainsaw-waving maniac biker couldn't have caused a bigger reaction.

Like they'd never seen a Goth before.

Like Didi's kind didn't exist in their Barbie Dream House reality. In that world, people didn't have skin that was hardly ever touched by the sun. People didn't have hair the deep purple hue of African violets, and glossy black fingernails, and pants with chains and leather straps.

Right now, though, Mr. Malibu Ken in his Catalina Island sweatshirt hardly seemed to notice or care.

"Val... Tiffy... Amber..."

"We'll find them," Justin said. "Mr... Brewster?"

"Stephen. Stephen Brewster."

"Sure. Stephen. Are you hurt?"

He blinked. "My wrist. My head. But... my wife, my sister-in-law, the girls!"

Didi heard The Brat again, hiccupping and blatting as Dad jabbered nonsense at him. Telling him not to worry, that they were fine, that in a little while they'd be out of the yucky dark cave and then they'd all go get ice cream. Wouldn't that be nice? Sam could have two scoops. Three, if he wanted.

A blonde girl stumbled into the unsteady circle of light, filthy and scratched up, missing both flip-flops and one barrette so that half her hair hung in wild straggles. Her flowered shorts and Cinderella shirt were torn. She clutched a stuffed bunny. Tears poured down her face, cutting clean trails in the dirt.

"Amberlyn!" Stephen Brewster shoved the lighter at Justin, then swept the girl into the crook of his good arm. "Amberlyn, baby, baby, it's okay, you're okay."

"Tiffy's gone, Daddy, Tiffy's gone!"

"I see something," Justin said. He turned, raising the lighter and striking a fresh flame. "It looks... oh, damn."

Didi hurried after him and saw what he must have seen. Legs and one outflung hand, protruding from beneath a pile of rocks. Scuffed white deck shoes. Blue capri pants. A wristwatch, the crystal smashed. A gold wedding band. Nice manicure. A few clumps of blond hair, matted with blood.

"She's dead," Didi said.

"No, look! She's moving!" Justin pointed. "See?"

With his free hand, he began sweeping away the rubble. Didi bit her lip and shook her head, but knelt to help. They moved rocks, moved rocks, exposing more of the woman's body. A fanny pack. A dented but not ruptured plastic bottle... Snapple, green tea flavored, half full.

A little girl. Huddled underneath the woman. The girl The Brat had been chasing, taunting with the bug on the stick. Yellow and pink striped sundress over stretchy pink tights, hair in pigtails held by pink scrunchies with fake flowers. Clinging to a doll in a princess outfit.

It wasn't the woman moving at all. The girl whimpered and squirmed, trying to get out from under the limp, slack deadweight.

"She saved her," Justin said. "Covered her when it happened."

Together, he and Didi hauled the body off and lifted up the trembling, terrified child. At first, she didn't want to leave, then she wrapped herself around Didi and clung with panicky tightness.

"Hey!" Stephen called. "We need the light over here. My wife's hurt. I think she's got a broken leg!"

"Take her back," Justin said. "I'll keep searching."

"Okay." Didi staggered to where they'd left Stephen and Amberlyn.

"And when we get home," Dad said, rocking The Brat, "we'll get that puppy you've been wanting, how does that sound? A puppy of your very own."

Amberlyn swayed on bare feet, hugging her rabbit. Her huge blue eyes gazed blankly at her father, hunkered down beside the other mom. Didi hissed breath in through her teeth when she got a look. One of the woman's legs lay bent at an angle no leg was meant to go.

"Take it easy, Val," Stephen said.

She moaned. Didi guessed that the bones below the knee must have snapped like breadsticks. There didn't seem to be any jagged ends poking out, but the skin was taut and tented. A lot of swelling and dark discoloration, too.

"Here," Didi said, setting her down by the other girl. "This your sis?"

They moved together, drawn like iron filings by a magnet, and put their arms around each other.

"My cousin," Amberlyn said. "Angelina."

"You take care of her for a while, can you do that?"

Amberlyn nodded. "Where's Tiffy and Britney?"

"I don't know. We're still looking."

"We have to get out of here," Stephen said. "Val needs a doctor. We have to find Frieda and the girls. Chad must be going crazy up there. He didn't come on the tour with us. Had work to do. Was it an earthquake, do you think? Was it the Big One?"

Didi shrugged and shook her head helplessly.

"Then what happened? What the hell happened?"

Again, she could only shake her head. They'd gone through a long tunnel with thousands of delicate-looking formations on the ceiling. Tiny hollow tubes of calcite, hanging down. Soda straws, according to Justin, and that part of the cave was called the Fairy Forest. She remembered how the little girls had loved hearing that.

Then they'd come to a much larger room, where the limestone formed a bizarre landscape that looked like hills covered with mushrooms, and castles made from dribbling wet sand. Discreetly-positioned light fixtures gave the whole thing a magical sheen, glistening with moisture and minerals. Rivulets, pools, trickles and creeks meandered all around.

"Goblintown," Justin had said. And yes, it was easy to imagine hosts of cunning imps and goblins living there.

He'd told them to go ahead and wander through, but asked that they stay on the marked path and not touch anything. Oils from human skin damaged the rock. Later, he said, there would be a formation that they'd be allowed to feel.

That was all she could remember. Goblintown, and then waking to Evanescence and the awareness that she was still alive.

She took a few steps back and tried to shine her meager light as far as it would reach. Which wasn't very far... but far enough.

Didi bit her lower lip. Hard. Drawing blood. The pain was sharp, sweet, intimate, immediate.

A hand fell on her shoulder. She jumped.

"Hey," Justin said. "Over here. I found one of the girls, but I can't get to her. I need your... Didi? What's the matter?"

"It's Grumpy-Jack," she said, in a voice that barely sounded like her own. "My grandfather. He's dead."

CHAPTER 3
Echo Gorge

It might be the only chance he'd get to kill the bastard.

But if he did, they might *all* die.

Griff didn't want to die. Not yet. Not until he'd done what he came here to do.

He stood in the echoing, noisy dark with the flashlight jittering in his grasp.

"Hold it steady," Dawes had said, thrusting it at him. Without a hint of anything to indicate he knew Griff, remembered him. "While I climb down to her, you hold that steady."

But his hands shook from adrenaline. The beam twitched, stuttering across stone in a strobe effect. Stuttering across the girl in the white top and red shorts. Her screams rebounded from the walls until it seemed like there were a hundred girls, a thousand, the cries so shrill and piercing that if there'd been bats in the caverns, those bats might have dropped stunned from the air.

"I said hold the fucking thing steady!" Dawes again, growling up from below.

As vulnerable as he was ever going to be. Clinging to the chasm wall. No rope, no nothing. Just his big hands hooked into cracks, and the toes of his boots feeling their way from one foothold to another. *If he slipped...*

All Dawes would have to do was slip. Lose his hold. He could have been a stunt double for Vin Diesel, all bulging muscles and gleaming shaved head, a hard iron jaw and cold don't-fuck-with-me eyes. None of that would matter against gravity, or against the churning river waiting at the bottom.

"Steady, he said! Just give it to me!" The Asian guy, slim and intense and still somehow neat despite everything, snatched the flashlight from Griff. He shined the beam down at Dawes, as the big man made his precarious way toward the ledge where the girl – the Asian guy's kid sister – held on for dear life.

Straight black hair framed an oval face dominated by enormous, frightened eyes. Eleven, maybe twelve. Tiny. Slender. Slow, spreading zigzags fractured the thin slab of jutting rock.

How she'd landed on it, and caught hold, had to be some kind of miracle. Or blind, dumb luck.

The old lady hadn't been so lucky, or didn't rate a miracle. She, a hale but hefty, ample-figured grandmotherly type in a lime-colored velour track suit and sneakers, hit headfirst. Griff saw her head wrench violently on her neck, saw her loose and boneless limbs flop, saw a chunk of rock break away and plunge with her into the chasm. Gone.

Her husband – stocky, ruddy, white-haired – knew there was no hope. But it didn't stop him from shouting her name, and fighting fruitlessly against the others as they tried to hold him back.

"Betty! No! Betty!"

Like Griff, all those years ago, when they told him about Kristin. Even seeing the proof with his own eyes, her poor dead body, he hadn't wanted to believe it. He'd shaken her, and held her, and rocked her back and forth in his arms as his tears fell. If he only *wanted* it hard enough, time would reverse and she'd be okay again.

Time didn't reverse. Terrible things didn't unhappen. Events couldn't be changed. Blame God... blame Fate... blame the forces of nature. Whatever. It made no difference. You couldn't get revenge on God any more than you could get revenge on a hurricane, tornado, earthquake.

Revenge was for people.

People could be held accountable for their actions. People could be blamed. Things still couldn't be changed, couldn't be made to *un*happen. But people could be made to pay for what they did.

Revenge… and justice.

Justice.

Griff swallowed a bile-bitter laugh.

Fucking *justice*.

"Betty!"

"Grandpa, she's gone!" The boy, tall and gangly, trying too hard to be cool in his baggy pants and untied sneakers, held the old man back from the edge. The redhead, the Asian guy's girl, helped him.

Dawes inched lower. Tattoos rippled as muscles flexed beneath his skin. Shoulders, back, chest, abs. He was shirtless, of course, having stripped it off to tie a tourniquet around an unconscious man's spurting stump of an arm. Quite the hero, our man Dawes. So gleaming with sweat in the backsplash of light that he might have been oiled before his big rescue scene.

The Asian fixed the light on the girl. "Kimmy, stay still. Don't move. He's coming to get you."

"What about us?" asked the man on the far side of the chasm, the one whose curious little boy had wanted to stop and inspect every formation. "We can't get across!"

"Stay back," Dawes said.

"But–"

"I said stay the fuck back! Unless you want to fall in and take your son with you."

The big hero. That was how he would come out of this. Brave Wallace Dawes, saving all these folks from certain disaster. Bruce Willis, eat your heart out. No one would care what he'd done in the past. If anything, it'd make the story even better. The press would have a field day. Ex-con redeems himself.

All Griff had to do was pick up a rock.

No shortage of rocks. When the cave lurched with that first shuddering, violent jolt, stalactites crashed from the ceiling and chunks tumbled down from the walls. Stalagmites shattered. Limestone formations millions of years in the making smashed across the uneven floor like pottery shards.

Pick up a rock.

Step to the edge.

Throw the rock.

Even if he failed to hit Dawes, a near miss would startle him into losing his grip. He'd fall. Fall like Betty had done, tumbling end over end, vanishing into the seething cataract.

No more Dawes.

Justice or revenge or whatever the hell you wanted to call it. Served at last.

Except…

He didn't want Dawes to just fall. That was too easy, too unsatisfying. Besides…

Griff had seen plenty of movies, read plenty of thrillers. He knew how this worked. Villain falls from a high place into a rushing river? Almost a sure bet that the guy would survive, and come back meaner than ever.

If he *did* hit Dawes, if his hurled missile was a perfect head-shot resulting in a busted skull and a spray of brains, that'd be *marginally* satisfying.

Not as satisfying as shooting the son of a bitch.

Dawes would be dead before his fingers uncurled from the stone and his body peeled back to topple into the dark. No chance of him washing up somewhere downstream, alive and hell-bent on payback.

If he shot Dawes, the girl – Kimmy – was as good as dead too. He could see her down there, bathed in the flashlight's beam, her face a carved ivory mask of terror.

She was probably good as dead anyway. Dawes, for all his action-hero looks and tough-guy determination, still might fall, or not be able to hold onto her, or fall with her. He'd end up being hailed a hero anyway.

More of the ledge split off with a sound like a cracking china plate. Kimmy screamed again. One of her feet – clad in a white sneaker that Griff first thought was polka-dotted, then realized was speckled with blood from her skinned knees and scraped shins – dropped over. She scooted backwards on her butt and almost went off the other edge.

"Kimmy, hold still, hold still!" Her brother nearly shrieked the words, but he kept the flashlight steady.

"I don't want to die!"

"You're not going to die," Dawes said.

"Oh, God." The redhead clapped hands over her mouth, muffling her words. "It's too far." She let go of the old man, leaving the teenager on his own in trying to restrain him.

"We need a rope," the Asian guy said.

"Yes, a rope!" The man across the chasm, standing well back from the edge as Dawes had ordered, held his son in his arms. "If we had a rope, maybe R.J. and I could get over to you."

"It's breaking more," Kimmy wailed from the ledge. "Makoto, it's breaking!"

"Hold still, Kim," Dawes said. "Can you grab my foot?"

"You said hold still."

"Stretch and grab my foot."

"What if we tore some shirts into strips," the teenager said, "and tied them all together? It wouldn't be very strong, but she's light. We could pull her up."

The redhead looked down at herself, at her tattered blouse, and ripped it away without a second thought.

"Kim, listen to me," Dawes said. "I'm going to lower my belt. I want you to wrap it around your wrist and hold on tight with both hands, okay?"

"Wait!" Makoto said, unbuttoning and untucking. "We're making a rope."

"Give me your shirts," the redhead said. She'd already spun-twisted the rags of her blouse.

"There's no time," Dawes said. He had both boots braced in footholds, and one hand clamped into a crevice.

Dawes would have to save the girl. Dawes would be the action-movie super-stud. Griff saw it perfectly in his mind. The instant she caught the belt, the ledge would crumble out from under her. She'd scream and swing and kick, dangling in midair. Dawes, the cords standing out in his neck, biceps bunching, sweat beading on his forehead and shaved scalp, would give a manly grunt of effort from between his clenched teeth. Maybe his feet would lose their purchase and he'd have to support their entire combined weight by one hand. Straining. Doing an arm-curl until she could clamber onto his broad back and wrap her little arms around his thick bull neck.

Then, a millisecond before his fingers gave out, he'd catch on with the other hand and force himself up, inch by excruciating inch, until the rest of them could reach down and help drag them to safety. A sobbing, grateful Kimmy would hug Dawes. Everyone else would crowd around him, clapping him on the back and shoulder, telling him how amazing he was.

What a hero.

The bastard.

Griff drew the gun from his pack. The flashlight's backsplash caught cold, dark metal in an ebony shine.

Dawes leaned down as far as he could. The end of the belt was about a yard above the girl, but she was either too afraid to reach for it, or unwilling to let go of her dubious clutch on the wall.

"I won't drop you, Kim," Dawes said.

"What if I can't hold on?"

"You can. Wrap it around your wrists like I told you, and I'll lift you up."

"Do what he says, Kimmy. He–" Makoto raised his head from the rope. He saw the gun. Griff saw him see it.

"Dawes," Griff said, aiming.

"He's got a gun!" gasped the redhead.

Dawes craned his neck to look up. There was no incomprehension in his flat reptile gaze. No confusion, no fear. If he had questions, they didn't show.

Similarly, there was no look of guilt. If he knew what this was about, it didn't show either. Or he didn't care.

"You out of your fucking mind?" The gangly kid's voice squeaked like he was twelve instead of seventeen or so.

Griff fired. Once. Twice. Three. Four. Squeezing the trigger again and again and again, the gun bucking in his hand. Deafening reports. Echoes boomed and rolled like thunder through the cave. The first shot slammed into Dawes' back, driving him against the rough stone.

Three years of grief and rage surged up inside Griff like a geyser. Freed at last. All this time kept bottled up, a boiling poison in his heart. Waiting for this. Waiting for justice, for revenge, for satisfaction.

Makoto and the redhead and the teenager grappled with him, trying to wrench the gun out of his hands and tackle him to the ground.

His fist, still curled around the gun's grip, swung around hard and fast. The barrel smashed Makoto in the mouth. Teeth exploded like porcelain plates in a shooting gallery, and he reeled back. The teenager jumped on Griff and knocked him flat. Griff heaved his entire body with a strength he hadn't even suspected he possessed. The boy flipped into the air like a tiddlywink. He landed with a dazed outrush of breath, tried to roll over and scramble upright, and blundered straight over the edge.

The redhead shrieked. Then a brutal hammer-blow met the side of Griff's head. A brilliance erupted inside his skull. His last thought was that it sounded like a bowling ball, hitting a perfect strike.

CHAPTER 4
Rock Garden

Chad Hinkel paused, fingers on the laptop's keyboard. With a faint frown, he took a surreptitious glance around the picnic area.

If no one else reacted, if it had just been a too-large, too-fast truck going by or the distant skyward rumble of a jet engine, *he* didn't want to be the one to jump up and ask, "What was that? Did anybody else feel that?"

He'd look like an ass.

Vacationers' vehicles crowded the asphalt parking lot: cars, minivans, SUVs, motor homes, even a trio of motorcycles canted over on their kickstands like insolent black-and-chrome gang members.

Nice cool cave plus hot California summer day evidently equaled a brisker business than he would have thought.

People milled about the gift shop, rest rooms and snack bar. Several picnic tables were occupied. A college-age couple sat unwrapping sandwiches on a blanket spread under a tree. Kids ran around, playing and shouting, throwing food to the wildlife or chasing them or both. A sunburned family posed grinning in front of a rock garden sculpture while one of the bikers, shaggy as a Viking, fussed with their camera in furrowed-brow perplexity.

Ready to dismiss the tremor as no big deal, Chad's frown deepened when he realized that he wasn't the only one who'd paused. He saw books and hotdogs lowered, saw heads turning, saw frowns similar to his own on more than a few faces.

The college girl on the blanket asked her boyfriend, "What was that?"

The sunburned dad, wearing a tacky-tourist Hawaiian shirt, called out, "Did anybody else feel that?"

"Earthquake," one of the other bikers, whip-thin and sharp-featured, said.

"Was not," someone else said. "I've lived in earthquake country all my life. I think I'd know."

A young mother, burdened with fold-up stroller and bulky diaper bag, paled and clutched her baby to her bosom. "Earthquake?"

"Easy does it, folks." A large man who could have passed for a retired dockworker stepped out the snack bar's side door. He had iron-grey hair in a crewcut, a drinker's nose, and Navy tattoos inked in blue on his thick arms. "No fault lines near here. No quakes."

"Bullshit," the thin biker said. "This is fuckin' California. Nothing but fault lines."

"Joe?" An apple-cheeked fiftyish woman leaned out the gift shop's ticket booth window. "Joe, what was that?"

"What if it was a cave-in?" the college girl cried.

A dozen voices rose at once. Shock, horror, denial. The young mother rushed over to the crewcut man, babbling about her husband and son still being down there. Parents corralled their kids. Some people shifted nervously from foot to foot, regarding the ground under them as if they expected it to suddenly split into great yawning black fissures or erupt in boiling lava. Others scanned the sky, as if waiting for an asteroid to streak down from space and pulverize them where they stood.

Chad slowly closed the laptop and got up.

Inside a motor home, a small dog began yapping like crazy. A large scruffy mutt tethered on a chain near the trailer answered with booming baying woofs.

"See?" The thin biker gestured toward the mutt. "Animals can sense quakes."

"It wasn't a damn quake," the earthquake-country-all-my-life man protested.

"Besides, that's never been proven," a pedantic banker-type said.

"Even if it was, they sense it *beforehand*," said the college boy. "I think Debbi's right. I think it was a cave-in."

"Now, wait just a second!" Joe raised his arms in a wide vee, palms turned out. "Let's not everybody panic."

"My husband's down there!" the young mother repeated. "My little boy! We were on the tour but Megan kept crying, so I brought her out. What if they're trapped?"

"Mine, too," Chad heard himself say. "My wife, our girls, my sister-in-law and her family."

Again, there was a rising commotion of voices. A pretty teenage girl, wide-eyed and breathless, ponytail bouncing, ran over from the gift shop. Like Joe and his wife, she wore khakis and a white polo shirt with the tour-cave logo. Chad only heard snippets of what she was saying to Joe, whom she addressed as 'Dad.' But he got the gist of it.

Frieda and Val had come up with the idea of taking their combined families on vacation, renting an RV and going for a long leisurely sight-seeing road trip. They'd wanted to do more than just hop from one theme park to another. They wanted to give the girls a variety of experiences. More than just Sea World and Disneyland, though of course those had been priorities.

On a travel and tourism website, Chad had discovered the extensive caves and caverns that central California offered. Some were only for the die-hard spelunkers and adrenaline junkies, requiring climbing gear and harnesses. Others, like Cornucopia, were family-friendly. Level paths, railings, adequate lighting, emergency exits, and nothing scarier than the occasional steep metal staircase. Enough to let the girls feel like they were doing something brave and adventuresome, while still being perfectly safe.

Provided that there wasn't an earthquake or a cave-in or something.

Now Chad heard the pretty teenager telling her dad that something had gone wrong with the fuses and she was fairly sure the power in the caves had gone out. She'd heard a lot of rumbling and crashing, and she'd felt everything shake.

"How many tours?" Joe asked his wife.

"Three," she said. "The one-thirties hadn't come out yet, the two-thirties just went in about fifteen minutes ago, and the two-o'clocks would have been about halfway."

"They're all right, though," Chad said. "Aren't they? I mean, they can get out with no trouble. Right?" Not waiting for an answer, he pushed past the crowd and headed for the entrance, a rustic gate of distressed wooden beams and a split-rail fence.

"Mister!" Joe's large, callused hand fell on his shoulder. "Hold on a minute."

Frieda, Val, Stephen and the girls had gone in at 2:30. The entire trip was supposed to take an hour and a half, so they wouldn't have gotten far. Barely into the caves at all. He was sure they'd be emerging any second.

But no one emerged.

This close, he could feel the chilly draft issuing from the depths. It smelled earthy and damp and mineral-rich, like well-water.

And he... he could hear...

"Shut up back there!" he shouted at the others.

For a wonder, they actually did. Even Joe ceased his objections, though he still had Chad by the shoulder. All of them listened, silent and intent.

Faint, far, and distorted... floating... dreamlike... came voices. Indistinct words. Screams. Calls for help.

"We have to go in for them," Chad said, whirling on Joe.

"We will. We will. Hold your horses."

"We have to go in there *now*!"

"Chloe," Joe said. "Where's Ed and Pete? And where's your brother?"

"I... I..." the teenager stammered.

"Ed took Lily into town," Joe's wife said, cell phone pressed to her ear. "She had a doctor's appointment today, remember? Pete brought out the one-o'clocks and then said he needed to..." She nodded toward the rest rooms. "Read the paper for a while."

"And Colin?"

"Went off someplace with Brandon, I think. Isn't that right, Chloe?"

"For Christ's sake!" Chad yelled. "There are people in that cave and they need help and you're standing around playing Where Are They Now? I'm going in there."

"Me, too," declared the shaggy Viking biker.

"Hell yeah," said his thin buddy.

The third biker, who had an extravagance of beard and an extravagance of gut, eyeballed the cave with doubtful apprehension. "Bear, Snake, you sure about that?"

The young mother looked torn between wanting to join them, and needing to stay with her baby. Some of the other men firmed up their chins and chests, and stepped forward to volunteer. So did the college girl and her boyfriend.

"Everyone, just wait a minute," Joe said. He renewed his grip on Chad's shoulder. "I know you're upset here. I am, too. We all are. But we're not going to do anybody any good by rushing in without knowing what's what. We need lights and equipment. We need those who know these caves."

A diminutive elderly lady with bifocals perched atop her fluffy blue-white perm came forward. She also wore the white polo shirt with the logo, over navy-blue slacks and under a crocheted cardigan. Chad had seen her at a table in the rear of the gift shop, making jewelry with painstaking care.

"What about Rory?" the bifocaled woman asked.

Joe's expression darkened.

Undaunted, she went on. "You need to give him a chance, Joe. He's your own nephew. Flesh and blood. He spends as much time in those caves as any of the guides. Probably knows them better than Chloe and Colin by now, for all they've lived here since they were babies."

The girl, Chloe, shrank back and gnawed on her fingernails. Her gaze darted this way and that.

"What about our families?" The young mother, her baby squalling and waving tiny fists, elbowed her way to stand beside Chad. "What about Rich and R.J.? They might be hurt!"

"Where's the end?" the Viking-biker named Bear asked. "Where does the cave come out at?"

"Around there," Joe said. "Behind the buildings. There's a path leads from the main exit back through the gift shop."

"Just like Disneyland," Chad said sourly. "What about the emergency exits? Your website said there were emergency exits."

The mother nodded. "R.J. is four and we told him the same thing, but he was loving every minute of it. I brought Megan up one of those emergency exits. It looped back to the entrance."

"They all do," Joe said. "Anybody coming out will come out one of those two ways."

"So we divvy up into groups," Snake said. "And we–"

"No," Joe said. He met the bikers' eyes firmly. "It's appreciated, but no one is going in there unless they already know the caves. If you want to help, then get these folks organized and start moving cars, so that when the rescue guys get here and the cops and the ambulances, they'll have room to do whatever they need to do."

"Ambulances!" The young mother staggered. Chad put an arm around her and she leaned into him, shivering.

The college girl made an offering-gesture. "Want me to hold your baby? Mrs....?"

"Carson. Melinda." Still shivering, she handed the red-faced, screeching bundle over. "Her name's Megan."

"I'm Debbi. This is Jim. You want to come over here with us and sit down for a while?"

Melinda Carson shook her head. "I want my husband and my son."

"It's okay," Chad said. "We'll get them. Don't you worry about that." His gaze challenged Joe to say otherwise.

Joe, confronted with that on top of the belligerent stares from the bikers, groaned a sigh and pinched the bridge of his nose. "Look, mister–"

" I understand your position here, Joe. But my wife, my sister-in-law, my brother-in-law, my daughters and my nieces are all in that cave. I didn't go with them. I stayed up here because I thought I had important work to do. I let them go down there alone. And now, I am going to do whatever I have to in order to bring them out safely. You got that?"

Mutters of agreement came from Bear and Snake. In the part of his brain still capable of viewing things with cool detachment, Chad couldn't decide whether to be impressed or irritated. He'd been sitting right at that picnic table when the three Harleys came snarling into the lot and the three bikers swung off, all gruff but jovial swagger in their jackets, boots, chaps and jeans. They'd gone straight to the snack bar and ordered half a dozen fully-loaded bratwursts.

Maybe they saw themselves as do-gooders, the breed of Hell's Angels that went around holding fund-raisers and doing charity work for the underprivileged to improve their bad-boy image. Maybe image was all it was, and underneath the long hair and studded leather and chains, they were just your ordinary bunch of guys. Maybe, for them, this was a chance to do a good deed. Maybe they were just of a genuinely helpful nature.

But they didn't have anyone in the caves. They had no personal stake in this.

Stephen had given him a sour, curled-lip look when Chad had announced his intention to "skip this one, girls... Daddy's got a lot of work he needs to do." Stephen hadn't been thrilled about this trip in the first place. He probably resented how his brother-in-law had already spent so much of the trip staying behind in the hotel rooms and the RV parks with his laptop and Internet connection, while he got the job of ferrying Val and Frieda and the girls around most of Disneyland and Disney California Adventure and Sea World and the San Diego Zoo.

It wasn't that Chad didn't enjoy spending time with them. He loved Frieda, and he adored Britney and Angelina – though in all honesty, he still wished he could have talked Frieda into other names for them. He liked Val and Stephen and Tiffany and Amberlyn, too.

When they all got together, though, it was a little hectic. Val and Frieda seemed to regress, becoming giddy giggly little girls again themselves. When they passed through the big castle there at the entrance to Fantasyland, and seen not only Cinderella but also Snow White *and* Jasmine, it had almost been a rampage. They went after those princesses like a raving mob, squealing and brandishing souvenir autograph books. Chad clearly saw the deer-in-the-headlights alarm in Cinderella's blue eyes, and the way Snow White's graceful throat convulsed in a nervous gulp before being surrounded.

He'd been annoyed at the time, and embarrassed. Feeling sorry for those poor park employees and hoping they got paid decently enough to put up with this kind of thing hour after hour, day after day. Shortly thereafter, he'd made his excuses and hopped the Monorail back to the Disneyland Hotel.

Now he kicked himself for his annoyance. He only wanted his wife and daughters again, wanted to see them happy no matter what.

"I should have been with them," he said, snapping himself back to the here-and-now with a vengeance.

Around him, activity bustled. Some of the tourists had taken off. Most, though, pulled together in the way people did in times of crisis.

The college girl, Debbi, and the elderly lady who made jewelry took charge of Melinda Carson and her baby. A grizzled coot who looked like a crazy old mountain-man prospector – Chad had seen him leading out the previous tour group, and thus deduced that this was Pete – emerged from the rest room and stood with Joe, jabbering and gesticulating.

The bikers tried to see about clearing space. Joe's wife, whom someone addressed as Kitty, announced that help was on the way from town and the nearest ranger-and-fire station. But with so many of the vehicles belonging to people who were currently on the tour, it was slow going.

And still, no one had come out. Not from the exit, not from the entrance.

"How far in could they have gotten?" Chad asked Chloe, who was still chewing the bejesus out of her fingernails. "They'd only been gone fifteen minutes! You must have a map of the caverns, and have the tour routes timed and everything."

"We do," she said around her fingers.

"So where would they be?"

She shrugged. "Fairy Forest... Goblintown... around there, I guess."

"Shouldn't they be able to backtrack?"

"Yeah, I mean, unless the roof fell in or something. Or the stairs got blocked. You have to go down a long twisty metal staircase near the start of the tour."

"What about the emergency exit tunnels? They had a guide, didn't they?"

"Sure." Chloe blinked several times, rapidly, as if fighting back tears. "Justin took the 2:30 tour. He's really good. He's a grad student. Geology. He does this summers. I hope he's okay."

"He'd know all the ways out?"

"Sure," she said again. She took a deep, watery breath and seemed to strengthen herself. "He knows the caves better than almost anyone, even better than Pete because Justin used to lead the advanced tour."

"Advanced tour? There wasn't anything about that on the website."

"We stopped doing it a year, year and a half ago. It was only for the really good climbers, see. They'd rappel down and crawl through shafts and go across chasms and everything. It lasted four hours and you could only go on it if you were in really good shape because you had to use pitons and carabiners and all that stuff."

"Why'd you stop offering it?" he asked, narrowing his eyes in anticipation of being told that there'd been a disaster, a cave-in, a collapse, deaths… and they'd discreetly hushed it up to avoid harming their trade.

"It cost a lot and it was hard," Chloe said with another shrug. "So, not many people ever went on it. Dad said it wasn't worth the trouble."

"But this Justin used to do it."

"All the time," she said.

"What about Pete? That's him, over there, isn't it? He knows the caves?"

"Oh, yeah. He's been working here since before I was even born. But he quit doing the advanced tours a long time ago. He's way too old."

From the direction of the road, sirens whooped. Chad briefly closed his eyes, giving in to a momentary sense of relief. The rescue workers were here. It would be over soon. Like one of those uplifting stories on the news all the time. Miners surviving against all odds. Toddlers rescued from wells. People emerging unscathed from the rubble of a quake-ravaged building.

Very deliberately, he did not let himself think about the disasters in which the ending was not so happy.

CHAPTER 5
Bunker

"Oh, wow."

Toni had been wrecked plenty of times before. That was kind of the whole point of doing drugs.

But she didn't think she had ever been *this* wrecked.

Had Nick or Rory slipped her something different?

It started the same. Felt the same at first.

Right up until the whole world went fuckwire.

Everything going suddenly dark, but not in any fading-out sort of way. Jarring. Abrupt. Noisy. Full of crashings and tumblings and a sensation like falling. The kind of thing you might feel in one of those dreams where you wake up with a gasp right before you hit. Except she hadn't woken up with a gasp. There'd been a bone-rattling thud, and hard heavy objects slamming down all around her.

Hadn't hurt, exactly. Hadn't been fun, either.

And the smell… whew, what a stink!

Could she blame it on the drugs? Hallucination, or nightmare, or something? Was this what the old hippies meant when they talked about a 'bad trip'?

Seriously, WTF?

The light throbbed. It waxed and waned, grew and shrunk, brightened and dimmed. Pulsing like the slow beat of a weird heart. The shadows of the rock formations expanded and contracted. Swelled and dwindled. Stretched and retreated across the stones, as if dark, misshapen fingers were reaching toward her and then withdrawing. Some of the formations even seemed to be moving on their own.

She remembered relaxing on Nick's thick green Army-surplus sleeping bag, flipping through some magazine or another by the glow of a camping lantern. She wasn't sure what she'd been reading. Didn't matter anyway. All the guys kept in the cave was comic books, porn, video game manuals and the military/survivalist stuff Nick collected. And she had been way too wrecked to make much sense of it anyway. She'd just been turning pages, looking at pictures, bobbing her head in time to the beat coming from the old CD player, and listening with half an ear to Brandon and Colin arguing.

She was still on the sleeping bag. Still on her stomach. But it hadn't been draped over a rock before. She hadn't been lying with her ass in the air and her limbs hanging. The magazine was gone. The music was gone. The argument was gone. The beer she'd been sipping from was gone.

Everything was gone.

Except for... Brandon...

Hallucination.

Toni knew it had to be hallucination. A 'bad trip.' It sounded lame, hopelessly hokey. Like saying 'groovy' or 'boss' or the other lame and hopelessly hokey things their parents said whenever they tried to be cool but really only ended up embarrassing themselves. Not to mention embarrassing their kids even more.

Bad trip. Lame, hokey... but it fit. It described what she felt.

And it was the only possible explanation for what she thought she saw. She wasn't *really* seeing her brother dead. Not Brandon. Not all crunched and mangled, like a clay doll given one quick, violent squeeze in a giant's fist.

Not Brandon.

Bad trip. Hallucination.

Fucking vivid, though.

The way his belly had burst open and splurted out a slippery tangle of guts... the way half his head dented in, the eye on one side obliterated in a gory socket and the eye on the other side looked about to pop from the pressure...

Way too fucking vivid.

She could even see the flare-and-dwindle reflection of that pulsing light in his single eyeball. It glinted on his braces and fillings.

A boulder the size of a Mini Cooper rested where Brandon's legs should have been. With a wide puddle around its base.

"Guys?" Toni swallowed. The stench, and the hideous hallucination, made her hiccup sour bile into her mouth. Her stomach lurched. She struggled not to puke. "Hey, guys, I'm not... not feeling so good."

Had they slipped her something? A roofie, maybe?

No. They wouldn't. That was stupid.

At least, Brandon wouldn't because he was her brother.

And Colin wouldn't because he was a wimp.

Nick wouldn't, because Nick was her boyfriend and so didn't have to.

What about Rory?

Toni frowned. Rory, she wouldn't put it past to pull a stunt like that. She noticed the way he watched her when he thought Nick wasn't looking. He wanted her. He couldn't do much about it with Nick around, and if he'd tried anything, Toni would have gone right to Nick and told him and then there'd have been trouble.

But Nick hadn't been with them. Nick went into town to meet with some people. Buying or selling or whatever, she didn't know. He wasn't supposed to be back until five.

So, Rory might have figured he could get away with it. Brandon and Colin might have objected, but they were scared of him.

She didn't feel like anything had been done to her. As far as she could tell, her clothes were on straight. So that was okay.

"Guys?"

Ugh, the smell.

Blood and shit and pizza.

Pizza?

Brandon.

He'd had pizza for lunch.

The hallucination of him lying there dead and gut-split was so incredibly detailed that she could even detect undigested sausage, mushrooms, olives and cheese. From his stomach. Awash in Coke. And the shit-smell was from his intestines.

Again, she hiccup-belched and threw up in her mouth a little. Beer. Doritos.

"Toni?" A voice, practically a whimper, but she was glad to hear it.

"Colin? Oh, jeez, Col."

"Where are you? Are you okay?" He sounded marginally stronger, marginally closer. "What happened?"

"I'm *so* fucking wrecked."

"You're hurt? How bad?"

"No, I'm okay. I think. I mean... you wouldn't believe what I'm seeing. It's a bad trip. Such a bad trip." She hitched herself off the rock, the sleeping bag dragging along with her. "What'd I take? What'd Rory give me?"

A short, pudgy, geeky shadow loomed nearby. Colin. The white logo on his dark *HALO 3* tee shirt and the lenses of his glasses caught each sullen pulse the same way Brandon's braces and staring eyeball seemed to. Cracks frazzled one lens and the glasses hung askew on his round face. Below his emo-kid hair, she could see a huge scrape on his forehead.

"Give you?" he asked. "Rory? Huh?"

"A roofie or something? Because I am really messed up here. Hallucinations and everything. You need to talk me through, okay?" She rubbed her temples. "It even looks like Brendan's laying there squashed, total roadkill."

"Toni..."

"What?"

Colin tugged off his glasses and wiped his eyes. "Toni," he said again, sniffling. "Brandon is dead. For real."

"Don't fuck with my head, Colin. That isn't funny."

"I'm not! You aren't... tripping. You took whatever it is you usually take, and you had a beer, but it's not like anyone gave you a roofie or... or LSD or whatever. This is real. Brandon's dead."

"I told you, that isn't funny."

"It's no fucking joke!" he shouted.

Colin, Mr. Good Boy, saying 'fucking' anything was so out of the ordinary that Toni faltered. She could blame hallucination for the red light, for the roadkill-Brandon. But not even in her wildest hallucinations could she expect to hear Colin Goddard cussing. Sometimes, Nick tried to get him to do it, because it cracked him up to watch Colin blush and stutter and squirm.

"You're saying I'm not..."

"You're not."

"But that means Brandon..."

"Yeah."

"What the fuck, Colin? What the fuck happened?"

"Rocks fall, everybody dies," he said in a bleak tone, and then laughed an even bleaker laugh.

Toni got goosebumps, which made her realize that for a change she hadn't been feeling cold, the way she always did down here in this damn dank chilly cave.

Weird...

Even when all bundled up in the sleeping bag, even when happy-drugged, she couldn't ever quite get warm enough.

But now, the shivers, the goosebumps, and the awareness she'd been warm for once. Almost too warm.

Hallucination, too? Except Colin insisted she wasn't tripping balls. Since he hadn't morphed into a cartoon character or something, and since their conversation – bizarre as it was – still made some kind of sense, Toni wondered if maybe he was right.

"Huh?" she said. "Rocks fall? What do you mean, rocks fall?"

"Look." Colin swung his arm around in a sweeping arc. "This isn't where we were, Toni. Part of the floor gave out, and part of the ceiling fell in. We must have dropped ten, twelve feet. We were up there. In the bunker."

He pointed up and back. She saw a rock-strewn slope of broken limestone and the flowing ridge-ribbon formations she liked to call mermaid-hair, but Colin and Rory said was called 'cave bacon' by the experts. Along the slope, mixed in with the rubble, she saw other familiar things. Shattered plastic and metal. Electronic components. Batteries. Magazines. Silvery pie-wedges that used to be CDs. Another sleeping bag, the dumb one with Spider-Man on it that Colin refused to give up no matter how much he got teased. A six-pack of beer, one of the cans punctured by a sharp rock.

Their stuff, basically.

The card table where the guys sometimes played Texas Hold 'Em lay upended with its spindly legs sticking up like those of a dead dog. A folding chair teetered on a slab of stone. The lantern had ruptured, and the pulsing light came from a guttering pool of flame feeding on debris.

"This is one of the lower chambers," Colin went on. "We sort of... slid down into it when the floor collapsed."

And Brandon. Battered to pulp. Legs pinned under that boulder. Flesh looking like cheap ground meat with little pieces of bone left in it. One eye a mangled hole. The other a bulbous, veiny horror.

"You're sure I'm not wrecked?" Toni asked in a faint, almost pleading voice.

Colin nodded, sniffled again and scrubbed at his face, smudging dust and snot and blood around, not improving anything. "Yeah, Toni. I'm sure. No more than usual, anyway."

"Brandon... Brandon's really... dead?"

He nodded again, then turned away. She heard him hitch a breath. Brandon was her brother, so if anybody should be crying it was her... but she couldn't wrap her head around any of this yet.

How could it be that Brandon was dead, while she and Colin weren't even hurt?

Well, mostly. Now that she was being forced to face reality, she became aware of assorted sore spots, and that her left knee and ankle ached, and that she'd skinned scrapes up her right arm most of the way from elbow to shoulder.

But still.

They were up and moving around, pretty much in one piece. And Brandon was...

Roadkill.

"What was it?" she asked when she figured Colin had gotten himself under control. "Earthquake or cave-in or what?"

"I think..." He gulped. "I think something went off."

"Went off?"

"Blew up. You know."

Her mouth fell open. "You mean like a nuke or a terrorist attack?"

"No. I mean something down here."

"Damn it, Colin! You guys said you were going to be careful with all that shit!"

"It wasn't *me*! None of this was my idea!"

"Not your idea?" She punched him in the arm. "It's your fucking cave, isn't it? And your idea to keep it down here!"

"Ow! Nuh-unh! It was Nick's idea. Him and Rory."

"You just went along with it."

"Hey, you know how they are," whined Colin, rubbing his arm. "I couldn't say no. Anyway, Nick's *your* boyfriend. Why didn't you stop him, if you thought it was such a big deal?"

"I never thought you assholes were serious. I thought it was another one of those stupid games, you know, because you got tired of playing Grand Theft Auto. Just this big tough-guy act. All talk and show and bullshit."

He just looked at her. A pitying look. As if marveling how anybody could be so impossibly naïve. To be looked at that way by Colin – Colin! – infuriated her so much that she almost punched him again. A loser whose idea of a hot date was a night alone with his Megan Fox poster and a bottle of hand lotion... having the nerve to look at her like that!

Except, of course, she knew better. She knew Nick. He had gone from frying ants with a magnifying glass to putting potatoes in tailpipes in the faculty parking lot. From egging houses to breaking windows to mailbox baseball. From flaming bags of dogshit to firecrackers poked through vent-slots in school lockers. In trouble with his folks, in trouble with teachers, in trouble with the cops.

While always, *always* talking with savage, gleeful expectation about how someday, he'd pay them back. Pay them *all* back. Them and the rest of the entire fucked-up society. Whenever there was a school shooting, like Columbine or the massacre at Virginia Tech, Nick had been the one to say that the gunmen had the right idea.

Colin was still looking at her in that infuriatingly pitying way.

"Okay!" Toni said. "Okay, fine, great, so... my boyfriend's a fucking psycho nutcase. Your cousin's no better!"

"My cousin's worse," Colin said. "Nick may be a psychopath, but Rory? Rory's a sociopath."

"Never mind. Who gives a shit? The big thing is what do we do now?"

"We've got to get out of here. If we can. If the rest of it doesn't come down."

"You are *not* telling me we're trapped in this fucking hole!"

"I don't know," he said. "Maybe."

She punched him again. "If you don't get us out of here–"

"I will!" Colin flinched from her. "Just chill out!"

"What about Brandon? We have to take him with us."

"Toni, we can't."

"You want to leave him here? I thought he was your best friend!"

"He is! But he's... and the rock... we couldn't carry... I don't even know if we could pick him up without... he'd fall apart."

She spun away, bent double, and retched up a splatter of puke. Beer. Doritos. Colin tried to put a hand on her back and she batted it away. Like he had any business trying to comfort her after making her imagine them picking up Brandon and having him come apart like a greasy overcooked chicken, the meat just sliding off the bone.

He shuffled back and waited. When she was done, he said in a timid sort of way, "When we do get out, we're kind of going to be in for it."

"Ya think?" She spat until her mouth cleared.

"If we tell the truth, I mean."

"Don't be a dipshit, Colin. They're going to come down here. Rescue guys and investigators and stuff. They'll have to, in order to get Brandon, and they'll want to know what caused this. They'll find whatever's left of your fucking stash–" She broke off, revolted at the idea that they'd also find whatever was left of Rory, wherever *he* was, and probably also splattered all over the place like those inkblots the psychiatrists used.

"Oh, jeez." Colin looked more horrified than revolted. "The tours. There could have been all kinds of people in the cave when it happened. What if someone got hurt, or killed?"

Her fist curled to give him yet another punch. *People possibly getting hurt or killed?* What did he think a stockpile of guns and ammunition and dynamite and plastic explosive and all that other shit was *for*? Did he really believe no one could actually get hurt?

"Who gives a fuck about the tours? What about us? I don't want to die down here. More importantly, I don't want to be stuck here with you for the rest of my life."

He looked wounded. "What did *I* do?"

"You're supposed to be the hot-shit cave expert," she said. "You're always saying how you know these tunnels better than anybody–"

"Hey," Colin said, still wounded. "I *do* know the caves. I've been crawling around down here since I was just a kid."

"So get us out already! Before we suffocate or something." She waved in the general direction of the flames. "In case you haven't noticed, brainiac, we've got a fire going on! It'll use up all the air and roast us alive."

"I don't think it'll spread. This is a cave. It's limestone and calcite and water and granite. There's nothing to burn. See? There's hardly any smoke."

"Would you save me the fucking science lesson and get us *out* of here?" Forget punching him. She was going to strangle him.

"Sorry." He pointed up the slope. "The way we came in is back that way, but the rubble's real loose and we might not be able to get out. If we are where I think we are, though, down by the armory, then we're near one of the old ladder-shafts. People used to use them on the advanced tour back when we were still doing that. They'd rappel down, explore the lower caverns, and then climb up."

"Great," Toni said. "So, let's go. Sooner the better."

"Let's see if we can find anything that might be useful." He pawed through debris until he unearthed a few cans of Coke that were dented but otherwise undamaged. A few minutes later, they had one working flashlight, some spare batteries, a couple of candy bars, and a hunting knife that folded into a decoratively-painted handle.

"Oh, right, and what do you think you're going to do with that?" Toni asked as Colin tucked the knife into his pocket.

"Just in case," he said again.

"In case of what? Rats? Monsters? Cave mutants?"

"It might be a good idea to have a weapon, that's all." He piled the scavenged supplies into a scuffed old olive-green backpack. Nick's, more Army-surplus. "Come on."

"My hero," Toni said, not bothering to hide the sarcasm. "Lead the way."

CHAPTER 6
Crawl Through

"Is that Todd blubbering for his daddy like a little baby?" Austin asked.

"Him or that other kid, the fat one."

"Yeah, well, they're both babies."

They sat back to back for a while, each with knees drawn up. Dallas played her flashlight beam over the cave walls, watching the shimmer of different colors in the rocks.

"We're gonna be in trouble, aren't we?" Austin finally spoke again.

"Probably," Dallas said.

"What do you think happened back there?"

"Dunno," she said, working her wad of gum from one cheek to the other. "It sounded bad, though."

"And nobody's come looking for us yet," he said. "Not Mom, not the tour guide, not nobody."

"Maybe they don't even know we're gone."

They sat quiet again, listening.

"It sure was some crash," Austin said. "Like an avalanche or something. Is Mom okay?"

"How should I know?"

"Is she dead?"

"Austin!" Dallas drove her elbow backward, into his ribs. "I've been here as long as you have, remember? What am I, psychic?"

"If she was, wouldn't we feel it?"

She scoffed. "Did you feel it when Dad died?"

"No. But I was only three." He paused. "Did you?"

"No."

"If she was okay, she'd be looking for us, wouldn't she? Or maybe she thinks *we're* dead?"

"Maybe she thinks we already got out," Dallas said.

"Or maybe," Austin added bitterly, "she's more worried about Greg. She likes him better."

"We're her kids. He's only her boyfriend."

"But she's gonna marry him." The rubber soles of Austin's Nikes squeaked on the slick rock as he shuffled his feet.

Neither of them said anything for a while. Far away through the passage, back the way they'd come, they could dimly hear the echoes of voices drifting in the darkness. Calling. Crying. Begging.

Not so many screams, though. The screaming had pretty much stopped.

"I bet somebody's dead," Austin said. "I bet the whole roof came down and smashed 'em flat."

Dallas didn't reply, but she figured he was right. The two of them had been at the head of the pack, wanting to be the first ones to see each new wonder that the caverns had to offer. And so that they didn't have to walk with Todd, who was an annoying squirt as well as being clumsy and funny-looking.

Just because he was a year older than Austin and a year younger than her, their mom and his dad thought they should all be the best of pals. As if anybody wanted Todd for a friend! Let alone for a brother.

He couldn't seem to get it that they just plain didn't like him. No matter how much they ignored him, he was always right there tagging along, telling them to slow down and wait for him, wanting to hang out with them at school and go with them when they went to the park or the mall or the movies. He was *such* a dork and *such* a loser.

She and Austin had tried earlier in the tour to sneak away, but the guide kept catching them and telling them they had to stay with the group. Everybody else was slow, stopping to look at everything. To ooh and aah like they'd never seen rocks before. Mom and Greg insisted on repeating everything the guide had said. "Look, kids! Sylvia says that one is called the Sleeping Angel!"

Like they were deaf or stupid or something. It was dumb, anyway. Giving names to a bunch of shapes that didn't look like what they were called. Sleeping Angel? Castor and Pollux? Far as Dallas could tell, they looked more like a bunch of wieners. Big blobby wieners.

"Someone will come find us, right?" Austin asked.

"No, they're gonna leave us down here to starve." She elbowed him again.

"Starve? Really?"

"Jeez. No!"

"Well, what if it takes them a while to rescue us?"

Dallas swiveled around toward him and held the flashlight under her chin so that it lit up her face like a monster-mask. "Cannibalism!" She snapped her teeth.

"Quit it!"

"We won't starve. I've still got pretzels and you have M&Ms. We can do okay without food for a few days as long as we have water, which we do because Mom made us bring water bottles and the creek's right there. So don't be a wussy."

"I'm no wussy!"

"Good." She flickered the beam around the chamber some more.

When they'd had come to the part called The Squeezes, Sylvia hadn't really wanted to let Dallas and Austin go first. She must've figured they would try and ditch the group again. Each time they came to a new cave room, they had to wait for everyone else to catch up. The fat guy, gasping like he was about to drop dead from a heart attack any minute… the people on their honeymoon who were more interested in making out than in hearing about how soda straws and stalacagamatites were made…

But at The Squeezes, Sylvia didn't have much of a choice. She made them promise-promise-cross-their-hearts to stay in the next room and not go any further.

"They will," Mom had said. "Won't you, Dallas? Won't you, Austin?"

Naturally, they'd agreed.

They'd scurry-crawled through the low, twisting tunnel, come out, and taken one quick glance around at the formations. Ribbon Falls was a ripple-ridged flow that reminded Dallas of those giant slides from the county fair, the ones that you rode down sitting on a burlap sack. Trickles of water ran in the grooves, then spilled into the Mermaid's Pool, which was round and deep and glimmering.

But then they'd gone looking for something even cooler and more interesting. Like the little arched hole in the far wall. A hole just barely big enough for a couple of kids to crawl through.

"I'm cold," Austin said, leaning against her and shivering. "Aren't you?"

"Sure. It's only like fifty degrees in here."

"And that water was freezing," he said. "How long will it take for our clothes to dry out?"

"As long as it takes."

The Mermaid's Pool looked super-shallow, just a couple of inches, because it was so incredibly clear that they could see every pebble on the bottom. An island rose up from the middle, with a formation on it that, if you really stretched your imagination, did kind of look like a mermaid sitting on a rock.

According to Sylvia, the pool was really almost four feet deep. Some cave water, she'd said, filtered through so much soil and rock that it was the cleanest and purest on the whole planet. It filled the pool right to the very brim, and spilled through, making a creek.

That creek, Dallas and Austin had immediately seen, vanished through the little arched hole.

All it took was a shared glance and a grin. No words necessary. They'd been over the metal-pipe fence and into the Mermaid's Pool cave grotto faster than monkeys on a jungle gym.

The wet limestone turned out to be extra slippery underfoot. Walking on it was a major no-no. A formation further along in the tour would be okay to touch, Sylvia said, but no one was allowed to touch the others. Dallas reasoned that the people who owned the place wouldn't be able to make any more money charging admission if everyone went and broke off their own souvenirs to take home.

She and Austin hadn't hesitated, though. The unspoken challenge and dare made it worth any amount of scolding they'd get later.

So, Dallas first, they had slithered and wormed their way into the creek tunnel. They were both wearing hoodies – Mom had made them, though it was practically a hundred degrees outside in the sun – and the icy water soaked right through. Their hands went numb. Hers still felt like blocks of frozen meat.

But once they'd gone over the fence, they had to keep going. Seeing as how they were going to be in trouble anyway. Might as well make the most of it.

"Dallas, what if they don't figure out where we went?"

"They will. Where else could we go?"

He hesitated, then said, "You think we maybe should have stayed on the path?"

"Are you wussing out on me?"

"No! I'm just... saying."

"Is that what you want, Austin? Stay on the path, follow instructions, do whatever they tell you?"

"I'm just cold," he said. "And wet. And hungry. And my butt hurts from sitting on this rock."

"Do you have to tinkle, too?" she asked in her most sweetly condescending tone. "Go ahead. I won't look. Unless you need me to hold your hand."

"Shut up."

"You shut up."

Austin did shut up, and Dallas went back to roaming the flashlight around. In the back of her mind, she wondered how long the battery would last, and if she should maybe turn it off for a while. In case they did wind up being stuck down here a long time.

She switched it off, plunging them into darkness. At once, the few sounds they could hear seemed louder. The trickling of the creek, the distant voices, the plink-drip of water from formations. Austin yelped. He fumbled around and, a few seconds later, his light came on.

"Doofus," she said. "I did that on purpose. To conserve batteries."

"But it's dark!"

"Yeah. That happens when there's no light."

"I don't wanna be here in the dark."

"You liked it in Hall of the Pharaohs when Sylvia turned off all the lights to show us what pitch-black looked like."

"C'mon, Dallas."

"What, you scared?"

"No," he said, offended. "Anyway, it uses more energy to turn a light on and off a lot than it does to leave it on. I heard that on a science show."

"What science show?"

"Um… *Mythbusters.*"

"Oh, you did not."

"Did so!"

"You heard that from Greg," she accused. "When you were messing around with the light switches that one time and he told you to knock it off."

"He shouldn't be bossing me around in our own house," Austin said, slashing his light around angrily.

"Go back!" Dallas said. "I thought I saw something."

"What do you mean?" He craned his head. "Bats? Spiders? What?"

"Giant albino centipedes," she said. "With big pinchers."

"Ha, ha."

"It looked like another opening, okay? Maybe we can get out of here and not have to wait around for them to come get us."

"But…" He aimed the beam at the tunnel they'd crawled in through, which was now partly blocked by a bunch of rocks. "What if the rest of it caves in on us?"

Dallas didn't like to be reminded of how close they'd been to being underneath those when they fell. She grabbed her brother's head, pointed it in the opposite direction. "Over there."

"Hey, yeah! Behind that big rock, the one shaped like a dog's head?"

"It's not a dog," Dallas said. "It's a horse."

"It's a dog. You can see the floppy ears."

"That's its mane. It's a horse."

"It's a dog! See? There's the nose, and –"

"Okay, fine, whatever, it's a dog, are you happy?" Dallas got up, staying hunched over so she didn't bang into any low-hanging formations. "Come on. I bet if we get out of here on our own, they'll be so glad we're okay that we don't even get in trouble."

Austin brightened. "We could get on the news!"

The rock shaped like a horse's head – and it *was* a horse; Dallas rode and had placed second in her age group last fall, so she knew a horse when she saw one – jutted out from the side of the cave. There was a space behind it, where the creek flowed into another passage that slanted down in a rounded, curving tube. The walls of the tube, smooth and almost shiny, caught the light in a sheen that made her think of the way oilslicks caught rainbows when it rained on the parking lot.

"Down that?" Austin asked dubiously.

"Just like the waterslides at Cascade Mountain," she said, hoping she sounded less apprehensive than she felt.

"What if we get stuck?"

"We have to do something."

"We'll get wet again."

"You can wait if you want," she said. "When I get out, I'll tell them where you are."

"I'm not staying here by myself!"

"Then let's go." She sat down in the creek, catching her breath as the icy water soaked through her clothes. "Brace yourself on the sides. Go slow. We don't want to go shooting over a waterfall or something."

Feet first, on her back, she worked her way into the tube. The walls were slick to the touch. She wasn't at all sure that she could stop herself if she did begin to slide. Wasn't sure if the tight stone throat would narrow even more, into a funnel. If it did, there was no way she'd be able to climb back up. It'd be just too slippery.

Austin wiggled along behind her. A couple of times, he kicked her in the head and she had to tell him to not follow so close. Her voice rang loud and weirdly hollow.

Drenched, numb and half-frozen, they continued inching her way down. The water swirled around them, sometimes splashing up onto their faces, making them sputter. Dallas couldn't see anything past her knees.

"Let's go back," Austin said. His teeth chattered so hard that his words were chopped into fragments. "Dallas, let's go back, huh?"

"It's getting steeper," she said. "And I hear more water. Didn't Sylvia tell us there was a river that went through the deeper part of the cave?"

"Yeah. That one lady, the fat kid's mom, asked if they did cave tubing. She said she heard they did it in Mexico or someplace. Riding on a cave river in an inner-tube."

"Right," Dallas said. "I remember now. Sounded like fun."

"This isn't fun."

The rushing of water was louder. Much louder than their feeble creek. A gusty draft eddied up past them. A river, all right. She and Austin were both excellent swimmers. The cold would be the real problem. They'd just have to find a place to climb out as soon as they could, and get dry and warm before they got hyperthermos, or whatever it was called.

Her heels came to a place where there wasn't any more floor. She told Austin to stop, and felt around with her feet.

"We made it," she said. "It opens up. The creek must make a little waterfall. I'm going to roll over and scootch on my stomach and see how much of a drop there is."

"Ok-k-k-kay," he said, chatter-chatter-chatter.

Getting the flashlight out of her sweatshirt's front pocket, she held it up as best she could to keep it out of the water. She twisted and rolled, slipping some. Her legs were out as far as her knees, sticking into empty air.

She scootched more, curling her body at the hips and waist so that her legs hung all the way into the larger space. The waterfall pattered on her sneaker-toes.

"I think–" she said.

Then she slipped again, clawed at the slick rock, couldn't get a grip, and fell backwards out of the passage with a startled cry.

CHAPTER 7
Wishing Well

"Where is she?" asked the Goth chick.

She'd taken the loss of her grandfather in stride. Better than the rest of her family had. Justin was impressed. Or maybe he shouldn't have been. Ms. Goth, after all. Nihilism, despair, bleakness, hopelessness. Death was something she probably contemplated every day.

Maybe more than just contemplated. Earlier, on the tour, he had noticed the network of scars on her left forearm when she'd pushed up the sleeves of her oversized black fleece jacket. Thin, delicate, clean scars. Regular cuts. Intricate patterns. Some straight, as if made by individual slices of a razor blade. Others whorled and looping. X-Acto knife?

"This way." Holding up the lighter, a cheap orange plastic one that didn't look like it had much fuel left, he led her across the shattered wreckage that had been Goblintown. Aftermath of a natural disaster now, like something seen on the news, in the wake of a tornado or quake or hurricane.

Poor Goblintown. Battered to crap. Chunks of granite, limestone and marble had come down from the ceiling in a furious bombardment. Stalactites that had taken thousands of years to form, drip by miniscule drip, were pulverized.

So much damage. It hurt Justin's heart.

Did that make him callous if the idea of destruction in the cave bothered him as much – if not more – than the human casualties?

It was only rock.

Except that it wasn't only rock.

It was time. It was the patient, painstaking work of nature. Millennia in the making. Water and stone. Erosion. The deposit of minerals in infinitesimal amounts. More exquisite and beautiful than anything that could be envisioned by the mind or crafted by the hand of even the best artists and artisans who'd ever lived. Flowstone, and travertine dams, cave pearls, soda straws, cave popcorn, helicite needles, gypsum flowers, crystals...

Damage like this was irreparable. It couldn't be fixed. Couldn't be restored. It could only be redone. Over ages and ages.

But still, only rock.

How could rock compare to even a single human life?

Inside, though he felt ashamed of himself for it, he knew what was more important to him. If the choice had been his...

"How bad off are we?" Didi asked. They had moved away from the rest of the group, but she still pitched her voice low to avoid being overheard. "We'll be able to get out, won't we?"

"I hope so," Justin said. "I won't know until I've had a better chance to look around. We weren't far. It all depends on how severe this was, and what condition the rest of the tunnels are in."

"They'll realize up top that something went wrong, won't they?"

"You bet. A tremor like that, they'll know."

"So they'll come in after us?"

"Eventually."

"Eventually?" she parroted, raising a dark eyebrow at him. It had a silver loop through it.

"My boss, Mr. Goddard, isn't going to let anyone rush in here without making sure it's safe. No use trying to stage a rescue until you're sure that the rescuers aren't going to end up victims themselves. They'll need to gear up. They'll need lights, and medical supplies."

"Well, they have all that, right?"

"Some. They'll also want experienced cavers, though. And the big problem with that is–"

"Lemme guess," she said. "The most experienced cavers are you tour guides, and you're already stuck down here with the rest of us."

"Bingo. I think Pete was between tours, and Pete's good. Taught me a lot. But Pete's not as young as he used to be. We might have to wait until Mr. Goddard can send for some outside help. That means, for now, it's up to us."

The cheap lighter heated up until he had to let go of the striker wheel and blow on his thumb. By the pallid blue-white glow of Didi's iPod, he made out the stone lip of the Wishing Well. It sat in the middle of what they called Goblintown's Marketplace, roughly equidistant between the White Cathedral and the Three Towers. Justin almost couldn't stand to look at the Towers, graceful spires snapped off into ugly stubs. White Cathedral had suffered less, sustaining only a few chips of the pale draperies that layered over its darker dome.

Justin approached the Wishing Well. Its natural stone arch, hammered to pieces, now lay strewn around the Marketplace. He struck a flame again and leaned over the knee-high rim. "Hello?"

The little girl's face peered up, a white blur in the shadows. "You said you wouldn't leave me in here! You *said!*"

"I came back. I had to get help."

The Wishing Well formed an ovoid hole, conical, tapering to a blunted tip about ten feet down. Like some negative stalactite, a cutout instead of a formation. Water filled it to a depth of just under three feet, with no current, the surface level unchanged except for by the minute displacement caused by several years' worth of pennies and other small coins tossed in by tourists. They were asked not to, of course, but for many, the temptation was too powerful to resist.

The Goth chick leaned over, long purple bangs swaying out from her brow. "Hey, kiddo. What's your name?"

"Britney. I fell down the stupid pit. It's cold. Get me out. I want out."

"I know you do. I'm Didi. Hang on a sec, okay?" She looked at Justin, both eyebrows raised now.

"I couldn't reach her. It narrows too much for my shoulders. But you can, if I hold your legs."

"You want me to... oh, hey, I'm not sure about that."

"We don't have a lot of choice. Nobody else is skinny enough and strong enough."

"Gee, lucky me."

"Look, Didi, we don't have a rope and even if we did, she might not be able to keep a grip on it long enough for us to pull her up. You need to get her by the hands or wrists."

"I tried to climb out," Britney said. "I couldn't hold on. There's no snakes in here, is there?"

"No snakes," Justin said.

"No prana-fish?"

"No piranha fish."

"No bugs?"

He paused, then regretted it as she started struggling and clawing at the sides of the well.

"There's bugs?" she squealed.

"There aren't any bugs," Didi said, and kicked him in the ankle.

Justin bit his tongue. Sooner or later in the tour, someone usually asked what kind of creatures might live in the caves. Cornucopia had no bats, like Carlsbad's great flocks, but it was home to a few varieties of tiny, blind, subterranean lifeforms. Nearly translucent crayfish. White spiders no bigger than the moon on his pinkie fingernail. Worms as supple and thin as overcooked angel-hair pasta. Occasional moths, a salamander or two. Sometimes pale minnows, fleeting-flash-quick in the creeks.

Somehow, though, he didn't think that information would prove particularly soothing to Britney.

So, he kept his mouth shut.

Didi unzipped her jacket the rest of the way, shrugging out of it and setting it aside. Her tee shirt was nearly small enough to have been a perfect fit on one of the younger girls. It hugged her, tight-white and scoop-necked. The picture of a round-faced, large-headed cartoon cat with devil horns and a devil tail and a pitchfork was done in red and black silkscreen. Beneath the cat, a spooky-looking font spelled out the words "Hell Kitty."

"Stay still, okay?" she said, smiling in at Britney. "You don't want to slide farther and get more wet. I'm going to lean way down and you grab my hands. Can you do that?"

She nodded soberly in the gloom. "Where's my mommy? Where's everybody?"

"Real close," Justin said. With his eyes, he cautioned Didi not to say anything more on that subject. Not yet. "You ready?"

"Uh-huh. You better not drop me, Justin," Didi said as she bent over the Wishing Well's rim. "And don't you dare grab my butt."

Britney giggled. The joking helped make the little girl less scared, he realized. That would help them get her out. Let her think of this as a silly bit of adventure now. She'd find out soon enough that it was anything but silly.

He moved behind Didi. "Are you ticklish?"

"You try it and I'll kick you in the nose."

"That might make me drop you."

"Then you better not tickle me!"

"Okay, okay, spoilsport." He took hold of her legs. Her pants were an airport security nightmare of clips, zippers, loops, chains, straps and clasps. Justin had no idea what function any of them served. Some of the zippers did close actual pockets, but most seemed to be there solely for decoration.

Her center of balance tipped forward, and if he hadn't had her legs she would have toppled in headfirst. "Don't even think about it, Justin."

"I can't even think about it? That's no fair."

Britney strained her arms up. Her fingers waved several inches below Didi's reaching hands.

"And don't go looking at my butt, either."

"Where'm I supposed to look?"

"Shut your eyes, then!"

"I bet she doesn't want me to see her tattoo," Justin said in a confiding stage whisper to Britney, who was still giggling.

"You're really asking for a kick in the nose."

He chuckled. Oddly, he found, the banter made him feel calmer, too. As Didi really stretched, her shirt rode up above the waistband of her pants, revealing that she did in fact have a tattoo. A tramp-stamp, smack in the small of her back, a black-purple-green symbol that looked vaguely like a cup with a flowered vine twining around it. Her skin was untanned and smooth and–

Justin cleared his throat and forced his gaze away. Banter or no banter, dire situation or no dire situation, he didn't need to be scoping out the ladies. Especially not someone who couldn't have been older than seventeen. No fooling around with underage tourists.

"Got her!" Didi said. "Okay, Britney, hang on tight and don't let go. I won't drop you. I promise."

"Pulling you up now." Justin took slow steps backward. "These straps on your pants make for pretty good hand-holds."

Wet slap-scrabble sounds came from the Wishing Well, and then Didi's shoulders were out, her purple-tinted head appeared, her arms... and then came Britney, barefoot and half-drenched with her shorts and Disneyland tee shirt stuck to her in dripping wrinkles.

Didi wrapped the girl in her jacket, which hung most of the way to Britney's shins. They led her back to the others.

Val Brewster, judging by her grimace of a smile, was doing her best to keep the pain from showing. Trying, Justin figured, to keep from upsetting the girls any more than they already were. The two little ones whimpered, leaking steady tears. Even when they saw Britney and jumped up in glad relief, the whimpers didn't altogether stop. Britney ran to them, in a confusion of hugging and questions and thank-God-you're-all-right.

"Damn," Didi muttered.

"What?" Justin asked.

She was looking past the Brewsters at another, smaller group. Her father and kid brother, he remembered. And a busty brunette with big hair, a gypsy's wealth of flashy jewelry, pricey hip-hugger jeans, a skimpy pale-blue silk tank top, and absurdly high, cork-soled sandals. Trophy wife once, shell-shocked survivor now, covered with so many scrapes she might have been rope-dragged down a half mile of bad road. Her fingernails were splintered ruin. She slumped with her face in her hands and a wide swath torn from somebody's shirt tied like a bandage around her head. Both sandals were off and flung aside, both ankles badly swollen and sprained.

"The Bitch," Didi said. "I was hoping... never mind."

Judiciously, Justin opted to not say anything.

"Didi! There you are!" her father barked. "Where were you, young lady? What did you think you were doing?"

"I was–"

"Didn't it occur to you that we might need you here? Can't you think of someone besides yourself for one minute? Is that so much to ask? How could you be so thoughtless? So inconsiderate?"

"Sir," Justin said. "I–"

"You can stay out of this," he said, not taking his indignant gaze from Didi. "I'm talking to my daughter. Who has to quit being a sulky, self-absorbed child and start being a responsible adult. Do you have any idea how terrified your brother was? Lost in the dark like that? And Ronette's been hurt."

Didi stared at the cave floor, purple bangs concealing her eyes. With her fists clenched and her pale arms bare, Justin could see the fine scars on her arm as shiny white lines. "You didn't ask me to help," she said tonelessly.

"I shouldn't have to ask. If you're going to be a part of this family–"

"Maybe I don't want to be."

"That's just about enough from you, Didi."

"Sir!" Justin said. "I needed her help to save that little girl. If you have to yell and make a stink, do us all a favor and save it until we get out of here."

"That's just about enough from you, too, pal," he said, leveling an angry finger at Justin. "You people… this cave… I'm going to sue your asses off. Bringing us down here when it's not even safe, and now my father's dead and my wife's hurt and my son is so traumatized he'll probably have nightmares for the rest of his life thanks to you!"

"Give it a rest," said Stephen Brewster. Didi's dad glared hotly at him. He glared back. He had one arm strapped to his chest with his own belt, and half his face was so glazed in dried blood that it looked like the blue paint Mel Gibson had worn in *Braveheart*. Despite that – or maybe because of it – his glare was the hotter, and it made Didi's dad back down.

When that was done, Stephen approached Justin and Didi. "We're still missing one. My oldest. Tiffany. We've been calling for her." He took a shuddering breath. "Calling and calling, but there's no answer. She was right near me when it all happened. She was right near me!"

"I'll keep looking," Justin promised.

"Me, too," Didi said.

"You most certainly will not," her father said, but they all ignored him.

"Stay with your family," Justin said to Stephen. "Nobody wander off. They'll be searching for us soon enough, and we're still pretty close to the entrance."

"I'll go that way, and work my way back around," Didi said.

"Okay, but be careful. It's bigger in here than it looks."

She eyed him. "Is the rest of it going to fall on our heads?"

"If it was going to, it already would have."

"That's what you said about earthquakes."

"Thanks for reminding me. Look, if it does, it does. There's not a whole lot we can do about that, is there?"

"No, guess not."

They headed off, shining their feeble lights as far as they could. Justin fought back a sinking feeling. He told himself to think positive. Maybe Tiffany got knocked out, and that was why she hadn't answered her parents. He really did not want to find the crushed body of a little girl. The woman, and the old man, were more than bad enough.

He went slowly, examining the sad wreckage of Goblintown, trying not to let himself brood about the devastation. Or about his almost-certain unemployment, because even if Cornucopia didn't wind up closed for good after this, it'd doubtless be shut down for a long time. And if it did reopen, the tourists wouldn't exactly be lining up for tickets.

"Justin?" called Didi from across the chamber. "I found a hat over here."

"Is it pink? A pink sun-visor?" Stephen Brewster's urgent voice reached them.

"Stay there, please, sir." Justin hurried toward Didi's voice and the glow of her iPod in the distant black. "Anything else, Didi?"

"Just the visor. Looks like it got dropped. I'm still–"

She let out a sudden cry, surprise and alarm. Justin saw the small, glowing square tumble and vanish. Heedless of the treacherous terrain, he broke into a run, the lighter's flame waving wildly.

Ahead of him, he heard a scuffling noise, a stifled yell, a meaty thud, a grunt.

"Didi!" He ran faster, kicking chunks of limestone and crystal out of his path.

The iPod's screen came back into view, lodged in a crevice where it had fallen. Though starred with fractures, its light still glowed. Near it was the visor, pink, with 'Tiffy' embroidered across the brim in silver and magenta thread.

Everyone behind him shouted questions. Justin skid-stumbled to a halt at the opening of a jagged crack in the cave wall. He knew all the ways in and out of Goblintown and this wasn't one of them. This was new.

Anything could be in there.

"Didi?"

Justin leaned into the crack, the blazing lighter held out in front of him and guttering in the breeze that wafted from the depths. He dreaded finding a shaft, a sheer pit plunging away, maybe lined with sharp edges that would do a far more severe job on Didi's skin than her razor blades and X-Acto knives ever could.

The first thing he saw was a series of steely-chrome glints. Links of a chain, caught on a spur of stone. A chain torn free from Didi's pants, as if it had snagged there as she went by.

The breeze gusted, teasing his nostrils with a rank, sulfurous smell entirely wrong for these caves. Cornucopia had no hot springs, no acid-pools, no bubbling mud pots as some caves in more volcanically active areas did.

The lighter whiffed out.

Justin cursed and spun the striker-wheel.

He heard... or sensed... movement. Danger. A threat. The hairs on the back of his neck rose up like prickling antennae.

Looking up, he could only make out a swift, large shape surging at him. Then something punched into his belly. Punched, and gouged, and wrenched in a cruel corkscrewing twist.

Searing pain exploded, expanded like a fireball through him. Blood gushed thick and hot down his legs.

Justin reeled, fell. He heard a revolting sucking sound as whatever had impaled him pulled back out. He felt things inside him unravel, a loose, hideous, sickening sensation.

He also heard and felt the solid-yet-brittle crunch when a ridge of stone shattered his shoulder, when his skull crunched down on rock.

After that, he didn't feel much of anything. Except for his head bouncing and bumping along as something hauled him by the feet, into the crack in the wall.

CHAPTER 8
Hall of Mirrors

"I want Mommy."

Rich Carson paced with his son in his arms. He'd soothed R.J. to sleep this way when he'd been little. He soothed Megan this way, now that she was old enough to be teething.

With one major difference. R.J. was a heck of a lot bigger than he'd been back then. Five now, and sturdy. Heavy. But whenever Rich made as if to set him down, R.J. got him in a strangling chokehold and started wailing again.

So, Rich paced and paced. His back ached. His arms felt like lead.

"It's okay, R.J.," he said. "It's okay."

Okay? What a bitter lie that was! *Nothing* was okay! He wasn't sure how it could get much worse than this. The only thing he could find to be glad about was that Melinda and Megan weren't here with them.

The baby's fussiness, her crying, her now-and-then shrieks of such ear-splitting shrillness, earned them disgruntled looks from others in the group. Rich suggested that all four of them cut their tour short. But such a stricken look of disappointment had brimmed in R.J.'s eyes that he hadn't had the heart to force the issue. Melinda saw it, too, and hastily said that she'd take Megan up and wait for them at the car.

"Next time, though," she'd told Rich, "it can be your turn."

"Deal," he'd said.

So she had kissed him, ruffled R.J.'s hair and told him to be a good boy for Daddy. She'd gathered up the assorted baby-stuff, and gone off in the direction of the discreet EXIT sign that the guide had pointed out.

That had been at least half an hour ago. At least twenty minutes before the earth bucked and leaped like a maddened bronco. Before boulders and slabs of rock had plummeted from the high arched ceiling with terrible shattering force.

Had they made it up and out in time? Were they safe? He'd last seen Melinda and Megan leaving the chamber their guide called the Hall of Mirrors, where formations of nearly transparent crystal made long slabs like sheets of milky glass. They hadn't been actual mirrors, of course, though when the lighting and the angle was right, it proved sometimes possible to see ghostly, distorted reflections.

They had to have gotten out. The guide said that the emergency exit shafts went straight up, all the way to an access tunnel that led back to the cave entrance. The switch-backed scaffolding of metal steps would have been a hassle, especially burdened by the baby and the stroller and the diaper bag. But Melinda often laughed about the stairs in their house, and how laundry and chores kept her running up and down them so much that they'd never need to spend money on a gym membership.

She would have been to the top long before the earthquake. Probably in a terror of panic over him and R.J., but at least she and Megan were all right.

"What's happening over there?" Rich called across the gorge, raising his voice to be heard above the tumult of the river coursing far below.

"He's tied up," the redheaded young woman called back. "I... I thought I killed him... but he's breathing. He's still alive."

Rich didn't know if that was supposed to be good news or not.

A slushy, mumbled string of syllables spilled from the Asian man's busted mouth. They were incoherent, but the tone seemed to say that in his opinion anyway, the redhead should have hit the gunman harder with that rock.

"The others?" Rich asked.

He could make her out fairly well, because the guide's larger flashlight was over there. All Rich had was a cheap little plastic one, with the name and number of a pharmaceutical company printed on the side. He collected crap like that by the boatload. Pens, keychains, pads of Post-It notes, calculators, executive stress-reliever squeeze-balls, tape dispensers. The pharm-reps never could seem to grasp the fact that a human-relations manager had no say in what brands of drugs the hospital purchased.

Though he could see her fairly well, and though she was topless but for her bra because her blouse made part of the crude rope binding the crazy son of a bitch who'd brought a gun, Rich didn't find anything erotic about the view. Not given the situation.

"Makoto's hurt," she said. "His face... his teeth... his jaw might be broken. The old man... I... I think he's dead. I think he had a heart attack or a stroke or something. First his wife, and then his grandson... oh, God!"

She hunched forward and covered her face, shoulders wracking with sobs.

"I want Mommy," R.J. said again. "I want Teddy Grahams and chocamilk."

"Soon as we're back to the car, kiddo," Rich said.

"Can't we go? Daddy, can't we please?"

R.J. had loved the cave at first, awestruck, agog, taking it all in with wide-eyed fascination, not wanting to miss a single detail or formation. He could have roamed the caves for hours, obediently not touching anything as the guide had directed, content just to look and look and look.

Between that, and their shared dislike for heights – not to mention cable-and-steel bridges dipping and swaying and creaking above black chasms with churning torrents of icy water at the bottom – they'd been at the back of the pack, bringing up the rear.

If Rich had simply hefted R.J. into his arms and lugged him, kicking and squalling, out onto the span...

"Hey... Miss... what's your name again?" Rich called.

"Shara," she said. "I'm Makoto's girlfriend. We came here with his sister, Kim, the one who... who fell..."

"Who else is over there? Who else is hurt?"

"There's this guy," she said. "The one whose arm got–"

"Right," Rich said, stopping her before she could say anything else. He winced at the memory, which he had seen but mercifully R.J. had not. The snapping cables, lashing through the air like snakes.

"He's still unconscious," Shara said, sounding steadier now. "And there's him." She nodded toward the trussed-up, motionless lump at her feet.

"That's it?" Rich thought back. How many of them had there been at the start of the tour? Fifteen? Sixteen? How many people were on the bridge when the massive chunk of stone had torn it from its moorings and taken it down into the river?

"We have to get help," she said.

"We have to get out or get rescued first," Rich said.

"What if they don't find us?"

"They will."

"What if they don't? We could die down here! We could all die! That man *is* going to die, going to bleed to death if a doctor doesn't do something about his arm!"

"They'll find us!" He felt close to hysteria himself, but R.J.'s tears against his collar gave him the strength to stave it off. "Stop it, Shara. Don't scare my son."

She broke down sobbing again. Makoto patted her back, but even from here the gesture looked pain-muddled and halfhearted, as if he was only barely aware of where he was or what he was doing. His other hand cupped gingerly around the ruined lower half of his face.

"Please Daddy please go now," R.J. whimpered.

"Shara, listen to me," Rich said. "We were near the end of the tour, right? Do you remember? The guide said we only had fifteen, twenty minutes to go. Just one more big chamber after this one, wasn't that what he said?"

They had taken a preliminary ramble through the gift shop while waiting for 1:30 to arrive, but Melinda had told

R.J. that he should see the caves first before deciding on what he wanted as a souvenir. That way, she said, he'd be sure to pick something special that would really remind him of the trip. Melinda-logic, which as a side effect meant that it'd be one less thing for her to end up carrying. She often griped good-naturedly about how a mother's purse was like a magnet for toys, crayon packs from restaurants, half-finished snacks, and similar detritus of kid-dom.

One of the items that Rich remembered was a booklet featuring a fold-out map of Cornucopia Caves. He should have bought it earlier. He would have given a lot to have that map right now.

"I think so," Shara said in reply to his questions. "The Queen's Palace, or something like that."

"Do you remember if there were any more emergency exits between here and there?"

She shook her head and shrugged. "What about the last one we passed? Where your wife went out?"

"Maybe." He stifled a grunt as he tried to support R.J. with one arm and direct the thin, weak little light back the way they'd come. "Hold on a second. I'll go see–"

"No!" R.J. seemed to grow extra arms to cling tight as a little octopus. "Don't put me down, Daddy! Don't leave me!"

"Wasn't going to, buddy. We just need to take a look, okay?" Rich fumbled one careful footstep after another across a tumbled litter of rocks. It would have been a lot easier – not to mention safer – if he could have led R.J. instead of carrying him. But he didn't even suggest it.

After a few turns of the passage, his light kicked back a fabulous spray of sparkles. Crystalline fragments lay everywhere. Thousands and thousands of them. Chunks the size of dinner plates, wicked blades like jagged razors, thorns of needle-fine crystal.

If their group had still been in the Hall of Mirrors when the disaster – whatever it was – had struck…

"My God," Rich said softly.

All those shards. Flying. Falling. Sharp as glass, *sharper* than glass. Anyone caught in that would have been shredded like cheese in a grater.

The muscles in his arms, back and shoulders felt like they'd been tied into white-hot knots. He retreated to a clear section.

"R.J., Daddy's got to set you down. No, hey, buddy. I'm not going to leave you. Daddy just needs to put you down for a minute. You stand right here next to me and hang onto my belt, okay? Both hands on my belt."

Snuffling, R.J. complied. He looked even younger than five, standing there in his dark green shorts and a tee shirt with cartoon raccoons on the front.

They both wore good, durable hiking shoes, not sandals. Rich had on knee-length walking shorts with many pockets, a plain tee shirt and a flannel shirt worn open like a jacket. He'd lost his ball cap somewhere, he realized. Not the best outfit for trying to pick his way through the vicious landscape of points and edges revealed by his sweeping beam of light. Crystals dazzled, sparkled.

Pretty. Pretty, but dangerous.

The Hall of Mirrors. And partway through it, the exit that Melinda and Megan had taken. Worth the risk?

What choice did he have, really? There was no way to cross the gorge. It might be hours, even days before rescue teams could mobilize with the people and gear they'd need to get everyone out of the caves. Days, trapped in the darkness. His cheap light wouldn't last long. The batteries in the bigger one that Shara had might, but what if they didn't?

And what about food, water? The snacks and drinks they'd brought down with them had been, of course, in Melinda's tote bag. He had part of a roll of hard candies – Werther's – in his pocket. That was it.

"Can we go out now, Daddy?"

"I'm thinking, buddy."

"'Kay."

Hunger and thirst. Claustrophobia. The cold. They could survive all that. Those of them, anyway, who weren't already hurt. The man whose arm had been ripped off was a goner. Makoto? Rich didn't have any idea. And what about the lunatic who'd pulled a gun? He was tied up now, but what if he got loose? There was no telling what a crazy person like that might do.

Whatever else, Rich knew, he had to think of R.J. first. His duty was to his own family. To R.J. To Melinda and Megan. He had to put them ahead of anybody else.

"Daddy, the light," R.J. said.

Rich looked down. The beam had dimmed, and gone yellower. The sparkles it struck from the crystal shards looked fainter already.

If he was going to do this at all, he had to do it now.

"Okay, R.J., listen to me," he said. "We want to get out of here and go find Mommy and Megan, right? To do that, we have to cross this room. Do you remember this room? The one that had all the funny rocks like mirrors? The trouble is, it looks like a bunch of them got broken. So there's pieces all over the floor. Like that time the shelf in the cupboard fell out and all Mommy's china smashed, remember that? And I wouldn't let you go in the kitchen because you didn't have shoes on?"

R.J. nodded.

"This time, we both have our good shoes on. We can walk. As long as we go slow and careful and don't fall down. That's why I won't be able to carry you. I wouldn't want to trip or anything."

Again, R.J. nodded. His chin quivered.

"You can keep holding right on to my belt," Rich said. "Walk behind me. Shuffle your feet so you push the sharp stuff out of the way instead of stepping on it."

"I'm scared."

"I know. Me, too. But we've got to try, okay? We can be out of here before that dumb light stops working. Ready?"

They ventured out into the long, winding cavern. Shards gritted and cracked and clinked and ground beneath them. In some places, entire slabs had fallen without shattering, lying tilted and askew like seesaws. In others, slanted edges made guillotine blades poised to whicker down and shear in half anybody who passed beneath them. Hooked crystal claws bristled out from the walls and up from the floor.

Pain sliced into Rich's foot, penetrating his shoe upper and his sock. He hissed through his teeth. The wan yellow beam faded, dulled.

Here and there, the Hall of Mirror's features remained relatively intact, and his heart kept jump-stuttering whenever he caught their reflections and allowed himself to hope for one wild moment that he was seeing an approaching rescue party.

"Ow! Daddy, it cut my leg."

"Just a little farther, buddy."

Their contorted images paced them, half-seen and bizarre.

"I got glass bits in my shoes."

"Almost there."

The flashlight died. R.J. crowded close. His breathing was rabbit-fast, and he'd be crying in another few seconds. Grumbling curses, Rich shook the light and tried it again. The bulb flickered, went out, flickered again, and stayed weakly on. Phantoms of shadow lurched, warped, retreated.

"Daddy, there's things in here, there's monsters."

"Only shadows."

"No, there's monsters."

"Hold onto my belt, R.J. Got to keep going."

"I wanna go back."

"We're almost out." He hoped. The side passage to the exit shaft had to be right around here someplace. Rich was sure of it. Almost a hundred percent sure. With the landmarks and formations all in ruins, he couldn't recognize much of anything.

A shrill scream burst from R.J. "I see it! I see it! The monster! The monster!"

"Settle down, buddy." Rich had almost screamed himself, adrenaline dumping by the gallon into his bloodstream. "Only a shadow, like I said."

But, damn... for a second there... it really had looked like a monstrous shape crouching and ready to pounce.

R.J. buried his face against Rich's leg. Rich shined the feeble beam in a circle. It found a frazzled but whole sheet of crystal and he saw himself, hair and eyes wild like some maniac asylum escapee from a horror story.

A brittle snap cracked loud in the stillness.

Behind them.

Probably a late-breaker giving way, or falling from the ceiling. That was all. Not an ill-placed footstep.

Another brittle snap, and fragments grinding under something heavy. A low, guttural huffing sound that made Rich think of Darth Vader's mechanized breathing from the *Star Wars* movies.

The light flickered.

"Daddy, please," R.J. said against his leg. "Make the monsters go away."

With his free hand, Rich reached down to stroke R.J.'s head. "It's okay. There's no monsters. Come on. Keep walking now."

The light dimmed to an ember. He shook it, with no results. The dull yellowish glow barely stretched three feet.

Snap. Grind. Huff-whoosh.

"This way." His voice had fallen to a harsh whisper. "Come on, R.J."

He shuffled, scuffing first one shoe and then the other through heaps of broken crystals. His hair, formerly wild, now felt like it stood straight out on end from his scalp. Every instinct clamored, shouting that R.J.'s childish perceptions were more on-target than his own adult logic.

Something was in here with them.

Something alive amid the shatters and shards and jagged bladelike slabs.

Crack-crunch.

Closer.

Rich shook the light again, shook it in short, hard jerks like it was an old-fashioned mercury thermometer. For one awful moment, it went dark. He thought that was it, all done, game over, no chance. But then the bulb came back with a renewed rallying effort. Its last gasp.

Grind... snap!

He turned. There wouldn't be anything. Or only his own reflection again. They'd jump and squeal, and moments later they'd be laughing. And then everything would be okay.

The yellowish light caught a visage as monstrous as any creature out of a nightmare. Snout. Horns. A single glaring eye that shone blue-green like that of an animal. A black, hulking shape as large as a man.

It lunged at him. Pain tore diagonally across his arm. Scything, horrible pain followed by a spurting gush. The dying flashlight – and most of Rich's right hand – spun off into the darkness. He glimpsed for one fleeting instant his severed fingers flying, and the raw slash so clean it could have been made by a machete's single swipe.

Then he could see nothing. He heard himself shrieking, heard R.J., heard those harsh, inhuman breaths. A large, powerful form grappled with him. Rich fought back blindly. His left hand struck against a toughness that was ridged and rubbery and repulsive in its cold, slick unnatural solidity.

He felt himself seized, spun. He felt R.J.'s fingers pulled loose of their terrified grasp on his belt.

R.J. screamed. "Daddy! Daddy! It's got me! Daddy! Help! It's got me!"

"R.J.!" He charged in the direction of his son's voice.

"Daddeeeeeeee!"

A brutal blow drove into Rich's chest. It felt like a horse-kick, the iron head of a sledgehammer, a battering ram. The force flung him backward as if he'd been hit by a car.

Spears of crystal slid between his ribs, punctured his lungs, impaled him.

"Daddeeee..."

Fading. Fading like the light had done. Fading away.

Fading.

And gone.

CHAPTER 9
The Mermaid's Pool

Were they all dead?

Everyone else, dead?

She hadn't heard any noises in a long time. Not since one of the boys, the one about Danny's age, fell silent instead of blundering around, crying and calling for his father.

Now, it was quiet.

Almost perfectly silent. Except for the trickle of water, a rippling murmur that was nearly subliminal.

Bob was dead.

Crushed. Like a grape in a press. All the juice squeezed out of him.

All the *whine*.

Ha!

Lindsey smiled, glad for the darkness because even without anyone else there to see, she knew it would have been a ghastly, unpleasant smile.

Bob was dead.

She certainly hadn't expected it to be like this. She'd figured he would keel over from a massive coronary one of these days, or suffocate in the night on his own neck-flab in a fatal case of sleep apnea. Or choke on a meatball and nobody would be able to perform the Heimlich because they couldn't get their arms around him.

All *those* eventualities she'd been prepared for.

This was a surprise.

Never, never in a million years would she have predicted Bob's death by violent crushing in a cave-in. He hadn't even wanted to go on the tour in the first place. For, she was sure, pretty much precisely this reason.

Well, not of being crushed to death in a cave-in. But of falling or getting stuck somewhere along the way. Of being embarrassed and humiliated by having to be unstuck, helped, rescued.

He was just as bad when it came to other kinds of vacation activities. Anything even remotely athletic? Out of the question. No hiking, no skiing, no hang-gliding.

Beach? Waterslides? Snorkeling? Never happen. Absolutely nothing that would require him to be seen in swim trunks. She would have loved to go scuba diving, but would he even consider it? Not a chance. No way would he so much as try cramming his blubber into a wetsuit.

They couldn't fly anyplace because no normal airline seat could accommodate him, and he was too cheapskate to go first-class. Or maybe he feared that even those roomy seats would prove too narrow. Or he'd have to ask for a seatbelt extender from some sweetly-sympathetic flight attendant who'd then go to the galley or cockpit and snigger about it to the rest of the crew.

Forget amusement parks, too. All because once, one single time, he had been turned away from a ride on account of how the lap bar wouldn't latch.

She was amazed he'd agreed to the cave trip. Amazed right up until they'd parked, and Bob had mentioned in that casual-offhand way of his that maybe he'd sit this one out.

Sit this one out.

Like always.

One look from her had done the job, though. If he'd stayed behind, Danny would have stayed behind. What was the point of doing this, of getting the two of them out of a buffet line or a hotel room or a food court, if they just sat in the damn car the whole time?

It wasn't like she was *trying* to be a bitch about things. He knew perfectly well what he was doing to himself. He knew what he was doing to Danny, too. That was the part that made her really crazy. He *knew!*

They'd talked about it, she and Bob. Dozens of times. Hundreds. He always agreed. Eating healthier. Being more active. For all of their sakes. Especially Danny's. With childhood obesity skyrocketing the way it was, they had a sacred obligation to their son. Besides, hadn't both of them been miserable as kids? Bullied and picked on and lonely? Was it so wrong of them to want Danny not to have to go through that?

And Bob always agreed. Bob always promised.

Then, the moment her back was turned, Bob always sabotaged.

She'd serve a good dinner with salad and vegetables and broiled chicken... and wouldn't you know, Bob would remember some errand he needed to do, invite Danny to go with him to keep him company... and they'd come back with burger breath, or ice cream smears drying on the corners of their mouths. She'd spend a Saturday morning at the gym and come home to find the two of them on the couch with game controllers in hand, surrounded by empty chip bags and pizza boxes.

Like he did it on purpose.

Like he resented her for having successfully shed the weight. Instead of being happy for her and proud of her. Whenever there was a special occasion – her birthday, their anniversary, her promotion – he'd be happy to celebrate with her, as long as those celebrations involved a restaurant. Not if they involved dancing or anything active.

Well, no more of that.

No more of him puffing and panting just from the effort of putting on his shoes. No more watching him wallow out of bed in the morning like a walrus on an ice floe. No more watching him shovel in enough food at one sitting to feed an ordinary person for two days.

Lindsey clicked on her keychain flashlight and inspected him again. Not to gloat. Only to...

Well, to make sure.

A while ago, Danny had been into these disgusting little toys... flexible plastic shells around some kind of stretchy fluid-sac interior, shaped like farm animals. A cow, a pig, a horse. With strategic holes. So that when a person compressed one in a fist, the inner sac bulged out through the holes, thereby giving the animal comically protruding eyeballs, tongue, and – the really gross part – a big bubble of it coming from the butt.

Bob looked a lot like that now.

At least, his front end did. She was glad she couldn't see the other. The thought alone was enough to make her feel sorry for the woman and girl who'd been behind him. What a view. Even before the collapse. His massive ass wobbling as he crawled. His belly dragging on the ground. Fat slapping on stone.

The crushing pressure forced the blood forward, into his neck and head, until her husband looked like a big purple bullfrog. His eyes and tongue bulged. Some blood had even sweated out through his pores. More formed a maroon puddle that spread slow, questing amoeba pseudopods. They oozed along the channels in the rock, mingling with the creek, and tinting the diamond-clear waters with swirls of pink and red.

Kind of pretty, in a way.

And Bob was dead.

He *had* almost saved their boy's life. Almost.

Unintentionally, of course, due only to his bulk. All that fat prevented the collapsed ceiling of The Squeezes from flattening Danny. He'd scrabbled his way out, into the chamber with Lindsey. Almost made it to safety. Almost.

Except for a limestone column that broke and toppled, slamming Danny to the floor as hard as any professional football player's tackle.

He lay there pale, not purple like his father. Just pale. His Cabbage Patch Kid face, all round chipmunk-cheeks and tucked little bow of a mouth, was turned toward her. His head dangled at the edge of Mermaid's Pool, strands of his hair wavering like kelp in the blood-tinged water.

Bob's limp hand curled over Danny's foot.

Both dead.

And she was alive.

No more arguing. Not over food, not over exercise, not over Danny.

Not over money, either.

Even the darkest cloud could have its silver lining.

She was...

She was *free*.

The weight was gone. In every sense.

She had shed the ugly, excess pounds that had clung to her for as long as she could remember. She'd emerged from a lifetime's fatty cocoon as a fit, healthy, athletic new person. Attractive. Sexy, even.

Now, she was shed of more encumbering weight.

The deadweight of Bob.

And Danny, okay, that was sad, but maybe even that was for the best. He'd already been a Bob-in-miniature, with all Bob's laziness and all Bob's bad habits.

This could be her new start.

Plenty of money. Whatever she got from the sale of the house... Bob's insurance policy... and compensation from *this* whole mess. Lawsuits, book deals... Oprah!

She would, for the first time in her entire life, be thin, single, unencumbered and rich. And free. *Free!*

Lindsey laughed aloud, then caught herself, then realized she didn't have to worry. Other people might not understand laughter under these conditions... but, what other people? She was alone. Alone with her dead husband and her dead son.

What about the others?

Dead, dead, and more dead.

Possibly not the brunette and her daughter. Those two, at the rear of the group and at the rear of Bob, had gone back to look for an exit. Maybe they'd gotten out already. Beyond earshot, at any rate.

The honeymooners? Who'd spent the whole tour groping, giggling, cooing, and sliding off into dark corners to make out? Oh, very dead. Very dead indeed. Mashed to paste together while trying to gain admittance into whatever you called the underground version of the Mile High Club. Hundred Under Club? Squish. Goosh.

Sylvia, the guide, had gone off looking for the two obnoxious tweens who'd ditched the rest of them – and good riddance, Lindsey remembered thinking at the time. Pair of spoiled snots with pretentious names.

Their mother talked non-stop from the start of the tour, bragging about this one's hockey games and that one's riding lessons, unable to shut up... until the cave-in, which shut her up once and for all.

So, really, there wasn't anyone to hear Lindsey laugh at her newfound sense of rushing, soaring freedom.

Except...

A hoarse, muddled voice groaned in the dark. Then, a word. "Mom?"

The laughter caught in her throat like a scarf on a bramble.

"Mom, that you?"

She moved the flashlight beam to Danny's face again. He looked at her, hurt and bleary and confused.

"Danny," she said.

He started to cry.

"Danny," she said again. "You... you're alive."

"I can't move. Mom, I can't move and I really hurt."

"There's a rock on you."

"Something's wrong with my legs. Where's Dad? Is Dad okay?"

"What do you mean, something's wrong with your legs?" Her gaze moved to Bob's dead fingers, curled around Danny's shoe. "Can you move them? Your feet? Can you wiggle your toes?"

"Huh-unh." His tears flowed faster. "I can't feel my legs or my feet, not at all, it's like they're gone."

Inside her, there was a second cave-in, a second rumbling avalanche. Everything changed. Everything came crashing down.

Danny, alive. Alive but with a crippling spine injury. Alive but crippled. Unable to walk.

She saw it all in an instant. Saw how it would be… how *he* would be.

Wheelchair-bound. Needing constant help and care. Needing to be shifted from bed to chair, from chair to tub. Possibly incontinent, needing to be diapered and changed like a giant baby.

Only wanting to eat junk food because it was his sole remaining comfort. Never exercising. She hadn't been able to get him to exercise even with two good legs. He'd sit in that chair and do nothing but eat. Eat until he was a loose mound of flesh, all rolls and jiggle.

For the rest of his life.

And what were her options?

Keep him at home with her, take care of him herself. Or hire someone. Or put him someplace where the staff could do it all.

Those places were astronomically expensive. So was hiring a caregiver. Either of those choices would drain away whatever she got from Bob's insurance like sand through a funnel. Eventually, the money would be gone.

If she kept him at home, kept the house, devoted herself to his care… she'd be able to hang onto the money then… but at the cost of her freedom.

She could have the freedom with no money. Or the money with no freedom.

"Mom?" Blubbering.

Or…

"Danny," she said.

"Will I have to be in a wheelchair?"

Lindsey patted his shoulder. "No, Danny. You won't."

"Really?"

"Really."

She seized him by the hair.

"Mom! Ow! Mom?"

She thrust his face into the Mermaid's Pool. Danny thrashed. Bubbles of expelled breath roiled up around him, mixing the clear water and the tendrils of Bob's blood.

He scrabbled at her. His fingernails gouged her forearm, but she barely felt the scratches. His upper body bucked and heaved. His lower body stayed limp as a rag.

She leaned. She pushed. She could feel the terrified struggling energy thrumming in him.

"It's better this way, Danny," she said.

Not that he could hear her, with his head under water.

The bubbles stopped.

At last, after what seemed like forever, the thrumming energy was gone. His neck drooped over the pool's rim. His hair floated in a corona. His arms drifted.

"It's better this way," Lindsey said.

CHAPTER 10
Heat

The girl he loved was holding his hand.

Holding his hand!

His hand!

Colin told himself to knock it off. He had to concentrate.

It wasn't like Toni held his hand out of any sort of affection. The footing was unsteady, and they didn't want to get separated.

But still.

The girl he loved was holding his hand.

Trusting him. Relying on him.

If he could save her, get her out of this... it could be the big change, the big chance. The event that finally made Toni Ashe *notice* him. She'd see that he wasn't just some loser. She'd dump Nick, and–

"God, it stinks, it reeks, what a fucking stench!" Toni said.

She'd pulled her collar up over the lower half of her face like a mask. It made her shirt-hem ride up, and he could see the soft curve of her tummy. Some of the guys at school called that a 'muffin top.' She had sweet hips and a sweeter ass, and the best pair of tits he'd ever seen outside of a magazine or a movie.

And her mouth – holy fellatio, Batman! Those plump, pouty lips. The things she did with a pen or pencil while struggling over a Sudoku... the way she ate a corn dog...

Toni. His best friend's sister. He'd had a wild crush on her since he was old enough to know the difference between boys and girls. Not that he'd said anything. Not to his own sister, not to Brandon, and certainly not to Toni herself. She would have laughed. Or pretended to gag. Or both.

"Not much farther," he said.

"Are you sure?"

Still holding his hand. Did she notice how moist and sweaty his palm was?

"That passage over there, it'll bring us to right outside the armory."

"What if it's caved in, too?"

"Then we'll find some other way."

"You better know what you're doing," she said.

"I do." *I hope.*

He did know the caves pretty well. Better than almost anybody. When one of the guides needed a day off or called in sick, Dad sometimes let him lead the tours. Him or Chloe, though Chloe didn't like the caverns these days. Once, she had been as into them as Colin, the two of them sharing that interest the way they – as twins – shared so much else. But not any more.

Why anybody would prefer to work in the gift shop, ticket booth or snack bar, or do boring stuff like help Mr. Baxley with the maintenance and Mrs. Baxley with the gardening, was beyond him. Especially with this whole fascinating world to explore, literally beneath their feet.

Because of Rory? Chloe said he was creepy. Which he was, okay. But it still wasn't a reason to avoid the caves, just because Rory liked them, too. Colin couldn't understand that.

Of course, if Chloe hadn't started staying away, she might have figured out what Rory and Nick were doing. She would have gone right to Dad, who would have gone right to the cops. They'd find the stash, the guns and drugs. They'd arrest Rory and Nick. Him and Brandon and Toni, too? Probably.

Much better being here like this. With Toni. Just the two of them, alone in the private dark.

With Brandon dead, flattened like a stomped-on cockroach back in the bunker.

With who-knew-how-many people trapped down here. Vacationers. Families. Kids. Old folks. Hurt. Scared. Even killed.

Mixed-feelings city.

He liked being alone with Toni, having the chance to prove to her what he was made of. Show her that a guy didn't have to be a bad-boy like Nick in order to be cool and interesting.

But his best friend was dead.

Other people, too. A Saturday summer afternoon meant peak time. Two or three tours, including guides, would be down here. As many as sixty people, give or take. Caught in the caves. Hurt, dead, dying.

And here he was, excited because Toni was holding his hand.

"We've got to climb some," Colin said, shining the light on a nearly vertical limestone face pocked with old piton holes. "I'll steady your feet and boost you."

Grumbling curses, she hooked her fingers into the lowest handhold. "I hated when we had to do this in gym. There better not be any fucking chin-up bars next."

He boosted. And stared at the candy-pink thong rising above her waistband. She was heavier than he expected. Or he was weaker. Or both. He tried not to grunt. She'd think he was commenting on her being fat or something, and then he wouldn't get anywhere with her.

"It'll level out into a low tunnel at the top," he said. "You'll have to crawl."

"What about the light? I can't see shit up there."

"As soon as you're up, I'll hand you the light."

"If a bat comes flapping out into my face—"

"No bats. There's hardly any animals that live down here. Only a few bugs and things."

"Slimy fucking bugs, I bet. Unh. Dammit. Give me a push, huh?"

Unable to believe it, he planted his palms on her ass. It felt firm and fleshy and warm and round through the worn, faded denim. Just that single layer of cloth between their skin, too, because the thong would ride snug and deep up her crack. His thumbs were almost in her crotch.

This was crazy.

His best friend, a pile of pulp back in the bunker. Dozens of people lost, hurt or dead. While he, Colin, had a double handful of Brandon's sister's buttcheeks.

He also had a zipperbuster of a hard-on. The semi-wood that he'd been fighting unsuccessfully to control ever since she'd taken his hand was a raging brute now.

He was *touching Toni's ass!*

More than just touching it.

Both hands, baby!

And she was squirming against him, flexing.

"Push, Colin!" she said. "Do it! Push hard!"

Every drop of blood surged right out of his brain and into his pants, because his imagination heard an altogether other context.

"Harder!" Toni demanded.

Dizzied, sure that he was going to pass out, Colin shoved with all his might. Then Toni clambered up, taking her weight off his hands, scrambling to the top. He held onto the rocks, trying not to lose his balance.

"Good," she said from above. "Now, give it to me."

His throat felt stuffed with dry wool. His voice croaked out, "What?"

"The flashlight, stupid. Give me the fucking flashlight."

"Oh. Yeah." He picked it up, fumbled, nearly dropped it. The beam swung across his body. Only the horrible thought that he'd be casting a gigantic crotch-level bulging shadow and she'd *see* it snapped his brain into focus again.

Toni leaned way over and reached. He had a quick but amazing view down her shirt. Full, swaying tits trying to fall out of a skimpy pink bra.

Is it possible, he wondered, *for a prick to explode?*

He stretched up on tiptoe and gave her the flashlight. She directed it away from him, into the new tunnel. Colin, cloaked in welcome darkness, leaned against the stone with one hand gripping his forehead and the other arm folded over his groin.

"Are you coming or what?"

"Huh?!?" He jumped. "No! I mean... what? I mean... yeah. Just a second."

"Hurry up already."

"Right."

He scaled the rock face, trying not to bump himself too much or rub against anything. It wasn't easy. But he managed to get to the top, where Toni hunkered over on her hands and knees with the flashlight pointing along the sinuous, low-ceilinged tunnel. Water dripped, collecting in basins. The thick, sulfurous smell they'd noticed before hung stronger than ever in the warm, humid air.

"Fucking stinks," Toni said, pinching her nose. "Is it gunpowder? Got that Fourth-of-July whiff. Did the ammo boxes blow up?"

"Maybe," Colin said.

He didn't know much about real-live guns, despite the survivalist magazines Rory and Nick brought around. He could use them if he tried, he was sure. He practiced enough. But he wasn't about to say so in front of Toni. She'd sneer and say video games didn't count.

Girls just didn't understand. It wasn't playing, wasn't goofing around, wasn't wasting time. It was *training*. The military used video games for training purposes all the time. Flight sims, first person shooters, tactical wargames...

If he or Brandon ever absolutely had to pick up actual weapons to defend themselves... say, in the event of zombie apocalypse or alien invasion or something... they'd be able to shoot with the best of them. They had it all planned out–

Wouldn't matter to Brandon now, though. Brandon was dead.

"Is it safe?" Toni asked.

"Compared to what?"

She thought about that, chewing her lip. Sexy. Never mind the sweat, the dirt, the scrapes, the smudges, the straggled hair and shock-hollowed eyes. Didn't matter.

Didn't matter one bit. He wanted her more now than he ever had before in his entire life.

This would be what brought them together. This tragedy. The shared grief. The ordeal. It'd make a powerful bond, intense, unbreakable.

Toni would finally realize that he'd been crazy in love with her since they were kids, desperately in love with her all these years though he'd never said a word. She'd see that he didn't care about her history – the drinking, the smoking, the partying, the slutty reputation. He saw past all that. And then she'd see past his shyness and social ineptitude. She'd see past his geek exterior. She wouldn't care anymore that he was no jock, no bad-boy.

When they got out of here…

Unless they ended up in jail…

There had to be some way to keep that from happening. He wouldn't be able to stand it if he got Toni, only to lose her again. It wasn't even their fault, it was Rory's, and Nick's!

A blinding glare seared his eyeballs. The flashlight. In his face.

"Are you going to sit there all day? I want to get the fuck out of here!"

"Sure," Colin said. "That way. You want me to go first?"

"You're the genius who knows where we're going." She flipped the light around and poked the handle end at him.

He crawled along, splashing through water that didn't seem as chilly as it should have. The air felt hotter, too.

Toni crawled behind him. "I almost wish this was a bad trip," she said. "At least then, when the drugs wore off, it'd go away. This bites. Creeping around in some dark, stinky cave with *you*."

Colin frowned. What about that bond? The bond of shared traumatic experiences? She was supposed to be appreciating how brave and resourceful he was. How he was saving her life and everything. Bringing them together. All bittersweet because of Brandon dying, but deeper and more profound because of that. Like in the movies.

So… why wasn't it working?

He deserved Toni, after what they'd been through! He loved Toni. He, Colin, was the one down here with her, rescuing her, taking care of her, protecting her. Where was Nick? Huh? Where was her bad-boy boyfriend? Off on his stupid motorcycle someplace, probably buying meth.

She wouldn't really go back to Nick after this, would she?

No. That was whack.

"We can stand up now," he said, rising first to a crouch and then to his feet. "Out into the other passage. That'll bring us to the exit shaft."

"Thank-fucking-God." Toni pushed past him, got up, and hurried in the direction of the new opening, kicking loose rocks out of her way as she went.

"Hey, slow down. Wait for me."

"You can take your time and hang around in here if you want, but I am through with this cave shit. I don't care if they throw me in jail for twenty years as long as it means I never have to be in a place like this again."

"Toni! There's a–"

–*low bridge*, was what he meant to say.

Her forehead found it before he could get the words out. Found it with a noise like a melon dropped on a concrete floor. She staggered back, dazed. Her feet blundered across the same loose rocks she'd just kicked aside, ankles splaying and turning.

Colin rushed forward, arms out, and caught her as she fell. At least, he tried. The impact jarred the flashlight from his hand and bowled him over. They both went down, landing on a hilly limestone slope, rolling-sliding-tumbling under the low bridge and all the way to the bottom. The air coughed out of his lungs. He came to rest, head spinning, on something soft.

On Toni.

He was lying on top of Toni. His face buried against her tits, their legs all tangled. One of her thighs was between his, pushing directly on his–

She took a deep breath, inflating her chest and half-smothering him. On the exhale, she moaned.

And one of his thighs was between hers, too... tucked against her–

"Whuhappn?" she said, her voice slurred.

Blackness surrounded them. He couldn't see her, couldn't see the cave, couldn't see anything. The flashlight must have broken.

But he could sure feel her. Warm and springy and deliciously cushiony. He'd never been this close to a girl, and the sensations shot through him like skyrockets.

Toni stirred beneath him. "Ouch. Shit."

"Are you okay?"

"Head hurts like a bastard," she said. "I think I broke my fucking ankle. I can't see. You're squashing me. And... what the hell is *that*?"

"What?"

She twitched up hard with her leg. "That!"

God, it felt so good!

"Oh. Um..." He had no idea what to say.

"Get the fuck off me, you little pervert!"

"Toni, I–"

"I said get off me!" She bucked her hips.

"Oh, jeez!" Colin gasped. He didn't mean to, couldn't help it, but it felt so *good* and he couldn't stop, couldn't stop.

"Dammit, Colin!"

"Toni, Toni, aaahhhh God!"

The world turned inside out, everything going from darkness to a sheeting white, and Colin heard his own helpless shuddering scream.

CHAPTER 11
Plutonian Shore

In science class, they'd experimented with liquid nitrogen, dunking objects into the smoking-cold stuff to see what happened.

A flower, frozen into a perfect sculpture. A racquetball that detonated like a bomb when hurled to the floor. A hotdog, set on a counter and struck with a hammer so it broke into chunks of pinkish-grey meat.

And cryogenics. Bodies being preserved at, or just past the point of death. The idea being that future advances in medicine and technology might be able to heal them, restore them. Didn't people say that Walt Disney was on ice in some secret catacomb underneath Disneyland?

Space-travel stories used cryogenics all the time. Cryo-sleep, they called it. Or suspended animation. Until the invention of faster-than-light propulsion, starfarers crossing the vast distances between solar systems might have no other way to survive such a long journey. It'd be more cost-effective, too. Sailing ships in the olden days had been forced to limit the length of their trips by the amount of food and fresh water they could carry. Consumables, weight, fuel, energy. A cryo-sleeping crew would not need to eat, or drink, or be kept warm. They wouldn't have to worry about boredom or illness or cabin-fever insanity. With the aging process canceled out, or slowed to an infinitesimal crawl, they could arrive at even far-flung galactic destinations without being decades older.

Cold did that.

Cold prevented decay. That was what ice-houses were for. And freezers. To keep things fresh for longer, to keep things from spoiling and rotting and going bad.

It worked on people, too.

Extreme cold could even help keep a person alive.

Like people who fell through the ice or were swept away in freezing rivers. Even if they drowned. Even if their lungs flooded. Sometimes, the doctors could revive them. Sometimes, they'd even be good as new. That slowing effect held off the deterioration of their cells and tissues. Their brains didn't shut off as fast. A minimal current stayed active. Not unlike the way a computer could be turned off, but keep its data.

She remembered other stories too, cartoons like *Futurama*, and silly things about cavemen or saber-tooth tigers or alien monsters found embedded in glaciers... then allowed to thaw out and run amok. She didn't believe those. There was reason, and then there was going way, way too far.

Extreme cold.

Freezing rivers.

Hypothermia.

The dramatic slowing of metabolism.

Was that what she was feeling?

Was that why she felt numb? More than numb. As if she had no body at all. As if only her mind floated in some lightless void.

Kimmy. Her name was Kimmy. Or Kim, since Kimmy was a kid's name, a baby-name.

The bridge. Crossing the bridge.

Right... the bridge... the bridge!

She'd hung back to look at a pearly-white rock formation shaped like a unicorn. The old couple and their grandson passed her, then Kim had followed, trying to catch up with Makoto and Shara.

Then the bad thing happened.

Everything shaking. A noise like cannons and thunder. The bridge lurching and swinging. Rocking back and forth, rollicking up and down. Like that famous old news video of the Tacoma Narrows Bridge. She remembered it from science class, too. When they'd been talking about resonance frequencies.

Everything shaking and everyone screaming. Missiles raining down from the vaulted cavern's dark heights. A golfball-sized rock bouncing off her shoulder. Another, larger, streaking past her head like a meteorite. People panicking. The guide yelling. Nobody listening. The guide grabbing people on the bridge, pulling them and pushing them and dragging them across.

Makoto. Shara. The grandfather. The grandson.

Kimmy remembered the grandmother. Clutching the cables. Terrified into paralysis. Praying in a shrill, incoherent voice. Blocking Kim's way.

A man shouldered past them both. Without a care, without a glance. Not stopping. Not trying to help.

Kimmy stopped. Kimmy tried to help. Even with the ominous cracking groan and sifting of grit, gravel and dust from above that warned her the worst was yet to come. She'd stopped. To help the old woman. To coax her along.

It almost worked. Only a couple more steps from the end, the guide extending his hand, urging them to move. Others stampeding close after them. Grownups. More shouldering, shoving. Not caring that they might knock over and trample a young girl and an old lady.

Huge slabs and boulders. A mountain falling on them. Kim felt the whistle of something that must've missed her by inches. The noise was tremendous, a gonging-clanging-banging-crashing, cast-iron cookware dumped from a cement mixer. The bridge gave way with a series of twangs like the snapping of a giant's guitar strings.

She'd fallen. Amid metal and stone. Amid bodies, mangled blood-sponge messes. Then the ledge. Then the old lady she'd tried to help, striking that same ledge hard enough to break right through it, leaving Kimmy with a tiny, crumbling perch.

It dawned on her now that she had been shrieking the entire time. Shrieking so that her throat had felt like splitting from the strain. Shrieking without even hearing herself because of the rocks, the river. In raw, instinctive, animal terror. Shrieking because she couldn't do anything else. Because she knew she was going to die.

But then, they'd tried to save her. The big bald man, climbing down, reaching for her.

And right as Kim thought she might not die after all...

Someone started shooting.

Shooting!

"Kim! Kimmy!"

Why was someone shooting?

Why shoot the person trying to rescue her?

"Don't you give up on me, Kim, goddamn it!"

She saw the bullets slam into him. Blood spouting. Impact tremors rippling through his torso. His body driven into the gorge wall, rebounding from it. Losing his grip on the rocks.

Not losing his grip on the belt. The belt she'd wrapped around her wrists so that he could pull her up. Instead, it yanked her over with him.

Falling. Falling in rocks, in darkness.

"Kim! You have to breathe!"

Into the river. Cold, so cold. A shock snatching her breath, stunning her heart. The water rushing and swirling, torrential and black. Swiftness. Power. Irresistible. At its mercy. A twig, a leaf, helplessly carried along.

Hypothermia. Drowning. Extreme cold.

Am I drowning?

Have I drowned?

Something covered her mouth. Thin, hard lips. Barely warmer than her liquid-nitrogen flesh. A gust of air blew into her. Peppermint air... curiously strong... and she remembered the grandmother offering around a tin of Altoids as they'd entered Echo Gorge's enormous chamber.

The air inflated her lungs like balloons. The hard lips lifted away. Something pressed down on her chest. An elephant, stepping on her. The air rushed back out. Through her mouth, through her nose. Peppermint stinging her sinuses.

Kim coughed.

"Good girl... breathe, Kim. Breathe."

When she coughed again, she choked on water. She felt herself turned sideways, and hacked and heaved as thin fluid dribbled out. Her ribs ached. Bone-deep shudders shook through her.

"Can you sit up? Here. Sit up."

Hands on her. Big hands. Maneuvering her as if she was a doll, a toy. Folding her up into a sitting position, bent forward over her own lap, head hanging. Wet slaps of long hair in her face. Streams running from them, running from her clothes.

"S'dark," she sputtered.

"Yeah. How are you doing?"

Her teeth clacked and chattered. "Cold."

"Shut your eyes."

"Why? Can't see anyway."

"Just shut them."

She did, then heard a clickety sound and recognized it as the striker-wheel of a lighter being spun. Not one of those flimsy disposable ones, but a sturdy one, a Zippo most likely. Their father carried a Zippo. Stainless steel with his initials engraved on the side. He didn't smoke, but he carried it anyway. Lots of his business associates loved their cigarettes, and their expensive cigars.

The striker-wheel sound was followed by a muttered obscenity, and then more clickety-clicking. A bright line dazzled at the seam of her eyelids.

Gingerly, head turned away, she squinted one eye open. When it had adjusted, she opened the other.

The flame gleamed on glistening rock, making a dim pocket of illumination in what seemed to be a vast cavern. Kim could have been tempted to believe she was outside, on a starless, moonless night... if she hadn't instantly known better. For all its size, there was a feeling of enclosure here. Of confinement.

She sat on a flattish, gentle slope. A yard or so below the heels of her waterlogged sneakers, the river flowed past, much tamer now than the wild and turbulent beast she remembered. Not channeled through a narrow gorge, but spread out, relaxed. Wide. Shallow. Almost smooth. The current no longer leaped and roared, but lapped and chuckled.

Hunkered beside her, holding the Zippo, was a large man with no shirt, tattered pants, a shaved head and a grim face. His eyes were shiny coins at the bottom of sunken hollows.

"Mr.... Dawes," Kim said. "But he... he shot you. Didn't he?"

The lighter's flame bent and flickered in a cool but constant breeze. Shadows undulated. She could see a gored, hamburger-looking hole in his side. Blood seeped from it. Not a lot of blood. Not as much as she would have thought.

"Don't worry about that," he said. He held the light closer, scowling as he scrutinized her. "We've got to get warmed up. Can you move? Can you walk?"

"I'll try," she said. Her throat hurt, as much from all that screaming as from swallowing and then choking up so much water. But it wasn't too bad. All things considered.

The feeling came back to her arms and legs, tingle-prickling into them, pins and needles. She looked down, saw starkly pale skin, fingernails gone dusky-blue. Her lips probably were as well. The immersion had washed her scrapes and scratches into pruny, bloodless, fishbelly crinkles.

The cold did it. The cold had drawn her blood to the core of her body, in a last-ditch attempt to keep vital organs warm. So there wasn't much near enough to her skin to leak out. Same for Mr. Dawes, though his wounds were a lot worse.

Cryogenics. Hypothermia.

He helped her up. As Kim rubbed her arms and stamped her feet, trying to get her circulation moving again, he raised the lighter as high as he could and turned in a slow circle, surveying what little there was to survey.

"Where are we?" she asked.

"Night's plutonian shore."

"I beg your pardon, Mr. Dawes?"

"I don't know, it just popped into my head. From some poem, I think."

"*The Raven*. By Edgar Allan Poe."

"How'd you know that?"

"How'd *you*?"

"Never mind."

A weak smile tugged at the corners of her mouth. "You mean, nevermore."

"When the hell did I end up on that Smarter-Than-A-Fifth-Grader game show?"

"I'm in eighth grade."

"Bullsh– crap," he said. "You're, what, ten years old?"

"Eleven."

"Eleven. And in eighth grade? What are you, one of those child-geniuses?"

"I like school," she said, jumping up and down in place though her feet were still so numb it was like jumping while wearing blocks of ice for boots.

"Too bad you haven't already graduated from med school. I could use a doctor right about now."

"I know first aid."

"Let me guess. Girl Scout, too."

She nodded.

"Don't happen to have any cookies on you, I bet."

"No cookies."

While they talked, which Kim knew was more to stave off fear and the dreadful hush of the cave as anything else, Mr. Dawes walked downstream with the lighter still held up. Twenty feet later, he came to an abrupt halt, and sucked in air through a clenched jaw.

Kim saw what he was looking at, and covered the lower half of her face with both hands.

The wide, shallow stretch of the river deepened toward this end, where curving spurs of stone bent around to make a narrowing kind of channel. Rocks and wood caught there, piling up. Almost like a beaver dam, only without the rudimentary logic and sense of purpose displayed by beavers. Especially now. Now that portions of the broken metal-and-cable bridge had snagged there, looking like a bizarre abstract modern-art sculpture.

And bodies.

The bodies of the people who'd been on the bridge when the rocks came down. They tangled through the wreckage, limbs moving in the current as if they were waving goodbye, or making pitiful, silent, pleading gestures for help. Blanched-white faces. Gaping mouths. Stringy hair. Torn clothes and battered flesh. Some of them were only...

Only...

"Pieces," she said, and everything went cloudy-grey.

When she opened her eyes again, it was to brighter light, and a welcome, baking warmth. It would have been nice to let herself think that she'd been napping and dreamed it all, that when she sat up she would see a sunlit lake and a picnic table, and Makoto grinning down at her asking her if she was planning to sleep her way through their entire vacation. Then Shara would offer her a sandwich and a grape soda, and they'd go for a stroll along the beach and gather interesting pebbles from–

–*night's plutonian shore.*

"Got to tie it tighter than that."

"I'm trying."

"Go on and pull, kid. You won't hurt me. Not worse than getting shot, anyway."

Kim sat up. No sunlit lake, no picnic table. No Makoto, no Shara. Instead, she saw a small but blazing campfire. And Mr. Dawes. And a teenage boy, the one from the tour, the one who'd been with his grandparents.

She understood right away. She had fainted, and while she'd been unconscious, Mr. Dawes had located another survivor. Had, possibly, fished him out of the subterranean river like a trout in baggy pants. Then they had scavenged for dry driftwood and anything else that might be useful in keeping the three of them alive, and started the fire with that trusty Zippo. Now, Mr. Dawes sat on a rock while the teenager tied long raggedy strips of cloth around him, to serve as bandages. Making a clumsy, amateurish job of it, too. Kim supposed that he'd never been a Boy Scout. But it was better than nothing.

"Grant," she said out loud.

The teenager started and looked at her. "What?"

"That's your name. That's what your grandmother called you. I'm Kim."

"I know."

He had a lot of long brownish-blond hair worn unkempt and in-the-eyes, damp and stuck plastered to his head. Fourteen, maybe fifteen. Chin stubble about as sparse as Makoto's, and she guessed he had to shave about as often.

"So you're saying the same assho–" Mr. Dawes stopped himself, curling his lip. "The same guy that shot me knocked you into the gorge."

"Dude was wild," Grant said. "When he shot you, we tried to take him down but he fought like a... pitbull or something. Strong, too. Crazy-strong. I jumped on him, and he just... threw me."

"But why?" Kim asked, hitching herself closer to the fire and holding out her hands. "Why would he do that? Why did he shoot you, Mr. Dawes?"

"Just Dawes, okay?"

"You know that guy?" Grant finished tying bandages and stepped back, eyeing them doubtfully. "He have some beef with you, or was he a random psycho?"

"It was me he was after," Dawes said. "He didn't pull a gun and open up on everyone indiscriminate. He wanted *me*, and he wanted me to know it, too. Said my name, waited until I looked up before he squeezed that trigger."

"Why?" Kim repeated. "*Do* you know him?"

Dawes worked his shoulders, rotating them, testing the bandages. "Didn't look familiar. But he had to have a reason. Maybe someone sent him. Maybe he figured he owed me some kind of payback. I don't know. Doesn't matter."

"Payback for what?" Grant asked. "Someone sent him? Like who? You have enemies? Is this a vendetta thing? Is he a cop? Are *you* a cop?"

"Drop it, would you? I'm not going to go into this with a couple of kids. In case you didn't notice, I'm kind of having a shitty day. Sorry. A bad day."

"It's all right if you swear," Kim said. "You saved us."

"I want to know," Grant said, jutting his chin belligerently. "Especially if it's because of you that me and Kimmy ended up in this. He hadn't shot you, you wouldn't have pulled her down and I wouldn't have got knocked in. We have a-"

A thick finger leveled at him. "You'd better not be about to say you have a right to know," Dawes said. "Or that I owe you the truth. This is no fucking courtroom, kiddo. All that matters right now is keeping ourselves alive until someone finds us or we can get the hell out of here. If you want to play Twenty Questions later, fine. Until then, shut up and let me think."

Grant bristled, but a single look from those hollow eyes evidently made him reconsider. He plopped down beside Kim, and rummaged through the small pile of salvage in search of something to do.

Dawes strode back and forth along the river's edge, with his head down and his expression stony. He flexed his big fists and probed at the bandages. Kim watched him. Maybe the cold water had stanched the bleeding for a while, but now that he was warmer, and moving, exerting himself... already, dark patches were soaking through.

"He's badly hurt," she said to Grant, pitching her voice low. "He should be resting."

"You tell him that."

"How many times was he hit? Are the bullets still in him?"

"Look, I don't know. He told me to cut up some cloth and tie those things on there. He's tough. He'll be okay. He's... like... Riddick. Or The Rock."

"No, he isn't. This is no movie."

"Guy gets shot, falls off a cliff into a raging river, drags himself out, rescues people, and he's still up and walking around as if he's got nothing worse than a paper cut? Hell yes, he's Riddick."

She gave up arguing. "I'm... sorry about your grandmother. She seemed like a very nice lady."

"Thanks." He fidgeted, uncomfortable. "My folks are having a hard time right now. Money and stuff. So they had me spend the summer with my grandparents while they try to work everything out. You know, driving around in the motor home with all the other golden oldies. I hope Grandpa Homer's okay."

They sat in silence a while, Kim thinking about Makoto and Shara, wondering how they were. They hadn't been on the bridge. Hadn't been hit by any rocks, as far as she knew. But did they think she was dead? Lost into the river and the dark? They had to.

Next, she thought of her parents. Her mother hadn't wanted Makoto to bring her on vacation with him and Shara. Her mother didn't like Shara very much, always trying to fix Makoto up with some daughter or niece of one of her own friends instead. But Father had overruled and given permission. What would they do when Makoto came home with this kind of news?

"Okay," Dawes said. "Here's the deal. We can't stay here. It might be days, hell, weeks before anyone finds us. That's assuming they even look. They're probably going to figure we're all dead. That means we have to get out of here on our own. It's no good going back upstream. The river's too dangerous that way, and we'd never be able to climb up the gorge. There may be side passages, other tunnels, but we have no way of knowing where they lead. We can't afford to waste time poking around in what might turn out to be a dead end."

"How big are the caves?" Kim asked. "The woman at the ticket booth told us that the tour only went through the thoroughly explored part, but that a lot of it was still unmapped."

"Pretty damn big," Dawes said. "But the river... the river doesn't run underground its entire course. It comes out at Little Elk Lake. If we follow it, if we can get through, we might be able to get out that way ourselves."

Several minutes later, carrying whatever they thought they might be able to use, they set out. Dawes left the fire going, saying that there was no danger of it spreading and if any searchers did come by, they might discover the smoldering coals or the ashes and realize that someone had survived.

He moved stiffly, and Kim noticed that he seemed to be favoring his right arm, holding it tucked against his side as much as possible. If he was in pain, though, he was steadfastly determined not to show any. The dark splotches on the bandages were bigger.

But what could she say? Even if she said something, what could they do? Getting out was their only chance.

Dawes wrapped the end of a gnarled driftwood branch in scraps cut from someone's jeans, tied the scraps with a shoelace, and ignited the cloth to make a torch. It burned dull and smoky, the denim too damp to really hold a flame. He also had his lighter.

The cave... the cave along the river... along night's plutonian shore...

Over time, an almost unfathomable eternity of time, the water had cut and worn and eroded its path through solid rock. It had smoothed away sharp points and jagged edges, leaving stone slick and smooth as sealskin, slippery as a freshly-waxed floor.

In some sections, the ceiling soared high above them. Once, it even broke through to a foliage-veiled skylight hundreds of feet over their heads, inaccessible and unreachable as the moon. In other sections, they had to get down and crawl in cold, slimy mud, coughing on the torch's smoke and trying not to hit their heads on the uneven ceiling.

For a horrible span that seemed to take hours to traverse, they had to wade through the freezing river in water that came up to Kim's hips. Other times, they were able to keep to the sides and to ledges, or use natural stepping stones that poked above the surface like turtle-backs. Dawes jumped across the wider gaps, leaning to help them. Kim saw him grimace once when he did that, the bandage on his side nearly black with bloodstain.

The cave and the river, the river and the cave.

Minutes? Hours? Days?

Night's plutonian shore went on forever.

They couldn't.

"Need a rest," Dawes said, finally stopping. "See if you can find any wood. We'll build up another fire."

"Hey! Hey! Hello? Is somebody there? Hello! Hey!"

The shouts made all three of them whirl around so fast that they nearly lost their footing. Two figures came stumble-rushing toward the sputtering, dying torchlight.

"Oh, shit," Dawes said as the dull glow fell upon the approaching faces. "Just what I need. More kids."

CHAPTER 12
Old-Timer

"Either go back up topside or stay out of the way. We've got enough on our plates without having to worry about you taking a fall and busting a hip."

"Dang it, I'm trying to help here," Pete said.

"I know you are. And you've done a great job. You did your part. Now let us do ours, would you?"

He wasn't sure which he hated more; the brush-off, the condescending tone of it, or the fact that it came from a kid young enough to be his own grandson. Or the way the rest of them shared glances when they thought he wasn't looking.

Bunch of kids. Bunch of damn, upstart kids. He'd been mining and spelunking when their mommies and daddies hadn't even been gleams in anyone's eye. He'd spent more time underground in his life than they had spent on this planet in the first place.

They thought he was old.

So what if he was? With age came experience. Came wisdom. Came know-how that this bunch would never even so much as bother to learn. Them with all their gear and gadgets. Safety checks and re-checks and triple-checks.

Which wasn't to say that Pete was against safety. Far from it. He was well aware of the dangers, the risks. More aware than this bunch would ever be. He had seen men die. Had seen men escape death who by rights should have died.

These kids had no respect for the caves. Didn't see them as what they were. Saw them as empty, unchanging holes in the ground. Bare, barren and lifeless. They thought that with their educations and equipment, they'd beat the cave.

You never beat the cave. You never beat the mountain. The earth couldn't be conquered. Everest didn't care if it was climbed or not. Hell, it wouldn't even notice. Anybody who believed different, who believed a man could pit himself against Nature and win, was a pure fool.

Challenge other men? Fine and dandy. Nothing wrong with that.

Challenge yourself? Even better. Because that was really what it was all about.

Challenge Nature? Plain, simple human arrogance and delusion.

But you did have to respect it if you wanted to survive.

Pete did.

He could step into any cavern or lava tube and suss it out in a matter of minutes. A listen, a breath of its air, and he'd know plenty. His gut would tell him. He didn't need any fancy degrees in geology or seismology or vulcanology or any other of those ologies.

Right now, what he knew was that Cornucopia had gone wrong.

He felt it.

Accepted it.

He wasn't going around like the so-called experts, pissing and moaning and arguing with each other as they tried to figure out what had happened. They swore there hadn't been any quakes, not even a super-localized temblor – whatever the sweet Jesus that was supposed to be. They went on and on about the geologic stability of the bedrock and how it shouldn't have collapsed. Indignant. Personally offended. If they couldn't make sense of it, if they couldn't explain it away, then they didn't want to admit it or acknowledge it at all.

When the fact of the matter was, it *had* happened. If they didn't know the reason, the problem was with them. Not with the event. It wasn't on purpose and malicious to make them look bad.

Nature didn't have to go by their rules.

Try and tell them that, though, and they would about cut you dead like you'd just insulted their mothers. Oh, no. Not when their egos, smarts, and very balls were on the line! They would solve this, beat this, win this. Because they were the *experts*, damn it!

Cornucopia went bad, that was all. Not because of anything that those poor trapped people had done to deserve it. The cave wasn't out to get them, wasn't a punishment from God or anything like that.

It just went bad.

And it troubled Pete down to the bone that none of these *experts* seemed to realize it. Troubled him that they wouldn't listen to him, either. If that was his own ego, he was not ashamed to own up and say so.

They hadn't even wanted him to come along, let alone lead the way. They'd been puffed-up and cocksure that they would be just fine without him. Worse, that he'd be a liability, a burden. Unable to keep up. Unable to do his share, pull his weight.

Joe Goddard had insisted, though. Never mind their computer-generated three-dimensional maps of the cave system and whatnot. Joe wanted them to have a guide who knew Cornucopia, who could improvise and think on his feet.

That was the thing about these kids. They relied on their gadgets and book-learning and their fancy computers. They put their full trust in the technology, and never stopped to consider what they'd do if it failed. Most of them wouldn't even entertain the possibility that it *could* fail. Suggest it, and they'd just laugh.

But they had gone along with Joe, however grudgingly. Treating Pete like some decrepit old hound dog, one lamed up with the arthritis and half-blind and half-deaf and toothless and palsied and incontinent, but one that still thought it could flush a pheasant or run a rabbit. They'd call him a good boy and give him congratulatory pats on the head, when really they were thinking he should have been taken out behind the barn long ago to be put out of his misery.

After he'd gotten them here and everything. Without hardly a single wrong choice or backtracking. In good time, too. They would have been ages finding their way down here if not for Pete. By the time they'd found these poor folks, they'd have had more corpses than live ones to deal with.

Good boy and a pat on the head.

Now stay out of our way, you used-up relic.

So, grumbling, he stayed out of their way. It chafed him, though. They were as finicky about their doctoring as they were their caving. Instead of patching up the injured enough to get them out in a hurry, they had to fuss and muss and finesse and bother over every little cut and sprained finger. While, elsewhere, others might be far worse off. Maybe dying. Better to get as many out as fast as possible, even if it meant jostling them around some.

And for the love of Christ Almighty, *now* one of them was taking the time to wrap gauze around a stuffed bunny-rabbit just to reassure a little girl. Someone could be bleeding to death or have a broken neck further along in the caves, but here they were wasting even more time.

Get them out first. Cheer them up later.

Pete wished that he hadn't deferred to Joe Goddard. He had been all set to come down here without delay. Not with a whole pack of volunteers, mind you. Certainly not with the frantic folks who had friends or kin on the tours. A small group, maybe those biker-fellows. Chloe or Colin, if Joe and Kitty would have allowed it.

And Rory. Provided Rory could have been found. Didn't it just figure that the one time that boy could have been useful, he was nowhere to be seen? He had almost as good a sense for the caves as did Pete himself. As if it was innate in him; as if Rory, who'd never so much as set foot in Cornucopia before last year, was born in its darkness, raised in its chambers and tunnels.

Just as Joe had insisted on the experts taking Pete, though, he'd insisted that Pete wait for the experts. Pete supposed that Joe had been hoping the groups would all come out under their own power. Scared, sure, and probably madder than hell. Threatening lawsuits. But alive.

Pete could have told him it wasn't going to be that way. He *had* told him, in so many words. Joe had replied by saying that Pete should have a little more faith in the guides. He had, after all, trained them.

He hadn't trained them for something like this. Not on this scale. A simple cave-in of a single section of passageway, sure. What to do if someone fell down a shaft, sure. Even how to find their way out in case of a power failure. But not for anything this big. He couldn't have imagined anything this big. Or this bad.

What had gone wrong down here?

"Stay close, old-timer," one of the whippersnapper experts called. "Don't go wandering off."

"I ain't *wandering* anyplace," Pete said. "How about you do your job and let me do mine?"

Without looking their way, he knew they'd be sharing those glances again. It rankled, but short of going over there and getting in their faces, there wasn't much he could do about it. He swiveled his head around, shining his lamp over the debris.

Goblintown was a sorry, sorry sight. It looked bombed. Not Baghdad-bombed, not Hiroshima-bombed, but London- or Berlin-bombed. Some places rubble, others untouched, others pocked by shrapnel.

Two dead. The mother of a couple of the little blonde girls, crushed to death while shielding one of her daughters. An older man, not Pete's-age older but in his sixties by the look of him. Respectably tough-looking, fit. Except that he'd taken a bad fall and most likely split his skull.

Plenty alive but hurt. The woman with the busted leg, mother of the other blondies, was the worst. She'd gone into shock. Her husband sported a broken arm, maybe a dislocated shoulder. The darker-haired woman had twisted the holy hell out of both ankles and banged herself a good one on the head.

The others, they seemed more-or-less okay. The children, mostly. They could be amazingly resilient, children. Pete and his brothers had tumbled off more roofs and out of more trees than they could count, and usually with nothing more than a bump or a bruise to show for it. They had taken line-drive baseballs to the skull and bounced up and gone back for more. He wasn't all that surprised to see that the kids were in fairly good shape, all things being equal.

Though Jesus-H, by the way that little boy was howling and carrying on, you'd think he had lost a limb.

Three missing.

This had been Justin's tour group, and one of the little girls said he'd helped her out of the Wishing Well. "Him and the purple-hair girl," she'd told Pete, before he got shunted aside so that the experts could see to splinting her auntie's busted leg.

Purple-hair girl. Pete remembered seeing her, oh yes. Kind of hard to miss, out there in the sunshine among all the bright summer-attire folks. Like a crow in a flock of parrots. He didn't see her now.

He was tempted to give a holler, but knew that if he did, the rest of them would panic, thinking he'd bring the whole rest of the mountain down on their heads. And never mind the way that one kid kept howling at the top of his lungs.

Justin missing. The purple-hair girl missing, not that her mom and pop seemed to be giving much of a good goddamn, occupied as they were with trying to placate baby brother. And one other girl, from the bunch with all the little blondies.

"We can't leave without Tiffy!" that dad kept saying.

"Mr. Brewster, we need to get your wife out of the cave. We've done what we can for her here, but there's an ambulance–"

"They said they were going to look for her," he interrupted. "The guide! And that punker-chick. But they never came back!"

"Which way did they go?" Pete asked, pushing his way closer and earning himself a couple of impatient glares.

"That way," the girl with the bandaged bunny told him, pointing off into the black recesses of the chamber.

"Don't even think it," the know-it-all expert said. "We don't need anyone–"

"Wandering off, yes, sonny, I know. Least of all a used-up old-timer like me. How about you tend your knitting and get these folks taken care of? I'll have a look around. I won't go far. Odds are, they're fine. Justin's pretty good. For a book-learned college boy, that is."

"I called and called," the Brewster man said. "I never heard any answer. Well, I thought I did hear something once. A yell. But..."

"But how could you hear anything, over that ruckus?" Pete jerked a thumb at the howling little boy. Earned a glare from that bunch, too. Oh, but he was making himself some popular down here in the caves today, all right.

"My son happens to be upset. In case you didn't notice, his grandfather's been killed and his mother is hurt–"

"In case *you* didn't notice," Pete said, "these little girls have been having just as much a hard time, but you don't see them throwing tantrums. And isn't one of the missing girls your own daughter?"

"I told her to stay here. She wouldn't. What more do you expect me to do? Go off searching for her myself? Abandon my wife and son? You don't know Didi. She's selfish, stubborn and irresponsible. She's probably already found some other way out and didn't think twice about the rest of us."

"Huh-unh," the blondie who'd been stuck down the Wishing Well said. "She helped me, and she helped Angelina, too."

"You hush up," the man said.

"Don't you tell her to hush," Brewster said. "At least your daughter was trying to do something for the rest of us, which is more than can be said for you!"

"I have my own family to think of!"

The argument escalated and the experts suddenly found themselves with even more problems on their hands. Last thing they needed was for a couple of the survivors to start punching each other and add to the injury-tally. Pete chose the moment to sidle away as surreptitiously as he could.

Of course, if any of them looked, they'd see him. He wasn't exactly hidden, not with the lamp on his hard-hat slicing a yellow-white beam through the darkness. But no one looked… or, if they did, they decided it would be a waste of breath to try and stop him… or just chalked it up to good riddance to an underfoot, pain-in-the-ass old man.

The usual tour-route path went through the more scenic sections of Goblintown. Back further, the formations weren't so pretty. The flow of water ran heavy with minerals that left deposits in dull-brown streaks, so that the farthest reaches of the chamber were filled with what looked like lumpy mountains of shit. Not the sort of thing that the Goddards wanted to put on a postcard, or have their paying customers take pictures of.

Even with the power on, there wouldn't have been much to see except for thick layers of shadow and the occasional half-discerned shape. Under his light, the fresh chips and cracks in the stone stood out in stark relief.

Pete's skin prickled. Now that he was away from the others, now that he'd left their noise and bickering behind, he could pay more attention to the cave itself. To the wrongness he'd been aware of, the wrongness that had intensified until it was a nearly palpable sensation.

The air didn't move the way it should. It didn't smell the way it should. There was a foulness to it. Like sulfur, like hot springs… but not. The boiling mustard-colored mud of a place like Yellowstone didn't belch anyone's idea of sweet perfume, but the odor was still somehow…

Somehow what?

He couldn't put it into words.

Worse than the smell was the *feeling*.

Cornucopia had gone bad, all right. It had gone very, very bad.

Twenty-six years, he'd worked here. More than a quarter of a century. He'd explored as much of these caverns and passages as anyone, and had his share of accidents and mishaps.

All of those, though, had seemed... ordinary. Normal. Clean. Natural.

What he felt now was anything but.

It was...

It was hostile down here now.

Hostile. In a way it had never been before.

Not indifferent. Aware, and hostile.

Which was absurd. Impossible.

He saw something pink against the rough brown chunks of broken stone ahead. A hat. A sun-visor. Pink as a flamingo, with 'Tiffy' stitched into the brim. Near it lay a smashed electronic widget about half the size of a pack of smokes. Chloe had one of those, Pete was pretty sure. Had about nine million songs on it. Amazing, what they could do.

"Hello?" he called. "Justin? Justin, it's Pete. Hello? Tiffy? Uh..."

What was her name? He couldn't very well call out for 'purple-hair girl.'

The beam roved over limestone and revealed a wide, ugly, jagged gap where two massive sections of wall must have been wrenched apart by the earth-splitting forces.

Here was where the smell was coming from... here was the source of the disturbance in the cave's air... here was the *wrongness.*

Pete looked into the gap, already feeling afraid and astonished at himself for the feeling. He'd been apprehensive in caves many times. Daunted, yes. He had thought the better of the occasional squeeze or climb that he suspected would prove beyond his abilities. But he had never, even during his worst experiences, felt actively and consciously afraid like this.

A cave was blunt indifference. Uncaring. A cave wasn't aware, wasn't hateful, wasn't out to punish intruders.

Same with Everest. Same with the ocean. Those things were not...

Well, they weren't entities unto themselves, so to speak. How come Cornucopia felt that way now?

It felt *alive*.

Alive, and aware, and murderous.

Christ on a crutch, but he was giving himself the world's biggest case of the willies right here and now!

He was letting it get to him, that was all. The pain and fear and confusion of all those people. Whenever there was some kind of serious disaster, people looked for reasons and cause and blame. They didn't want to think it was only random and meaningless.

Earthquakes, volcanoes, floods, hurricanes, cave-ins, avalanches... huge and random and meaningless. Tornadoes, now, those were capricious, evil, and malevolent as a wicked witch in a fairy tale.

Caves were... not like this. Never, in his life, had a cave been like this.

Pete stepped over a jumble of shattered stalactites and stalagmites. "Hello?" He angled his head to shine the beam into that jagged, ugly crevice.

No right-thinking person would have gone in there, and Justin was more than a right-thinking person. He may have come to them straight from college, strutting like a peacock, but he'd been willing to listen. He had respected Pete's experienced advice. He'd acknowledged that you couldn't learn everything from books and schooling.

He'd also loved the caves the way some people loved one-of-a-kind works of art. Boy could go on and on about the incredible *time* it took to form them, ages and ages of time that humans could only barely comprehend. Pete figured that it must just about have wrung Justin's heart like a wet rag to see Goblintown hammered to junk.

Justin wouldn't have gone into a new and unexplored passage. Not without a damn good reason. He was too smart for that. Too smart by half.

If he'd *had* a damn good reason...? Say, because someone who didn't know any better, like a little girl, had gone in there first? In that case, wouldn't courage and heroism get in the way of smarts and common sense?

Usually did, as Pete remembered all too well from his own piss-and-vinegar younger days.

He moved closer and saw the blood.

Everywhere. Dark and tacky-wet. Puddled on the ground. Splashed across the rocks and up the walls. Like one of those crazy paintings that were just streaks and blobs flung from a wildly-waved brush, except that this time, there was only one color. He could smell it, too, mingling with that not-sulfur stench.

A cigarette lighter, the cheap disposable kind, lay nearby with rusty red-brown beadlets drying on its orange plastic casing. He saw snarls of blood-matted hair, and scraps of cloth, and a grisly blood-trail leading into the crack.

As if someone had crawled...?

Or...

Or been dragged?

His knees popped as he crouched to pinch up one of the cloth scraps. White, originally. And the weave was familiar. *Very* familiar. Hell, he was wearing one of the same shirts right now, though he had an old many-pocketed chambray on over it.

Next, though he didn't want to and screwed up his face into a knot of distaste as he did so, he tweezed a clump of hair between thumb and forefinger, and brought it into the headlamp's beam.

Blond. Not the silky flaxen-blonde of the four little girls, but coarser, and sandy. Justin's hair.

If he'd fallen... no, if he'd fallen badly enough to do this kind of damage, lose this much blood, leave clots of his own hair stuck to the rocks... then he'd still be here. And if anyone – the two missing girls, say – had moved him, they wouldn't have taken him into the crevice, would they?

Someone had. There was no way Justin could have gotten up on his own and stumbled or crawled. Someone must have moved him. Dragged him. None too gently, either.

A shudder started in Pete's jaw and worked its way through his entire body.

Wrongness about the caves.

Wrongness very close to him.

He could just about hear it breathing.

CHAPTER 13
The Throat

"How's everybody doing back there?" Sylvia armed sweat from her brow. "Still with me? Sound off. Mr. Morris?"

His reply was bone-weary and bleak with despair. "I'm here."

"Todd?"

"Me, too," said the kid.

"Ms. Enzio?"

"How much farther?" With a quaver.

Ignoring the question for the time being, Sylvia said, "Phoebe?"

"Yes." Much calmer than her mother. As if she'd decided that she had to be the grownup right now.

"Okay. Good. We've got what looks like a tight spot up ahead. It's kind of ugly. But after that, things should open up enough for us to stop and have a short rest. I'll go first. I want Todd and Phoebe to follow me, since they're-"

"Tight spot?" Ms. Enzio cut in. "What do you mean? How tight? Worse than those Squeezes? Oh, God. Do we have to crawl? What if we get stuck, like that man did back there?"

"Mom, it'll be fine," Phoebe said.

"I can't do this. I swear, I can't handle much more of this. I can hardly breathe."

"Ms. Enzio, take it easy," Sylvia said.

"I don't want to die down here!"

"Are we gonna die, Dad?" Todd asked.

"Just stay calm," Sylvia said.

"We are, aren't we?" Mr. Morris asked. His voice was dull, slow, droning. "All of us. Like Audrey, only she went quick. We'll be trapped. We'll starve, or die of thirst, or exposure to this wet cold. It'll be slow. They'll never find the bodies."

Ms. Enzio began to gasp and wheeze. "No-no-no-please-God-I-don't-want-to-die!"

"Mom! Mom, stop it!"

"Everyone, please, calm down," Sylvia said. "We're okay. We just have to keep our cool. I don't want anyone running off in a panic. We've come this far already, haven't we? A little more. Then we can rest, and I can get a look around, see how close we are to an exit. There's one by the Hall of Mirrors. We should almost be there."

She hoped.

She had experienced some of the most dangerous situations the planet had to offer. She'd descended on a line into glacial ice caves in Greenland, rappelled down canyon walls to openings never before explored by humans. She'd gone cave-diving in the Yucatan, suspended in the eerie silence of subterranean rivers.

This was worse.

Those other times, she'd always known what she was in for. She was always trained, prepared, equipped, and in the company of people who were likewise trained, prepared and equipped. People who knew the risks and knew how to cope with them. She'd seen accidents. She'd lost friends. She'd been hurt more than once herself, broken fingers and a broken collarbone. She'd watched her own sister die while BASE jumping.

This was still worse.

"A little farther," she said. "Soon as we get to a big enough space, we'll have a rest. We'll have some water. I know you all must be thirsty. I know I am. I'll even crack a glowstick so we can have some more light. How's that sound?"

Gradually, Ms. Enzio's frantic wheezing settled back into regular, if still rapid, breaths. Todd kept sniffling, but seemed calmer than before. And if Mr. Morris sounded like someone delivering a boring stock-market report even when he said they were all done for, at least he was conscious. He hadn't been when Sylvia had found him.

"Only a little farther," she promised again, and hoped she wasn't lying.

The opening in front of her made the smallest of The Squeezes look like a railway tunnel. Under other circumstances, she would have relished the challenge and thrilled to the expectation of what she might find on the other side. She would have been confident that the rest of the team knew what they were doing, that someone had her back. You literally had to trust your fellow cavers with your life. It wasn't a trust given lightly.

"I'm going in now," she said. "Looks like it's about five, maybe six yards. Don't follow me until I say so. When you do, you'll go flat on your bellies. Keep your heads tucked down so you don't bang them on the ceiling. Push with your elbows and feet. Like they do in the army, in boot camp, you know what I mean?"

A couple of mumbled assents, and Todd said, "When they crawl in the mud under the wires and stuff?"

"Yeah, that's it exactly. And it's an uphill slope, so it might be kind of hard, but just keep going." She took a glowstick from her belt, snapped it, and shook it. Luminous yellow-green bloomed in the darkness. "Todd, hang onto this until it's your turn, then pass it to the next person. That way, you can each watch whoever's ahead of you, and see what to do."

She squirmed in, feeling stone scrape against her hardhat and shoulders. Feeling the unyielding earth surrounding her, and moisture soaking through her clothes.

A squeeze. More than a squeeze. This was a throat. Like being swallowed alive by a giant boa constrictor. Working her way along its gullet.

Claustrophobia had never been a problem for her. If anything, she'd been the opposite, ever since she was old enough to get out of her crib and hide under it. Her parents were always finding Little Sylvia in cupboards and closets and laundry hampers. On a rainy day, she'd be happy for hours in a fort made from sofa cushions and a sheet. When her sisters – who liked to climb up on things and jump off of things – wanted to build a treehouse, Sylvia would be the one lobbying to dig an underground clubhouse instead.

All the same, she never would have done *this* on her own. Alone, without so much as a cave-buddy, was not cool and not daring. It was suicidally stupid.

Doing this with a bunch of unschooled tourists? All of whom were scared and in shock?

Beyond suicidally stupid.

Not that she had a lot of choice.

If she didn't get them out of here, they would die. If the cave-in was as drastic as she thought, it'd be days before any rescue teams could make their way this far in. Her tour had been halfway through Cornucopia, in the deepest part open to the public.

"Sylvia?" Ms. Enzio's anxious voice floated up. "Are you still there?"

"I'm still here," she called. "Where else would I be? Hang on. I'm almost through."

She reached the end of the long, constricting squeeze and stuck her head out. The light twinkled across a dazzling landscape of crystals, flickering back at her in coruscating, scintillating winks and flashes. It took her several moments of staring around trying to place landmarks and orient herself before she could recognize the chamber.

The Hall of Mirrors.

What was left of it.

The Hall of Sharp Pointy Shards, now.

But she knew where they were, and she knew the way out from here. Relief washed through her like a long cool swig of iced tea.

The angle was tricky, and she had to boost and heave and scramble to get out without falling down the flowstone slope and into the glittering debris. Once she'd found a good perch with stable footholds, she leaned back in.

"Okay, I'm out. Todd, can you see my light?"

"I see it."

"Give Phoebe the glowstick and come on through. I'll be waiting right here for you at the other end."

There were a few exchanges, words she couldn't make out. The tones were clear enough. Todd hesitant, afraid. The others coaxing, encouraging.

Sylvia had found him huddled against his dad's motionless body, eyes glassy, thumb in his mouth, like he'd regressed from age ten to two in his terror. Ms. Enzio and Phoebe had still been at the start of The Squeezes, unable to go further because of the wedged – and then crushed – blockage of Bob Kemp. They'd groped their way around through the alternate passage to the chamber where the routes rejoined.

She regretted having to leave the others, but there wasn't anything she could have done for them. Most were dead, or too seriously injured to risk moving, or impossible to reach beyond the unstable piles of fallen rock. The only reason Sylvia herself hadn't been in there, or under one of those rockfalls, was because she'd hurried ahead to try and find the other kids, the Texas-named ones, who had taken the first opportunity to sneak away.

People dead, people hurt, people missing somewhere in the dark.

All she could do was help these ones as best she could, get them out of here, and worry about other survivors later. When and if there was a later.

Plaintive whimpers came out of the squeeze. Kitten-caught-in-a-pipe noises.

"Todd?" she said.

"I don't like it."

"I don't blame you. Nobody says you have to like this."

"I'm scared."

"That's okay. I'm right here. There's a whole big space on this side. Plenty of room to stand up."

The headlamp's beam caught his small, pale, dirty face. Sylvia reached in and helped him the rest of the way. He curled himself into a nook between two formations, knees tucked up to his chest and arms wrapped around them, rocking back and forth on his butt and trembling all over.

One by one, the others came through. Phoebe, outwardly calm but betrayed by the reddish smears on her lips where she'd chewed them ragged. Ms. Enzio, creeping along the entire way murmuring prayers in what sounded like Spanish. Finally, Mr. Morris. He was the largest, not a big man but still a man, with wider shoulders than the women and kids. But he forced himself through, at the cost of some skin and torn clothing.

"Where are we?" Phoebe asked, sitting with her arm around her mother.

A tiny light went a long way in subterranean blackness. Between Sylvia's headlamp and the glowstick, the shattered crystals sparkled like something from an alien world.

"It used to be the Hall of Mirrors," Sylvia said. "Whatever happened smashed the hell out of it. We'll have to be careful. Don't trip, try not to brush against anything or grab onto anything."

Ms. Enzio and Phoebe looked down at themselves and frowned. They both wore knee-length culottes, short-sleeved summery blouses, and slip-on canvas deck shoes with no socks.

Sylvia passed around a water bottle, and shook a palmful of trail mix into everybody's hand. The nuts, dried fruit, pretzel bits and chocolate chips only woke up her stomach and informed her that she was ravenous. She could have eaten the entire package herself and still had room for a full meal. But she sealed it up again and put it away.

"Okay," she said as the rest of them nibbled. "The regular tour route is right over that way. There's an emergency exit. Watch your step."

They only watched her with a bland helplessness that she found unnerving. It wasn't a look of trust and confidence. It was a look that said they had given up any initiative and would, like sheep, be placidly led wherever she led them.

She wanted to be irritated, or even pissed off. She didn't let herself.

As she made her way by the least hazardous-appearing course, pieces breaking like glass and grinding like gravel under her hiking boots, Sylvia scanned the chamber for anything familiar. She heard a yip and a curse from behind her as someone strayed too close to a cluster of miraculously untouched crystals that resembled a short, squat cactus with long transparent needles.

"This way. The exit's over here." She trained the beam of her headlamp on a distant sign that, if the power was on, would have been illuminated red with the letters E-X-I-T.

"Hey, what's that?" Todd asked. "I think it's a flashlight."

"Stay with the group, Todd," his father said.

"I just–"

Todd screamed and sprang back. He lost his footing and went down hard, with a brittle crash. He screamed again, a shriek of pain.

"Todd!" Mr. Morris yelled.

Ms. Enzio, clinging to the glowstick as if it was a talisman or good-luck charm, pointed and added her shrieks to the boy's. Sylvia's head swung that way. Brightness gleamed across a crystal sculpture that could have come from an artisan's gallery, then struck something at its base.

A small penlight, some company logo imprinted on the plastic. And stains. Dark, reddish stains. Not far from it was something that Sylvia couldn't immediately identify. Her mind tried out a few options. Bundle of driftwood. Spindly cave-crab. A torn gardening glove.

Part of a hand.

Part of a human hand.

Stiffly-curled fingers. Bluish-purple crescents of nail. A ring band, glinting silver through the splatters of blood. More blood, pooled around a clean-sliced gash where the hand had been severed from the rest of its owner.

Just a hand, lying there. As if it had dropped the flashlight.

But then... where...?

She began a slow rotation.

"Hold still, Todd, hold still!" Mr. Morris tried to pick him up, his own hands getting cut and gouged.

Todd kept shrieking, also bawling and blatting and caterwauling. He paused long enough to suck in a breath, caught a glimpse of the glassy slivers sticking out of his palms and forearms like porcupine quills, and started in again.

"Mom!" Phoebe cried.

Sylvia turned toward Ms. Enzio, who had averted her gaze from the dismembered hand. Her knees buckled. She swayed drunkenly, on the verge of fainting. Phoebe rushed to catch her. Staring past them, Sylvia saw the even more gruesome discovery Ms. Enzio had found.

The man's body had gone backward onto the jutting crystal spikes. He lay stuck there, a bug on many pins, propped at an angle halfway off the cave's floor. His arms dangled. Blood soaked his clothes, stained the spears protruding from mangled flesh, formed a lake beneath him. His shirt tented out on points that had not quite gone all the way through.

"Mom, no! Someone help me!"

Sylvia looked back to see Phoebe struggling with her mother. Not to hold her up now and keep her from fainting, but to hold her in place and keep her from running. Ms. Enzio, wild with hysterical panic, batted Phoebe away.

Even as Sylvia took a step in that direction, the woman lurched into a clumsy run.

"Ms. Enzio, stop!" Sylvia shouted.

"Mom!" Phoebe plunged after her, heedless of the shards that slashed at her bare shins and calves.

"Phoebe, don't! I'll get her!" Sylvia plunged after Phoebe.

"Hey, the light!" Mr. Morris yelled, as Todd continued screaming.

The headlamp's beam bobbed and weaved as Sylvia ran. It reflected from crystal planes and angles, turning the cave into a strobe-stuttering disco ball. Suddenly, it caught the sheen of a thin, nearly clear slab that slanted askew between two boulders, directly in Ms. Enzio's path. Like a line of light on the blade of a sword.

If she saw it at all, she saw it too late to stop.

The edge caught Ms. Enzio under the chin. Clotheslined, her head snapped back as momentum carried her feet and legs forward. A scarlet fountain sprayed high in the air, blood like glistening rubies before it rained down.

Ms. Enzio dropped to the cave floor. Crystals broke with brittle crunching sounds. The slab's bladelike edge hadn't decapitated her. Not quite. Her throat was gashed deep, from ear to ear and all the way to the spine. In the stark light, the wound was hideous and unmistakably, instantly fatal.

Sylvia seized Phoebe, wrestled her to a halt. "No, Phoebe, don't, don't look."

"Mom! Mom!"

"She's dead. I'm sorry. She's dead."

"No! No, she isn't!" Weeping, Phoebe crumpled against Sylvia.

"Come on," Sylvia said, as gently as she could. "Let's go."

CHAPTER 14
Monster Faces

Where was Mommy? Why wouldn't she come?

That was her job. That was what mommies were for. To make lunches, and fix toys that got broke, and give kisses to boo-boos so they'd get all better fast, and take care of him when he was sick. To wash his hair when he had a bath, and watch cartoons with him, and let him lick the spoon when she baked cookies. To tuck him in and read him a story.

And to be there when he had bad dreams, to make the scary go away.

She wasn't there.

She didn't come.

She didn't make the scary go away.

That time there was a spooky shape at his window, Mommy showed him how it was only the streetlight outside putting a tree-shadow on his curtains. When he was sure there was a creepy-evil snake hiding under his bed, Mommy turned on the light and they had looked together, and there wasn't anything underneath except some Hot Wheels cars, a coloring book, and a shoe. The time there was a ghost in his closet, she put on a nightlight so that it couldn't come out and get him in the dark.

It was her *job*!

Daddy could do those things too. But Mommy was better at it.

So, when he had bad dreams and woke up crying, he wanted Mommy and he called for Mommy.

Before, she always came.

Now, she didn't.

Why not?

R.J. scrunched his eyes shut tight-tight-tight and clenched his fists and thought really-super-duper-hard about waking up.

As soon as he did, he'd get out of bed and go to them. They would be sleepy but not mad. Mommy might even make warm milk for them, with nilla and cimmanin. She'd put the milk for R.J. in his favorite cup, the one with the panda bears. Daddy would ruffle R.J.'s hair and say that yeah, dreams sure could seem real, couldn't they, but they weren't. They were like stuff on TV. Only pretend. And R.J. would see that Daddy was right. Daddy wasn't hurt at all. Nothing had happened to Daddy.

All he had to do was wake himself up. All the scary would go away as soon as he woke himself up.

He peeked.

It was still the scary. It was still the bad dream.

Quickly, he shut his eyes again and tried harder. He even prayed to Baby Jesus and to Santa Claus, Baby Jesus' daddy. If Santa Claus could put all the animals on the ark and bring presents to everybody's house in one night on Christmas, then he could make the bad dream stop.

Sometimes, he dreamed about falling. Sometimes, he dreamed that mean dogs were chasing him and he ran as hard as he could but his legs were all slow and heavy and he couldn't go very fast. Sometimes, he dreamed that he was in a big bright noisy crowded place like a shopping mall and he hadn't held Mommy's hand like he was supposed to and kept seeing people he thought were her but they weren't.

This dream was scarier than all those.

He screamed and cried, and Mommy still didn't come. He prayed to Baby Jesus and Santa Claus, and he still couldn't wake himself up.

The scary was still here. All around him.

It was bad when the monster carried him through the dark. Bad because he couldn't see anything at all. Couldn't hear anything except for himself, and the monster's breathing. He fought and kicked, scratched and bit. Like

Daddy always told him he should do if some stranger ever tried to grab him. He'd done it. But it hadn't worked. Not even when he bit. His teeth wouldn't hardly sink in, and the monster's skin tasted ucky-awful. Like boiled spinach and chewing on a rubber tire.

Then the monster had brought him here. Where there was light. Kind of. A yellow, nasty-yellow light.

Yellow light on monster faces.

Monster faces all around him. Way up high. Looking down at him with their weird eyes. Snouts and horns and snarling mouths. Wanting to eat him. Wanting to chomp him like a chicken nugget.

R.J. sneaked another peek, and they were still there.

Whimpering, he closed his eyes again and curled himself up into a pillbug.

Why wouldn't Mommy come and make it stop?

Why couldn't he wake up?

He wouldn't even care if he wet the bed. He wouldn't care if everybody at Kidderclub found out and teased him. He just wanted it to be over.

What if it was real?

He pushed that thought away. Fast. Mad.

It wasn't real. It was a dream. A bad-scary dream. Not real.

Couldn't be real. He wouldn't let it be real.

Because if it was real, then Daddy...

No!

It wasn't real.

Daddy wasn't hurt. Daddy was fine. He'd just dreamed what the monster had done to Daddy's fingers. Dreamed how the monster had snatched him away so he couldn't hold onto Daddy's belt. Dreamed how it had knocked Daddy down on the sharp glass rocks so that the blood had come out of him.

Dreamed it.

Dreamed about being carried through the dark like a bag of laundry, unable to get loose no matter how much he bit and kicked.

He was still dreaming. Dreaming this place, with the yellow light and the horned monsters wanting to eat him up. Dreaming the yucky-gross smell.

Once, he and Jacob found a duck nest that was old with no ducks anywhere around and one egg left in it, and Jacob broke the egg to see if there was a baby duck inside but instead there had only been slime and it smelled almost this bad. Another time, riding in the car, they'd seen a skunk that had got runned over. It was the stinkiest thing in the world, even stinkier than Megan's diapers.

This was almost that stinky.

Hot, too. Steamy-hot. If he went in the bathroom right after Daddy got out of the shower, when the mirrors were all fogged up, he could see the steam hanging in the air and making the walls look sweaty.

This was almost that hot, too.

Stinky and steamy-hot.

In a… yellow kind of way.

The light was yellow, and the smell was yellow.

And there were other people in his bad-scary dream.

They weren't the tall strangers from the lost-in-the-shopping-mall one. Those people, he never saw their faces because he always ran up to them from behind thinking they would turn out to be his parents but then they weren't. He wasn't even sure if those dream-people even had faces at all.

These ones did.

They weren't grown-ups, either.

One of them was almost a grown-up. Old enough to be a babysitter. Like Lisa. Lisa sometimes came to their house and stayed with him and Megan when Mommy and Daddy went out to have dinner at a place where they didn't have kid-menus. This girl could have done that. Only R.J. didn't think Mommy and Daddy would let her. Lisa was a normal person, with curly brown hair and glasses. This girl's hair was crazy purple and there was jewelry in her eyebrow. Her pants were loopy-strappy with chains on them, and she had chains wrapped around her big clunky black boots.

The purple-hair girl was on her side with her arms back, and she was sleeping. With her neck and head bent all funny and no pillow. His mommy would say she didn't look comfable at all.

How could someone sleep in a dream? That was weird.

The other person was a kid. Bigger than him. He bet she went to the real school like Jacob's brothers, instead of to Kidderclub. She had stripety shorts, a shirt with a princess on it, pigtails, and a pink fuzzy purse-thing shaped like a poodle.

She was not sleeping. Her eyes were open and she was sitting up, and she was looking right at him.

"Are you dream-people?" R.J. asked.

"I'm Tiffy. Who are you?"

"R.J." He glanced up at the monster faces again. They were still there, still snarling down.

Monster faces in the rocks. Monster faces in the cave walls that went way up high almost to a ceiling where drippy rocks hung down like half-melted crayons.

Monster faces big as trucks. Big as houses. Just the faces. Black pits for eyes. Mouths like doorways full of teeth. Horns sticking out of their heads. All kinds of horns. Thick curly-down ones, branchy-poky-uppy ones, long skinny-twisty ones. Horns like deers, and horns like dinosaurs, and horns like bullfighting-bulls and boy-sheep. Nose-horns like rhinocerosusses and curved tusky tooth-horns like effelunts.

The faces were dark rock, but in the places where the cave walls were smooth, the dark was streaky-yellow and glowed. That was where the light came from. Yellow glowing streaks and lines and swirls on the dark stone. Like someone had used glow-in-the-dark fingerpaints.

R.J. could say his ABCs and he could count all the way to a hundred. The glowy-yellow lines on the walls up there didn't look anything like the letters and numbers he knew.

Was that where the hot was coming from?

In Kidderclub at recess, they sometimes played Hot Lava and tried to get across the playground without touching the dirt because they pretended the dirt was hot lava and would cook them if they stepped in it. Jacob was real good at that game, because Jacob could climb way up on the monkey-bars and go on the rings. R.J. didn't like to do that.

Was the glowy-yellow stuff lava in the walls? Would it cook them if they touched it?

"What is this place?" he asked. "I don't like it. I don't like this dream. Why can't I wake up? I want Mommy. I want Daddy."

Tiffy shook her head, her pigtails flipping back and forth. "Not a dream."

"Is so! A bad one."

"It's bad, yeah. But it's not a dream."

"But... there's monsters!" He sneaked another quick look up, then away. In case they came alive and gobbled him up or something. They'd have to whip out long tongues to do it, snaring him like anteaters going after ants, or frogs catching flies.

"We're not asleep."

"She's asleep."

"She got magicked."

R.J. stared at Tiffy. "Magicked?"

"Zapped by a magic spell."

"Who is she? Is she your sister?"

"No way! My sister's Amberlyn. We were on the cave tour. Me, and my mom and dad and sister, and Auntie Frieda, and Britney and Angelina. Uncle Chad didn't want to go in the caves. He had work to do on his laptop. He stayed up. That girl, she was on the same tour as us."

Not wanting to, but doing it anyway, R.J. nodded. "Megan didn't like it. So Mommy took her out, but me and Daddy..." His face cramped up and he tried not to cry. "Me and... Daddy... stayed... and then... and then..."

"Something bad," Tiffy said. "An explosion, maybe a earthquake. The roof fell down, and the lights went out, and everyone was yelling. I thought my dad was right next to me but then he was gone and I was lost." She hugged herself and shivered. "I remember someone grabbed me, but it wasn't my dad. It was the Cyclops."

"The what?"

"A big black troll with no face and only one eyeball," she said, shivering even more.

"Does it go like this?" R.J. asked, and imitated the hollow, huffing breaths.

"Uh-huh."

He did start to cry. "It hurt my Daddy! I hate it! I hate the skylops!"

"It brought me here, and it brought her here – magicked her, too – and it brought you here."

"Why-y-y?" he wailed.

"I don't know." She looked really scared. "Maybe it wants to eat us."

"Can't we go? Can't we go hoh-oh-ome?"

"We can't get away. See?" Tiffy moved her legs and there was a clinky noise.

"There's handcuffs on your feets." He looked down. "There's handcuffs on my feets too."

"I told you. We're chained up. See? They hook to those rings in the rocks."

He didn't want to believe Tiffy, but even with only the dim, weird, glowy-yellow light and the shadows everywhere, he could see that she was right.

Mrs. Wozlewski, the lady who lived next door to them, had a great big dog named Thor. Thor was friendly and wouldn't bite anybody, but a lot of people didn't know that and were afraid of him. So Mrs. Wozlewski kept him chained up. She had a metal corkscrew-spike with a loop on top, and that was where the other end of Thor's chain went. He could run all over the yard, but only as far as his chain could reach.

Poor Thor… now R.J. knew exactly how he felt.

The things around his legs did look like handcuffs, kind of. A length of chain went between them, so that if he tried to walk he could only scootch his feet. Or hop. But he couldn't hop, because there was another chain that went from the one between his ankles to a metal ring pounded into the rocks.

He remembered. He didn't want to do that, either, but he did. *The monster – the troll, the skylops – carrying him through a terrible darkness. No light. No light at all. The darkness of the deep cave.*

When their guide warned them and then turned everything off, R.J. had been holding Mommy's hand with one of his and Daddy's with the other, safe between them. So, *that* dark hadn't been too bad. It was safe because he could feel them, squeezing his hands to let him know they were there and everything was okay. Safe but exciting, dangerous but safe. Fun and scary at the same time. Like going on a ride, a rollercoaster.

The dark with the skylops...

That hadn't been safe or exciting or fun. He had kicked and kicked. Struggled. Hit. Bit. Shrieked. Nothing had stopped the skylops.

And then there had been some light. The glowy-yellow.

The glowy-yellow, and the monster faces.

Worse than the dark.

Worse than anything.

R.J. shut his eyes and put his hands over them like he did sometimes during movies. It should have made the bad-scary go away. When he looked again, the bad-scary should have been all gone.

But it wasn't gone. The monster faces were still there. Hungry in the glowy-yellow.

So he covered his eyes again. He'd tried to make himself wake up. Tried really-super-duper-hard. Wished for Mommy. Wished for Daddy. Prayed to Baby Jesus and Santa Claus and Superman.

He'd felt the skylops set him down on rock. Rock that wasn't cool like the rest of the caves, but rock that was like a sidewalk that got sun on it all day so that it stayed warm for a while even when the sun went down. He'd felt the skylops doing something to his feet, and he'd heard the same kind of clinky-noises that there'd been when Tiffy moved her legs.

The skylops put the handcuffs on his feet and hooked them to the loop. So that R.J. was stuck. The way Thor was stuck in Mrs. Wozlewski's yard, only R.J. got hardly any chain so he couldn't move hardly at all.

Then the skylops went away.

"Is the skylops coming back?" he asked Tiffy.

She shrugged. "Probably."

"What's it gonna do?"

"I told you, I don't know." She swallowed like someone had given her a spoonful of icky medicine, and said, "There's a dead person over there."

"You mean... a... a ghost?"

"No." She swallowed again. "I think it's Justin. The guide for our group. The Cyclops brought him. Dragged him in by the legs and dumped him in a pit."

R.J. didn't look. "He's really dead?"

She nodded. "He was all... stabbed... and bloody... and stuff. You can just kind of see... parts of him... his elbow, and his foot... sticking up." Tiffy bent over, holding onto her tummy, and made trying-not-to-throw-up noises.

The big girl groaned. Her eyes opened, and she coughed. "What the hell? What happened?" She saw R.J. and looked confused, then saw Tiffy and looked surprised. "What's going on? Where are we?"

They all started talking at once. Then, suddenly, Tiffy hissed for them to be quiet.

"Do you hear that?" she whispered.

Something moving. Something big. Getting closer.

And scuffing-sounds. Like a heavy bundle sliding over rocks.

"It's the skylops!" R.J. put his hands over his face again. He wanted the awful dream to be over, the bad-scary gone. He wanted Mommy and Daddy and Megan.

He peeked through his fingers and there it was. Entering the cave where the monsters snarled down from the walls. A big black shape with a snout. Horn-tusk-things curved back around its head. It had one shiny, greenish eyeball. He could hear it breathing – *hhheeee-khaahhh, hhheeee-khaahhh.*

A body dragged behind the skylops. Bony stick arms stretched over a loose, flopping head. Legs limp. Feet trailing. It looked like a scarecrow, but R.J. knew it was a skinny old man.

A skinny old man, and he was dead.

Chapter 15
Topside

Chloe Goddard wondered if this was what they meant when they talked about chaos theory. About pattern and sense in what initially looked like randomness and inherent contradiction.

Hectic, but organized.

Slow, but urgent.

Desperate, but careful.

Hasty, but deliberate.

Calm, but frantic.

Vehicles jammed the two parking lots to capacity and beyond. More lined the road for as far as she could see, some on the dirt shoulder tilted almost to the point of toppling into the ditches on either side. Police cars and paramedics and ambulances. Jeeps with the decals of state and county agencies. News vans. An old refurbished school bus that had disgorged volunteers. Highway department trucks and earthmovers. Motorcycles and a couple of mountain bikes.

And, of course, there were plenty more vehicles belonging to locals who'd come to help or to gawk. Not to mention the cars, motor homes, minivans and SUVs that waited for their owners to finish the cave tour.

The western sky looked airbrushed with streaks of orange and gold and violet. A bright point – Mercury? Venus? – sparkled near the sinking, fiery globe of the sun. To the east, half a pale moon hung overhead against an indigo backdrop.

Darkness was not a problem even with night coming.

Enormous portable lights bathed the area in a harsh white glare. Everything threw multitudes of conflicting, competing shadows. Headlights beamed. Revolving bursts of color came from roof-mounted flashers. Television lights centered on soberly excited reporters broadcasting live up-to-the-minute accounts of the ongoing and unfolding drama.

Large emergency tents and open-sided shelters covered the picnic ground. Equipment had to be organized and stored. Searchers had to be outfitted. There had to be a place for triage, a place for first aid, a place to perform impromptu surgery... a place to put bodies if it turned out to be too late for even those heroic measures.

Inside a long pavilion were folding tables that held cases of bottled water, restaurant-sized coffee urns, sandwiches, donuts, and energy bars. There were also cots, benches, and blankets.

The command center held portable computers, maps, seismometers, and other items the purpose of which Chloe couldn't even guess at. Someone from the county had brought rescue dogs, trained to sniff out survivors or bodies in the wreckage of collapsed buildings. Someone else had brought a robot with cameras on long jointed arms, like the kind used in bomb squad disposal.

The noise level was almost unbelievable. Chugging generators, power tools, engines, and the clamor of a hundred conversations all going on at once. A little while ago, a helicopter had *whupped* by, getting an aerial shot for the evening news.

The trained dogs might be well-disciplined, but Zeke, the Baxley's large mutt, had started barking shortly after the disaster and moved on to howls by the time the rescue effort reached full swing. No, not just howls. *Baying.* Chloe had never heard Zeke make a sound like that in his entire life.

A much smaller dog carried on ceaselessly from within one of the motor homes, a shrill and earsplitting yip-yip-yip-yark-yark-yap-yip-yip-yip. Chloe considered herself an animal-lover, but before long even she would have happily throttled the damn thing. With the motor home locked tight, though, there wasn't much that could be done about that.

Nevada, the Goddard's cat, had been spooked enough or sensible enough to get the heck out of dodge. Same for the chipmunks, the deer, and probably every other living thing within a five mile radius, except for Maribel, Lily Baxley's goat, who had the temperament of a yogi on Valium. With everything going on, Maribel simply stood in her pen, head stuck through the fence slats, tufted chin working in slow rotations as she chewed.

Almost six hours had gone by.

Chloe knew she had to talk to her parents.

Had to tell them about Colin and Rory.

For a while, she'd held onto the hope that she wouldn't have to. She'd let herself believe that maybe her brother and cousin had just gone off to spend the day at the lake, or at the movies.

Or doing whatever else they did, the stuff she didn't ask about and didn't want to think about.

This wasn't about looking the other way, turning a blind eye anymore. This wasn't about beer, or pot, or shoplifting, or fireworks. This wasn't about whether or not someone might get in trouble, or even get arrested.

Her dad emerged from the tent, walking with one of the rescuers, someone smudged and grimy, and angry. *Still angry about Pete taking off on them and then disappearing,* Chloe guessed.

"—first priority is making sure we don't get anyone else lost or hurt or killed down there," the rescuer said. "Believe me, Mr. Goddard, I'm as eager as you are to find and help those people. But we can't rush this."

As she headed for them, Chloe was brought up short when a hand curled into the crook of her elbow.

"The fuck you think you're doing, Chloe?"

The voice was low in her ear, raspy. The hot gust of breath smelled like cigarette smoke. Fingers dug into her soft flesh in what was not quite a pinch, but could easily become one.

"Let go of me," she said, pulling free.

"You were going to tattle to your daddy."

Nick Westlund had lean, vulpine features and coarse, darkish-blond hair. He thought he looked like that guy Sawyer on *Lost*, and did everything he could to make the most of it. Tan, tough, stubbled, with hard and narrow gunslinger eyes. Faded jeans, tank top, black lightning-bolt tattoo on his upper arm. No wonder that a slut like Toni had gone for him like a moth to a bug zapper.

"Nick, if they're in the caves, they could be in trouble. They could be hurt." She wasn't willing to acknowledge out loud any worse possibilities, but they swirled at the back of her mind anyway. "The rescuers know how many were on the tours, but they wouldn't even know to be looking for anyone else."

"If you tell, people are going to want to know what they were doing down there in the first place."

"Forget about your stupid secret hangout already! This is more important."

"You want to go to jail?" He asked it flat, and cold.

Chloe hesitated. "Jail? Why?"

"Our stupid secret hangout." Nick shook his head without breaking his gaze-lock on her. His mouth bent up on a slant. "You know what's in that stupid secret hangout, Chloe? Do you? I bet you think it's just harmless little shit, some beer, some pot, nothing big."

Her throat went dry, her eyes went wide. "What do you mean?"

"We could be looking at twenty-to-life," he said. He gripped her arm again, a crude homemade tattoo of a scorpion in blue ball-point ink riding the back of his hand. "You don't tell anyone. Got it?"

"We have to help them! Don't you care what happens to them? Toni's your girlfriend! Colin's my *brother*!"

"Colin's a dink."

"He's still my brother!"

"He's a dink and a loser."

"Are we supposed to just leave them to die? "

"I didn't say that. We do it ourselves, that's all. You and me. Right now. We go in, we find them, we bring them out. Nobody has to know."

Chloe stared at him, narrow-eyed with suspicion. "So you do care what happens to them?"

"Sure. And I care about getting rid of the evidence, making sure nobody can find it. But I can't walk right in there with all these assholes around. Since Rory's not here and neither is your dink of a brother, that means it's you."

"Are you kidding? The disaster... Nick, there's been rockfalls and rockslides and cave-ins... the power's out so there's no lights... whole sections are destroyed and impassable! There's no way!"

"There better be. Your dink brother was always mouthing off about how you and him grew up in those fucking tunnels."

"Not when half of it's fallen in. I'm not that experienced a caver, especially not under those kind of conditions."

"Too bad. You're doing it."

"I'm telling you, it's too dangerous!" She flung her free hand toward the medical tent. "Sylvia barely made it out alive, and she's done this lots more than I have. It's a miracle she was able to bring those people up."

"If she got up, you can get down. Save your brother's dink life. Isn't that what you want?"

He released her wrist, which bore red welts from the pressure of his fingers. A daredevil Sawyer-grin creased his face and crinkled his gunslinger eyes. If she hadn't known better, she might have thought he was good-looking. But all that grin did was churn her stomach.

She took another look at the rescue workers, the piles of safety gear, the lights and commotion. Go in alone? Her and Nick? It was crazy.

It might be Colin's only chance. Not to mention Brandon, Toni and Rory as well.

The searchers had more than enough to do already.

Her parents would have a fit if they found out. They wouldn't want her setting one foot in those caves, not now. Not even to find her brother.

They wouldn't want Colin to go to jail either, though.

"Okay," she said. "Okay, I will, all right."

"So let's go," Nick said. "Grab yourself one of those stupid hard-hats from the gift shop if you have to, and move that pretty little ass."

CHAPTER 16
Cold Justice

"He's dead."

The words rolled past Shara, and it took her most of a minute before their meaning registered. She looked up.

The man she'd hit with a rock lay on his side, trussed hand and foot like a roped rodeo heifer. Dried, matted blood caked his hair. A rusty brownish crack-glaze of it coated half his face. But he was conscious, both eyes open. He'd been the one to speak.

"What?" Just talking hurt her throat. The rest of her felt stiff, achy. A pervasive chill seeped into her bones, despite having Makoto's windbreaker spread between herself and the cave's hard, stony floor.

She'd read or seen on television somewhere that ground cover was the key to preserving body temperature. The earth stole heat a lot faster than the air. She figured that was even more critical when down in a deep cave, right on the bedrock, than it was when out in the wilderness where there might at least be an insulating layer of soil to help a little bit.

So, she'd spread out the jacket and sat on it, with Makoto cradled in her lap. Sharing warmth. Sharing comfort. Being together. It might not make much difference in the end, but it made a difference now. Being alone would have been worse.

"Him." With his chin, he gestured. "He's dead."

Not at Makoto. Makoto was sleeping. The painkillers she'd dug from the bottom of her carryall had kicked in. Aleve. Three cheers for Aleve. Just the thing for when a guy had a broken jaw and most of his front teeth smashed out into little white chips.

His perfect teeth, so white and straight and even. His perfect smile, so cute and charming. Ruined. Thanks to the man who now challenged her with his gaze as if asking what she was going to do about their latest problem.

Makoto didn't stir. He slept with his mouth agape, breathing in wet, sloppy snores. His lips were puffed, split. His face was swollen and discolored. He looked like he'd been attacked by hornets.

She didn't even dare touch poor Makoto above the collarbones for fear of disturbing whatever relief the pills had given him. As long as he could sleep, he didn't have to deal with the misery his mouth had to be. Or with the fear and dread.

Or with the grief.

"Are you listening to me?"

She shot him a slitted glare. "I can hear you."

That the injured man had died was no big surprise. The surprise was that he'd held on as long as he had. With most of an arm torn off, he'd needed immediate medical care. Not a half-assed tourniquet cinched on in a hurry.

Shara wondered what was the matter with her. Someone else had died. She didn't feel much of anything. *Does that make me a bad person?*

It didn't make her a bad person.

Did it?

"We have to do something," the tied-up man said.

"Haven't you done enough?"

He had the decency to look ashamed. "Hey, I know what you must be thinking. I swear, I'm really sorry about hitting your boyfriend."

"Is this where I'm supposed to say I'm sorry for bashing you with a rock?"

"No." His gaze shifted, downcast. "But it wasn't necessary. None of that was necessary. They didn't need to jump me. I wasn't going to hurt anyone else."

Incredulity seemed like too much of an effort. So did arguing. She just didn't care anymore. Let him tell himself whatever he wanted. She had seen what he did.

"My name's Griff," he said. "You're Shara, right?"

"Don't talk to me. Don't try to make friends with me. It isn't going to work."

"I'm not. Just… listen, okay? We can't sit here and do nothing."

Listen? She didn't want to listen. She wanted this whole terrible ordeal to be over. She wanted to turn back the clock. Turn back the calendar by a day. Never come here in the first place.

We shouldn't have come here. We shouldn't have stopped. It had seemed like a fun side trip. Why not? They'd been making such good time on their drive. They were ahead of schedule. It'd be something neat to do. Kimmy would enjoy it. They all would enjoy it.

So they'd said. The stated reason.

Not the real reason. The real reason, unspoken but hanging over them like a cloud, was that she and Makoto grasped at any delay, any reprieve, to put off the awkwardness and confrontation they knew would be waiting for them in Boise.

"Shara, we have to face facts here," Griff said. "It's been hours. If any rescuers were going to come for us, if they were able to get to us, they would have been here by now. We're on our own."

How come, when it's Makoto's parents having objections to our relationship, it was excused as being 'traditional,' but when it's my folks, it was racism?

Whose business was it, anyway? Besides hers, and Makoto's? They didn't strictly need the approval and permission of their families. They were adults. It wasn't like she was all entitled, expecting that her father pay for a lavish wedding.

"The batteries in that flashlight aren't going to last forever," Griff said.

The meeting with Mr. and Mrs. Yidori had been tense enough. Makoto warned her ahead of time that his mother still clung to hopes that he would marry the daughter of one of Mr. Yidori's business associates. A nice, demure, lovely Japanese girl he'd known since grade school. Mrs. Yidori even whipped out pictures of her, with all the speed of a Vegas cardsharp, to show Makoto how much Eiko had grown up.

All very traditional.

Very polite.

Nothing you could really take offense at.

The reception they'd get from Red and Sue Ellen Holcomb, on the other hand...

Griff kept talking. Shara tuned him out. *Blah-blah-blah* food and water *blah-blah-blah* cold *blah-blah-blah* damp.

It wasn't to say that her parents were out-and-out bigots... she'd never thought so before, anyway...

"Hey! *Hey!*" Griff shouted. "Damn it, listen to me! Do you want to die down here? Because that's what's going to happen if we don't do something. We'll die. You, me, him... like everyone else. Is that what you want?"

In her arms, Makoto twitched. He mumbled mushily through his broken mouth.

"Stop it!" she said to Griff. "You'll wake him up."

"You'd rather he dies in his sleep?"

"He's not going to die!" Her voice splintered into a sob. She had cried earlier, cried until her eyes felt like sandpaper, and the new rush of tears felt like an acid bath.

"He is, unless we get ourselves out of here."

"Someone will come for us."

"Yeah? When? Hours, Shara. It's been hours."

She wanted to say that if it had been so long, then surely Mr. Carson and his little boy would have gotten out by now, and told the rescue parties where the rest of them were, what had happened with the bridge and everything.

Had it been hours?

It simultaneously seemed as though days had gone by, and mere minutes.

"We can't be that far from the exit," he said. "We could make it out. With the two of us helping him–"

"No."

He paused, looking taken aback. "Well, then… if you went–"

"And leave him here?"

"I could take care of him until you get back, or send help."

"Either way," Shara said, "I'd have to untie you, wouldn't I?"

"I know you have reasons for not trusting me–"

"You *shot* the guide!" She stopped it from being a shriek only because she was too aware of Makoto's labored breathing and the fitful fluttering of his eyelids. "You shot him, you murdered him!"

"I did, but–"

"And you killed Kimmy!"

"I didn't!"

"He was trying to save her and you shot him. You might as well have shot her, too, you murdering bastard!"

"That wasn't what I wanted."

"What about that boy? Grant? You threw him over the edge!"

"It was an accident."

"Like what you did to Makoto?"

"Shara, please, you have to understand."

"Oh, I understand just fine."

"I killed Dawes, yes. That's why I was here, in the caves. That's why I had a gun. To kill him."

Makoto coughed. The effort opened the cuts on his lips again. Shara blotted them with a bunch of tissue. His dark eyes swam open and fixed on hers. Muddled at first, without recognition. Then they cleared. He slurred a sound meant to be her name.

"I'm here, Makoto."

He tried to say something else.

"Water?" she guessed.

Weakly, he nodded.

She rummaged in her carryall, for once thankful that she was a packrat by nature and couldn't go anyplace without ten pounds of junk slung from a shoulder strap. Most of it was useless under the circumstances, and some of it was laughable – sunglasses, sunblock, one of those little battery-operated gadgets that had a fan attached to a misting spray bottle.

But there were some useful things in amid the junk. The tissues, for example. The Aleve and other random over-the-counter remedies. A package of dried apricots, a small tin of smokehouse almonds. Books of matches and handfuls of mints, both of which she routinely grabbed whenever they went to restaurants.

She dug out a plastic bottle, popped the nozzle, tipped it, and squeezed to dribble water into Makoto's mouth.

When he signaled her with a wave that he'd had enough, Shara took a couple of sips. Her throat sighed with relief. She wanted to guzzle down the rest, but wouldn't let herself do it. Though she refused to believe Griff's assertion that no help was coming, she couldn't quite overcome the urge to conserve what scant resources they had.

Griff watched her, and swallowed hard. "Can I have a drink? I'm... really thirsty."

The conservation urge rose up strong, mingled and partly overpowered by something even older. Age-old, territorial. Primitive. She wanted to curl her arm over the carryall and growl at him, like an animal warding off another predator from its kill.

She could hardly believe it. Where was the generous and giving Shara, the Shara who made regular donations of everything from time to money to blood? This grab-and-snarl Shara, this selfish and savage Shara, was new and unexpected. She wasn't sure she liked it. Look out for Number One... protect yourself and your mate... your injured mate...

"Please," he said. Softly. As if reading her expression.

But why should I help him? Why should I do anything for him? He's a murderer! Maybe what he'd done to Makoto and what he'd done to the boy, Grant, really had been accidents, unintended and in the heat and desperation of the moment.

What he'd done to their guide was anything but accidental. He'd admitted it. He brought that gun down here with the intention of killing that man. He hadn't let anything stand in his way. Never mind that the cave had collapsed on them, that the bridge had fallen. Never mind that several people had been crushed or swept to their deaths in the river, that others were hurt or trapped, and that the guide was their best hope at making it out of here alive.

No, he hadn't let any of those considerations stand in his way, had he? He'd seen an opportunity to shoot, and he'd taken it. In doing so, he'd also killed an innocent girl.

For that, she should give him water? She should help him? Save his life, when he hadn't given a single thought to the rest of them? To Kimmy?

"A sip," he said. "One sip. Please, Shara."

Next he'd want her to untie him instead of letting him lie there hogtied on the dank limestone with the circulation cut off in his arms and legs. He'd want her to share the food. Then he'd ask for some of the Aleve for his head, the implication being that she owed him, seen as how she was the one who'd brought that rock down on his skull. Hard enough to draw blood. Hard enough to knock him out. She could have given him a concussion, or amnesia. She could have cracked his skull open and killed him. When she'd felt that gruesome crunching sensation, she'd been sure that she had.

He was a murderer. She couldn't trust him. She'd be crazy to untie him.

"I just want a little water." He tried to smile. "Besides, you've got the gun, remember?"

Shara shuddered. She *didn't* have the gun.

She had picked it up – pinching it gingerly between thumb and forefinger like it was something nasty, which it was – and returned it to Griff's small backpack. Which now sat on a pile of rocks at the furthest reach of the light's circle. She'd been tempted to chuck it into the gorge.

She hated guns. She always had. One more big way in which she differed from Red and Sue Ellen. Right along with opposing war and thinking that the government should keep its collective nose out of everybody's sex lives.

"One drink," he said.

Why should she be kind and merciful? Why should she give him the consideration he hadn't given anybody else? Didn't he deserve everything he got?

"All right," he said, and turned his face away as well as he was able. "I'm sorry."

She put the water bottle away in her carryall, and saw that despite his averted gaze, he watched her closely as she did so.

"I made a mistake," Griff said. "I shouldn't have shot him then."

Her eyebrows went up. "*Then?*"

"You don't understand." His face contorted. "I had to do it. I did it for Kristin."

"Don't," Shara said, amazed by the steel and ice in her own voice.

"He was a criminal! *He* was the murderer!"

"I said, don't."

"Wallace Dawes killed my wife," Griff said. Not looking at Shara. Trembling all over, perhaps with anguish more than cold. "He killed her. For no reason. No reason. Killed her because she was in the wrong place at the wrong time. Killed her for the hell of it, for the thrill of it, killed her because he could."

"I'm not listening!" she cried.

Griff uttered a maniacal little laugh, either not hearing her or ignoring her the way she was unsuccessfully trying to ignore him. "And he got away with it. How do you like that? My Kristin, my wife, the sweetest woman you'd ever meet, so gentle, such a wonderful sense of humor, so beautiful... maybe most people wouldn't have said so, but to me she was beautiful... and Wallace Dawes killed her. They just couldn't prove it. The other charges, yes. Not the murder. So he went to jail. Do you know for how long? Twenty-six months. A month for every year of Kristin's life, how do you like that? Then they let him out."

Makoto lay in her lap, pain-fogged but awake. He could hear everything Griff was saying, his dark and worried gaze found and held Shara's.

"They let him out," marveled Griff, and did the maniacal laugh again. "A tap on the wrist and there you go. Like it never happened. Like it didn't matter. Like *she* didn't matter. So much for the justice system, huh? Where was Kristin's justice? He gets away with murder. He ends her life, ruins mine, and then goes on his merry way. To end up here. I guess there's no background checks for a job like this. Or maybe there is and they just didn't give a damn. I found him, though. Oh, yeah. I found him."

"Why right then?" Shara asked, more because she read the question in Makoto's eyes than because she herself cared about the answer. "Why did you have to do it right then, when we were already in so much trouble?"

"If it turned out we couldn't get out of here alive, I didn't want the cave to have the privilege of killing him. If we did get out alive, then he'd be the hero. He'd be redeemed. No one would care what he'd done in the past. They'd say he more than made up for it. I might never have gotten another chance."

"This is your idea of justice? Letting innocent people die so you could get your revenge?"

He hitched a deep breath, and shook his head sorrowfully. "You're in love. You should be able to understand. I only did it for Kristin. Can't you see that?"

What she saw, with skin-crawling horror and vivid clarity, was that she and Makoto were the only people left who knew what Griff had done. What were two more deaths, give or take?

CHAPTER 17
Troglobites

He stood naked and sightless, utterly still.

The only sounds he made were the involuntary noises of his body. Shallow breaths slipping in and out of his nostrils. The slow thump of his pulse in his ears. Burbles and gurgles from his stomach as his digestive system went about its ordinary business.

This was what it was like for them.

Blind. So blind that they did not even know what it meant. Not blind*ed*. Not deprived of a sense. Not robbed of one. How could you be robbed of something you'd never had, never imagined?

Like emotion.

They had never known sight. Never had eyes.

Why should they? Unnecessary here. A waste. No need to squander precious biological resources on something that wouldn't have done them any good. No need for distinctive coloration to find a mate or ward off a predator. No need for protective camouflage to hide or blend in.

Vision was beyond them.

No.

They were beyond vision.

Eyeless. Never seeing. Nothing to see. No light by which to see.

And they got along just fine. Better than fine.

They were adapted.

He wondered sometimes if he had that backwards, as well. What if it was the other way around? What if this was the way it had begun and the way it should have been? The way it would have stayed?

Kaleidoscope colors flitted past, but they weren't real. He dispelled them with an almost offhand, casual flick of his will. Just his eyes and his brain sputtering, grasping at straws. So accustomed to sight that, in its absence, they felt like they had to make something up to keep from going crazy.

Would it be different if he had no eyes at all?

Possibly. Probably.

Should he scoop them out?

It would hurt, but that didn't matter. Pain was temporary. A flare in the void. Just sensation. Meaning nothing. Like rage, like sex, like hunger.

Flares in the void.

As unreal as the colors that had spun and flashed.

Without my eyes...

No use. Removing something was not the same as never having had it in the first place.

By denying himself the use of his eyes, his other senses would learn to compensate. To adapt. To change, and develop. And evolve.

Eyes closed or eyes open, it didn't matter. The same black surrounded him. A void. Not an empty one, though others might have made the mistake in thinking so.

Not empty, no, not empty at all.

He could feel it.

The longer he stood there, naked in the dark, he could feel it.

The cave air...

To some it would seem stagnant and motionless. Hanging there like a held breath. The temperature constant, the cool humidity unchanging. Against his bare skin, he felt it moving. Stirring. Making the fine hairs quiver. Subtle gradients of heat, so subtle that only the most precise thermometer might have detected them, became tantalizingly discernible.

To the ones who dwelled here, who had never known any other world, those gradients would have been as obvious as the difference between the drafts from an open freezer or an open oven. They had senses that made his look crude and blunt. Nerve clusters. Antennae. Specialized organs that registered stimuli he couldn't even begin to imagine.

He could hear them. Almost.

Nothing specific. No sound he could single out and identify and name. Not a splash, not a chirp, not a flutter, not a step.

An undercurrent. A susurration. The faintest whispering-slithering-crawling.

The cave was anything but empty and barren and dead.

The cave was alive. Alive, and teeming. Full of motion. Full of purpose and instinct.

Thousands of years. Millions. In this subterranean world. With no awareness of anything else. Eyeless and ghostly. Albino-white or even translucent as gelatinous glass. They were thin-skinned, soft, with no need for shells or carapaces or other defenses.

If he stayed down here in the dark for the rest of his life, he knew that he would not become like them. His children would not be born pallid and blind. Neither would their children.

But after thousands or millions of years... gradually... over time... so, so much time...

Troglobites.

That was what the scientists called them. Cave-dwellers. Exclusive cave-dwellers. Not bats or bears or other interlopers who might use a cave for shelter but still ventured out to hunt. These were the creatures who had never known any other reality. Creatures with no concept of light. If you shined a light on them, they couldn't see it, but they would feel it. As a searing, inexplicable agony.

Rory was not one of them.

He could never *be* one of them.

In other ways, though... in other ways...

As far as most people were concerned, the creatures of the deep caves and the deep sea were more alien than anything from another star, for all that they shared the same planet. Alien and strange. Cold, loathsome and revolting. Though they were as natural as anything else on Earth, they seemed hideously unnatural. Hideously malformed, deficient, wrong.

When, really, they were perfect. Perfectly adapted to their environment, to their function. Beautiful in their economy and efficiency. Exquisitely specialized.

He admired that. Envied it. Wanted to emulate it, and knew that the best he'd ever be able to do on his own was a bumbling approximation.

There were other ways, though. Ways that might get him closer to what he wanted and where he belonged. Ways he could stay down here forever. Survive, and adapt.

The wet limestone felt simultaneously slick and coarse against his toes, his callused heels, the more tender soles of his feet. He stepped with confidence but with care, feeling his way. Rills of water wended their courses through channels, pooling against rimstone dams, trickling from ledges. Imperceptibly eroding and building as they went, fractions of inches over centuries.

Had he switched on a light and trained its beam into one of those streams or pools, small aquatic and amphibian cave-dwellers would scatter, fleeing from that blistering brightness. Cavefish and crayfish, salamanders looking half-formed from blobs of tallow. He could have turned the light on the rocks and seen arachnids strutting on long, hairlike jointed limbs, millipedes creeping in a ballet of undulating legs.

He didn't. Like them, he could make his way without light. Without sight. He would follow his other senses, the way they did.

The moist air warmed as he moved, though he knew the change would be imperceptible to anyone else. It began to feel less like mist and more like vapor.

His toes met a rimstone ridge with shallow water sluicing over it in a rippling sheet to merge with one of the creeklets. Rory eased his foot over and dipped it into the pool. The cave's chill never bothered him. The water felt pleasant. Not bathtub-temperature, but pleasant.

Knowing that the pool's floor would be slippery, Rory did not even try to wade out. He lowered himself instead, crouching and then stretching out so that he could slide into the water on his stomach the way salamanders did.

Its scent and taste were clear, clean, and mineral-rich. Like well-water drawn from a deep artesian spring. With a hint – the barest hint – of something else, something heavy and thick. Against his naked skin, it felt like enveloping satin, like having a girl's long silky hair swept along his entire body.

He crept deeper into the sump, an underground watercourse where the cave ceiling dipped to below the surface. As Rory moved, half-floating and hand-walking to pull himself along, the floor sloped down at a gradually steeper angle.

At last, he came to a point when he could only keep his nose above water by supporting himself on the very tips of his fingers. Ahead of him a yard or so, he knew, was the cutoff where stone met sump.

This part of Cornucopia had no official name and did not appear on any of the stupid photocopy maps that his aunt and uncle sold in the gift shop. Not even the experienced cavers who used to explore the other routes and passages had ever ventured down this far. They had no idea it existed. Only Rory.

Those experienced cavers would have been shocked if they'd known. They would have thought he was out of his mind. To be down this far, alone, with no buddy and no back-up and no safety equipment... to make a swim like this without a guideline or breathing apparatus... it went against everything they would have been taught.

He had never hesitated, not even on his first time here. So what if he hadn't had any idea how far the sump extended, or how narrow it got? So what if he didn't know whether or not there were air bells along the way, or if the air in them would even be breathable?

The sump could have led to anything. It could have dumped him into a raging current that smashed the life out of him. It could have teased him with the promise of an air bell, only to pop him up in a chamber of stale or toxic gases.

So what?

He'd gone in. Not like this, true. Not naked and sightless. That first time, he'd worn trunks and mask and fins, and carried a dive-light. He had kicked his way through slowly, cautiously.

Now, he just raised himself up enough to take several full breaths, inhaling and exhaling to saturate his system with oxygen. After one final chest-swelling lungful, Rory gripped the undercurving stone and propelled himself down.

Submerged, the sensory deprivation was almost complete. He not only couldn't see, but he couldn't hear, couldn't smell, couldn't feel anything at all but that satiny rippling over his skin, and the occasional bump of his back or butt against the ceiling as he went. The water-smoothed stone was like polished marble.

Pressure throbbed at his eardrums. His held breath burned low in his chest, a good burn. His hands patter-tracked ahead of him, feeling for familiar landmarks. A spherical nodule, a nearly-perfect globe the size of a bowling ball, told him that he was almost out. The stone ceiling rose sharply a few feet beyond that. Rose toward what would have looked, if he could have seen it, like a shimmering puddle of mercury suspended at the top of the water.

Rory gave a couple of final powerful kicks and sailed upward, letting bubbles stream from his mouth. His head burst through into open air. With a reflexive, seal-like gesture, he swept his hair out of his face and boosted himself onto a ledge.

The sump dead-ended further on, in a breakdown of fallen rocks. He had poked around in there a few times with his mask and his light, though never with complete diving gear. There might have been other outlets, but they would have been nothing more than cracks and crevices far too small for him to get through.

It didn't matter, anyway. What mattered was what he had seen the first time he popped up into this space. What mattered was the ledge he sat on, more polished marble under his butt. And the ledges above it, notches in the stone. Too regular in shape, too even in spacing, to be entirely the work of nature.

Steps. Stairs. Climbing up from the sump's air bell, showing it to be not just an air bell at all but the end of a chimney shaft.

Someone had chiseled and smoothed those steps into the rough rock. Someone else had left a collection of items on a recessed niche that made a convenient shelf. Clay pots, stone knives, tools of bone and antler. Artifacts. Untouched for who-knew-how-long. Rory didn't know. What was he, an archeologist?

What he'd known was that this was important. Secret. The stairs had been carved for a reason. Those objects had been stored for a reason. It wasn't the kind of thing anybody would do on a whim, regardless of how dull and tedious life in this back-hills dump could be.

He had climbed up then no less eagerly than he did now. Maybe more eagerly now, because now he knew what he would find at the top.

His eyes had seen only blackness for so long that the dim glow from above made him squint as if pinned in the spotlight from a police helicopter. He adjusted to it quickly enough, able to make out the shapes of his hands and arms, and the close-in rock walls around him. Most was dark streaked with darker, but a single damp and slow-dripping flowstone formation ran down the shaft in a vein the color and knobby texture of cottage cheese.

By the time he'd hauled his weight all the way up, he was trembling with exhaustion and exhilaration, and his eyes had gotten accustomed enough to the change in light so that he could see but no longer felt glare-blinded.

She was there. Waiting for him.

Gnarled and twisted. Grotesque. Fishbelly white. Glistening. Sheened with a faint luminescence. Hugely fat, an albino mound of loose fleshy rolls and swells and sagging, drooping obesity. Massive hips, monstrously bulbous buttocks, dimple-pocked thighs.

Her face drew up in a crinkled, wrinkled leer. Horns bristled from her head, curling down like a ram's, branching like a deer's, spreading wide like a bull's, pointing up like a goat's, jutting out like the spiky tiara on the Statue of Liberty. A long single spiral sprouted from the middle of her forehead, and a thick tapering rhinoceros curve thrust up from the end of her snout. Rows of short, blunted bony nubs dotted the sides of her neck, ran the length of her backbone and rose into vicious spikes atop her round shoulders.

As she hunched, crouching forward, her pendulous pairs of breasts hung like six half-deflated water balloons. Fluid dribbled from them, thin and palely radiant. It splattered into a hollow in the floor between her wide-braced hooves. Some overflowed, oozing in a slow ribbon to the flowstone vein that descended the shaft wall. The rest of it pooled beneath her, making milky swirls around little hummocks of round white clusters.

They looked like sparkling pearls, like bunches of grapes made from gypsum crystal. Each was no bigger than a pinball. Rory knelt at the pool's edge, gazing at them, counting them.

He raised his head.

"Six," he said. "Yes. I'm ready. I'll do it."

CHAPTER 18
Measureless to Man

They were killing him, fucking killing him. His head was going to explode. He would go nuts and rip out his own throat with his bare hands. He would find a deep shaft of howling dark wind and hurl himself into it.

Anything.

Christ!

They were killing him.

It was enough to make him wish that the asshole with the gun had been a better shot. At least if he was dead, it'd be fucking quiet.

She started over. *"In Xanadu did Kublai Khan a stately pleasure dome decree...* something-something-something about a sunless sea. Darn it! I can't remember how it goes."

"Give it a rest already, would you?" That was the other girl. "Jeez, like anybody cares about some stupid old poem."

"Who asked you?" The older boy. Belligerent.

"Who asked *you?"* The younger one. "Huh? Who? Nobody, that's who."

Dawes pinched the bridge of his nose and didn't say a word. He didn't open his eyes. He breathed steadily.

"Oh, shut up." The older boy.

"Don't tell my brother to shut up!" The girl. What was her name again? Some city.

"Yeah!" The younger boy. *"You* shut up!"

"I should be able to remember it. I read it in school last year." Kim. Distressed.

"Big whoop, bookworm." Dallas. That was it. Dallas. "Little miss teacher's pet."

And her brother was Austin.

Their parents needed a good swift kick in the ass for hanging those names on them. What did they call their other kids? Houston? Fort Worth? Abilene?

"Leave her alone." Grant. The teenager with the unkempt hair.

"There was something about caves," Kim said. "I'm sure of it."

"So what?" Austin. "Dumb poems aren't gonna do us any good. It's cold, it's dark, it's wet and I'm hungry. And I gotta pee."

"So pick a spot and go," Grant said.

"That's gross." Dallas.

"Well, hey, pardon me but it isn't like there's a bathroom anywhere down here."

"What about the empty bottles?" Kim asked. "We could use those."

"That's even grosser!" Dallas cried. "Pee in a bottle? What if we get them mixed up? I'm not drinking anybody's pee!"

"Yeah," Austin said. "And what about when we gotta... you know... number two? How do we wipe?"

"Austin, jeez!" There was a smack, as of a sister backhanding a brother in the fleshy part of an upper arm.

"Better hold it, then," Grant said.

"How long?" Austin sounded whiny, the kind of whine that went straight in through a person's temples like twin diamond-tipped drill bits. "We've been here forever. What if we can't ever find the way out?"

Forever. It sure as hell seemed like that to Dawes. Hours had gone by since he'd been leading the 1:30 tour group. Right near the end, too. At Echo Gorge. Another fifteen minutes and they would have been on their way back up. Twenty minutes and he could have deposited them all at the gift shop, then retired to his camper for a break before his next tour.

Instead...

Here he was.

Hours later. Lost. Somewhere in the bowels of the fucking earth.

Shot.

Shot!

The irony of it just about staggered him.

He had never been shot before. Not once. He'd been knifed, sure. He'd been pepper-sprayed and stun-gunned and clobbered with everything from baseball bats to wooden kitchen chairs. He'd taken more kicks and punches than he could count. There was a metal pin in his knee (car bumper) and a thin white scar along the side of his shaven scalp (broken bottle) and two toes missing from his right foot (pit bull).

But he'd never been shot until today.

Some fucking irony there, all right.

Honest job for once in his life. Actually trying to save a little girl.

Bullet in the back, dropped into a gorge, nearly drowned.

If it was a message, it was a cynical one. One that said he might be better off going back to his old ways.

God was a real wiseass comedian.

Stranding him down here with a pack of kids.

Kids who fully expected that he, Wallace Dawes, would by virtue of being the grown-up, take care of everything and lead them to safety. Who wanted to know why he hadn't done it already. Who seemed to have mistaken him for some kind of action-movie hero.

The four of them moved on to arguing over who was the hungriest. Austin claimed it was him, which was a barefaced lie because Dawes had seen the sneaky little bastard popping M&Ms into his mouth when he thought nobody was looking. At least his sister, snotty though she was, had offered to share out her stash of crushed pretzels.

Not that it mattered. They were all hungry.

Thirst wasn't a problem... an immediate problem anyway. They'd refilled their various containers when they'd moved away from the river. Even if they drained those, there were other sources of water. Creeks. Hell, even the driplets and puddles from the rock formations. They wouldn't die of dehydration. Dehydration would be the least of their concerns.

Food, okay, food was much more of a problem. He'd scrounged among the bodies, but hadn't had a lot of luck. A couple things of trail mix, one of those fruit-rolls that looked like weird skin and tasted like sour sugar, a zip-top baggie of apple slices, half a package of Chips Ahoy that had shipped water and turned into mush.

Thanksgiving dinner, it wasn't.

Enough to sustain himself and four kids?

It wasn't that, either.

With a genuine longing that surprised him, he thought of his camper. Nothing fancy. Just a cap on the back of a pickup truck. Mattress and tangle of blankets up above the cab. Propane stove. Portable television. A radio. Indifferent heaps of clothes. A shelf of tattered paperbacks. Photos, postcards and pictures torn from magazines taped to the walls.

Compared to a jail cell or some of the other places he'd lived, it was the Ritz.

He wished he could be there now.

Home.

Tipped back in his chair with a beer and a sandwich. Maybe a hot serving of pork and beans from his dented cookpot, instead. Or even a take-out dinner of fried chicken, slaw and biscuits.

His stomach growled. Loud. Prolonged.

The kids broke off their bickering and laughed.

Dawes pried open an eye to see them all looking at him.

In the guttering firelight, they could have been refugees from a hurricane or flood or other natural disaster. Muddy, bedraggled, bruised, scraped, wet. The cave's high humidity saw to that, and the damp fabric wicked the heat away from their bodies with stealthy, deadly persistence.

So far, though, none of them appeared to be showing obvious signs of hypothermia. No numbness, no disorientation, no forgetfulness or hallucinations. Least of all, no speech problems. He might have almost welcomed speech problems.

"I guess that means you're still alive, huh?" Grant asked.

"Haven't died yet." Dawes stretched. He groaned. All the exertion and climbing and crawling, not to mention the holes in his hide, hadn't bothered him as much while he'd still been moving. Stopping, and resting against this cold hard rock, hadn't done him a lot of good. Only let the stiffness settle in.

"The wood's almost gone," Kim said. "Should we go find more?"

"No." He pushed himself up, groaning again. "We need to keep going."

"Where *are* we going?" demanded Dallas. "You don't even know, do you?"

"Does it matter? Anywhere's better than here."

"No shit," Grant said.

The initial idea of following the river all the way until it emptied into Little Elk Lake would have been a good one, except for some problems. Waterfalls. Rapids. Boulders the size of houses. A place where the current dove in a foaming, churning whirlpool sump under a forbidding barrier of solid rock. They wanted to come out the other side alive, as opposed to having their mangled bodies eventually surface in the lake.

They had flashlights, though who knew for how much longer before the batteries died? They had torches... sort of... but those weren't much good when they had to worm their way through narrow squeezes. Dawes had his trusty lighter, and a sinking feeling that it was low on fuel.

Even those pathetic light sources hadn't been able to illuminate the biggest cavern they'd found so far. Dawes had heard of cave systems in Europe that boasted chambers that huge, and there was Mammoth, and Carlsbad. But he didn't think California had anything else to rival the vast space he and the kids had entered by way of a cramped uphill crawl.

From a tight stone-walled maze into that...

How large a space? He couldn't get a sure sense. Caves had a way of screwing with the perceptions. A formation that looked the size of a car and fifty feet away might really be as big as a building, and a hundred yards away.

Football fields. Airplane hangars. Sports stadiums.

No way to guess.

That cave had prompted Kim to recite the Kublai Khan poem, with some line about caverns measureless to man.

Pretty much summed it up, in his opinion.

Fucking measureless to man.

Dawes didn't even want to know how far underground they must have been at that point. And still, the massive chamber's floor had dropped into a chasm that made Echo Gorge look like a roadside ditch. From way, *way* below, he'd been able to hear rushing water. Was this where they might have washed up if they'd tried to continue along the river? Or was this some other subterranean watercourse entirely?

Either way, it didn't matter. They had no chance in hell of getting down there. Not without rappelling gear and plenty of rope.

The ceiling soared so high above them that stalactites probably forty feet long looked like tiny little soda straws. One immense flowstone formation looked, with its tiered layers and glittering calcite frosting, like some kind of half-melted wedding cake. Another, dark and looming and pocked, was so reminiscent of a termite mound he'd seen once in Africa that it wouldn't have surprised him if giant insects had come whizzing and clicking out of it to swarm them into a stinging death-agony.

He and the kids made their way along ledges that turned out to be wider than some city streets, hugging the walls and huddling together in the small radius of their light. The enormity of the chamber awed even the Texas Two into a welcome respite of a hush.

The chatter and the bickering had started up again once they were back in areas where everything was more reasonably to an understandable scale. Once they felt less like tiny ants creeping through a giant's house.

"Now what?" Dallas asked when they had all gotten up, stamping their feet and slapping their arms. "Can we get out this way?"

Dawes hoped so. He didn't want to have to backtrack through that cavern and search for other passages. He didn't want to try and traverse any gaps or cross any of the slippery-looking arches he'd noticed.

This was not really his area of expertise.

What did he know about caves?

Not much, that was for sure. What little he'd picked up from books or from the other guides. Justin the college boy, Pete the old-timer, Sylvia the adventure hound. Sometimes, especially in the mornings before the day's tours began, the three of them would sit around swapping stories. Dawes often listened in but never contributed.

Hell, I only took this job on impulse. It seemed like a good way to lay low for a while. Out here in the boonies, where nobody would have any reason to come looking for me.

See how well that had worked?

His thoughts flicked back to the man who'd shot him.

Would have been nice to know who the fuck he was. Dawes didn't for a second tell himself that it was all a big misunderstanding, a case of mistaken identity.

But who the fuck was he?

And how the fuck *did he find me?*

Idly, as an afterthought, he also wondered why. That there was a reason for finding him, even shooting him, Dawes had no doubt. *Which reason, though?*

"Hey," Austin said. "Hey, do you feel that? There's a wind."

"Big deal," Grant said. "There's been wind ever since that humongous cave."

"Yeah, but–"

"No, he's right," Dawes said. "There was a breeze before, but this is different. It's blowing past us."

He struck his lighter and held it up, observing the way the flame bent. It pointed toward a crack in the stone. A thin, twisting crack. The kids would have no trouble, but Dawes himself...

Sidling in sideways, feeling his way blindly with his leading foot, Dawes worked his way into the crack. Rough stone rubbed along his chest and back. Even when he exhaled, deflating himself as much as possible, he left layers of skin at the tightest spots.

Claustrophobia infiltrated his brain like icy wires. He breathed in a shallow, panting series of puffs. He expected to hear the heavy grinding sound and feel the unimaginable pressure as the walls closed in, flattening him. *Ribs crackling. Skull bursting like a pine knot in the fireplace.*

"I don't want to go in there," Kim said.

"It's okay." His voice emerged as a pained whistle. "You kids... you're... skinny. You'll... be fine."

The bandages Grant had tied around him hadn't been terrific to start with, and the trip through the caves had already reduced them to ragged mummy-wrappings. He could feel them getting a further shredding now as he forced himself between viselike pincers of sharp rock. Blood dribbled down his torso. *More blood. How much have I lost? How much more can I afford to lose?*

Then he was through, wrenching out of the stony clamps and into a chamber about as roomy as a phone booth, or small elevator. He struck the lighter again but saw no passages.

"Oh, fuck," Dawes muttered. Was he going to have to go back?

"What's the matter?" Dallas emerged, followed by her brother.

"There's no way out from here."

"But the wind," came Grant's voice from the other side of the crack, where he'd been waiting to bring up the rear. "You said–"

"Look." Austin pointed. Straight up.

Dawes raised the Zippo as high as he could reach. "You're fucking kidding me."

Kim and then Grant joined them. They stood in a ring around Dawes, all of them looking up. The elevator-sized chamber was really an elevator-*shaft*-sized chamber, and they were at the bottom of it.

For several blissful seconds, none of the kids said anything. They studied the rising shaft by the lighter's flame and the wan beams of the flashlights. It made a narrow chimney, not smooth-walled but bumpy with protruding rocks and ledges.

"We can climb it," Grant finally said.

"Sure," Dawes said. "Climb it. With no ropes, no harnesses–"

"I can climb it," Dallas said.

"Yeah, me too!" Austin stuck out his chin as if daring anybody to call him a liar. "I'm a good climber. I don't care how high it goes. I'll climb all the way to the top."

"Kimmy?" Grant asked.

She bit her lip, her brows drawn together in fine black arches. "I don't think we have a choice."

He didn't like it, but Dawes figured they were right. There wasn't a whole lot else they could do. Climb this and hope it led to a way out, or go back and search for other passages in hopes that one of those led to a way out. Any option was as good at this point as any other option.

"Okay," he said. "One at a time, and when you get to the top, you get just far enough out of the way so the next person can come up. Do *not* go any further, got that? Stay *put*. I'll boost each of you up, and then I'll go last. Everybody clear?"

They nodded.

"Keep three points of contact at all times," he added, remembering what Sylvia said about 'chimneying.' He showed them his hands, indicated his feet. "One, two, three, four, see? Whenever you move, you only move one hand or foot, and the other three keep contact with the rock. Use your back, your shoulders, your – your butt as much as you can. Push against the sides. It'll help keep you from slipping."

Grant went first. Dawes waited underneath, as if he'd actually be able to do anything if the kid fell. *What, catch him? That'd be a good trick. Break his fall by giving him something softer than limestone and granite to land on?* That was more likely.

But Grant made it, scrambling up so that his baggy pants and ratty sneakers vanished from sight. "I'm up," he called. "It's not so bad. Maybe fifteen feet."

"What do you see?" Dawes asked.

"Dark. You guys have the... hey, wait a minute. There's... yeah. There's light. There's a tunnel, and way down it, there's light. Kind of yellow."

"Sunshine?" Dallas clawed fruitlessly at the nearest handhold, still two feet above her reach. "Is it daylight? Is it the way out? Boost me up!"

"Remember, you get up there and you *stay* put." Dawes hooked his hands into her armpits and lifted.

"I will, I will, jeez." She went up the stone chimney like a squirrel on a rope. "I see it! Like he said! Light!"

"Stay there!" Dawes barked.

"I *am!*" She did the sort of exasperated heaving sigh that Dawes figured would be accompanied by an elaborate preteen eyeroll of disdain. "Whew boy, it smells weird."

"I think I hear people, too," Grant said. "Voices. Or maybe it's the wind in the rocks. Sure sounds like voices, though."

"Stay," Dawes said yet again.

"We are, we are. Right, Dallas?"

"Right already, jeez."

"You next, Austin." Dawes leaned conspiratorially close to the boy. "I need you to keep an eye on your sister. Can you do that?"

Austin nodded, eyes bright. He climbed almost as well as Dallas had done. Then it was Kim's turn.

"What if it isn't the way out?" she asked.

"What else could it be?"

"I don't know." She bit her lip again.

"Whatever it is, it's got to be better than staying down here, don't you think?"

Reluctantly, she nodded, and raised her arms. Dawes picked her up, and watched as she climbed. She was slower, less sure than the others, even with the Texas Two shining their flashlights down to guide her. She did slip once, and he lunged as if to catch her, earning a stabbing twinge in his back, but she recovered, and made it.

Dawes leaned against the wall, pressing his hand to the folded pad of cloth beneath the unraveling bandage. *Hot and wet and sodden. Bleeding again.*

Again? Hah. He hadn't stopped bleeding.

Now he was just bleeding *more*.

CHAPTER 19
The Pit

Everybody else slept.

Not her. Not Tiffy.

If she slept, she could miss something. A chance, maybe.

A chance to do *what*, she didn't really know. So far, she hadn't exactly come up with any brilliant ideas. She'd yanked at the ankle-lock things until she thought she was going to rip all the skin right off her foot and still couldn't get free. They were too tight. Then she'd tried getting the other end of the chain unhooked, but that hadn't worked either. And then she'd tried to pull the metal loop out of the rock. It was on a spike. She'd wiggled it and wiggled it like a loose tooth but it was in there too good.

Stuck. Totally, totally, a hundred percent stuck.

No way she was going to be able to escape.

Unless she got an opportunity.

In the stories, the bad guys always gave you an opportunity. It was in the rules. They would catch you, and hold you prisoner, and explain their whole evil plan. Then they would go away. They'd go away and leave you in the dungeon, or hooked up to their doomsday-deathtrap-machine or something.

That was the way it always worked in the Kim Possible cartoons. Tiffy didn't like that show as much as she did the other Disney stories, the ones about princesses and fairies, but this place she was in seemed a lot more like something Kim Possible-ish.

Anyway, in the princess and fairy stories, there was supposed to be some hero to come to the rescue. Because he was in love with the girl and wanted to save her from the villain. Tiffy didn't even have a boyfriend yet.

Well, there was Adam Trasker. The cutest boy in her class. He would sit with her at lunch and she was one of only five girls he'd invited to his birthday party. On Valentine's Day, he had written 'Love, Adam' in her card, and he hadn't written that in anybody else's. So he was maybe-kinda her boyfriend.

Adam wasn't going to come rescue her, though. If she wanted to escape, she'd have to do it herself. And she couldn't do that if she went to sleep. She had to be awake and ready for when the Cyclops came back.

What was the Cyclops going to do with them?

Feed them to the imps in the pit?

She didn't want to be imp-food.

That would be awful.

But if the Cyclops wanted to put her in the pit, then he'd have to unchain her feet first. As soon as he did that, as soon as he unchained her feet and tried to pick her up, Tiffy would kick him in the nuts and run like heck.

Kim Possible wouldn't have kicked him in the nuts. Kim Possible never kicked anybody in the nuts. Neither did Snow White, or Cinderella, or Belle, or Princess Jasmine.

Real life wasn't very much like the cartoons.

No fancy leaping cheerleader moves. No cable-shooting guns or kim-municators or naked mole rats to help save the day. No fairy godmothers or talking candlesticks or flying carpets. No princes to the rescue.

Only Tiffy. On her own.

So, she'd do the nut-kicking thing and run like heck.

What she would do after that, she didn't know.

Get lost in the caves, probably.

The Cyclops grabbed her near Goblintown, covering her mouth so she couldn't scream. He'd carried her through all kinds of dark and scary twisting passages, sometimes slinging her over his back so he could climb up or down, all in the pitch black so she couldn't see anything.

He made her lose her hat, too, and that really annoyed her. It was brand-new, a visor from Disneyland with her name right on it and everything.

She did still have her poodle-purse. There were five or six dollars and some quarters in it, and her souvenir autograph book with its matching pen. There was a little velvet bag of fake jewels from a Fantasyland gift shop. Part of a sugar cookie – shaped like Mickey Mouse, only she had bitten his ears off – wrapped in a paper napkin. A pack of watermelon-flavored bubblegum. A couple Tootsie Rolls. Her folding hairbrush with the mirror in the handle. Some elastic hairbands and butterfly clips. A bouncy ball, all white and glittery pink swirls. A folded up placemat menu that she'd drawn a flying horse on, and the three-box of crayons from the restaurant.

No cable-shooting gun. No kim-municator. Her mom and dad wouldn't even let her have her own cell phone until she was thirteen, never mind that everybody else in her school had one.

No magic unlock-any-lock key, either. She did find her diary key way at the bottom of the poodle-purse, but it didn't work in the ankle-locks.

Hungry, she snapped off half the cookie and nibbled at it, making sure not to drop any crumbs. She wanted fish-and-chips. She wanted spaghetti. She wanted a strawberry milkshake.

She ended up eating all that was left of the cookie, and still felt hungry.

Maybe she should have saved some to share?

Oops.

Too late.

Feeling guilty, she shook the napkin over her mouth to catch any last bits.

Sharing was nice. But when you didn't even have enough for yourself, wasn't it okay to not share? She wasn't trying to be mean or anything. This wasn't like when she saved some of her Easter candy on purpose so that later after Amberlyn's was all gone, she could make a big show out of enjoying the jelly beans and malted milk ball eggs.

This wasn't like that.

If the others had been awake and watching her, she might have done it anyway. It would have felt really hoggy and selfish to sit there munching on a cookie while they had nothing. She didn't know how she could have given them pieces. She couldn't reach. If she'd tried throwing, what if she'd missed and the cookie had landed too far away? Then nobody would have had any!

But they were asleep.

Didi had struggled and yelled for hours and hours, calling for somebody-anybody to come help them. Calling the Cyclops names, too, and using more bad words than Tiffy had ever heard. Words that should have been bleeped out. Words that Kim Possible and Disney princesses *never* said!

No one came. The Cyclops didn't care. He maybe didn't speak English. Maybe couldn't talk at all. No matter what Didi called him, he only ignored her.

The little boy, R.J., cried and cried until he just couldn't cry any more. Cried himself to sleep. He had his thumb in his mouth and around his nose was gunked up with snot. In the yellowish light, it looked like he'd dunked his face in a bowl of raw eggs.

The bigger boy was also asleep... or maybe still knocked out, the way Didi had been before. They had heard him coming long before the Cyclops pushed him into the cave room, making him trip and fall.

"Hey what's going on where's Tony what did you do with Tony where are you taking me oww that hurts don't hurt me where are we going what's that light what is this place if you hurt Tony I'll–"

And flop, onto the rocky floor. Ripping his pants and skinning his knees. He looked like a high-schooler and a geek. Geeky hair. *HALO* tee-shirt. Like a bigger version of some of the boys in her class, not the cute ones like Adam but the ones who spent their recess time trading Pokemon and Yu-Gi-Oh cards.

When he'd hit the floor and looked up, his eyes about bugged out of his head and his mouth fell open. He wore glasses, broken and cracked ones hanging crooked, and he fumbled them straight with one hand.

He'd stared around at the giant carved heads, the horrible demons with their fang-filled jaws and spiky horns sticking out in all directions. Stared at the glowing yellow lines in the walls. Stared at the imp-pit, which still had some body parts hanging over the edge. He stared at Tiffy and Didi and R.J., the three of them chained to the floor and Didi with her arms tied behind her back.

"Get him!" Didi had shouted, thrashing around in a clank-clink-clankety of chain. "Get him, kill him, kill the son of a bitch and help us! He's crazy!"

Tiffy and R.J. joined in, their voices and echoes making it sound like there were fifty kids in here and not just three. "Help us get us out of here look out look out it's a monster it's a skylops don't let it hurt us get us out of here please please help us save us!"

Amazingly, the boy in the *HALO* shirt had jumped up, spun around, and thrown himself at the Cyclops. Arms flailing, fists smacking at the black shell, the single glassy-green eyeball in the middle of that weird face.

Bubbling excitement, like a fizzy gulp of 7-Up, had filled Tiffy. The *HALO*-shirt boy was no fairy-tale Prince Charming, no handsome hero like Cameron Mack. But he would beat up the Cyclops and rescue them.

Instead, the Cyclops punched him hard in the tummy. The big boy went "Whoof!" and fell on his butt. The Cyclops hit him again, on the side of the head so that the boy's glasses flew off. There'd been a *bzzt* noise and a blue flash, and a quick smell like the time Amberlyn stuck a fork in a light socket when she was just learning to crawl. The boy in the *HALO* shirt flopped on the floor again and lay there, eyes half rolled back in his head, drool on the corners of his mouth.

Didi, R.J. and Tiffy quieted down then, afraid that one of them might be next. They didn't move, didn't say anything as the Cyclops hauled *HALO*-boy to another metal loop hammered into the stone, and chained him up the same way they were.

Then the Cyclops left again. He'd been gone a long, long time.

The boy in the *HALO* shirt woke up for a while, real confused, and only getting more confused when each of the rest of them tried to tell him what was going on. All he'd say was that his name was Colin, he had been in the caves with his girlfriend – Toni-with-an-i, not Tony-with-a-y – and they'd had a fight.

"She kind of got upset at me for something," he explained, looking how Lyle Figg had looked after Mrs. Zimmerman caught him sitting on the copy machine in the principal's office with his pants down. "She was really mad and wouldn't listen when I told her we had to stay together, that she couldn't go off by herself."

"What'd you do?" Didi asked, her eyebrow with the silver hoop in it going way up.

"I tried to follow her," he said, avoiding Didi's gaze. "She doesn't know the caves at all. It's dangerous. She could get hurt. But she wouldn't wait. She ran away in the dark. The flashlight was busted, and I didn't have any matches. I couldn't find her. She wouldn't answer me. After whatever happened, the cave-in, everything was different and screwed up. It kept getting hotter and the smell... fumes or gas or I don't know what... messing with my head. I got lost. Turned around or something."

He'd had a ratty old backpack on, but all it had in it was some spare batteries for the broken flashlight that he didn't even have anymore. He said there'd been some Cokes and candy bars, but that he'd drunk and eaten them while he was wandering around trying to find his girlfriend. There'd been a knife, but the Cyclops found it and took it away.

Nobody said much after that, and eventually the rest of them had gone back to sleep. Everyone but Tiffy.

Still hungry after the cookie and thirstier than ever, she unwrapped a piece of gum and chewed. Sweet juicy watermelon flavor.

She was really, really tired.

Couldn't close her eyes. If she did, if she went to sleep too, that would be when the Cyclops would come back. She wanted to be awake and ready in case that opportunity came.

How long could a person go without sleeping? In a sweaty-hot cave where the air felt heavy... like a muggy summer day when there would be thunderstorms later... and all that anybody wanted to do was relax on a shady porch or in a hammock. With lemonade. Pink lemonade. Ice cubes. Her favorite Wakky-Straw, the one that did the swoops and curlicues. The sprinkler going hishka-hishka-hish on the lawn. Somewhere, off in the distance but coming steadily closer, the ice cream man. "Yankee-Doodle-Dandy" playing on his speakers. Orange Creamsicle. Drumstick with a coating of chocolate and chopped peanuts.

Her head drooped. The watermelon gum-wad plopped out of her mouth, onto her hand, sticky like a slug. Tiffy gasped and sat up straight, realizing that she had almost let herself drowse right into a dream of hammocks and ice cream.

And the Cyclops was coming.

She could hear him breathing.

He entered the chamber and she thought of those antique posters for horror movies. All black and white with drippy scary-font letters spelling out titles like "Mutant Cannibals from Outer Space" and "Graveyard of the Vampire." Always, on those posters, the picture would be of some cheesy monster that you just knew was a guy in a rubber costume. And he'd always be carrying some half-fainted girl in his arms... and her clothes would always be torn in just the right places to make it look like her boobies were about to spill out.

The Cyclops came in looking like a cheesy monster in a rubber costume, carrying some half-fainted girl with her clothes torn and her boobies almost spilling out. She moved and groaned as he brought her into the hot-yellow murk. Her eyes opened. She had on lots of makeup, streaky-smeared on her face.

She blinked, peering up at the demon heads and the glowing symbols in the walls. In a thick, mumbling voice, she said something astonished-sounding, with the f-word in it. There was blood and a puffy bruise on her forehead.

Tiffy didn't know what to do. *Yell? The way they had yelled at HALO-boy? But that hadn't worked out so well, had it?* She doubted that this girl would do much better. She wished the others were awake. Wished she could reach them to shake or kick. They were chained too far apart.

When the Cyclops set her down at the base of a rock-column, the girl slouched there, still looking around. She scowled when she saw *HALO*-boy, and said the f-word again. Angry-sounding this time.

"There you are, Colin, you little pervert bastard creep!"

Her gaze roved the rest of them – Didi, R.J., Tiffy – and the scowl morphed into a hard-math-test frown.

The Cyclops reached for her leg with a silvery hook. Another ankle-lock, with chain leading to another loop in the stone. She bent her knee, drawing her foot away, and demanded to know what the f-word he thought he was doing.

He reached again.

She crab-scuttled sideways, sounding freaked out as well as angry, saying more bad words. He grabbed her by the shirt and she slapped. Hard. Wrenched out of his grasp, ripping the shirt right off herself so that the Cyclops was left with a torn scrap hanging from his hand and the girl was left with a teensy pink bra.

The shouting and bad words woke Didi and *HALO*-boy Colin. Not R.J., but Tiffy remembered how when Amberlyn was that little, she'd been able to fall asleep on Daddy's shoulder and stay that way even while they were on a sidewalk watching a parade with marching bands and horses and everything.

They started shouting and fighting their chains. Tiffy joined in.

The girl – *HALO*-boy's Toni – lashed out wildly as the Cyclops jabbed something toward her. Whatever it was flew halfway across the cave and hit a tall cone-shaped rock. There was another blue flash, another *bzzt*. It was a taser-thing! A black handle with little metal prongs poking out of the end. Not magic. A taser-thing.

The Cyclops got his big arms around Toni and lifted her feet off the ground, holding her with her arms pinned at her sides. She slammed her forehead into his single staring eye, then howled with pain. Blood poured down her face.

"Toni! Toni! Let her go, you jerk!"

"Kick him!" Didi and Tiffy screamed together. "In the nuts!" Tiffy added.

She did. *Bullseye*. With a sound like a volleyball player smacking a high lobbing serve.

The suck-blow of his breathing hitched with a grunt. He dropped her. She landed on her heels, danced crazily for balance, couldn't find it, stumbled backward.

"Look out!" Didi cried.

Toni's foot came down on an arm that hadn't gotten dragged all the way down into the pit. The arm was yellowish-pale, the fingers curled like they were clawing at nothing. It turned under her, just as she almost steadied herself.

"Toni!" Colin threw himself to the limits of his chain.

Toni tottered, cast a wild sideways glance, and saw the pit. Saw what was in the pit. A screech of pure terror exploded from her throat as she fell in.

She landed with a squelchy thump on the bodies, making their stiff limbs jump with the impact. Watery stuff that wasn't water splashed out. It was reddish-pink, yellowish-white, greenish. Like something squeezed from a yucky sore. Smoky steam rose from it when it hit the limestone.

The Cyclops said a bad word. He started to reach for Toni, then pulled his arm back and said the bad word again.

Still screeching, Toni lunged halfway out of the pit. She came up drenched in the yucky liquid, covered with blood… and covered with imps. They were all over her. Pinchers and little claws helping them cling and stick and hold on. Like pufferfish, like thorny ticks, like living burrs. Piercing her with their horns and stingers, with their long sharp needle-beaks. With their barbed scorpion-tails and mandibles and fangs.

Imps swarmed. Imps burrowed. Imps sank their horns into Toni's arms, her stomach, her cheek, her neck. Sharp. Hooked.

She pawed at them, slapped at them. Seizing one, she tore it from her chest. It came off with a Velcro noise, taking a clot of meat with it. And it stuck to her hand. Toni shrieked again. She beat her hand against the edge of the pit.

The imps were eating her alive. They buzzed and chittered. They seemed happy to have their dinner so fresh. The others had already been dead by the time the Cyclops dumped them in.

The liquid…

It was melting her skin away. Dissolving it like acid.

And the imps swarmed and stung and bit and stabbed.

And Toni screamed, screamed, screamed.

CHAPTER 20
Jacob's Ladder

Cornucopia made a great hide-out, but damned if Nick was ever going to like all the creeping-around-underground shit. Couldn't see the sky, couldn't tell what time it was, couldn't be sure which way was north-south-east-west. Landmarks weren't as helpful as they should have been, since everything looked different depending on what direction you were facing from.

Aren't there stories about people taking balls of string down into caves? Or making chalk marks on the walls so that they could find their way back out?

He asked Chloe, and she shook her head.

"String wouldn't do much good," she said. "It'd just snag and tangle, or break. As for chalk arrows, yes, people did used to do that in the olden days. Chalk, or they'd use smoke from candles to smudge marks on the walls. Cavers don't do that anymore."

"Why the hell not? They enjoy getting lost?"

"They don't want to damage the cavern. The formations are fragile."

"The formations are rock," he said.

"They're still growing. A wet cave is an active cave. Chalk, paint, smoke, even the oils from your hands could damage the limestone and prevent future layers of minerals from being deposited. That's why we tell the tours not to touch, and why we have the Petting Zoo at the end. The stalactites and stalagmites there have already been ruined, so there's no harm done on those ones."

"Sorry I asked," Nick grumbled.

Probably the biggest speech she had ever made in his presence, but the way she said it made him think it was something she'd memorized for the tour. Afterwards, she lapsed back into silence. Not that he minded the quiet. It was a real change of pace from what he was used to. *A quiet chick. Fancy that.*

At home, he had to listen to his mother yakking away non-stop. Nagging at the old man, nagging at Nick. When he wasn't at home, he had to listen to Toni. That girl always seemed to need to be doing something with her mouth. If words weren't coming out of it, other things would be going into it. Which did have its benefits.

Chloe, now, Chloe hardly ever talked to him at all. She didn't like him. No secret about that.

Too bad. He wouldn't have minded nailing her.

They took advantage of the activity out front to slip unnoticed around back of the gift shop. A dirt and gravel trail led between snarls of weeds and sticker-bushes to a side entrance blocked by a metal gate with a sign on it, reading: "Staff Only No Trespassing."

"I think we should go back," she said, after they'd proceeded well into the dark.

"What's the matter?" He grinned his most wolfish grin. "Nervous about being alone with me?"

"It feels wrong down here. All wrong."

"Well, no shit. What do you expect after a fucking earthquake?" He knocked on the hard red plastic shell strapped to her head. "That's why you have your special hat."

Chloe twisted away. "Quit it."

"I can't help it. You look so cute in your special hat with the special little headlight on the front."

"So sue me if I don't want a cracked skull or a concussion," she said. "If a rock lands on your stupid head, you'll wish you had one."

"I'll risk it. Better than looking like an idiot."

"Fine. Suit yourself. Whatever."

"Shit, Chloe, I didn't think you cared," he said, his grin widening.

"I don't."

"Then what's the problem?"

"The problem is, this is too dangerous. We shouldn't be down here. We shouldn't be doing this."

"I thought you wanted to find your brother."

"I do, but..." She blew out a sigh and looked around. "I don't know if we can."

Not all of Cornucopia was something that anybody would pay good money to look at, including this section. The formations were ugly, brown, dry, old, chipped, broken off. Metal U-brackets bolted to the ceiling held corrugated black tubes with power lines running through them, leading to a utility room full of fuse boxes, switches and levers, and control panels.

Or they *used to* lead there, anyway.

Half a mountain's worth of boulders clogged the passage. Even now, hours after the collapse, gritty dust still hung in the air. Motes drifted like dull glitter in the beams from Chloe's headlamp and flashlight. It glued itself to their sweaty faces. It got up Nick's nose and made him sneeze, got into his mouth and made him feel like he'd been eating dirt.

Nick tried shifting some rubble, but triggered a small avalanche. He damn near sprained his ankle getting out of the way, still not quick enough to keep a bowling ball of a rock from mashing his foot. He thought at least one of his toes was broken. It hurt like a bitch.

"You're limping," Chloe said. "Are you sure you're okay?"

"Yeah. Something in my shoe."

Something in his shoe, all right. A broken fucking *toe* in his shoe. Not that he was going to let on.

Five minutes further in, he whacked his head a good one against the jagged stub of a stalactite. He muffled a curse of pain, since the last thing he needed was to prove Chloe right about the hardhats and have her do the whole told-ya-so thing. When he sent his fingers probing through his hair, he found a spot tacky with blood, and a swollen bump split by a gash maybe three inches long.

Stitches. Great. A broken fucking toe, and stitches in my head. What else?

"I really think we should go back," Chloe said.

"What about Colin?" Nick asked.

Not that he gave a shit about Colin. Or Brandon. Dinks, the both of them. Dinks with resources, okay. Dinks who were desperate pathetic kiss-asses, which was sometimes nice to have around. He didn't give much of a shit about Toni, either, for all that she was supposedly his girlfriend. Wasn't like he was going to *marry* her.

He did give a bit of a shit about Rory. Rory might be a flat out bugfuck lunatic, but he was the closest person Nick had to an actual buddy. Rory understood about the guns, the pipe-bombs, and the rest of it.

And he *did* give a shit, a very big shit, for that. Almost two years, it had taken him and Rory to build up that arsenal. They had fucking *everything* in there. Not just weapons. They had flak jackets, gas masks, night-vision goggles, sniper scopes, motion detectors... you name it.

The others might sit around bullshitting about how cool it would be when civilization imploded and anarchy reigned and only the tough, the strong and the ready could survive. Truth was, none of them would be worth a piss in the shower. They would crack and fall apart. Only Nick and Rory had what it would take to make it in a harsh new post-apocalyptic world.

"I want to find him, I really do," Chloe said, worry filling those big brown doe-eyes of hers. "But I just don't know if we can, Nick. We might not even be able to get to the bunker."

"You said there were plenty of ways. This one was just the easiest. So we go around. What about that ladder you mentioned?"

"Jacob's Ladder. The emergency shaft near Queen's Palace, yeah... it comes out kind of close to where we want to be."

"Then let's go."

She continued the worried look, and started in nibbling on her fingernails.

"Don't chicken out on me, Chloe."

Nibble-nibble-nibble. Her lips weren't as full as Toni's, but they looked soft and sweet. She had that innocent, good-girl quality to her face that would make it even more dirty and exciting to see her down on her knees. He wondered if she was a virgin, then nearly laughed out loud for wondering.

"They're counting on you," he added.

Her gaze sharpened as she looked at him. "We both know you don't care about them. All you care about is the stuff you have stashed in the caves, and getting rid of it before the police find out."

"Yeah, so?" He dug into his pockets and found one last, lonely, slightly bent cigarette in the crumpled pack.

"You shouldn't smoke down here."

"Why? I'll damage the fucking cave? Take a look around." He lit up. "This place is finished. *El finito.*"

She glared, whirled, and stalked off. Nick chuckled, letting out a thin stream of grey smoke, and followed her, watching her cute little ass switching indignantly back and forth.

The arsenal had to be taken care of. Not all of it was illegal, but there was enough to ensure him a hefty jail term. *Have to dispose of the evidence.* Down a bottomless pit or into the underground river or something. Maybe into one of those wells that Rory called sumps. Where it'd never be found.

And the witnesses? The others? If they'd survived the cave-in?

Rory wouldn't talk. Rory was in it as deep as Nick, if not deeper. Toni? Toni was a tough chick; she'd tell the cops to cram it up their asses. Colin and Brandon? Fear might keep them silent. Or it might make them blab. One round of Good Cop/Bad Cop and those two would break like pinatas.

Be better if they hadn't survived. No chance then of anybody squealing.

And Chloe?

Damn. Really, he should get rid of her.

What a waste.

It'd have to look natural, in case they did find the body. A fall or something. Push her over an edge. Bash her head in with a rock. Make it seem like an accident.

Just then, she looked back at him. The headlamp flashed white-hot in his eyes. He flung up a hand to shield it out, squinting in protest.

Shit... could she read his mind, or what? Did she know what he'd been thinking?

"Here it is," she said. "Jacob's Ladder."

"Fucking blinded me with that thing."

"Sorry." She moved the light out of his face. "The shaft hasn't collapsed. It's clear. I can hear echoes from the river down there, and I can feel the air moving."

"Great." He blinked until he could see again.

Chloe stood at the edge of a hole. A barrier chain hung between metal posts, supporting a sign that advised, "Caution!" A darkened EXIT sign with an arrow, mounted on the wall above her, pointed to a nice even-floored tunnel that curved up in a switchback and out of sight.

"This will get us to the Queen's Palace. After that..." She shrugged.

Nick moved closer and aimed his flashlight down. "Fuck," he said. "This is your idea of a ladder?"

The hole, maybe six feet in diameter, went a good thirty feet deep. Metal rungs like enormous rounded staples poked out of the coarse stone wall at intervals, making a long corkscrew spiral. Looked like a fucking DNA strand.

"The rungs are secure. They'll be cold, though. Wet and slippery. Be careful how you put your feet, and get a good grip before you transfer any weight."

Could he make it the rest of the way on his own? If, say, he gave her a shove right now? She'd carom down that shaft, battering herself on stone and iron. Probably break her neck.

Such a waste. I really would have liked to nail her first.

Too risky.

She was looking at him again. Warily.

"What are you thinking about?" she asked.

God, she was fucking creeping him out. Like she *could* read his mind.

"Nothing," he said. "Come on. Let's do this."

He didn't push her as she maneuvered past the chain. As convenient as it would have been, he wasn't sure if he'd be able to find the armory on his own. He still needed her. There'd be plenty of opportunities later.

She'd been right about the rungs. The iron felt slick and cold. Rusty moisture came off on his hands, leaving a smelly, reddish residue uncomfortably similar to bloodstains. Blood on his hands, how about that?

Well, shit… it isn't like I've never had blood on my hands before.

Chloe climbed down first, moving with surety and grace. Nick faked it, hanging onto the rungs with white-knuckled strain. He couldn't stop thinking about the drop below his feet.

A clammy breeze rushed up from the depths, flapping his clothes and hair, whistling in his ears. It made a whooshing, thunderous sound. Like jet engines heard from very far away.

The cold metal and the death-clutch of his grip made his hands ache. His foot shot sideways off a rung. He scrabbled, clung there with heart hammering a mile a minute.

"You okay?" Her headlamp did weird things to his shadow when she tipped her head back to look up at him.

"Yeah," he gasped. "I'm good. Go."

A couple minutes later, she called, "Off ladder!"

"Huh?"

"I'm down. You've got ten, twelve more to go."

Finally, he stepped not onto slippery metal but onto stone. Then he had both feet firmly on good solid ground again. He tossed his hair out of his eyes and did his best to look nonchalant. Mr. Bravado. He hadn't been scared. Not scared at all.

"This way," Chloe said.

The Queen's Palace, without its hidden spotlights and their gels of different colors to throw rainbows across the glistening formations, looked less like Disneyland and more like a fucking spooky graveyard catacomb.

When Chloe clicked her headlamp off, swallowing them in a suffocating black where the echoes roared, it got ten times spookier.

"The fuck?!" he blurted.

"Shh! I saw something!"

"So you turn out the fucking light?"

"It *was* a light I saw!"

He wanted to grab her and throttle her right then. Forget making it look like an accident. The little bitch was messing with him, and he wasn't going to take that from her. He'd choke her, he'd–

"There!" she said.

A flicker. A light. A moving light.

"Someone must be at Echo Gorge!" Chloe sounded giddy. "Maybe it's Colin!"

She snapped the lamp on again and was off like a shot before he could stop her. Almost running. Ponytail bouncing from under her hardhat. Calling her brother's name.

"Colin? Col? Is that you? Colin!"

Growling curses, Nick hurried after her before she could completely vanish and leave him stranded in the dark with only a half a book of matches in his pocket.

He burst into the next chamber, a high-arching one cut down the middle by a deep chasm. The bridge was gone, rocks and rubble heaped everywhere, and Chloe gaped in shock at the strangers who gaped in shock right back at her.

"Oh, my God," a red-haired woman said, getting to her feet. "Oh, my God, thank God, you found us!"

CHAPTER 21
Mud Pots

Dallas was right. It did smell weird. Gross. A Brussels-sprouts-for-dinner kind of smell. A smell you could almost taste, and it made you want to throw up.

Yuck.

Stupid cave.

It just kept getting worse and worse.

Tired, hungry, cold, wet, sore, needing a pee, lost, and now this. Gross Brussels sprouts smells. Stupid boogery cave.

He'd liked it at first. Thought it was really neat and cool and different. Going down that skinny spiral staircase was exciting. Being underground. Being in the dark, seeing the secret places where plants didn't grow, and the only animals were weird creeping bugs. *Cool!*

Too much boring old talk from the guide, though. Nobody cared how the rock-shapes got made. Nobody cared how long it took, bazillions and bazillions of years. Nobody wanted a history lesson about who found the cave. It was too much like being in school. Who wanted that? This was summer vacation. He wasn't supposed to think or learn or anything.

His teachers might say that he didn't think or learn very much when he was in school anyway. Making it sound like that was his fault. Like he didn't listen and pay attention. When really it was their fault. Boring old talk, boring old talk. Except for recess time, school was nothing but a big lump of boring old talk.

And reading. Boring old talk and reading. Books with more words than pictures in them. Book reports. Tests. They didn't only expect you to read, they expected you to remember. They thought you'd give a darn about fractions, and vocabulary, and people who died two hundred years ago, and what was the capital of Argentina.

Like any of that crap was important.

Softball and hockey were important. Karate and swimming were important. Real things. Things that you could *do* and be good at. Things you could *win*. Oh, sure, the coaches sometimes gave speeches about teamwork, and fair play, and sportsmanship. They didn't mean it. They wanted you to play hard, not give up, not back down, and win. *Win, win, win.*

So Austin barely listened when Sylvia talked on and on about the caves. He and Dallas only wanted to get to the good stuff. To climb rickety ladders like they did at Mesa Verde last summer. To crawl under low spots and squeeze through tight spots. To drop rocks into holes and see how far they fell. To see bats, bugs, and spiders. To find gold or buried treasure or dinosaur bones.

To *do* things.

To be good at things.

To be better than Todd, show him up. Todd was such a loser and a scaredycat and a wuss. A nerd. A bookworm. Teacher's pet. Academic Olympics. Ha! Olympics was for sports. Olympics was for skiing and pole-vaulting and boxing. Sports! Not spelling, not geography. *Jeez, and if their mom married his dad that would make them almost brothers... brothers with some nerdy wuss...*

Doing things was what mattered. Not *knowing* things. *Doing* things.

Right now, though, he'd had pretty much enough of doing things. He wanted to sit down. He wanted to eat something. A chili dog and fries and a root beer. A grilled-cheese sandwich. Pizza. Chocolate cake.

Anything but Brussels sprouts.

Yuck.

Dallas fidgeted. "What's taking so long?" she asked, fidget-fidget. "Can't we go already?"

"Mr. Dawes said to stay put," Grant said, and she glared at him like she would punch him.

Austin thought it'd be funny if the bigger boy and Dallas got into a fight. Dallas would beat the snot out of him. The same way she'd beat the snot out of Mitch Nelson at the park one day.

"But there's light! And voices! It's the way out!"

Kimmy finally reached the top of the shaft and climbed out. "It doesn't look like daylight to me," she said, wiping her muddy hands on her shorts.

"How would you know?" Dallas challenged.

"I know what daylight looks like as well as anyone," Kimmy said.

If *they* got into a fight, it wouldn't be as funny. Kimmy was a lot smaller than his sister. Shorter and skinnier and weaker. She'd be toast.

Unless she was a secret ninja or something...

Austin surveyed Kimmy more closely. He and Dallas watched *Ninja Warrior* every week. Sometimes, there were ladies on the show. Sometimes, even girls. There'd been a girl who was twelve, and a girl who was nine. Maybe Kimmy was tougher than she looked. Maybe she *was* a ninja. Why not? She *was* Japanese, right? She even said her brother's name was Makoto. Like Makoto Nagano, the best ninja warrior guy of all time.

"That doesn't mean you know everything," Dallas said.

"I know it's got to be way after sunset by now."

"Hey," Grant said. "Don't argue."

"Don't tell us what to do." Dallas gave him her Death Look. "You aren't the boss of us."

"Yeah," Austin said.

"Whatever." Grant combed his hair back from his face with his fingers. It fell right back down, over his eyes. He leaned and called, "Mr. Dawes? She's up. We're waiting."

There was a silence.

"Mr. Dawes?" Grant repeated.

"Okay." His voice came up. It sounded... rusty. "Be right there. Stay put."

"We *know!*" Dallas said, rolling her eyes. "You already said. Jeez!"

"He's really hurt," Kimmy whispered. "I'm worried about him."

Grant patted her on the arm. "It's cool. He's fine. He's Riddick, remember."

"Totally!" Austin grinned. "He's totally Riddick, yeah! Badass!"

Grumbles and mutters rose from the hole. "... damn kids... too many... fucking movies..."

"He *is* hurt," Kimmy said, still whispering. "He shouldn't be exerting himself."

"It's not like we've got a lot of choice," Grant said.

"Well, we could be doing something," Dallas said. "We could be going for help. It's dumb to just stand here when there's light and voices right over there. I bet it's the exit. I bet there's all kinds of people right outside."

"Cooking Brussels sprouts," Austin said, and made a face.

"It isn't day-"

"And if it doesn't look like daylight," Dallas went on, her tone turning triumphant, "it's probably because they have floodlights and emergency flashers on ambulances and stuff. That's why it's all yellow. It's nighttime, and those are ambulance flasher lights."

"You okay down there, Mr. Dawes?" Grant asked, leaning over the hole again.

A hand appeared, groping for a handhold. It left bloody hand marks on the rock. Then another hand. Bare arms, knotted with muscle and shining with sweat. Each of his biceps was as big around as Austin's whole leg. Mr. Dawes boosted himself up with a terrific flex. Bald head and bare chest, also shining. Also bloody. The bandages looked more like scraps and rags. Austin could see what they'd been covering, and it was raw meat oozing red.

"Give me a second," Dawes said, slumping against the wall. He left a big smear like a snail-trail on the rocks.

Kimmy fussed around trying to patch him up again, while Mr. Dawes kept his arm above his head, his eyes shut and his teeth gritted so hard that bulging veins stood out in his neck.

"Hellooooo!" Dallas suddenly yelled. She had her hands cupped around her mouth to make a megaphone, facing down the passage in the direction of the yellowish light.

Everyone else jumped.

"Hey, don't do that," Grant said.

"Why not?"

"Someone might hear you."

Again, she did her famous eye roll. She copied it from their mom, who was really excellent at it. "That's the idea, genius," she said to Grant. "We want to be rescued, don't we? Hellooo! Somebody! Anybody! We're down here! We need help!"

"Dallas, stop it," Kimmy said.

"Oh, let her," Dawes said. He sucked a deep breath through his nose. "Can't do any harm."

"What if..." Grant trailed off and shifted his feet.

"What if what?" Austin asked.

"Nothing."

"What if there's something else down here?" Kimmy said, finishing it for him. "Besides us?"

"For cripes' sake!" Dallas cried. "Some*thing* else? Like what? Ghooooosts? The boogeyman?"

"Giant albino centipedes?" Austin chimed in, trying to joke, remembering how Dallas had teased him back when they were hiding in the room beyond the Mermaid Pool.

"Come on," Grant said. "Knock it off, huh?"

"Let's go." Dawes got up, squaring his jaw and pushing away the pain to become entirely badass again.

That gross Brussels sprouts smell intensified as they made their way carefully along the damp, musty tunnel. Dawes reminded them to keep using the flashlights so nobody tripped or stepped in a hole, or walked face-first into a hanging formation.

Austin stubbed his toe and smacked his shin, but to show he could be as badass as Mr. Dawes, he didn't whine about it. He didn't whine about the stink either, not even when it got so bad he could taste it, like a greenish-yellow slime on his tongue and in his throat.

"It's getting warmer," Grant said. "Do you feel it?"

Kimmy nodded. "And I thought… for a minute, I thought I heard someone… yelling?"

"Well, that proves it, then!" Triumph rang in Dallas' tone. "Daylight! Rescuers! I told you so… we're coming out!"

They went up and up. It got warmer, steamier. The smell got stronger, and grosser. Austin realized he could hear something besides their own breathing and their footsteps. A kind of thick, bubbling noise. Like Mom's automatic coffee pot, the one that could be programmed to start brewing before their alarm clocks went off. It was kind of like that. Not totally like that. But kind of. Thicker. Maybe more like stew or chili, cooking in a pot.

Chili.

He would kill for a chili dog.

Three chili dogs. Extra-large fries. A super-king-size root beer.

Heck, *five* chili dogs.

"I'm starved," he said. "I hope they have food ready."

"You and me both." Grant wiped his forehead with his sleeve. "I could eat a whole McDonald's. I mean, the entire restaurant."

"Maybe you could, but this smell makes me want to puke," Dallas said. "Rotten eggs, diss-guss-ting."

"No, it's Brussels sprouts," Austin said.

"Boiled cabbage." Grant grimaced. "My grandma makes… made… boiled cabbage."

Dallas held her nose, which made her voice funny when she spoke next. "And what's with the noises? Double diss-guss-ting. Fartapalooza."

The thick bubbling had gotten louder, going *blurt-blurp-gurble-blaaarp* and *plut-plut-plut* and *blorrrrp-thp-thp-thp-thp.*

Austin laughed. Totally crude and obscene. Like an entire roomful of guys having a belch-and-fart contest.

"Look," Kimmy said. "The light. It's not coming from outside. It's coming from the walls."

She walked forward, and the rest of them followed. They came to a place where the passage ended, opening out onto a ledge above a wide oval-shaped cave room. That murky yellowish light filled the chamber, from the floor way far below to the ceiling so close they could have reached up and touched it. The ledge ran along one wall, sloping down from where they stood, all the way around to what looked like another opening over on the far side.

Not outside. Not an exit to the surface, and comforting view of fire trucks and police cars and ambulances. Not light from rescuers.

The light came from the walls. Yellow light. The color of... what? Not orange enough to be school bus-colored. Not browny enough to be mustard-colored. Not lemony enough to be lemon-colored. Kind of like all those things, and not really like any of them. Like... a bottle full of old dog pee... or the sky on a day when there'd been wildfires. In patterns and veins, making weird designs in the stone.

Light in the walls.

Light in the ceiling.

Sort of.

Light in the big blobby thing that hung from the ceiling.

All five of them stood rooted to the spot, just staring around.

The big blobby thing in the ceiling...

What *was* it?

Austin's brain struggled to find the right words.

It was roundish. Blobbish. Mostly yellow with swirls of brown and orange and red. It looked kind of like a wad of gum that someone had blown a bubble in, and then pinched shut and stuck to the underside of a table. It looked like when you breathed out through a runny nose and the snot bulged to just before it would pop, or when you hocked a really good loogie.

He didn't know what the heck it was.

Mud puddles filled the whole bottom of the cave. Brown and grey and yellowish. *Bubbling* mud puddles. Some were all fast and small, brisk, like in a boiling pot of water. Others were slower, the entire brownish surface welling up, up, up and then giving way – *blurple!* – with a truly classic gross-noise. Scalding-hot water gushed from the tops of cones like little volcanoes, or seethed out of cracks in the walls.

"What is this place?" Grant asked.

They all looked at Mr. Dawes. Who was the grownup, and who was also, according to Grant and Kimmy, a cave guide. But he only shook his head, as amazed as they were.

"The goddamn devil's sauna," he said.

"Sulfur springs," Kimmy said. "Like at Yellowstone."

"You mean geysers, Old Faithful, like that?" Grant wore a skeptical frown.

She nodded. "The mud pots, the heat, the boiling water, the smell. It all makes sense."

"And that thing?" Dallas pointed at the blob hanging from the ceiling. "What's that, then, little miss know-it-all?"

Kimmy looked at it. "Some kind of formation... I don't know. It's like a Dale Chihuly nightmare."

"A what?" Austin cocked his head. "What's a *daylchy-hoolie*?"

"He's an artist," she said. "From Portland or Seattle or someplace up north. He works in glass. Bowls, and spheres, and decorative ornaments. He's very famous."

"You mean that's glass?" Grant's frown turned even more skeptical. He glanced at Mr. Dawes. "You didn't know about this?"

"Nope. There aren't supposed to be any hot springs around here. That's what I heard, anyway. But she's right. It is like Yellowstone."

"What about those marks in the walls?" Dallas asked. "The glowy ones. What are those? They look like... what-do-you-call-thems… caveman paintings, with mammoths and saber-tooth tigers and stuff."

"Pictographs," Kimmy said. "There's also petroglyphs, stone-carvings, like the Mayans used. And hieroglyphs, of course, which ancient Egyptians used for their writings."

"Hold the fucking phone," Dawes said. "You're not seriously suggesting that those lines are man-made."

"Yeah," Grant said. "And why are they lit up like neon bar signs that say Budweiser or Heineken or whatever?"

"Phosphorescence? Chemical reactions in the stone? Maybe they're caused by bacteria and invertebrates, extremophiles–"

"Ex-what-o-whats?" Dallas interrupted.

"Life forms that live in extreme environments where nothing else can survive. Deep caves, ocean trenches, places like that. Sometimes, they develop bioluminescence. They glow, they light up. I read about it."

"Hey, yeah," Austin said. "I saw that on TV. Like those fish with all the teeth and the lightbulbs on their noses. When something swims up, thinking it's food…" He hooked his hands into claws and snapped them together. "Chomp! Gotcha! And then *it's* the food!"

"Never mind all that," Dawes said. He glanced at Kimmy. "Is it safe to be breathing this shit?"

"Aren't you supposed to know?" Dallas said before Kimmy could get her mouth open. "You're supposed to be the guide."

Dawes didn't take his gaze away from Kimmy, though he was talking to Dallas when he said, "Hey, I just work here."

"It's not exactly… healthy," Kimmy said. "Not for breathing it long-term or for any extended length of time. But in small doses? We should be okay. At least, if we can get across reasonably quick."

"Across that?" Grant wrinkled his nose. "Do we have to?"

"You wanna go back the way we came?" Dawes asked.

"Uh… no… guess not."

Slowly, single file, with Mr. Dawes in the lead and Kimmy right behind him, they made their way down the ledge. It was tricky, scary. Sometimes there were only a few inches of width, and a long way down to the *blop-plbbt-blorp*ing mud.

The lower they went, the worse it stunk and the hotter the air got. Austin sweated like crazy, and the fumes made his eyes water. He felt dizzy, queasy, light-headed. A repainting-the-house feeling, a sniffing-Sharpies feeling. Headachy, and sick to his stomach. The thought of a chili dog now only made him want to barf.

Rocky paths led through the bubbling mess of mud-pots. It reminded Austin of those maze books, where you had to trace the tangled strings to find out which kite belonged to which kite-flyer.

"Man," Grant said. "It's like being on another planet."

"Which way do we go?" Dallas asked.

"This way," Dawes said. "But be careful. This shit looks slippery. Don't get too close to the edges."

"We're not gonna fall in," Austin said, offended.

"Good. But look at the way it's splattering up and squirting out. Get any of that on you, kiddo, and it'll hurt like a son of a bitch."

Dawes went first, trying to pick the widest paths, the least-splattery ones, or the ones that went past the tamest-looking mudpots. The rest of them followed, girls and then boys. All of them sweating. Hot. Holding their noses, not that it helped. They could taste the bad smell.

The burpy-farty noises were pretty funny, though. Really, really gross. Despite the stink and the heat and everything, Austin couldn't help snickering, even laughing out loud when there was an especially ripe, wet, prolonged one that sounded like an elephant having a mad diarrhea attack.

Dallas, in front of him, turned to give him a god-you-are-*so*-immature look. She even said it. "Jeez, Austin! You are *so*–"

"Watch it!" Grant, behind Austin, yelled.

As she turned, she stepped in a runny smear of grey mud. Her sneaker skidded off the edge. Her foot plunged into the mud pot all the way to the knee.

She screamed, but she was already falling sideways, arms waving, accidentally slapping aside Austin's hand as he tried to grab her. She fell on her tummy, arms scrabbling at the rocky path, both legs in it now.

Austin grabbed for her again and missed, slipped, tottered. Dawes couldn't get past Kimmy without knocking *her* in... then he picked up Kimmy and spun around with her, setting her down hard. Grant yelled again and caught Austin by the back of the shirt before he went headfirst over the side.

Dallas howled. "It hurts it huuuuurts!" She thrashed and kicked and splashed, sending thick gobbets of hot mud flying all over the place. Some splattered Austin. One hit him on the cheek and clung there like a melted slug.

He screamed too, pawing at it, smearing it around.

Dawes seized Dallas by the collar of her tee shirt, but it ripped, and he lost hold and she fell in even more, only one arm still clawing at the path. Her other arm came up, gloved in gooey mud that oozed and dripped.

Austin saw boiled-red skin puffing with huge blisters, already sliding off in places like skin from a boiled chicken. He saw her eyes, not the eyes of his sister but the eyes of some panicked thing... the rolling, wild, white-rimmed eyes of an animal. She wasn't his sister anymore. She was a crazy screaming animal.

Everyone screamed and shouted and yelled. Austin felt Grant holding him back, maybe trying to turn him around so he wouldn't look, so he didn't have to see as the mud came up higher on Dallas' chest, all the way to her neck.

Dropping to his knees on the path, Dawes thrust his arm into the cauldron. He roared with pain but fished around, and got something. Her hoodie. She'd taken it off when they got to the warmer part of the cave, and knotted it around her waist by the sleeves. Austin had done the same thing with his. Now Dawes had a handful of fleece, and hauled, towing Dallas toward the edge.

Then the sleeves must have come untied or something because he rocked back in a sudden jerk, with the mud-caked hoodie hanging from his scalded arm, and almost went over backwards into the mud pot on the other side before getting his balance.

Dallas screamed some more, dog-paddling through the gluey boiling gunk, and it was all over her face like warpaint and coating her hair. A giant bubble welled up right in front of her and popped with a *plpt* noise, spitting mud in her eyes. Her chin went under. Mud flowed into her mouth. Her screaming stopped in a gurgle.

Then her head went under.

Dawes cursed, pounding his fists on the stone.

Austin stared at the mud pot. Grant had him by both arms but he wasn't trying to get loose. He only stood, and stared. Watching the bubbles bulge and then pop. Because any minute now, one of them would rise up but it wouldn't be a bubble at all. It'd be Dallas, surfacing like she did in the pool.

But she didn't come up.

Didn't come up.

He knew she could hold her breath a long time. She was good at that. Proud of it. She could swim all the way from the shallow end to the deep end and back again without coming for air once.

She still didn't come up.

She wasn't *going* to come up.

She was gone.

Gone!

When Austin finally looked around at the others, disbelieving, he saw something that wasn't right. It took him a second to figure it out, because it didn't make any sense.

Kimmy was also gone.

Chapter 22

Discovery

Get some rest, indeed.

Grace Goddard sniffed indignantly.

As if anyone would be getting much rest tonight. The only ones sleeping at all were those who had either been sedated or simply succumbed to overwhelming physical and emotional exhaustion.

Well, the children. The children slept. Poor little dears.

No one else did. No one else could. Fueled by caffeine, sugar and anxiety, it was no wonder. With the floodlights blazing bright as high noon... with the noise of generators and earthmovers and twenty different conversations going on at once... with the news people underfoot poking their cameras and microphones into the faces of whoever they got near... sleep? Ha!

Yet her daughter-in-law Kitty had told her to get some rest. Told her to go upstairs and lie down for a while, take a nap.

What about Joe? If anyone needed some rest, it was Joe. He needed to take a nap, or at least a break and a sit down. He needed to have a hot meal instead of just grabbing a bite of this or that here and there, and swilling cup after cup of coffee.

Joe's father, God rest his soul, had been like that. No matter how tired he was or how much pain he was in, Victor had passed it off on various excuses. Until one day he had keeled over in their driveway from a heart attack while washing the car. It was quick, they told her. Painless. He most likely never even knew what hit him.

Grace remembered nodding, smiling, thanking them for their kindness. While all the while, she'd been sure that Victor had known perfectly well what was happening and hadn't been willing to acknowledge it. Chest pains? What chest pains?

The stubborn horse's ass.

How she missed him!

Now here was Joe, being the same damn way.

Randy, on the other hand...

Grace veered her thoughts away from her elder son and returned her attention to the view from her window, which overlooked the hustle-bustle in the parking lot and picnic area. She could see the experts getting ready to make another descent into the caves. Medical people tending to the injured survivors. Volunteers and reporters and the simply curious from town, all gathered and eager for news.

She still did not see her grandchildren. Not a single one.

Where were they?

Grace had been in the gift shop, working on a necklace of hematite and malachite beads, when it happened. When the ground lurched and shuddered, and that awful noise came rumbling-grinding up from below. She remembered that Chloe had been at the cash register.

Where is Chloe now?

And where is Colin?

Colin hadn't been around all day. Joe and Kitty thought he was off someplace with his friends. With Brandon, and Brandon's trashy sister, and the trashy sister's no-good hoodlum of a boyfriend.

Grace wasn't so sure.

Even if Colin had been at the lake, or in town at a movie, he would have come home by now. He would have heard the news by now and hurried back. His friends as well, eager to see what was going on. They had neighbors from all over, and complete strangers who'd driven ninety miles to rubberneck and cluster like vultures eager for a whiff of death and disaster.

Joe and Kitty didn't know, but Grace did, that the kids sometimes sneaked into Cornucopia when they thought no one was watching. Maybe even that they had a hideout or clubhouse down there.

She never said anything about it, figuring that if they were drinking beer or smoking pot, better they did it close to home than out driving around in the hills. If it kept them off the roads and out of trouble, that was good enough.

If Colin and his friends were in the caves...

But she had seen one of them a while ago. That no-good hoodlum Nick. Grace remembered seeing him talking to Chloe. Not that she'd seen either of them since... strange, as Chloe had never been shy about hiding her likes or her dislikes. She wouldn't have gone off with Nick.

And what about Rory? Her other grandson, Randy's boy?

Rory hadn't been around all day, either. But then, he usually wasn't. He preferred his own solitary company to that of anyone else. Even family. Perhaps *especially* family. Rory was...

She rejected the word 'disturbed.'

Rory was troubled. Rory could be difficult sometimes. Randy hadn't been able to provide the steady supply of love and understanding the boy needed. Or security, stability, attention, discipline, affection, a steady income, and everything that went along with being a father.

At Grace's insistence, Rory came to live with Joe's branch of the family last year. And, yes, at first none of them had been very optimistic about how it'd work out. Rory wasn't thrilled at being shipped off to the middle of nowhere, to stay with his uncle and aunt and grandma and cousins. Joe and Kitty were sure that Rory would run away, hitch a ride with an interstate trucker or something, and never return.

The caves changed that.

The caves, for Rory, changed everything. He took to them like a duck to water. He might have lived in them if Joe allowed it. Never once in the nineteen years of his life had Grace known Rory to be so at home anyplace else. He spent all his spare time down there.

Grace leaned close to the window again and scanned the crowds, hoping against hope that she would spot her grandchildren. She saw none of them.

What if they were in the caves? All three? And their friends?

If they were, they could be almost anywhere.

Could they get out?

If anyone could get them out, it'd be Rory.

But that was assuming they were together.

What if Chloe and that no-good Nick had up and decided to go looking for the others?

What if they were trapped? Hurt? Killed?

She closed her eyes. *Not killed. Please, God, not killed.* Not her grandkids.

Unable to stay still – and certainly unable to relax and 'get some rest' – she left her room and paced the upstairs hall.

The sounds of conversations and kitchen activity rose from downstairs. She could hear that nice Carson woman sobbing in the den, which she'd been doing ever since they'd found her husband's body near the emergency exit from the Hall of Mirrors.

Such a terrible way to die. The pain must have been excruciating. She wished they hadn't let Melinda Carson see him. He'd been grey from blood loss, and his expression…

Of their boy, there had been no sign.

Grace wasn't sure which must be worse for that poor young woman. Knowing the fate of her husband, or not knowing the fate of her son. No comforting her, that was for sure.

Her shoes scuffed on the faded Oriental runner. The window at the end of the hall let in the false day of the floodlights. Her door was open, so was the one to the upstairs bathroom, revealing a pie-wedge view of hexagonal tiles and blue bathmat. The door to the master bedroom Joe and Kitty shared was ajar. The others were all shut.

Grace paused at Colin's door. *Has anyone actually checked?*

"Colin?" She tapped.

No answer. Of course.

Silly. He wouldn't have stayed in his room this whole time. Not with sirens and flashers and television news vans.

She twisted the knob and pushed, and stuck her head in for a peek just the same.

Lordy, what a mess. Dirty clothes, science fiction paperbacks, comics, video game hint books, other teenage boy debris. Posters of actresses and supermodels covered the walls. The bed was unmade. The computer screen cycled through a series of images, unrealistically-proportioned cartoon women in skimpy costumes.

No Colin.

No Chloe, either. Chloe's room was tidy but cluttered, the top of her vanity strewn with make-up and nail polish and hair accessories. A stack of fashion magazines sat on her nightstand, beside a purple cell phone in a holder shaped like an elegant female hand. Pretty-boy movie stars and framed prints of horses hung on the walls, and a stuffed palomino pony with lilac ribbons braided into its mane sat on the pillows of her neatly-made bed.

Grace hated feeling like a snoop, but she kept going. The last room, formerly a den, was Rory's. The door closed. The door was always closed. Even when he was in there.

She tapped. "Rory?"

His father had always flown into a rage if she or Victor invaded his privacy. Going into his room without knocking, looking at his mail, poking through his belongings, talking to his teachers without him present... he would rant and rave and shout. Sometimes he'd even throw things.

"Rory, it's Grandma. I'm opening the door."

When she still got no reply, Grace did just that. She pushed it open.

Rory's room was submerged in gloomy dark shadow. Its windows faced toward the hills and with the shades drawn, so no light came in that way. She could make out shapes but no details.

An odd, vaguely rotten smell tickled her nose. As if something half-eaten had been left to go moldy. Not rotten-egg... or at least, not just rotten-egg. It had an undertone, or an over-smell… something tangy-spicy-pungent-sour. Like mustard and garlic and vinegar. Egg-salad, a forgotten sandwich, perhaps.

She flicked the switch, and the overhead fixture came on. The light was weak, wan, dim. As if the ordinary bulb had been replaced with something low-wattage.

Grace expected to find Rory's room at least half as messy as Colin's, and instead, it was even tidier than Chloe's. Bed made, dirty clothes in the hamper. She saw some pictures taped to the wall above the desk, and a row of books lined up between two thick chunks of polished agate that served as bookends.

Funny. She had never seen Rory as much of a reader. She crossed to the desk for a closer look. Her nose wrinkled as the egg-mustard-garlic-vinegar smell grew stronger on that side of the room.

The pictures taped to the wall were maps and photographs, most of them photocopied or torn from magazines. Topographical maps, and survey maps. Maps of caves and caverns. Mammoth Caves in Kentucky. Carlsbad Caverns in New Mexico. The Oregon Caves. Others from elsewhere in America, from the Yucatan, from Europe. Pictures of limestone formations, of bat-flocks whirling out of openings, of underground waterfalls and rimstone pools.

She peered at the books. Caves and cave exploration, manuals on caving and spelunking and equipment. As she could have guessed. But there were some that made her eyebrows go up. Books on mythology and folklore.

Mythology and folklore?

Rory?

Grounded, unimaginative Rory? Who, as a boy, had never professed belief in Santa Claus or the Tooth Fairy or ghosts?

There were also books about history and archeology… hieroglyphs… idols… the stone carvings of ancient Central Americans… prehistoric cave paintings…

Rory?

Since when had Rory been interested in anything academic? The only reason he hadn't flunked out of high school was because he had dropped out first. Many of these looked like college textbooks.

Grace slid open the kneehole desk drawer and looked inside at the usual litter of pens and pencils. She tried the topmost side drawer, and found a battered spiral notebook, warped as if exposed to moisture and then allowed to dry.

As she picked it up, she hesitated.

Coming in here, she'd had the valid excuse of looking for Rory.

Going through his desk was definitely snooping.

Peeking into his notebook would be even more of an invasion of his privacy.

That bad smell clung to the notebook. Not as if the notebook were the source, but as if the cardstock and paper had absorbed the miasma.

She riffled the pages. Some stuck together, the pre-printed wide-ruled blue lines smeared, smudged and blotched. She saw lines and characters drawn in heavy black ink. Not letters, not numbers. Strange symbols, squiggles, doodles she couldn't make heads nor tails of.

Frowning, puzzled, she flipped through the notebook from the beginning. It was more of the same, more of the same.

She came to a page that had a bold black square traced in the middle. Inside the square were words. At least, she assumed they were words. They were in ordinary alphabet letters, anyway. The ink had only been partially spotted, leaving them legible.

Legible, but not understandable.

Some kind of secret code?

That seemed insane, but then, so did an entire notebook full of incomprehensible squiggles.

The words had an unclean look. She didn't want to read them aloud. She had the oddest sensation that if she did, saying them would leave a foul-tasting residue in her mouth. Hearing them would make her break out in goosebumps.

Even seeing them made unease resonate way down deep in her mind. She felt as though she should know what they meant. As if she almost did know what some of them meant.

Black letters. Bold strokes. Block capitals.

Echidna. Hel. Guhaiya. Ixchel. Hades. Niflheim. Tiamat. Lillith. Xibalba. Shul.

A code?

Not a code?

Some other language?

What would Rory know about other languages? Or about secret codes, for that matter?

Lillith... wasn't that a woman's name?

And Hades... wasn't that another word for Hell?

Hel with one L was on the list... not Hell with two... so it couldn't be that.

The rest of the words made no sense to her whatsoever.

Except, on some level below conscious reason, they almost did.

She replaced the notebook and shut the drawer, then stood for a moment in indecision before reaching for the lower drawer's handle. As it slid open, the foul smell wafted up into her face and nearly made her gag. She recoiled, fanning the air in front of her nose and mouth.

Such a *yellow* stink. Reeking and revolting.

Good God, what had Rory left in this drawer? A full carton of rotten eggs? Cracked and oozing a putrid slime?

Inside, she found a stack of clear compartmentalized hard-plastic boxes of the kind used to store and display rock collections. Each compartment held a specimen, with a tab identifying the mineral. Amethyst, turquoise, pyrite, rose quartz, smoke topaz, petrified wood, and so on. They sold similar items in the gift shop.

Something that looked like half a broken bowl caught her eye, and she picked up a chunk of clay or ceramic. The inner curve was plain greyish-brown. The outside might have once been glazed with red ocher, but most of it had worn away or flaked off. She could make out black and yellow markings... symbols... the same kind as the ones she'd seen in Rory's notebook. As if he'd copied them from this fragment of old pottery.

A plain cardboard box with tape-sealed edges seemed to be the source of the odor, so Grace went ahead and lifted it out. She set it on the desk, slit the tape with a pair of scissors from the kneehole drawer, and unfolded the flaps. Beneath wads of crumpled newspaper and a layer of bubble wrap, she discovered three small spherical objects, each cradled in its own hollow sort of nest in the packing material.

They were round and whitish, nearly the size of mothballs, and they had a similar porous and granular look to them... but the smell was nothing whatsoever like mothballs.

Grace touched one, and instantly recoiled, rubbing her fingertip against her cardigan.

Rough, like coral or pumice.

But soft. Almost spongy.

Geodes?

She had seen countless geodes over the years. The gift shop sold them, cracked them on demand to reveal the inner cavities full of glittering crystals or colorful bands of agate. These were not geodes.

Cave pearls?

Those were delicate formations, not to be removed from the cave, and absolutely not to be sold. She couldn't see Rory doing that. And these didn't seem much like cave pearls, either.

One of them had a fissure that ran in a long hair-thin zigzag. She touched that one.

The two pale pieces fell away from each other with a brittle noise, revealing the darker inner core.

No cavity of glittering crystal. No bands of agate. The larger piece looked like a cross-section of a nut, or a seed, or a fossilized egg with the embryo still curled inside.

"My God," she breathed, fumbling her glasses from their perch atop her hair. She picked up the chunk and held it in her palm for a closer look.

The tiny form, no bigger than a nickel, nonetheless had clearly defined features. A body. Limbs. A tail. A little head with budding horns or tusks or egg-teeth.

It twitched.

Moved.

Pinpricks of stinging fire sank into her hand.

She tried to scream but her voice was snagged in her throat. She shook her hand, wanting to fling it away, get it *off.* It stuck like a burr.

As she recoiled, she knocked the box to the floor. Pain shot up her arm. It felt like she'd seized a handful of nettles. She shook her arm harder, doing a helpless frantic shuffle.

Newspaper crinkled and bubble wrap popped. Mothball-sized round objects crunched beneath her feet. She trampled them heedlessly, blundering around Rory's room, bumping into furniture and rebounding from the walls.

Finally able to scream, she pounded her hand against the desk in a futile effort to dislodge the dark thing that had hooked into her palm with miniscule fishhooks and barbs. It clung, clung… digging, gnawing, chewing through her parchment-frail skin.

With her other hand, she clawed at it, scratched, gouged, drew blood. She heard her shrieks as if they belonged to someone else. She heard startled, questioning outcries from downstairs… downstairs in the kitchen…

The kitchen!

Grace lurched for the door. She could no longer feel her left hand and that was all right because it wasn't hers anymore. Wasn't hers. Was a stranger's hand now. There were knives in the kitchen. Joe's electric carving knife. A meat cleaver. A butcher block. Whatever it took to get rid of the thing that was burrowing into her flesh.

People rushed up the stairs and their own screams joined hers as they saw blood streaming from her outstretched hand. Some reached to help her. Others scattered out of her way. She ignored them all. Ran toward them, past them, through them.

Down the steps at a breakneck plunge. Elbowing Kitty aside with a strength that seemed inhuman. Into the kitchen.

The knives... where... the cleaver...

She wheeled, desperate. Her entire lower arm hung dead. Except for the way the fingers on that hand flexed, clutched, clenched. Not hers. Not hers anymore.

Kitty was making soup. Piles of chopped carrots and celery. A mound of peeled potatoes by the sink. Where were the knives?

No time.

She flung herself against the counter and drove her left arm into the sink. Into a coarse-slimy-starchy mess of potato peelings. Pushing them down. Rubbery black gasket parting like flower petals. Fingerbones snapping because her traitor hand wouldn't close, and she heard them go, like pencils, but she felt nothing.

Into the drain. Into the hole. Wet black rubber and cold wet steel.

Everyone screaming at her to stop. Women. Strangers. Friends. Lily and Kitty. Some were grabbing at her, trying to pull her away from the sink as she pushed her arm deeper. She swatted them away as if they were gnats.

Her right hand hit at the switch. With a furious gnashing of metal, the garbage disposal roared to life.

CHAPTER 23
Lies Beneath

They came closer, the bright headlamp blazing in the darkness, and Makoto's first flare of hope faded as he saw that there were just two of them. Hardly a rescue party. Other trapped tourists?

The girl with the red hardhat was a teenager, the guy a little older and not appearing happy to see them. Rangy and tough-looking, long-haired, denim-clad, he was composed of lines and angles and narrow-eyed suspicion. A fresh cut marked his forehead and he looked muddy, irritated and disgruntled. When his gaze fell on Griff, his expression settled into a scowl.

"Why the fuck's he tied up?" he asked, pre-empting the girl just as she seemed about to speak.

"He's crazy," Shara said. She had risen to greet them, holding the flashlight. Its diminishing batteries let it cast only a feeble beam.

Rangy guy looked at Shara; Shara in her bra because she'd used her blouse as part of the makeshift rope. A different sort of expression replaced the scowl.

Makoto pushed himself up as best he could. As long as he was careful when he moved, it didn't hurt. Much. If he tried to talk, eat, drink, or do anything else that involved opening his mouth, that was another story.

"Where's the rest of your group?" the hardhat girl asked. She had a long brown ponytail, and as she came closer Makoto saw that she wore a polo shirt with the Cornucopia logo stitched on the breast pocket. "You were on the 1:30 tour, right? With Wallace Dawes?"

Shara nodded. "You work here?"

"My mom and dad own the place."

"Why," the tough guy cut in, "the fuck is he tied up?"

"I told you, he's crazy." Shara stared imploringly at the girl. "Can you get us out? We've been stuck here for hours. My boyfriend's hurt."

The girl moaned, catching sight of the stiffened corpse of the man whose arm had been ripped off by the whipping steel bridge cable. "I knew it was bad, but…" She turned her head and saw the old man in the track suit, his skin ash-grey, his lips and eyelids twilight purple.

"Everyone else is dead." Shara took an unsteady breath. "It's just us."

Griff struggled as if trying to sit up, but after so long left lying tied hand and foot on the hard, cold stone, he wasn't able to do much. "Help us," he said.

"Why the fuck are you tied up?" the rangy guy asked him. "What are those, torn-up pieces of clothes?"

"We had to," Shara said. "We didn't have a choice. He's crazy!"

"That's what you keep saying, lady."

"Nick—"

"Shut it, Chloe." Nick looked at Makoto, and one eyebrow went up. He let out a low whistle as he surveyed the swollen, malformed, blood-encrusted mess that had replaced Makoto's mouth. "The hell happened to you?"

"He's hurt," Shara repeated. "How many times do I have to tell you? We've been trapped here for hours with hardly any food, hardly any water, and it's freezing, and I didn't know how long the light would last, and nobody came to find us and I was sure we were all going to die, so can we please just go already?"

"Don't let them leave me here," Griff said. "I'm not a danger to anyone. I promise. I swear."

"He shot our guide!" Shara said.

"What?" gasped Chloe.

Shara related the events, while Griff sputtered and protested that it wasn't as bad as it sounded. He launched into his previous speech about Dawes and justice, and claimed he never had any intention, or any desire, to hurt anyone else.

Makoto could hardly bear to listen. Remembering hurt worse than his fractured jaw, split lips and shattered teeth. Remembering Kimmy. His burst of horror at thinking she'd gone into the river, his wild relief upon seeing her on the ledge, the terrible tension as Dawes tried to reach her, and the resurgence of horror when the gunfire erupted, the blood flew, the bodies plunged.

"I had a feeling about that Dawes asshole," Nick said. "Mean fucker. Always looked ready to punch the shit out of someone. Nice going. I would have shot him, too."

"So, you mean you hit him with a rock and tied him up and he's been like that ever since?" Chloe asked.

"I didn't know what else to do," Shara said.

"Where's the piece?" Nick asked. When Shara looked blank, he added, "The gun? Where is it?"

As she began to raise her hand to point, and open her mouth to speak, Makoto saw Chloe give a quick, urgent shake of her head, her large eyes filled with alarm.

Shara saw it, too. Her motion faltered. "I... uh..."

Trepidation spread through Makoto like tendrils of frost along the pathways of his nerves. Even Griff seemed struck with a sudden wariness. As if a premonition had passed, unspoken, from one of them to the next, and the next. A sense, indistinct but strong, that if anyone here was truly dangerous, it was Nick. Not Griff.

"Yeah?" he prompted Shara.

"I threw it in the river," she said, the words all in a rush.

She was lying, and Makoto was pretty sure that everyone could tell. Shara was among the world's worst liars. She said what she meant, she didn't hide her feelings, and she never played mind games. He loved that about her, but right this instant, he found himself wishing she was a little better at deception.

Nick chuckled. "Fibbers go to Hell."

"It's true!" squeaked Shara. "I threw it in!"

"Why don't you just let me carry it until we're out of this fucking cave?" Nick advanced on her, holding out his hand. "Give me the gun, Red."

"I don't have it!" She backed away.

"Let's see what's in the bag. Toss it to me."

She clutched her tote bag. "It isn't in here."

"Toss me the fucking bag!"

Makoto got up. He was in no shape to fight, but he hadn't been able to save those other people, he hadn't been able to help Kimmy and damned if he was going to sit around and do nothing while this son of a bitch threatened his girlfriend. He nudged her, nodded encouragement.

Chin quivering, Shara lobbed the tote bag. Nick caught it and dumped it upside down. Out spilled a mostly-empty water bottle, sunglasses, snacks, postcards, a state map, a ring of keys on a souvenir Golden Gate Bridge keychain, tissues, a package of allergy pills, loose change.

No gun. No weapons of any kind, unless Shara's nail clippers counted.

"Nick, stop it," Chloe said. "Let's just go, okay? Let's get them out of here. We can go back the same way we came."

"And what? Be heroes?" The sarcasm in his tone sizzled strong as acid. "Gee, Chlo, you think we could end up on television?"

"I... I guess..." Chloe threw an anxious look at Shara and Makoto.

"Bullshit. I didn't come down here to rescue people, Chloe, and you fucking well know it."

"But we found them. We have to–"

"We don't *have* to do jack shit." He quit glaring at Shara and started glaring at Chloe instead, squinting into the shine of her headlamp so that his eyes turned into tiny slits.

"You never planned to even try and find Colin!" Her voice splintered. "You were just using me to get to your stupid armory!"

"Armory? What?" Shara asked.

Makoto gave her hand a warning squeeze, but by then it was too late and the question was already out.

"We kept some stuff hidden down here," Nick said in a casual, conversational kind of way, not taking his attention from Chloe. "But her asshole cousin had to go and fuck it all up for me, setting off those explosions."

"Are you saying it wasn't an earthquake?" Griff asked from the ground. "It was a *bomb*?"

"A bomb, two bombs, ten bombs, how the hell should I know?" Nick shrugged.

"Wait, what?" Chloe crossed her hands back and forth in front of her. "You mean Rory? That's crazy!"

"That's Rory. Him and his fucking devil-worship. I'll tell you one thing, though... if he used up all my C-4, I am going to kick his ass so hard he'll walk funny for the rest of his life."

First an armory, and now this mention of devil-worship out of the blue... Makoto looked at Shara again, and she returned his gaze with matching bafflement.

"You might have been able to talk Colin and Brandon into going along with you, but not me," Chloe said. "I'm going back. I'm taking these people with me. You can do whatever the heck you want."

Nick darted forward. Chloe yelped as he spun her into an arm-lock, forcing her wrist high behind her back. A switchblade materialized, seemingly out of nowhere. It jutted from his fist like a steel fang. He poised the tip against Chloe's stomach.

"I don't think so," he said, speaking low and directly into her ear so that his breath stirred loose wisps of her hair. "Don't fuck around with me, Chloe. You really don't want to do that."

"Let go of her, you bastard!" Shara tried to tug free, but Makoto held tight to her hand.

"You want me to break her arm?" Nick asked Shara. "I can. I will. Want me to? Or should I stab her a little? You want me to stick her?"

Shara subsided.

"Now what?" Makoto enunciated the words as clearly as his mouth would allow. "What about us?"

"Kind of have to kill you," Nick said. "No hard feelings. Nothing personal. Chloe just had to go and spill her guts. Like I could do... right now... if I have to." He prodded with the knife point, dimpling her shirt.

Chloe stood rigid and trembling, pale as milk, eyes shut tight with tears flowing from beneath her lashes.

"Oh, God, don't hurt her," Shara said, on the verge of tears again herself. "Please, don't. We won't say anything. None of us."

"Wish I could believe you."

"Really! I mean it! We only want to get out of here and go home. That's all we want."

"For sure," Griff said. He uttered a rueful half-laugh. "I know I sure as hell don't want to talk about any of this. You think I want the world to know what I did?"

"Riiiight." Nick drew out the word, his narrow gaze shifting to Griff. "You shot Dawes, you've got a good reason to keep quiet. You, I could almost believe. Where'd your gun wind up again? Maybe we can work this out together, you and me."

Shara made a wordless anguished sound. Makoto felt his spirits sink.

Griff smiled. Considering that he was hogtied, with dried blood all down the side of his head, it was a very winning smile. "You wouldn't repay my honesty by shooting me with my own gun, would you?"

"Hey, I think we understand each other."

"Okay," Griff said.

"No! Don't tell him!" Shara yelled.

"Screw you!" Griff shouted back. "Why should I give a damn what happens to you, Red Sonja, leaving me tied up and freezing, not letting me have any water? You think I want to die?"

Nick laughed. Makoto pulled Shara against his chest and waited for it to be over. Once Nick had the gun… well, it'd be quicker than starving down here in the cave, quicker than dying of exposure.

"She threw it over there." Griff gestured with his chin. "It landed somewhere behind that big pile of rocks."

Shara went rigid in Makoto's arms. Her eyes widened. For a moment, she almost blurted out something that would have given it all away. He gripped her hand in an urgent squeeze.

Still laughing, propelling Chloe ahead of him without releasing her arm or moving the knife away from her stomach, Nick headed for the spot Griff had indicated. "Good man. Nothing wrong with being a selfish prick looking out for Number One."

Still holding onto Shara, Makoto edged sideways. He was keenly aware of Griff's eyes on him. They burned like coals. He could almost feel the other man's will urging him on.

"I heard it bounce and clatter," Griff called to Nick. "It might have fallen down between a couple of boulders. Hurry up, though, would you?"

"Don't get your panties in a twist," Nick said. "I'll find it. And you, Chloe, no bright ideas, okay?"

"Nick, please. You don't have to do this."

"Yeah, actually, I do," he said. "Turn your head back and forth. Nice and slow. I need the light."

Griff's pack still lay where Shara had left it, propped on some rubble several yards from the place they'd been sitting. In the opposite direction from where Nick investigated, using Chloe's headlamp as a searchlight.

The gun was in the pack.

Can I do it? Point the gun? Pull the trigger, if it came to that?

Morally speaking, he was fine with the idea.

Physically?

He wasn't sure.

His jaw throbbed in steady whacking drumbeats, making him think of old movies with galley slaves chained to oars, hauling in backbreaking tandem as some sweaty, obese, shirtless slave-master pounded out the rhythm on an enormous kettledrum. His whole head reverberated. Jags of pain shot like lightning bolts from the remains of his front teeth.

Hold a gun steady? Unlikely.

Actually hit a target? Very unlikely.

Deal with the battering recoil? Forget about it.

What choice do I have?

Not much. None at all, really.

He couldn't make Shara do it. She hated guns. One more difference between her and her parents. She had struck Griff with the rock, that was true... but that was in the heat of the moment. She wouldn't be able to bring herself to shoot a person.

"I'm not seeing it," Nick said from over past the piled rocks. Sounding impatient, and beginning to get suspicious.

"Well, it didn't get up and walk away," snapped Griff. As good a liar as he might have been, the stress strained his voice.

Makoto opened the pack and groped inside. His fingers found the butt of the gun. He grasped it. Pulled it out.

"There's still no fucking gun over here," Nick announced.

Shara looked at Makoto. For a moment, he thought she would ask if he was sure he wanted to do this... or tell him not to... but instead, she met his gaze and mouthed, "Shoot him!"

Just... shoot him? Just like that? Without warning? Without saying a single word? Shouldn't he at least give Nick the chance to release Chloe and let them all go unharmed? *Shouldn't I make Nick force his hand?*

To just haul off and shoot him, in the back, before he had any idea of the danger… it seemed *unfair* somehow. Dishonorable. Dirty fighting.

"You wouldn't be lying to me," Nick said, turning to Griff. "You wouldn't do something stupid like that."

"Why would I do that?" Griff countered. "Don't you think I know whose side I should be on? These people cracked me on the head and tied me up!"

"Shoot him!" Shara hissed through clenched teeth. "Shoot the son of a bitch!"

Nick turned around, perhaps to come back, perhaps to shake the truth out of Griff or Shara. As he did so, Chloe stumbled. Nick wrenched at her arm. It jerked up at a sharp angle and the girl screamed like a nail screeching across glass.

"Shit!" Letting go of her, Nick sprang back. His expression was barely visible in the gloom but he looked both shocked and revolted. "Her shoulder, I dislocated her fucking shoulder, I felt it go, shit did you hear the pop?"

Chloe went to her knees, and pitched headfirst onto the rocks. One punched into her headlamp. With a flash and a stutter, it snuffed out.

By only the wan glow of the dying flashlight, Makoto aimed the gun at Nick and pulled the trigger.

Recoil hammered through him, setting off earthquakes of pain along every fault line in his body. The gun dropped from numb, nerveless fingers that suddenly couldn't have held on to anything. The cavern seesawed and swayed. His ears rang. He couldn't see.

Then things cleared, and he found himself leaning strengthless against a slope of limestone wall. Shara had him by the upper arms, shaking him gently, calling his name.

"I'm okay," he said, mumbling mushy word-shapes through the aftershocks in a haze of agony. A lie, of course. He had never been less okay. "Did I get him?"

"You got him," Griff said. "In the throat."

Griff's words made him gag. In his mind's eye, he could see Nick's throat splitting apart in wet, fleshy wedges. Could see the dark red spray of blood.

"He went into the gorge," Shara added.

"Chloe?" Makoto asked. Tried to ask. He croaked out a sound that was almost an approximation of the girl's name.

"Her arm... he did dislocate it... it's all... there's a lump like a doorknob sticking up at the top of her sleeve. She's out cold. Banged her head. If she hadn't had this hardhat on... God, she could have fractured her skull on the rocks. But she's breathing."

"Believe me now whose side I'm on?" said Griff. "Come on. Untie me, let me up, let's get the hell out of here."

CHAPTER 24
Helldark

Riddick would save them.
Well, Dawes would anyway.
He had to.
Right?
That was kind of his whole thing.

Even if he didn't want to. Even if he didn't particularly like them. He'd save them. Because, down deep under his gruff tough-guy exterior, he sort of *did* like them.

A little.

At least, he wouldn't just go and let them die.

He'd save them. He would come busting in here, kick monster ass, and lead them out into the daylight and the open spaces again.

Grant could see it in his head as if on a movie screen.

The cave entrance as a big pile of rubble. Suddenly, a rock comes loose and rolls down, revealing a hole. A man's hand gropes out. Dirty. Scratched. Pushing more rocks away. They go bouncing down the slope. The hole getting bigger. People nearby turning to look. Gaping and gasping and pointing in astonishment. And then the first of the kids is boosted out. Grimy but alive. One by one, the rest of them follow. Last of all, bone-weary and about to fall over from exhaustion, out climbs the hero. Shirtless. Injured. Carrying the littlest of them in the crook of his elbow. There's a tearful, joyful scene as everyone rushes over to them... but in the moment before the kids are whisked away to the care of the doctors or the waiting arms of their families, all of them rush to give the hero one final fierce group-hug. And then, at the very end, his hard, strong face softens into a smile.

Yeah. It would be exactly like that.

It had to be like that.

He would save them.

Even if he wasn't really Riddick. Riddick was make-believe anyway. Dawes was real. Dawes was even badder-ass than Riddick, because Dawes wasn't some destined and enhanced super-dude with mutant see-in-the-dark vision. He was more of a regular guy. Like the guy from the *Die Hard* movies, only not so old. Like Jason Statham, who totally kicked ass.

Any minute now. Any minute now, Dawes would come busting in here and save them.

Any... minute... now.

Now.

Now?

Please? Now?

Before anyone else had to die?

Grant knew he had done a stupid, stupid thing.

Dawes told him to do it, but he shouldn't have listened. He should have stayed. *They* should have stayed.

He hadn't wanted to.

He'd been glad at the time. Glad to go. Glad to get away from the horror, the death by boiling mud. Glad to get Austin away from it. Nobody should have to see something like that. Not at all. Not ever. Especially when it was a person you knew.

Triple-especially when it was your sister.

"Get him out of here!" Dawes yelled.

Austin only stood there like a store dummy, staring at the spot where Dallas had gone under.

God, how awful!

All the screaming and sinking and her eyes had been so *aware* right up until the moment her head went under. Swallowed up by the thick yellow-grey glop. Just some strands of her hair still visible. Then... stuff... stuff that bubbled to the surface... thin and watery, foamy... like scum on top of soup... *pinkish* stuff...

"Get him out of here!" Dawes yelled again, with boiling-hot mud caking his arm most of the way to the shoulder.

They should have stayed together. Should have stayed with Dawes. No matter how horrible it was. They never should have split up.

But Kimmy had already vanished. Grant thought she'd fled rather than have to see any more. Part of him wished he'd done the same. He didn't want to be there when Dawes tried again to reach Dallas.

It was way too late for her already. It had probably been too late as soon as she fell in. Even if Dawes could find anything at all, the most he'd be doing was pulling out her body. What was left of it. Maybe only bones, a jointed skeleton held together by stringy cooked flesh.

Grant hadn't wanted to see that, and he sure didn't think Austin should have to see it either. So he did what Dawes wanted. He shoved Austin, propelling him along the twisting maze-paths. Steering him like a shopping cart because Austin was in shock or something.

He really expected to find Kimmy in the next passage beyond the cavern of the mud pots. Hiding her face against the rock wall. Crying in the dark.

She wasn't there.

And it wasn't dark.

The eerie luminescent streaks and markings continued down the passage. Like pulsing veins with some kind of radioactive yellow liquid in them.

He saw something moving. A shadow. A shape. *Kimmy?* Looked too big and too bulky, but...

"Kimmy!" He called her name anyway and followed, pushing Austin ahead of him.

Austin went without protest, without resistance. He sobbed and whimpered and made mewling little hurt-puppy sounds, and Grant didn't even think he realized he was doing it. The younger boy also smelled like he'd wet his pants, a sharp and bitter smell that cut through the cave's rotten-egg funk like a splash of ammonia.

"Kimmy!" Grant called. "Kimmy, where are you? Wait for us!"

Then the shadow-shape rushed at them. Blotting out the glowing yellow streaks in the walls. Its shape insane, upright like a man but with horns or growths or tubes or something bristling out of its head.

Grant remembered a raspy intake of breath, and a reflected sheen across a single huge glassy eyeball. It snatched Austin. Grant held on. Austin screamed, pulled in a brutal tug-of-war between them.

A tug-of-war Grant lost.

Strong. Jeez, it was strong.

"Help, Grant, help!" Austin shrieked.

Grant threw himself onto its broad back, feeling something that was hard and rubbery, clammy-moist, segmented, and inhuman. Something he couldn't get a grip on, either with his hands or with his mind.

He felt a quick jab and a jolt, a brief but total sizzle-snap throughout his whole body. Like the time when he'd been eight or nine, goofing around with the stripped wires of his bedroom lamp, and he'd damn near electrocuted himself. His mouth zinged with the same metallic biting-on-foil taste and sensation.

After that...

Nothing. Nothing until opening his eyes to this yellow-glow weirdness. To this cave of nightmares, where he lay chained with six other, similarly chained-up, kids.

Giant heads loomed from the cavern walls around and above him. Deep black pits for eyes. Dark. Scaled. Fanged. Horns jutting-branching-curling-spiraling. Dinosaurs and dragons and demons. The T-Rex head on the *Jurassic Park* ride at Universal Studios, the one with the jaws that seemed about to snap shut on each boat just before the plunge down the waterfall. Godzilla and Ghidrah.

But not really any of those. *Almost, but not really.*

Stone heads. Stone carvings, like... like tiki gods, like those monuments on that one island... bulging out of the walls... totems, masks... idols.

As his head cleared, he realized he could see more. And that he didn't *want* to see it. That pit... that seething pit full of bodies and acid and...

What are those things, anyway?

He couldn't tell without a closer look.

He *did not want* a closer look.

What he could see from here was more than enough to convince him of that.

"Can you get loose?" the Goth-girl asked him. "Try. See if you can."

"I already tried," Grant said. "No good."

Just to be sure, though, he tried again. The cuffs on his ankles attached to a chain and a metal spike driven deep in the rock. Another set of cuffs held his wrists above his head, that chain looped behind a thick formation. His arms and shoulders already ached from the awkward position.

The seven of them made a rough semi-circle around the cavern, beneath the monstrous stone visages. Each of them was tethered to ringbolts in the floor, or handcuffed around limestone columns, or both.

Prisoners.

Victims.

Sacrifices?

Grant shuddered.

Besides the Goth-girl – who was, he couldn't help noticing even under the circumstances, about his own age and absolutely gorgeous – he could see Austin and Kimmy, a blonde girl of maybe eight, a little boy even younger, and another teenager, a guy seventeen or so, with a pudgy face and the kind of squinty look of someone who normally wore glasses.

"We're stuck, then, until he comes back," the Goth-girl said. "Shit. Shit, shit, shit!"

"It's a skylops," said the little boy. "Tiffy told me."

"Cy-clops, R.J. Cyclops," the blonde girl said.

"Is not," said the teenager. He spoke in a low and doleful voice, the kind of voice that seemed designed to suck the hope right out of anybody that heard it.

"Is so," Tiffy said. "It's a monster that only has one eye, so it's a Cyclops."

"There's no such thing as monsters." Kimmy's know-it-all tone was not as sure as it used to be, Grant noticed. She seemed even smaller and more delicate than he remembered.

"And what the hell is with those things?" The Goth-girl, unable to point with her hands behind her back, used the toe of one big clunky black boot to indicate the looming stone heads above them. "What are those, hieroglyphs?"

"They aren't–" Kimmy began, exasperated.

"Not right now, okay, Kim?" Grant said. "Does anybody know what this place is, where we are?"

"And how do we get *out*?" Goth-girl yanked and clanked on her chains again. "Who is that bastard, I'm going to kick him in the nuts!"

"Can't hurt the skylops," R.J. said. "He's got magic powers."

"I told you, it's not a Cyclops," the teenager said. Sulky. He had on a *HALO 3* shirt that had seen better days. "It's my cousin."

Goth-girl raised an eyebrow with a silver hoop through it. "You must come from one screwed-up family."

"Cousin?" said Grant. "Like a creepy mutant cousin raised in the caves since he was a baby so that they wouldn't take him away and study him in a lab or something like that? Are we talking *The Hills Have Eyes*?"

"Awesome," the Goth-girl said, making a face.

R.J. started to cry again. "I don't wanna be eaten by the monsters."

"He's not a monster," *HALO*-boy said. "Not the way you think. I mean, he's... you know... human. Not a freak."

They all looked at him.

"Not physically a freak," he amended. "Okay, yeah, he's crazy. I know that. But he doesn't have... like... two heads or something."

"Um, excuse me?" Goth-girl said. "You see the thing that brought us here? Shiny black carapace, one big green eye, breathes like an obscene phone call... that thing?"

"Body armor," *HALO*-boy said. "A gas mask, night vision visor. Rory – that's him, my cousin – Rory and Nick, they're into all kinds of weird stuff. Anarchy and bomb shelters and what to do when the terrorists set off biological and chemical weapons, end-of-civilization time. They stashed a whole bunch of supplies down here. Food and water, but also weapons, military surplus."

"Stun-gun," Grant said. "That's what he zapped me with."

"Yeah!" Goth-girl nodded. "But anyway, fine, okay, so it's your whacked-out headcase of a survivalist cousin... what's his deal with us?"

"Seriously," said Grant. "What does he want? Why's he holding us prisoner? What about the glowing letters and the giant devil-heads? Did he do those?"

"Who cares?" Tiffy kicked at the spike fettering her to the floor. "We have to get loose. We have to escape. He's gonna feed us to the imps if we don't."

Imps. Grant had been trying not to think about the imps, trying not to notice the pit where unspeakable things crawled and slithered and chattered.

"And what the hell *are* those?" Goth-girl asked. "No way your cousin ordered a bunch of little bug-monsters off the Internet. Not even eBay goes there."

"They're probably just ordinary cave-dwelling life forms," Kim said.

"Ordinary?" *HALO*-boy scoffed. "My parents *own* these caves and those are no way ordinary!"

She started in again about extremophiles and whatever, but trailed off under their combined looks.

"Imps," Tiffy insisted.

Goth-girl shifted around again to peer at *HALO*-boy. "Your parents own these caves?"

"Uh-huh. I was down here, me and some of my friends, when... when..."

"Your *friends* the ones who collect weapons and army surplus?" asked Grant.

"It was cool," *HALO*-boy said. "Me and Brandon, we only thought it was for if something happened, a zombie outbreak, you know? We wanted to be ready. We didn't know Rory would freak out and set off a bomb! He killed Brandon! He killed *Toni!*"

"He killed lots of people," Goth-girl said.

Austin finally stirred. "My sister's dead, too. And our mom, probably."

"My daddy..." R.J. started sniffling, big tears rolling down his cheeks.

Even Tiffy, who'd been trying to stay all tough and brave, got a quiver to her chin.

"Guys, come on," Grant said. "We can't focus on that right now."

But he thought about Grandma Betty, who'd fallen into the river gorge and ended up broken in the pile of debris. He wondered about Grandpa Homer. About Kimmy's brother and his girlfriend, and the crazy dude with the gun.

And Dawes... where was Dawes? Was he dead? He couldn't be dead. It didn't seem possible. If he hadn't died from being shot, and he hadn't died from falling into an icy, raging river, then he wasn't going to die from sticking his arm in hot mud, was he?

Unless something else had happened to him.

Rory-the-Cyclops, maybe?

"They're never going to find us," *HALO*-boy said, slouching against the limestone formation. "Never. We're going to die down here. Whether Rory kills us or not, whether he feeds us to those things, or sacrifices us, or what... we're going to die and they won't ever find us. Maybe our bones, someday."

"Knock it off," Goth-girl told him. "You're scaring the little kids."

"Aww, too bad."

"Hey, she said knock it off," Grant said.

"Go to hell."

"I think I'm already there."

"Then just shut up! Can't you just shut up?"

"Both of you shut up!" Goth-girl snapped.

"I've got an idea," Dawes said, stepping into view. "How about you all shut up?"

"Mr. Dawes!" Kimmy nearly sobbed with relief.

Grant knew precisely how she felt.

"*More* kids. Give me a fucking break already." His arm was still clumped and swathed with greyish mud, but where it had flaked away, his skin was the color of a bad sunburn. Scarlet bordering on maroon. He held it stiffly out to his side, as if it hurt to move or bend.

Austin raised his head again. The hope in his eyes was terrible. "Did you get her? Dallas? Did you save her?"

"No." Dawes heaved a sigh. He looked around, his pain-filled and exhausted gaze taking it all in. The cuffs, the chains, the demonic idols glaring down from the cave walls, the pit of half-devoured corpses. Then he settled his attention on *HALO*-boy, his eyebrows arching in surprise. "Colin? What the–"

Tiffy screamed. "The Cyclops, look out, the Cyclops!"

The Cyclops – now Grant could see that it really *was* a person in bulky black body armor, with a mask and tinted-glass visor and breathing apparatus that seemed more suitable to space travel or deep sea diving – charged in and slammed against Dawes in a full bone-jarring tackle. Their bodies, both big, both heavy with muscle, grappled and staggered and fought. The cave's weird yellow light made monstrous shadows writhe around them.

Action movie. Boss battle.

Roundhouse and uppercut and knee-jab to the groin. Dawes ripped off the front of the mask and the Cyclops wasn't a Cyclops after all. Just like *HALO*-boy, Colin, had said. Just a guy, nineteen or twenty, but with a furious snarling grimace of fury and total psycho eyes bulging.

Back and forth, struggling, wrestling. Punching and kicking. Chained kids scrambling as best they could to keep from getting trampled. Dawes determined, but injured, a bullet hole in him, his arm scalded to the shoulder from the boiling mud, worn down, tired, reeling. Rory-the-Cyclops enraged. Grabbing something from his belt. Something Grant first thought was a knife, a long wicked hunting knife, but the shape was wrong. The color was wrong. An old-ivory twisted thing, a horn, a fang. He clenched it in a fist, raised it high, brought it down in a savage stabbing arc.

The point punched into Dawes' chest. Dawes bellowed in pain. Rory bellowed in victory. They both went over with a colossal crash, inches from the pit. Rory reared up and hurled his full weight down on Dawes, on the protruding butt of the sharp horn-fang spear-knife whatever it was. He hammered at it with both hands like a man trying to stake a vampire.

The old-ivory spiral gored into muscle and through rib. Blood spouted everywhere. Dawes bucked and heaved and tried to throw Rory off him. But, with a maniacal grin as evil as those of the demon idols on the walls, Rory ground the horn deeper and deeper.

Dawes went limp, and lay there motionless with the horn stuck in him so that only the last couple inches remained visible. A river of blood coursed sluggishly away from him, down the slope and toward the pit. Some of the imp-creatures crawled out to sample it, and follow it to its source.

Rory got up, leaving the horn impaled in the body. Again, like a vampire... like if he thought removing it might bring Dawes back to life.

The four younger kids – Kimmy, Austin, Tiffy, R.J. – wailed and cried. Goth-girl looked as shocked, as thunderstruck, as Grant. They all knew this wasn't the way it was supposed to go.

Dawes was supposed to win. Dawes was supposed to save them. He was the action movie hero! He was Riddick! He was Jason Statham, for crying out loud!

But Dawes was lying there dead. Dead. No mistaking it.

"Hey... Rory..." *HALO*-boy said in a trembling voice. "Rory, it's me. Colin. Hey... you don't... you don't have to..." He fumbled and faltered and tried a feeble grin.

Ignoring him, ignoring all of them, Rory left the cavern. But before any of them could so much as begin to hope he was leaving again, he was back. Carrying something.

A clay pot?

An old clay pot.

With something sloshing in it. Water? Acid? Blood?

"I have seven of you," Rory said in a thoughtful, musing tone. "I only need six."

Colin immediately began to babble. "Let me go, Rory. I'm your cousin. We're family. Let me go. I won't tell anyone. I swear. Not about Toni, not about anything. Swear to God. Kill them all, sacrifice them to the Devil or these horn-gods, whatever, I don't care. Just let me go. Okay?"

Rory reached into the pot with one black-gloved hand, and brought out something small held between thumb and forefinger. It looked like a frosted white marble, wet with what might have been milk. He approached Grant, and Grant could smell it.

Milk... but sour... spoiled... bad. And that frosted white marble, what the hell was that? Rory held it out to him. Like someone offering a sugar cube to a horse.

"Take it," he said. "Take it or I'll put you in the pit."

Grant pulled his head back as far as he could, the curve of his skull pressing against clammy limestone. "What is it? What happens if I do?"

"You only need to know what happens if you don't," Rory said, and inclined his head meaningfully toward Dawes.

The imps had reached the body by then. Grant could see them swarming over him. Stripping away his skin. Eating him. He knew Dawes couldn't feel it... but it still looked like it hurt worse than anything imaginable.

"I'll do it," Goth-girl said. "Give it to me."

"But maybe it's poison," Tiffy said.

"I goddamn well hope so."

"Wait!" Grant looked at Rory. "I'll go first. So they... so they can see... they can know what... what it does."

"Grant, no, it's bad," Kimmy said. "Whatever it is, it's bad."

"I know," he said. Maybe if Rory gave him a chance, he could bite–

Rory didn't let his fingers stray within biting distance. He flicked the grape-sized ball into Grant's open mouth.

"Spit it out and I'll pop your eye with my thumb," Rory told him.

He almost spit it out anyway. The taste… sour milk and rancid butter and the kind of outrageously expensive moldy cheese that only real snobs would pretend to enjoy… his stomach lurched.

Somehow, though, somehow he managed not to reflexively spit or puke.

The thing had a hard shell and he thought of gumballs, he thought of jawbreakers. Was he supposed to swallow it whole? Crunch it between his teeth and chew it up?

Before he could do either, it broke apart on its own. Something hot and squirmy and alive writhed on the soft tissue of his tongue.

Then piercing barbs of pain hooked into the roof of his mouth, and the whole world went away.

CHAPTER 25
Vigil

"Show caves," Lavonne Schwartz said, moving with slow, even strides as the camera panned to pace her against a backdrop of golden hills, green underbrush, craggy grey boulders and clear blue sky. "Sometimes called commercial caves or tour caves, they are a popular destination for weekend vacationers."

She kept her expression somber and serious, though she knew that through most of this part, they'd be running her as a voice-over with stock footage stills and film clips of caverns, stalactites and stalagmites, and gypsum crystals.

"With constant temperatures averaging in the mid-fifties year round, a cave can be a welcome refuge from wind, weather and summer sun. The variety of rock and crystal formations, sculpted over millions of years by erosion and mineral deposits, form spectacular landscapes that can be seen nowhere else on Earth."

A shame, because she was looking very good right about now. This story was her long-awaited break, her stepstool to bigger and better things.

"Some show caves are located in national parks," she went on. "But most are on private property, privately owned and operated, and open to the public for a fee. They feature paved walkways, lighting, stairs and handrails."

Lavonne stopped and faced directly into the lens. Beside her, framed in the shot so as to be a tantalizing hint, was the painted edge of something large and wooden.

"But how safe *are* they?" she asked her viewing audience.

At that point, she knew, the camera would zoom out to reveal her – tall, slim and shapely, the sun lending an indigo sheen to her impeccable black hair – beside the 'Cornucopia Caves' sign. The painted background was yellow, the lettering dark red. Both instances of 'o' in 'Cornucopia' were stylized into cave openings, with disembodied white cartoon-character eyes peeking out. Underneath were the days and hours of operation.

"I'm standing here," Lavonne said, "outside of Cornucopia Caves. Until recently, this was just one more of a dozen or more show caves dotting this part of central California. During the height of the tourist season, thousands of people... families... pass through these caves every single day."

The camera followed her as she resumed her slow strides. The heels of her fashionable boots crunched on gravel, crossing toward the closed gift shop, and the ticket booth with its window covered by plywood.

"Two weeks ago, disaster struck here with tragic consequences. It happened at the worst possible time, when three full tour groups were deep underground, exploring the chambers and passages of Cornucopia Caves. Fifteen people were either able to escape or were rescued, some of them with critical injuries. Thirty-one more, over twice that number, were not so lucky."

She stopped again, this time in front of the impromptu memorial that had grown with each passing day. Framed photos, flowers, ribbon-bedecked crosses, stuffed animals, handwritten letters and pleas and prayers. *Good footage. Emotional. Touching.*

"Thanks to the tireless efforts of search-and-rescue workers and cave experts and an army of volunteers, twelve bodies have been recovered from the subterranean depths. The rest, unfortunately, remain lost. And those same experts must now reluctantly conclude that they might never be found."

A gripping tragedy, and right during a lull when there was just the same-old-same-old from the government, when no celebrities had done anything more outrageous than normal. It landed right in her lap like a blessing from heaven.

"With me here now is Ed Baxley, caretaker and groundskeeper for Cornucopia Caves," Lavonne said, walking over to the man where he waited with obvious anxiety.

Some people just weren't cut out for the spotlight, and Ed Baxley was one of them. He wore brown workman's coveralls and had a cap over the worst of his thinning hair and sunburned scalp.

"Mr. Baxley," Lavonne said. "You've worked here for how long?"

"Fourteen years," he said. Long, skinny, leathery face. Bad teeth. "I've known the Goddards – Joe, Kitty, the kids – a long time. They've always been good people. It's a shame to see this happen."

"You weren't here the day of the quake, is that right?"

He nodded. "My wife, Lily, had an appointment to see the doc. We're expecting our first in a few months. So I drove her into town. We were at the doc's office when we heard the news, and I rushed right straight back. But it wasn't a quake."

"Oh?" She gave the camera a conspiratorial glance.

"Region's seismologically sound," he said. "No fault lines."

She prided herself on covering up her surprise at hearing him get that ten-dollar word out of his mouth. "But the caves were structurally unstable?"

"No," Ed Baxley said. "Solid as could be. That's the thing about caves, at least, that's what Pete always said."

"Pete Fisker, one of the guides," Lavonne said for the sake of the audience keeping score at home. "He became separated from one of the rescue parties and subsequently lost in the caves himself, isn't that right?"

Baxley frowned. "Something must have happened to him, all right, but I can't believe Pete would have just gotten lost. He might've taken a fall or got hurt somehow. Lost? Not Pete."

"You were saying what he told you about the stability?" she prompted.

"Sure." He launched into a boring ramble about how natural caves were so much safer than anything man-made; it was a mine or a tunnel that was more likely to fall in on a person, because a cave took forever to form, and anything that was going to collapse would have done so a long time ago.

Lavonne kept her attentive, interested expression even though she was sure most of this would be cut and edited down to pertinent sound bites.

"If not an earthquake, then, Mr. Baxley," she said when she could seize a chance, "what do you think could have caused the disaster? What about the other caves in this area? Are they safe? Are we likely to see a repeat of what happened here?"

"I'm no geologist," he said, squinting at her as if thinking that she was trying to lead him into a trap. "All I know is what they've been saying."

"Which is?"

"That they're stumped. It shouldn't have happened. Those caves had been fine for thousands of years and they should have been fine for thousands of years more."

"A fluke?" She let a hint of skepticism creep into her tone. "A random one-in-a-million?"

"Well," he said, sounding a little truculent, "what else could it have been?"

The moment she'd been waiting for. She pounced. "Some people have speculated about explosions, underground gas pockets, even sabotage and terrorist attack."

"I've heard some of that." He glowered. "I think it's all hogwash. Trying to whip up a scare for folks. Nobody would want to bomb a cave. That doesn't make any sense."

She plodded through a few more exchanges with him, then thanked him for his time. He scuttled away from her like an animal that had just escaped a close call with an eighteen-wheeler, heading back toward the ramshackle little trailer that he and his wife called home.

Lavonne signaled the cameraman to pack it in, studying the larger house on the hill as he loaded up his gear. She felt unsatisfied. Disgruntled. The more she looked at the house, the stronger those feelings grew.

The Goddards had stopped talking to reporters. A devastating cave-in on their property... their business and source of income closed for the foreseeable future... talk of lawsuits... the loss of three of their guides... their teenage son and their nephew among the missing.

As if all that wasn't burden enough, Joe Goddard's mother had some kind of nervous breakdown during the crisis. Screaming, hysterical and irrational, she stuck her arm into the kitchen garbage disposal. Grace Goddard now clung to what could only technically be called life, comatose in the intensive care unit.

The only bright spot for the Goddards in the entire mess was the stalwart heroism of their daughter and one of their guides.

Sylvia McCain managed to bring out three survivors after a harrowing hours-long struggle. Rumor had it that despite her reputation as a thrill-seeker, adventure junkie and daredevil, she'd been so shaken by the ordeal that she planned on giving up caving altogether.

Chloe Goddard, sixteen, barely trained and with no equipment but a gift shop hardhat, had gone the brave-but-foolishly-reckless route, venturing into the caves to try and find her brother and his friends. Who, as it turned out, had been using one of the cave's less-spectacular chambers as a secret clubhouse. More young lives lost, more numbers for the mounting tally of grief. The names of Brandon Ashe, Toni Ashe and Nick Westlund had been added to the list.

Lavonne would have given an important body part to interview either Sylvia or Chloe, but both remained unavailable. The Ashes hadn't even known their son and daughter were in the caves until after, and Nick Westlund's father had only called her a nosy bitch and slammed the door in her face.

Really unfair. And damn annoying. Whether the public had a right to know or not wasn't the point. The public *wanted* to know. The public was eager to know. The public was willing to pay good money if that's what it took. Magazine articles up the wazoo. Talk shows. Soon there'd be books. Made-for-TV dramas.

And Lavonne Schwartz wanted to be right there riding the wave. She *deserved* to be. Hadn't her crew been the only ones to film the startling, miraculous appearance of Chloe Goddard, Makoto Yidori, Shara Holcomb and the guy called Griff when they had stumbled out of the caves hours after the accident?

God, what an epic moment! All of them battered, looking like war zone survivors, with Chloe leading the way despite her dislocated shoulder... a few minutes of footage, and Lavonne's hasty commentary, flashed around the globe to make them all famous.

None of them would consent to be interviewed, either! Lavonne just could not understand it. If she had been in those caves, if she had lived through the quake or explosion or collapse or whatever... if she'd survived and been able to claw her way out on raw luck, grit and determination... if she'd been trapped down there and had to be lugged out on a stretcher...

Hell, she would have told the whole world all about it! Every detail, every emotion, every nuance. She would have turned her experience into a book. Or at least a 'Drama in Real Life' essay for *The Reader's Digest.* She would have gone on Oprah's show, or Dr. Phil's, or Montel's, or all of them. She would have worked hand-in-hand with the people who made that *I Shouldn't Be Alive* show to do a faithful recreation of what she'd been through. There might even have been a movie deal in it.

Had the survivors given off *that* vibe, the vibe that said they were holding back because they intended to do those very things, Lavonne would have understood. She wouldn't have liked it, but she would have understood.

The thing was, she didn't get that feeling off of them.

Well, off most of them.

Ronette Alpert, who'd survived along with her husband and little boy but lost her father-in-law and stepdaughter, seemed disappointed to find out that Lavonne's crew was only from a local affiliate. She wanted CNN, or Fox News, or one of the major networks.

The Hinkel and Brewster families consented to some press conferences and statements, but no private interviews. Each time, it was a feeding frenzy of cameras and microphones and shouted questions. Those three girls with their matching blonde hair and adorably grief-stricken little faces were media gold. The missing one of their quartet, Tiffy, was the closest thing the Cornucopia disaster had to an official poster-child.

Lavonne wandered around the site, scrutinizing everything and hoping to see some single overlooked detail... anything... a scrap, a bone with some meat left on it. Something that hadn't already been picked over and stripped bare by her fellow hyenas and sharks.

All the accessible human-interest angles had already been covered nine ways from Sunday. The couple on their honeymoon, found crushed together so thoroughly that they were buried in a single casket. The woman who had succumbed to hypothermia in the cold, wet cave before the rescuers could reach her... found in the company of her dead husband and son.

Even Pepper the dog made the news, after being saved from Homer and Betty Crane's abandoned motor home by the volunteer rescue biker gang of Rumble, Snake and Bear.

The 'examining accidents and injuries in other local caves' shtick had been done. So had the 'what should *you* do if trapped underground?' shtick. And the 'earthquake and disaster preparedness' shtick.

There'd been interviews with people who had taken the tour before it happened, and people who had purchased tickets for a later tour that same day. Those stories boiled down to basically the same two things: "those poor, poor families" and "thank God it wasn't us."

Damn.

Two weeks, and things were milked dry. Nothing new. No miracles. No more bodies retrieved from the caves. No "in an ironic twist, one of the rescuers was killed today when..." developments.

She didn't want to believe it.

To Lavonne, it didn't feel done yet. It didn't feel finished.

What did the miners say?

It wasn't played out. Like a vein of ore. There was still good stuff to be found, if she only did enough digging in the right place.

How many times can I show them the boarded-up ticket booth? The Goddard house with its curtains drawn? The staging area, with fewer and fewer tents and volunteers each day as the experts concluded there wasn't anything more to be found? The memorial? The cave entrance and its surrounding piles of rocks and dirt, all barricaded off with sawhorses and bright orange tape? She couldn't keep showing that. The viewers had seen it. They'd be getting bored with it.

Films of action, now, those could be rerun again and again. Nobody ever got tired of those. The grainy footage of the Kennedy assassination... the Space Shuttle bursting apart in a fireball... the World Trade Center coming down... those were action. Those were dynamic. The aftermath, the debris and rubble... that got dull because it never changed.

Lavonne sighed.

There had to be more.

If she could get into the cave itself...

No such luck. She'd begged, threatened, cajoled, bribed. Five minutes in there. *I'm not asking for exclusive shots of the bodies, for God's sake. Some blood on the limestone at the most!*

With another sigh, she leaned her elbows on a sawhorse and propped her chin in her hands.

"Von?" her cameraman called from the parking lot. "We going?"

The sound guy already waited in the van, with the cute perky intern who had the cute perky tits and the winning smile and the attitude saying she thought she could do this job better than Lavonne.

Her crew, impatient. Probably more bored with this cave story than their audience by now. *It was old news. Done. Over.*

"Yeah," she said. "Give me a second."

"Sure." Bill sounded like he was checking his watch.

She gazed at the dark gap in the stone again. "Damn it," she muttered. "Just a little more. That's all I want. A little more. What do you say?"

Something moved, there in the darkness.

Lavonne straightened up, excitement prickling the fine hairs along the nape of her neck.

Movement. Yes, movement!

A figure. A person. Coming out of the cave. Coming out of the cave and into the daylight.

"Hey," Lavonne said. It was meant to be a shout.

One person. Two. Four. Half a dozen.

Kids.

Alive.

Survivors!

Kids!

Pale and dirty and looking half-starved. Their clothes hanging around them in flaps and filthy rags. Wincing as sunshine fell on their faces, stung their eyes, for the first time in two weeks.

"Hey!" Lavonne did shout that time. She gestured for her crew, barely able to contain herself from jumping around and dancing in place.

No miracles? Was I really just thinking that? No miracles?

Had she ever been wrong!

"There is a God!" she cheered, scrambling over the sawhorse to run and meet the kids as they emerged from the cave.

CHAPTER 26
Fault Lines

"It's so nice being able to go out like this," Ronette said. "We can have a leisurely dinner, a few drinks, relax, talk to people, and enjoy our evening. Without having to worry about anything at home. Isn't that nice, honey?"

Larry Alpert nodded and went, "Mmm-hmm," keeping his eyes on the road. Not so much on the road as on the other drivers. The ones that weren't maniacs were idiots. *Does nobody comprehend the purpose of a turn signal these days? Does nobody realize that there are rules of the road for a reason?*

"It always used to be on my mind," she said. "The worry. Keeping me from having a good time. I always felt so guilty about leaving Sam. Just knowing that Marcela is there puts my mind so much more at ease."

"Well, it isn't like we ever left him alone," Larry said. He resisted the urge to lay on the horn as some ditz gabbing on her cell phone allowed her hybrid to drift halfway into his lane.

"Oh, I know, honey. Marcela's just so wonderful with him, that's all. She really pays attention to him. Sam adores her. She's so devoted."

"Mmm-hmm."

"Don't get me wrong, it's not like I'd ever say anything bad about Didi."

"Mmm-hmm."

"But you have to admit it did seem like she was more absorbed in doing her own thing than in looking after her little brother. Listening to that awful depressing music, and doing God-knows-what on the computer, and just completely ignoring Sam the whole time we were gone."

"Teenagers," Larry said, in a what-can-you-do kind of voice.

"Marcela never acts like we're imposing on her precious freedom when we ask her to do something."

"That's because we pay her, babe."

"Are you saying that we should have offered to pay Didi? What next? Bribing her to clean up her own messes? You were the one who kept telling her how being part of a family meant sharing chores and responsibilities. Now you're saying we should have paid her? To take care of her own little brother? Her own flesh and blood?"

"I'm not saying that."

"I certainly hope not. You spoiled her more than enough already."

"Me?"

"Larry. Honey." Ronette patted his knee. "You were only trying to be a good father. You felt bad for her, losing her mother so young, and you just wanted to make it up to her. I understand. It's a shame that she was so selfish and couldn't see how much pain *you* were in. The more permissive you were with her, the more she tried to get away with, and when you finally tried to reassert some authority, it was too late. You decided it was easier to let her have everything her way than it was to argue with her all the time. It's perfectly understandable that she would take full advantage of that."

This was a familiar tune, background noise, part of the elevator music of his life, and Larry nodded and went, "Mmm-hmm," again. Next would be the clothes or the hair or the nose ring...

"Those horrible clothes, the jewelry and tattoos, what she did to her hair... I'm sure it was all to see how far she could push the limits. It's like she was hoping to pick a fight. Wanting one of us to say something so that she could get mad."

"Mmm-hmm. But, babe–"

"You really should have put your foot down with her, Larry. I wish you'd taken my suggestion about the camp for troubled teens. It wouldn't have been sending her away. It would have been getting her the help she needed. My God, when we heard from the school counselor about her cutting herself? I have never been so embarrassed. That woman practically came right out and accused us of being bad parents. That we should consider family therapy!"

"Babe," Larry said, and did hit the horn this time as a jackass on a motorcycle roared around them to speed through an intersection as the yellow turned to red. "Can we not talk about Didi? You know, under the circumstances?"

Ronette fell silent for a moment, then patted his knee again. "I'm sorry, Larry. I... I guess I wasn't thinking."

"It's okay." He smiled at her to prove it.

A couple of minutes later, they pulled up the Parshmans' long curving driveway and waited in a line as the hired, crisply-jacketed parking attendants took charge of the cars one by one. When it was their turn, Larry got out quick and hurried around to get the crutches from the back seat. The valet, a kid who looked like he was only doing this until he got his big break as an actor, helped Ronette out.

She was a vision in her sleek black cocktail dress and diamonds, hair spilling to her bare shoulders in soft dark ringlets, makeup expertly applied. The effect, as well as her mobility, was somewhat hampered by the plaster casts encasing both lower legs. The other arriving guests stopped to watch as Larry and the valet got her onto the crutches.

Normally, Ronette would have been mortified to appear in public with so much as a Band-Aid on display. She had gone to great lengths to conceal the scrapes and bruises. But the casts, she didn't mind letting the whole world see.

At home, she complained endlessly about them. So bulky. So uncomfortable. She couldn't take a decent shower without wrapping them in plastic. She fretted about what her feet would look like when the plaster finally came off. Pale and wrinkled. Atrophied. She'd need careful tanning sessions to even everything out again. The itch of healing bones was maddening. And so on.

You'd never know it to look at her now, maneuvering deftly on the crutches. Up the steps, across the marble entryway, graceful and gracious as she moved through the crowd. People flocked around her and her smile was sweet and sad and humble as she soaked up their condolences, their compliments.

Very sorry for your loss.

Such a tragedy.

How brave you must be, to be bearing up so well.

If there's anything we can do, Ronette, anything at all…

Larry didn't want everyone comforting him on the loss of his father and his daughter. He didn't want them telling him how strong he must be, to bear up so well under the weight of that double tragedy. When he had only just begun to put his life back together again in the past few years after Susanne's death, remarrying and starting over, et cetera, et cetera. He didn't need to cry about it or get grief-counseling to help him cope and come to terms. He didn't need to see a psychic to work through any 'unresolved issues' with his dad's spirit.

Anything he had to work through or work out, he would do it on his own, thanks. He'd take care of himself, and Ronette, and Sam. He didn't need, and didn't want, any help.

They mingled their way into the party. It was *the* event, no expense spared and no holds barred. Exquisite catered buffet, circulating waiters, musicians, full bar. Impressive guest list, drawn from business and politics, society and entertainment. This was where it all happened. Where connections were made. Where deals were made. Where *money* was made.

They'd sent in their RSVP weeks ago. Before the vacation. Before Cornucopia. Larry was tempted to skip the party, but Ronette had been through so much. Suffered so much. If coming to the Parshmans' party would make her happy, fine. He could hardly tell her no.

So, he mingled. He chatted. He drank. Probably too much. To counter the effects of the alcohol, he munched on appetizers snagged from the silver trays that went by, half the time without even noticing what it was.

Ronette staked out some central territory, surrounded by sympathetic women who fawned and cooed and hung on her every word. Larry recognized a senator's wife, a famous fashion designer, and a chick-flick star among them. By Ronette's gestures and her well-practiced saintly-martyr expression, he knew she was once again telling their harrowing tale of disaster and escape.

Larry talked briefly with a lawyer who'd heard about the pending lawsuits. He talked even more briefly with a slick studio-type who seemed to want to turn their ordeal into an action movie starring Ben Affleck. He talked for a longer while with a lovely silver-haired congresswoman who'd known his father, reminiscing.

His cell phone rang, one more electronic warble among many. Privately, he hated the things. Great for emergencies… but a pain in the ass status symbol, convenience, dependence and frivolity.

The screen showed the home number, though, and Larry knew Marcela wasn't one to call for no reason.

"Yes, Marcela?" he said into the phone.

The housekeeper – Ronette preferred 'au pair,' though Marcela's duties included far more than taking care of Sam – spoke very fast, breathless and excited, losing much of her English in the process. Larry needed several repetitions before he thought he fully understood what she was telling him, and even then he could barely believe it.

Fifteen minutes later, he found Ronette and shouldered his way into her circle of admirers. He leaned down close.

"They found Didi," he said, low, into her ear.

"Oh, honey." She looked up at him, dewy eyes brimming with sorrow. "Honey, I'm so–"

"She's alive."

Ronette's face froze. She very slowly set down a mostly-empty champagne flute. In a voice that was almost as fragile and brittle as the crystal stemware, she asked the others to excuse her for a moment.

Larry moved to help her from the chair, but she brushed him aside and got the crutches situated on her own. They wove around groups out onto the Parshmans' terrace. A warm salt-scented Pacific breeze wafted over them. Ronette leaned on the rail and propped her crutches beside her, and when she looked at him this time, her eyes were sharp rather than dewy.

"*What* did you say?" she asked.

"They found Didi," he said again, shaking his head in stunned amazement. "Ronette, babe, she's alive. My daughter's alive!"

"Larry, that's impossible. It's been two whole weeks."

"It's true. And not just her. Five other kids made it out of there. This afternoon. They just… walked out of the cave. Walked right out."

"The experts said that no one could have survived this long," Ronette said. "That there was no hope for the rest of them, the ones that hadn't been found in the first couple of days."

"I guess the experts were wrong."

"It must be some kind of mistake, Larry. Or it's someone's idea of a cruel, cruel joke."

"Babe, I talked to a doctor at the hospital where the six of them were taken. He says they're a little malnourished, some bumps and bruises, but that basically, they're okay."

"What about dehydration and hypothermia and everything else they were talking about?"

"There was water in there. I don't know about the rest. We can get the details and ask questions later. I'll have them bring the car–"

"Ah-ah-ah!" she said, raising her hands, palms out. "What? The car?"

"Ronnie, babe, we have to go!"

"Now? Tonight? This very minute?"

"It's a long drive."

"Larry, slow down. We can't just leave! We haven't even been here an hour yet. How would it look? What would people say? What would we tell everybody?"

He blinked at her. "It's only a party."

"I can't believe what I'm hearing." She shook her head, incredulous. "Only a party?"

"We're talking about my *daughter.*"

"Exactly! Once again, your selfish spoiled daughter can't stand to let us enjoy a single evening out! It's always got to be about her! Didi and her drama! She's always got to ruin things for us!"

"She was trapped in a cave!" His voice climbed over the melodic rushing of the surf, and he reined himself in as a couple of curious heads swiveled in their direction.

"It's always something with her," Ronette said. "I wouldn't be surprised at all if it turned out this was all some kind of stunt to get attention. *Ooh, let's hide down here for a couple weeks and make everyone worry, give them a good scare!* She has no regard for anyone but herself, Larry, and you know it. Of all the days to suddenly reappear, she picks today?"

"You think this was... what? Staged? Deliberate?"

"She *knew* the Parshmans' party was tonight. She knew we were planning to go. It's been on the calendar for over a month. We'd even arranged with her ahead of time, being far more considerate than she deserved, to make sure she'd be able to keep an eye on Sam. Well, she got out of *that* responsibility, didn't she? And as if that wasn't enough, she also got to spoil our evening!"

He could only look at her, shocked, open-mouthed. "Ronette..."

"Oh, Larry, honey." Ronette heaved a sigh that tested the seams of her sleek black dress. She laid her palm on his cheek. He smelled the subtle fragrance of the expensive perfume she'd daubed on her tender inner wrist. "You're a good man, and I love you, but sometimes you really have your head stuck in the sand. You've seen Didi pull this kind of thing before. You know how manipulative she can be. But because you're her father, you can be blind, or pretend to be, when you don't want to deal with the truth."

He shut his eyes and tipped his face into her hand. He took a long, deep breath. Perfume and sea air. "She's still my daughter," he said. "I can't just leave her there, sitting in that hospital, while we drink champagne."

"Serve her right," Ronette muttered, then said, "What I mean is, maybe she needs a drastic lesson to get the message, to show her that she can't keep playing these games. If you drop everything right now and run to her, she wins."

"What else can I do?"

"And what about Sam?" she asked. "You're ready to jump in the car right now and drive us way out into the middle of Nowhere, California... and leave Sam alone?"

"He's with Marcela," Larry said. "She lives in. She'll–"

"That isn't the point, Larry. What would it be saying to Sam? You know how upset he's been since the accident. He needs reassurance. He needs to know that we'll be there for him like we say we're going to be. If we suddenly just take off like that, he'll think he's not important enough for us to care about. He'll think you love Didi more than you love him."

"Well... what, then?" he asked, feeling lost, feeling helpless.

"Tomorrow," Ronette said. She rested her other palm against his other cheek so his face was cradled in her hands. "We'll go first thing tomorrow, all three of us. Okay, honey?"

"Okay," he said, exhaling heavily.

"Good." She drew his head down, and gave him a long, lingering kiss. "It's the right decision, honey. You'll see."

CHAPTER 27
Burial Ground

"What if I don't want to stay at your house? What if I want to stay at my own house? In my own room? Why do I have to stay with you?"

Greg Morris looked at Audrey's son, wishing he knew what to say. What he *could* say. Something, anything, to make this easier on all three of them.

The doctors who'd treated the kids after their miraculous reappearance said Austin was fine... physically. Better than anybody had any right to expect, given what he'd been through. He'd lost some weight, he'd lost most of his bronze summer tan, but had no injuries more serious than a sprained thumb. Nothing that couldn't be cured by a few good meals, a few good nights' worth of sleep, sunshine, fresh air and exercise.

Mentally and emotionally? That was a whole other ball game.

Poor kid.

Lost his mom, lost his sister, damn near lost his life.

Greg and Todd only spent a matter of hours trapped in the caves before Sylvia led them to safety. Even that had seemed like forever.

He could hardly imagine what it must have been like, down there in the dark for two weeks. In that black, wet, subterranean hell.

Forever-multiplied-by-infinity. A lifetime squared. Infinity to the nth power.

"Can't go home to your house right now, buddy," he said as he got out the cutting board to begin dinner preparations.

"Why not?"

"Well… without your mom… You know… since she's…"

"Dead," Austin said flatly.

"Yeah. There's nobody at your house to take care of you."

"I can take care of myself." The belligerence in his tone made him sound for a moment almost like his old self again.

Audrey always said that the quickest way to get either of her kids to do anything was to tell them they couldn't. Nothing made them rise to the occasion faster than a challenge or a dare. And she'd always said it not with exasperation – which was what Greg would have felt – but a sort of perverse pride.

"I'm sure you could," he said, being sure of no such thing. "But, you are only nine, and the law says a nine-year-old can't live alone."

He expected a litany of "that's not fair!" and "what, you don't trust me?" and "my *mom* would have let me!" None of them came. Greg glanced around to see if the boy had simply walked out.

Austin stood ramrod-stiff in the doorway between the kitchen and hall, head lowered, hands bunched into fists at his sides. His hair – the same rich brown as Audrey's – fell around his face. His eyes, peering up through the too-long bangs, narrowed. His mouth was a hard line, nostrils flaring as he breathed.

"Hey," Greg said, forcing a laugh, "I don't make the laws, buddy. You need a place to stay where there's a grown-up. No use getting mad about it."

"You aren't my father," Austin said. "You aren't anybody to me."

"Right now, I'm kind of an emergency foster parent. You wouldn't want to have been sent to live with strangers."

"I hate it here."

"Is it really that bad?" Already wishing he hadn't asked it, Greg reached for the lettuce. "You've stayed over at my house before. Remember that time you and Dallas and Todd all camped out in the living room? We moved the couches to make a big clear space and put up the tent, and you guys toasted marshmallows in the fireplace. That was a lot of fun."

Austin said nothing. His unwavering stare made Greg's skin crawl, and it took an effort to keep his hands steady as he shredded the lettuce for taco-toppings.

"After such a traumatic ordeal," the child psychologist had told him, "their shock, their stress, could manifest in any of a number of ways. Some of them are evidencing partial memory loss about their time in the caves. There's bound to be anxiety afterward, depression. Nightmares, perhaps phobias, irrational behaviors. They might have episodes of withdrawal or even outbursts of hostility."

In other words, be ready for anything.

"It's all going to work out," Greg said. "This is only temporary right now. Since your mom and I hadn't gotten married yet, your Aunt Vicky is still listed on all the paperwork as your legal guardian. It'll really be up to her."

"Then why am I here with you?"

"Like I said, buddy… you can't stay on your own. Vicky will be back from Paris as soon as she can. Until then, we thought it'd be best if you stayed here with me and Todd."

Normalcy. The psychologist had emphasized that. Not that they should try and pretend it had never happened, not that they should discount or devalue the horror of the experience. But neither should they dwell on it, make a big deal out of it, turn it into the center of their universe. Normalcy, routine, stability, security. These, she said, were what kids needed most in times of crisis.

"Dinner in ten minutes," he said to Austin, finishing with the lettuce and picking up a block of cheese to grate. "Hope you're hungry. Why don't you go out back and play with Todd for a while? I'll call you guys in when it's ready."

He thought Austin might protest, the way he often had at any suggestion to 'go play with Todd.' Greg knew that to Audrey's accomplished, athletic, energetic pair, Todd came across as a nerd and a klutz.

Austin surprised him by crossing to the back door without a single objection. He only paused long enough to don sunglasses and a ball cap before heading out into the burnished-copper afternoon.

Still with the sunglasses, Greg saw. *Still with the aversion to bright light.* He said it hurt his eyes, gave him a headache, made him want to throw up. Anything more than a dimly-lit room could do it, but sunshine was the worst. A holdover from all that time in near-total darkness, the doctors explained. Most likely psychosomatic.

Seasoned beef simmered in his huge cast iron skillet, and refried beans bubbled in a pot. Greg set the bowl of grated cheese beside matching bowls of shredded lettuce and diced tomato. He arranged the taco shells on a baking sheet and slid them into the preheated oven, then got salsa and hot sauce from the fridge.

He paused at the window to check on the boys, saw them at the bottom of the yard in a bar of shade cast by the fence. Todd had his toys and shovels spread out around a dirt-mound landscape of roads, tunnels, hose-fed rivers and bridges. He'd worked at it all summer, patient excavations and careful construction.

Even from here, Greg read nervousness in his son's face as he talked and gestured. Todd knew that Austin didn't care for such sedentary play. Neither had his sister. They'd always dismissed it as dull and boring, sit-on-your-butt stuff. Both of them preferred to be up running around, kicking a ball or throwing a Frisbee.

But Austin plopped himself down in the shade by Todd, picked up a spade, and started scraping at the loose earth.

It was a start. Better than nothing. Greg exhaled with relief and allowed himself a glimmer of hope. They might be okay here, until Audrey's sister returned from France.

The phone rang as he pulled golden-crispy taco shells from the oven. Greg slung a dishcloth over his shoulder and went to get it from its cradle in the hallway phone nook. "Hello?"

"Greg, hi, Stephen Brewster here. From, you know, the caves? Tiffy's father?"

Like I would have forgotten? They'd all met in the aftermath, bonded the way survivors of disasters sometimes did. The grief, the loss, the helplessness... and then, for some of them, the miraculous good news when that reporter spotted the six kids after all hope had been abandoned.

"Stephen! Hey. How's it going? How's Val? Her leg healing good?"

"Yeah, she's doing all right. Listen, Greg... how's Austin doing?"

The question, and the tone of it, made Greg uneasy. "He's fine... pretty much. Why?"

"Is he still having eye problems? Headaches?"

"Well, yeah, but the doctors said those would go away."

"Claustrophobia?"

"No," Greg said. "I was worried at first, especially because the guest room here is a lot smaller than his room at home, but it hasn't seemed to bother him at all. Why? Is Tiffy okay?"

"About the same," Stephen said. "Bright lights, headaches. She keeps rubbing her head, and she'll eat baby aspirins like they were M&Ms if we don't lock them up. But she's been acting, well..."

"What?"

"Kind of... weird the past couple of days."

"Claustrophobia?" Greg repeated Stephen's question back at him.

"Far from it. The opposite. She's always tucking herself in the corner or sitting under a table, and the past few nights I found her bed empty and Tiffy curled up asleep in the closet."

"That is weird," Greg said. "What would you call that, anyway? What would be the opposite of claustrophobia? Claustro... claustrophilia?"

"Agoraphobia is fear of being out in the open," Stephen said. "Val looked it up online."

"Does she go outside?"

"Not if she can help it. The girls – you know we've got Brit and Angie staying with us until Chad's in better shape?"

"Yeah."

"Anyway, Brit and Angie and Amberlyn wanted to go to the park yesterday, and Tiffy absolutely refused. I mean, threw a *fit*."

"Huh," Greg said.

"I was just wondering if Austin was having anything like that."

"No. He's outside in the back yard with Todd right now. Have you talked to anyone else? The other parents?"

"Not yet. You think I should?"

"Might not be a bad idea for us all to keep in touch," Greg said. "Do-it-yourself support group. I don't know if everybody would be interested, but I bet some would."

"Maybe I'll give it a try," Stephen said.

"But hey, don't worry too much about Tiffy. That kid-shrink said they could have all kinds of oddball reactions. So far, it sounds like we've come off lucky. I was expecting nightmares and waking up screaming in the middle of the night."

"Hell, *I* do that. So does Val. The girls are a lot tougher than us in that regard."

They said their goodbyes and Greg hung up. He went to the back door to call through the screen.

"Dinner! Come and get it or go to bed without it!"

No answer. Frowning, he pushed open the screen door and leaned out.

"Boys? Guys?"

He saw Austin, hunkered in the shade by the dirt-mound, with his ball cap pulled low, pulled all the way down to the top of the sunglasses. Austin didn't turn in response to Greg's voice. Didn't even glance around. He just scooped and dumped spadefuls of earth, patting them into place.

Todd wasn't out there, so Greg listened in the direction of the downstairs bathroom, thinking he must have come in already to wash up.

The bathroom door stood open, the bathroom beyond empty. No Todd.

"Hey, Austin, where's Todd?"

Scoop. Dump. Pat.

"Austin!"

Greg pushed open the screen and stepped out. Lazy, humid heat... the drone of bees... the heavy syrup scent of honeysuckle. He didn't see Todd anywhere in the yard. Only his favorite shovel and a bunch of cars, scattered in the dirt. Austin continued scooping, dumping, patting.

"Austin? I asked you where Todd was."

"Playing in the dirt," Austin said without raising his head.

"No," Greg said. Patiently, he thought. "He's not."

"Yes, he is."

"Austin, I'm right here looking at the dirt and he's not here."

"He's in the dirt." Austin finally looked up, or at least tilted his cap's brim and the sunglasses toward Greg. A strange smile curved his lips. "He wanted to know what it was like. Being down there. Underground. Where it was dark. Where there was hardly any light, hardly any air. So I showed him."

"What do you mean, you showed him?" Greg felt numb, felt cold. If this was Austin's idea of a joke...

With the spade, Austin pointed at a large pile of freshly-turned dirt.

"That isn't funny. Now tell me where he really is."

"I did."

"Damn it, Austin–"

"Look. You can still see part of his arm."

Part of...

Greg stared. His mind stuttered in disbelief and shock. At first he couldn't move, his feet seemingly rooted to the spot, his body seemingly paralyzed. Then, with a convulsive yell, he flung himself to his knees and pawed-scratched-scraped at the dirt.

"Todd! Jesus, Jesus, Todd!"

"He wanted to know," Austin said, standing to move out of the way. "But I don't think he liked it very much. He probably would have screamed if there hadn't been so much dirt in his mouth."

"Todd!" He uncovered a limp hand with a Hot Wheels car still loosely grasped in it. "Oh, you little bastard, you sick little fuck, you buried him? You buried him alive?"

"No," Austin said.

Greg caught movement out of the corner of his eye. Austin's arms going up. Out of the shade. Into the sunlight. Briefly. Just briefly enough for the hazy light to glint on the spade before it came down hard and fast.

The dirt-caked metal edge chopped into the back of Greg's neck. Pain flashed through him, stunning and intense. Greg pitched forward onto his face. His mouth, open to cry out, plowed through loose earth. Rocks hit his teeth. He tasted dirt. He breathed dirt.

The spade hit again. Small of his back. Biting deep.

Greg struggled to push himself up but his arms didn't seem to want to be working right. His face was full of dirt. He couldn't breathe. He was suffocating, smothering in dirt, smothering in the dirt of his son's own grave, and he couldn't get up.

Couldn't get up as the spade chopped, chopped, chopped. It furrowed the side of his neck, releasing a gush of blood to soak into the dirt in a wide muddy maroon blotch. It grazed the curve of his skull, shearing off scalp like some half-assed tomahawk.

He fell full-length on the ground, hugging the pile that covered Todd. And still the spade chopped. Between his shoulder blades. Cleaving into a kidney.

At last, the chopping was over. But he still couldn't get up... couldn't even move. He could only lay there, choking on dirt... listening to the sounds as Austin started digging again.

Scoop. Dump. Pat.

Scoop. Dump. Pat.

CHAPTER 28
Hard Candy

Tiffy wasn't the same.

She looked the same.

Mostly.

She still *looked* like Tiffy. She still *sounded* like Tiffy.

But she wasn't the same anymore.

Mommy and Daddy said not to worry. They said it was because of what had happened to Tiffy in the caves. Getting lost like that. Being down there for a long time like that. Tiffy would need a while to 'get over it.' Because it was worse for Tiffy than it had been for the rest of them.

Not counting Auntie Frieda. Auntie Frieda got killed covering up Angelina so Angelina wouldn't get hit by the rocks. Amberlyn figured that was the worstest-worst there could be.

Right after it happened, everybody told Mommy and Daddy they had to 'prepare for the worst.' That it was probably pretty sure Tiffy was *dee-eee-ayy-dee.* Dead. Like Amberlyn wouldn't know what they were spelling. She wasn't a dumb baby. She was six.

She wondered if Mommy and Daddy even noticed how much Tiffy wasn't the same. She wondered if they cared.

It was bad when they thought Tiffy was dee-eee-ayy-dee dead. Auntie Frieda and Tiffy both. Killed by the rocks. The cave people were able to take Auntie Frieda's body out, but they couldn't find Tiffy. Tiffy was gone. Disappeared.

Like Fuddles. One day, Fuddles was there eating his cat food and playing with his clump of feathers on a string. The next day, Fuddles was gone. Fuddles *stayed* gone. Fuddles didn't come back. They looked everyplace. They put up signs at the park and the grocery store. They went to the pound to see all the lost doggies and kitties, but there was no Fuddles. He was just... gone. Probably dee-eee-ayy-dee dead. Run over by a car or bit by a dog or something. Gone and dee-eee-ayy-dee dead. They didn't know for sure. They couldn't have a cat funeral for Fuddles the way they had for Tweeter-Bird.

Same with Tiffy. Gone like Fuddles. Just gone. Auntie Freida was more like Tweeter-Bird. With a funeral and everything, a funeral with a fancy wood coffin instead of a cardboard box, and at a real cemetery instead of under the peach tree.

Tiffy being gone and not even knowing for sure... yeah. It was bad. When poor Mommy was in the hospital, all she could do was cry and cry. Cry for Auntie Frieda, and cry for Tiffy, and cry because her leg was all broke. The only time she didn't cry was when the nurses gave her medicine, and that made her sleep. Uncle Chad cried a lot, too. So did Britney and Angelina, because they didn't have a mommy anymore.

But then, all of a sudden, Tiffy wasn't gone anymore. Tiffy wasn't dee-eee-ayy-dee dead. Tiffy was found and alive and okay. It made Mommy and Daddy super-duper happy. So super-duper happy that they didn't really notice how Tiffy was different.

She was, though.

She wasn't hardly the same Tiffy at all.

Amberlyn didn't like it. Tiffy felt like a stranger now. A stranger living in their very own house. In the room right next to Amberlyn's room. Wearing Tiffy's clothes and sitting in Tiffy's chair. Like Goldilocks. Except that she wasn't eating Tiffy's porridge because porridge was oatmeal and Tiffy never ate oatmeal.

And she wasn't sleeping in Tiffy's bed. She was sleeping in Tiffy's *closet*.

The stranger who looked like Tiffy didn't hardly ever play with Tiffy's toys. Not even the Barbies and the My Little

Ponies. The stranger who looked like Tiffy didn't want to watch *Kim Possible*, or color with crayons, or dress up in princess costumes.

She didn't want to go outside, either. She wouldn't go to the park, she wouldn't run in the sprinkler, she wouldn't rollerskate or hopscotch on the sidewalk. All she wanted to do was sit in the house the whole day. With the lights off and the shades pulled down.

Mommy and Daddy said to give her some time. They told Amberlyn not to bug Tiffy, not to expect Tiffy to be just like her old self right away. They were just so glad to have Tiffy back that they didn't care what she did. Tiffy was alive, Tiffy was home. That was what counted.

There were sandwiches for lunch, and carrot-celery sticks, and cheesy goldfish crackers, and green Kool-Aid. After, Daddy gave them pudding cups and said they could play in the family room because it was maybe going to thunderstorm.

Britney and Angelina didn't want to play with dolls or a board game. They were still all sad about Auntie Frieda. So was Amberlyn, but she figured she'd be a lot sadder if she was them, and it was *her* mommy who was dee-eeee-ayy-dee dead. She got out the art stuff instead. Construction paper, kid-scissors, glue, markers, glitter-pens, stamps, stamp pads, stencils, everything.

Tiffy sat on the couch instead. Looking like Tiffy – except that her pigtails were funny, not far back on her head like usual but toward the front and way up high almost to the part in her hair. There were fat blue sparkly scrunchies on them, and they stuck almost straight up.

Looking like Tiffy, but sure not *acting* like Tiffy. Of the four of them, Tiffy was the one that liked arts and crafts the most. She was good at it, too. She was 'specially good at drawing and coloring. Her pictures always stayed inside the lines.

"Don't you want to color, Tiffy?" Amberlyn asked. "You can go first with the new color book Grandma got us, if you want. See? It's all fairies and butterflies and stuff. You like fairies."

"No," Tiffy said.

"But there's fairies. Look. These ones live inside flowers. And these ones make shoes! That's silly. Shoe-fairies."

"I'm watching TV."

Amberlyn glanced at the screen. "That's a boring show. Put on something else."

"I'm watching this."

"Hey!" Britney said, looking up from her project to see what was on. "Isn't that Didi? The girl from the caves? The one who got me out of the hole?"

Amberlyn looked closer. It was one of those shows that just had people sitting on chairs in the middle of a stage, talking, while some guy went around to other people on benches in the audience. When Daddy was at work, Mommy liked to watch those shows. Sometimes there was bleeping because people said no-no words. Sometimes there was fighting and people throwing their chairs instead of sitting in them.

Britney was right. The girl in one of the chairs was the girl from the caves. The one who had been in their tour group, with the freaky pants that had all the straps and chains on them. The purple-hair girl. Lost in the caves like Tiffy, thought dee-eee-ayy-dee like Tiffy, and found like Tiffy.

"Uh-huh," Angelina said.

"Why's she on TV?" Amberlyn asked. "Why's she on this show? Is she gonna throw a chair at somebody?"

"What's she got on her head?" Britney abandoned her construction paper and scissors to scootch closer to the television.

Just then, the screen showed the audience people, because a lot of them were yelling and booing. The yelling-and-booing ones were weirdoes like the purple-hair girl. They had black clothes, staples in their lips and noses, tattoos, dog collars and dark makeup on their eyes. They seemed really mad at the other lady who'd been sitting on one of the stage-chairs, and the picture swung around to show her next.

"I 'member her, too," Amberlyn said. "She was in the caves with us. She fell and broke her feet."

The lady in the chair had dark hair and was dressed like she was going to a party. Both her feet were in casts that covered them like fat white booties.

"Yeah," Britney said. "Didi's mom."

"Stepmom," Tiffy said.

Mom or stepmom, she sure seemed mad at Didi. She was talking fast and waving her hands around. She looked all upset. Practically crying.

Didi, the purple-hair girl, didn't seem mad at anybody. Or upset. Or practically crying. She just sat there. She looked calm and kind of bored. Her hair was still purple and all kind of swept up and spiked and pinned. She had on a black tube dress with a short jacket over it. The jacket was shiny and silvery-black. It looked like snakeskin. She had silvery chains hanging from her ears, a hoop in her eyebrow and a jewel in the side of her nose.

And on her head...

"Cool," Britney said, grinning for one of the first times in days and days. "She's wearing devil horns! How do you think they stay on? Are they on a headband? A clear plastic one or something? Do they stick on with glue like those pretend fingernails Mrs. Hamilton at school wears?"

Tiffy didn't say anything else, but she slid to the edge of the couch cushion and used the remote to turn up the TV sound so they could actually hear it.

"Didi," said the talk-show guy, who had dark skin, inky-black hair, a grey suit, a black shirt and a white tie, "How long were you missing again?"

"Two weeks, Raul," Didi said.

"Two weeks," he repeated, raising an eyebrow at the audience. "Fourteen days trapped underground. In the dark, in the cold. You had water but not much food. You didn't know if you'd be able to get out. You didn't know if you'd see your friends and family again. You didn't even know if you would survive."

"That's right, Raul."

"Not only that," he said, "but you were trying to take care of how many other people? There were how many of you who made it out?"

"Six of us, Raul."

"The rest of them younger than you. Children. Children who were hurt, scared, homesick. But you all knew that you had to stay together if you were going to have any hope of getting out alive."

Didi nodded.

"You made it through," Raul said. "Two weeks. Fourteen days of misery, terror, near starvation. Against all odds, you and those children came out alive."

"That's just it, Raul!" Didi's stepmother cut in. "Against all odds, you said it yourself! All the experts said there was no chance they could still be alive down there."

"So, Mrs. Alpert, you presumed your stepdaughter was dead? You gave up hope?"

"We had to," she said, with a pouty face. "After so long–"

"How long?" Raul thrust the microphone almost up her nose. "How long did you wait before you gave up hope, Mrs. Alpert? How long until you boxed up and gave away all of Didi's possessions and redecorated her room for your live-in nanny?"

Furious shouts, jeers and boos came from the audience. Raul waved them to shut up.

"That... that isn't..." stammered Didi's stepmom.

"How long, Mrs. Alpert? Exactly?"

"We waited a whole week!" She said it fast, and she sounded the same way Amberlyn did when Daddy asked her why she ate all the cookies and she said there was still *some* left... when there was really only two or three.

"A whole week," Raul said, as the weirdoes in the audience booed again and even some of the nice-dressed people looked all shocked and frowny. "I'd like to bring out another guest now, Dolores Mitchellson. Mrs. Mitchellson's daughter Zoe disappeared on a camping trip eight years ago, and she still keeps Zoe's room exactly as–"

Amberlyn decided she didn't want to watch any more and left the room. She was only six and she knew there was going to be more yelling and maybe fights on that show. It was okay when it was on cartoons. It wasn't funny when it was real.

She peeked in at Daddy, who was going through the mail. She peeked in at Mommy, who was asleep with her leg-cast up on pillows and the book she'd been reading fallen on the floor. She peeked out the window on her way upstairs and saw the sky all dark and low and mean-looking, and some rain-spots on the sidewalk.

Her room was nicely messy. Not *bad*-messy. Not *boy*-messy. There were just lots of toys not put away. She couldn't put them away until she was done playing with them, could she? And she wasn't ever done playing with them. Big Lego blocks that made castles with princes and princesses. Dolls. Stuffed animals. Storybooks piled on her fuzzy mushroom-shaped stool. Puzzles.

When she heard someone else in the hall, she looked to see if maybe Angelina had gotten bored with the talk-show TV too. But she didn't see anybody. She heard Tiffy's door open, then shut. Tiffy kept her door shut a lot now.

If Tiffy went to her room, that meant they could watch something good, or put in a movie. *Alice in Wonderland*, or *The Little Mermaid*.

Then Tiffy's door opened and shut again, and Amberlyn heard footsteps going back to the stairs. She poked her head out and saw Tiffy walking away. Outside, thunder made a rumbling noise. The window lit up. The rain started smacking hard on the glass.

A thunderstorm might mean the power would go out. She didn't want to be upstairs alone when the power went out. Not even if it was still daytime. It'd be spooky. It wouldn't be so bad if she was with everyone else. Daddy would get out the candles and the flashlights.

Like in the caves?

Amberlyn shivered. She wished she had a bleeper in her head that would do to those kind of bad thoughts what the bleepers on TV did when someone said a no-no word.

She hurried back down to the family room. The TV was off and the craft stuff was where they'd left it, but... where was everybody? She opened her mouth to call her cousins' names. Before she could, she heard Tiffy's voice coming from under the big table where Mommy put out her Christmas village every year.

"Don't be a baby scaredy-cat," Tiffy said.

The table was dark wood with fold-down sides that almost reached the floor. It was a great place when they had friends over and played hide-and-seek.

"What's it taste like?" Britney asked. "Is it gonna be gross like those Harry Potter jellybeans?"

"No," Tiffy said. "Just try one."

Amberlyn tiptoed around to the end and bent down to look underneath. She saw the three of them in there, sitting in a triangle. Tiffy had her hand held out toward Britney and Angelina like she was offering them something.

"Whatcha doing?" she asked.

Tiffy looked around at her. Amberlyn thought Tiffy might be surprised, or annoyed, but she didn't act like she was either one. "Come on in," she said. "I've got treats."

"Really?" Amberlyn perked up. "Is it candy? What kind?"

"A special kind."

"Are they sourballs?" Angelina wrinkled up her nose. "Sourballs are ucky."

"They're not sourballs. Go ahead."

Wedging her way in among them, turning the triangle into a circle, Amberlyn tried to see what was in Tiffy's cupped palm. There were three round, white things. As big as maltballs but not chocolate-coated like maltballs. Gumballs? Gobstoppers? Jawbreakers?

Britney picked one up and sniffed it. "Tiffy, it smells funny. Are you sure they're okay?"

"You're always mad at me when I don't share," Tiffy said. "Now I'm sharing. Here. You can each have one. Just put them in your mouths already."

"But they do smell funny," Amberlyn said. "Eew. Old cheese and feet."

"Eew!" Angelina agreed.

"Do it!" Tiffy said.

The rest of them looked at each other. Nobody wanted to be a baby scaredy-cat. And if they refused this time, Tiffy might never share with them again. She could be bratty that way, after Halloween when she had candy left, or a birthday party where there was a piñata and she came home with a goodie bag full of Jolly Ranchers and butterscotches and Tootsie Rolls.

Britney sniffed again. "Is this crystally stuff on the outside sugar? It isn't salt, is it? A joke candy with salt, you know, like there's that joke garlic-gum?"

"It isn't salt, so would you just hurry up?" Tiffy was finally starting to sound annoyed.

Amberlyn hesitated. The candy was in her hand, held between her thumb and two fingers. All she had to do was pop it in her mouth.

But...

Should she?

It was only a piece of candy. And Tiffy gave it to her. Tiffy. Her own sister.

Except Tiffy wasn't the same anymore.

Tiffy was... well... kind of almost like a stranger now.

And taking candy from strangers? That was bad. That was one of those don't-ever-ever-do-it things. Don't take candy, don't get in the car, don't go with a stranger even if they say they're only looking for their lost puppy.

That was for *stranger* strangers, though!

Tiffy was her sister! Tiffy was Britney and Angelina's cousin. She had never been mean to any of them. She never picked on them, played jokes on them, or anything like that. The worst things she ever did was tease sometimes, and not share.

Angelina brought the candy close to her mouth and stuck out her tongue, but didn't quite dare lick it until one of the bigger girls tried it first.

Britney sighed. "Okay, okay, I will."

Candy... stranger... no... bad... Tiffy... stranger!

"No!" Amberlyn slapped the candy from Britney's grasp. It fell on the carpet. She grabbed it, then grabbed the other one away from Angelina.

"Ammmm-berrrr!" Angelina and Britney squawked together.

"Stop!" Tiffy said.

Amberlyn scurry-crawled out from under the table with the three candies in her fist. They clicked and scraped against each other.

"Amberlyn!" Tiffy darted out after her, snatched at her hair and got a handful, and yanked. Really hard, too!

It hurt! Tiffy had never pulled her hair like that, never-ever!

"Let go!" Amberlyn flailed and smacked Tiffy's arm. It hurt even more as some of her hair ripped out of her head, still tangled in Tiffy's fingers. But she was free, and she bolted for the door.

The clicky-scrapy-scratchy round things almost felt like they were moving around against her hand. Something sharp like a thumbtack poked at her skin. She heard Tiffy chasing her, and Tiffy was older, bigger, had longer legs, could outrun her every time they had a race.

She had a head start, though. And she didn't have to go far.

"Don't you even, don't you dare!" Tiffy hollered.

The bathroom off the family room was a little one, with no tub and no shower. It was really just for when somebody needed to go potty during a commercial. Amberlyn banged her funnybone on the edge of the door and it hurt, her hair hurt, her hand hurt where the thumbtack thing was jabbing. She had tears in her eyes so she could hardly see, and the bathroom rug slipped on the tile when she stepped on it, and she nearly fell down.

Tiffy screamed a big howling "Nooooooo!" that was like the time she had accidentally dropped her favorite Barbie into the pigpen at the fair and the Barbie got all gunked with mud and pig-poop.

Amberlyn threw the round things into the toilet. Two of them drop-splashed into the water, which was blue because Mommy put special cleanser cakes into the tank. They sank like pebbles in a pond, and clinked against the bottom.

The third stuck to her hand.

Its white surface, which sparkled under the bathroom light as if it really was coated with salt or sugar, had a bunch of tiny cracks running across it. A long dark bristly thing hooked out of the largest crack and into her skin.

She thought of eggshells. She thought of spiders.

"No!" Tiffy slammed against the door, which Amberlyn had tried to swing closed but it hadn't latched. It flew open so hard it hit the wall. A picture of a knight riding up to a castle where a lady waited in the high tower fell down. The glass broke and pieces went everywhere. Tiffy shouted again and it was a no-no word that should have been bleeped on the TV.

Amberlyn tore the round egg-seed-thing from her hand, tore the long dark bristly thing out of her hand. A bright red bead of blood oozed up. She threw.

Into the toilet. *Splash. Clink.*

Screaming and howling more no-no words, Tiffy knocked her aside and stuck her arm into the toilet bowl. Amberlyn swatted at the flusher. Missed. Gasping and panting and sobbing all at once. Tiffy scrabbled, blue water up to her elbow. Amberlyn swatted again.

Hit!

Flush!

Water swirled. Tiffy screeched and just about tried to shove her whole body into the toilet. The top of her head butted Amberlyn in the hip. A hard sharp pain stabbed her, like Tiffy had pencils in her hair-scrunchies instead of pigtails.

Tiffy rocked back on her heels, then collapsed onto the toilet seat with her forehead on her crossed arms. Her breathing was big sloppy slobbery hiccups.

"You stupid!" she said, suddenly whirling on Amberlyn with vicious fury in her eyes. "You stupid-stupid-stupid! I hate you!"

As Amberlyn goggled, so shocked she couldn't even cry, Tiffy jumped up and ran from the bathroom. Past Britney and Angelina. Past Daddy, who'd heard the ruckus and come to see what was going on. Not even glancing toward the room where Mommy was calling questions. She went straight for the front door, opened it, and plunged outside into the thunder and lightning and rain.

CHAPTER 29
Basement Dweller

"Tupp! Dude. Your brother? Creepy."

Douglas Tupper hadn't gotten two steps through the front door of his apartment, arms loaded with grocery bags and a twelve-pack, when Ozzie's voice greeted him. His keys, on which he'd had a precarious grip at best, escaped his grip and jangle-thumped to the worn, stained carpet.

"Ozzie? What the Christ are you doing here?"

"Needed a place to crash."

"I thought you were living at Tink's."

Ozzie shrugged. He sprawled on the futon, one of Tupp's last beers leaning open against his knee. Game controller in one hand, PB&J in the other. "Problem."

"Yeah?" Tupp nudged the keys out of the door's path and hooked it shut with his foot. "She finally dump your butt?"

"Dude." Ozzie looked hurt. "Nothing like that. It's her roomie. She and Tink had some huge fight. Clarissa was all *we agreed when you moved in that your boyfriend would only stay over one or two nights a week.*"

"I remember." Tupp carried the bags into the kitchenette, which was roughly the size of a public bathroom stall, and about as clean, but it did have a sink that worked most of the time, a fridge only partly taken over by colonies of mold and fungus, a microwave, and a two-burner stove with an oven that looked like it had been bought used from a crematorium.

He elbowed some dirty dishes out of the way, knocking over an aluminum can Leaning Tower of Pisa to make enough cleared counter space to set down the bags.

"She made it sound like I was mooching," Ozzie continued around a mouthful of sandwich. He had a purple jelly-smear at the corner of his mouth. "Said I didn't chip in or help out or any of that shit."

"Right." One of the grocery bags held frozens – frozen pizza, frozen burritos, frozen dinners. Tupp crammed them in the freezer wherever they'd fit. "What, she wanted you to pay rent? Just because you were living there?"

"Exactly! And Tink, she didn't want to move. So she said I should crash someplace else for a while."

"And here you are?"

"And here I am. What kind of Hot Pockets are those?"

"They're *my* Hot Pockets." Tupp opened the fridge. Nothing attacked him. The colonies were biding their time. Some night when he shuffled out half-asleep for a snack, that was when they'd pounce. "Listen, Oz, you can't stay here. The couch is spoken for. Grant's–"

"Creepy. Like I said."

"Where is he, anyway?"

"Went downstairs."

Tupp arched an eyebrow. "Downstairs? You mean, in the laundry room? Grant's doing laundry?"

"I should run a load. Can I bum some suds? And some quarters? Takes quarters, yeah?"

"Yeah, but–"

"This is pretty sweet. Apartment manager. Free rent and access to a laundry room. Nice." Ozzie grinned. "You, uh, get a lot of service calls from that babe on the third floor?"

"Anyway!" Tupp raised his voice. "Oz. Sincerely. You can't stay here. Grant, he's been through some severely major shit. Remember I told you about our grandparents?"

"Died in that cave collapse, and he got stuck down there. Two weeks yada-yada. What about your folks?"

"They're having their own problems right now," Tupp said. Talk about making a long story short. "Probably they're going to get a divorce."

"No big. Mine split when I was eleven, and I turned out fine." He drained the beer, crunched the can against his forehead, and tossed it on the floor amid a litter of similarly crunched empties.

"Anyway," Tupp said again, "Right now they can barely take care of Grandma's dog, let alone Grant. The fact that they sent him to stay with me proves how bad the situation is with them. He's been kind of messed up since the cave thing."

"Messed up? Yeah, no shit. What's the deal with the hoodie and the shades? Who's he think he is, the Unabomber? Though, hell..." After some consideration, Ozzie laughed. "Being the Unabomber would be pretty sweet. Fame, fortune and Jennifer Tilly? Dude, where do I sign and who do I have to kill?"

"Hey, Oz? You do know that the original Unabomber was a terrorist? One of those nutjobs who lived out in Montana or someplace, writing threat letters to the government?"

"No shit?"

"No shit."

"Huh." Ozzie took another bite. "Not the poker guy?"

"Not the poker guy."

Tupp eyeballed a heap of duffel bags, milk crates and lumpy pillowcases beside the futon. "You brought your stuff."

"Just for a couple days, dude. You won't even know I'm here. Hey, toss me a beer? You buy any chips? Oh, and I ate the last Pop Tart."

"Did you talk? You and Grant?" Tupp fished a beer from the fresh twelve-pack and lobbed it to Oz, who caught it without missing a beat on the video game.

"Nah. I mean, he let me in, but like I said, he was on his way downstairs."

"You mean he hasn't come back up?"

"Small apartment, dude. If you don't see him, he ain't here."

Not quite suppressing a groan, Tupp grabbed his keys from the carpet and headed for the door. "Keep out of my Hot Pockets, Oz. If you so much as open the cheese steak ones, I guarantee I will kick your ass to the end of the block."

"Jeez, dude. You don't have to threaten me. Just say so."

"Right."

The building was old, creaky, shabby, and architecturally unsound. The exterior brown brick had trim that was white once upon a time... back in the Reagan era, probably. These days, the real trim was graffiti in predominant shades of black, scarlet and orange. Rats and roaches inside, roof and fire escapes were infested with territorial pigeons. The pipes were rusty and the heating was a joke. The previous manager was shot in a dispute between rival neighborhood drug dealers and the only reason the babe on the third floor wasn't in jail for prostitution was because she had an ongoing business arrangement with the alcoholic cop on the fourth floor.

There was an elevator, but Tupp never used it. He didn't trust it. Visions of a cable snapping with a twang like a guitar string, and the box plummeting to the bottom of the shaft, went through his mind whenever he so much as glanced at it. The stairwell echoed and stank of piss, cigarette smoke, burnt greasy food, and mildew.

Hell of a fine place to live. Hell of a finer place to be in charge of. The pinnacle of his career. Manager of this festering shithole.

He had graduated – if you could call scraping by in the lowest ten percent of his class – high school and moved out while his brother had still been just a kid. At the time, he'd been convinced that success was out there, ripe and ready to be picked. All he'd cared about was getting away. Getting away from small-town poverty and small-town ideas and small-town people. Mom dragging them to church every Sunday. Dad expecting them to join him in running the hardware store, and take over for him someday. Tupper and Sons, family owned and operated. Jesus-please-us. Until the Wal-Mart had opened a few miles away.

The stairwell doors were supposedly kept locked, something that was done more in theory than in practice. Tupp passed a few new graffiti murals and blew out a breath, knowing that he should get down here and paint over them before the next time the owners did an inspection. He saw a dead rat in the corner of the bottom floor landing and a pair of soiled panties draped on the handrail.

"Grant?"

His voice echoed in the stairwell the way he imagined it would in a submarine. Not that he had any idea what a submarine would be like, except for what he saw in the movies. *God, I hate it down here.* Like he could feel the whole weight of the structure pressing down on him. Six floors of cheap apartments and thrift store furniture.

"Yo, Grant! It's me."

The L-shaped cinderblock laundry room had a single tiny street-level window near the ceiling. Anyone trying to look through it – good luck, given the current state of grime – would only have seen feet and ankles going by. Of the five washers, three worked on a fairly reliable basis. Only one of the dryers had an 'Out of Order' sign pasted to it today. Humidity-waterlogged old boxes of detergent and dryer sheets sat on the shelves and a small trash can overflowed with wads of lint scooped from the dryers.

"Bro! Hey! You down here?"

One of the washers was in its spin cycle, juddering and straining like it hoped to pull free and jounce across the room. A pink plastic laundry basket wobbled around on top of it.

A short flight of concrete steps – four of them altogether – led down even further, half-a-level to the actual basement. Pipes crisscrossed the ceiling, several of them dripping into puddles on the cracked concrete floor. The air was wet and earthy, with whiffs of musty upholstery, mold, newspaper, paint, turpentine and other less identifiable smells mixed in.

"Grant?" Tupp groped in, feeling for the light switch. He found it, but nothing happened. Cursing, he squinted until he saw the fixture. No bulb.

Terrific.

He peered around until he could make out the dim shapes of the boiler, the furnace, the breaker-boxes and gauges. Pipes and wires and tubing went every which way. He could see the shelves where various tools, paint cans and cleaning supplies were kept. He could see discarded furniture, boxes, twine-tied bales of newspapers.

What he couldn't see was Grant. *Or anybody else down here in this dank nasty–*

"Hi, Tupp."

His brother's voice, coming out of the blackness right as Tupp had been telling himself that Grant wasn't down here after all, made him jump.

"Christ! What are you doing down here?"

"Nothing. Just… sitting."

"In the dark?"

"Yeah," Grant said. "In the dark."

"Why?"

"I like it."

It was Grant's voice. Tupp was sure of that. But there was something in it… or something absent from it… that gave him the willies.

"You okay, bro?"

He heard a long, slow sigh. "I don't think so, Tupp. I really don't."

"Uh… you know… if I'd been through what you had… you know, in the caves and all," Tupp said, gingerly feeling his way down the steps, "this is about the last place I'd want to be. Doesn't it freak you out?"

"It wasn't so bad," Grant said.

"Why don't you come on up to the apartment with me? I shopped. There's food. As long as we get back before Ozzie eats it all."

"Can I talk to you, Tupp?"

"Sure, bro."

"Come over here."

Tupp swallowed. "Where? I can't see for shit. Where are you?"

"Over here."

"Let me replace the bulb. Some clown–"

"I took it out," Grant said. "I like it better this way."

"Okay," Tupp said. Chills ran up and down his spine like mice on a piano. "How about if I get a candle or something?"

"I have a candle. I'll light it… if you want."

"Uh, yeah, I want." He flinched as something wispy tickled his cheek, and brushed it away. "I mean, if you're okay. You said before that bright light hurt your eyes, gave you a headache."

"Only a little now."

He heard the scratch of match head on rough surface, and then a small flame flared, turning the black to deep gloomy greys and purples. Grant touched the match to a fat candle stub sitting in an upended jar lid.

"I kind of set myself up a place here," Grant said. "Found this chair, rearranged some of this old furniture." He patted his chair, an avocado-green recliner with vinyl so cracked and split it looked mauled by a tiger.

"Yeah?" Tupp asked, inching forward. He found a tubular chrome stool with a red leatherette seat, the kind of thing that had probably been salvaged from a going-out-of-business diner, and swung it around to sit across from Grant.

"I didn't think anyone would mind." Grant sat forward in the recliner, elbows on his knees. He wore baggy, too-large jeans, unlaced high-top sneakers, and a navy-blue fleece hoodie with a St. Louis Rams logo in faded yellow on the front. The hood was up, shadowing his face.

Not shadowing it quite enough for Tupp to miss the fact that he still had his sunglasses on. Shit, he *did* look like the Unabomber.

"Grant… bro… what's going on? What's up with you?"

"I don't really know," Grant said. "Not for sure. Something… Tupp, something's happening to me."

"Do you need a doctor?"

"No. I saw doctors."

"Yeah, they said you were fine. Great, all things considered. I meant more of a psychologist-type doctor."

Grant smiled. "You think I'm going crazy?"

"Bro, you're in a dark basement with sunglasses on. Tell me how that's anywhere near normal."

"Tupp, do you believe in the devil?"

He rocked back on the stool a little. "The devil? As in, the Bible? Hellfire and brimstone, red guy with a pitchfork and a pointy goatee?"

"Or whatever. Devils, demons. Do you believe in them? Do you believe in demonic possession?"

"Whoa, hey, hang on." Tupp laughed, but it was forced and he knew they both could tell. "I hope you're not trying to tell me you think you're possessed by the devil. That you're going to start spewing green puke and spinning your head around like that chick in the movies."

"No," Grant said. "No, I don't think that."

"Then... uh... what?"

Grant leaned further forward. "There are life forms that can survive in environments so hostile to humanity that we can't even imagine what they'd be like."

"Sure," Tupp said. "In the deep oceans and–"

"In caves."

"Yeah. In caves. Grant, what's this all about?"

Grant stuck his hand into the hole in the cylindrical part of a threadbare carpeted cat tree beside his recliner. He brought it out slowly, carefully, and extended it toward Tupp. As his fingers uncurled, the candle's meager light revealed something in his palm.

Something no bigger than a hamster, but nothing like a hamster. Spiny like a porcupine, like a prickly pear... but not a porcupine, not a prickly pear. Covered with dark, shiny chitin like a bug... but nothing like a bug. It had clusters of tiny horns like a desert lizard... but was no lizard.

Tupp frowned, thinking it was a toy, thinking Grant was playing some weird joke on him with a freaky little plastic monster he'd picked up at a novelty store or from a cereal box.

Then it stirred. It moved. It raised its head and flicked out a tiny greyish tongue.

"What is it?" Tupp whispered.

"An imp. I call him Spike."

"Grant... bro..."

"You wanna see something else?"

I don't. But he nodded, unable to speak.

Grant pushed back his hood. His hair hung like a shaggy mane, unkempt, tangled, tousled and long. It still couldn't cover, couldn't *hide*, the thick horns that curled down from the sides of his head.

CHAPTER 30
Metamorphic

Nine messages. Nine! Nine messages on her machine, all from that Lavonne Schwartz woman. The reporter. Nine messages! All of them saying the same thing. Wanting more. Always wanting more.

How is R.J. 'adjusting' to being home again? How are they 'adjusting' to Rich's death? To R.J.'s miraculous return? How are she and Megan 'adjusting' to their own close call?

'Adjusting.'

The word made Melinda Carson want to scream.

How do you 'adjust' to being a widow before age thirty? How do you 'adjust' to raising two young children without their father?

How *do* you 'adjust' to having your husband's body brought up from a cave, bled dry and full of puncture holes from being impaled on jagged crystal spears?

How *do* you 'adjust' to fourteen days of anguish, not knowing the fate of your precious little boy and being told by everyone that you had to prepare for the worst?

When she brought in the mail, she found letters from more reporters. Requests for interviews, offers to fly the three of them to Los Angeles or New York to be on this show, that show. A fat manila envelope turned out to be notes, an outline, a cover mock-up and a sample chapter from someone who wanted to ghost-write her story and rush it into publication as a true-life novel. Another turned out to be a package from a children's clothing company, gifts for R.J. and a slick-worded invitation to have him appear in their commercials, with the implication being that their brand of sneakers had contributed to his survival.

Trash, trash, trash. She chucked all of it in the trash.

All that mattered now was R.J. He was alive. He was with her again. *We're home. The three of us will just have to do our best to pick up the pieces and move on, build a new life without Rich.*

At least she had her son back. At least there was that. R.J., safe and sound. Fine and well. Good appetite. Sleeping through the night with no bad dreams.

Well, he did prefer sleeping *under* his big-boy bed instead of *in* it now, but was that so irregular?

They would be all right.

Not wonderful. It could never be wonderful with Rich gone.

But all right. They would be all right. They'd get by.

They passed an evening as ordinary as an evening could be. Routine dinnertime, Megan's bath, all of them cuddling up on the couch for a story. Then R.J. went to play in his room while Melinda got Megan settled for the night. Within minutes, the baby conked out with her fingers in her mouth and her blankie clutched close to her cheek. Awake, Megan looked more like Melinda. Asleep, the resemblance to Rich came through.

Melinda went to look in on R.J., who sat on the floor surrounded by blocks, Fischer-Price toys, and dinosaurs. "How's it going, sweetie?" she asked, sitting on the end of his bed and hugging a stuffed raccoon to her chest.

"Okay," he said. "My feets hurt."

"Your feet?"

"Uh-huh. They don't like my shoes."

"Do they pinch your toes?"

He shrugged. "My feets just hurt."

"Well, you're probably outgrowing them. Why don't you take off your shoes? It's almost jammie time anyway."

"They look funny."

"What do, sweetie?"

"My feets."

The doctors had checked over all the kids, and proclaimed them amazingly healthy, considering. No serious injuries. Bumps on the head, skinned knees, like that. Electrolytes out of whack, minor malnutrition. The headaches and aversion to bright light? Chalked up to eyestrain, or psychological stress.

Nothing to worry about, they said. Nothing at all to worry about.

Melinda worried anyway. She couldn't help it. She was a mom. It went with the territory. Who knew what kind of strange germs and viruses might have been down in those caves? What if R.J. came down with something that took a while to incubate?

So far, he'd been okay. *Until this.*

"What do you mean, sweetie? What's wrong with your feet?"

"They just hurt and look funny." R.J. moved a spiky-shelled dinosaur to menace the Fischer-Price airport. "My toes click when I gots no socks on."

"Your toes... click?"

"Uh-huh." He scratched his head. "And I'm itchy."

Her spirits sank. Last year, there'd been an outbreak of head lice at the Kinder-Club. A huge hassle. Special shampoos, washing everything, stuffed animals sprayed and sealed up in plastic bags.

But R.J. hadn't been back to Kinder-Club yet. She wanted to keep him home until she was sure he was ready, and until she felt able to let him out of her sight again.

Germs and viruses. What if he'd been exposed to something in that cave? What if he was allergic, and it had taken this long for the symptoms to really show up?

R.J. set down the dinosaur and dug both hands into his hair, really scratching away like mad. His eyes went half-lidded and he reminded her of a dog she used to have. When Sparky got scratched in exactly the right spot, his hind leg would twitch and his eyes would go exactly like that.

Melinda winced, imagining nits and lice being shed all over his room. "Mommy better check your hair," she said. "Remember the lice? Oh, I hope we're not going to have to go through that again. Come here and let me look."

He shrank away, holding his hands protectively splayed over the top of his head. "I'm okay!"

"Let me see, R.J."

"No lice-bugs!"

"Mommy's got to check to make sure."

With a big despondent sigh, he hitched himself over so that he was within reach. Melinda put down the stuffed raccoon and bent to inspect his hair. He'd been washing it himself in the tub lately, combing it himself, so proud of his big-boy accomplishments that she and Rich agreed to overlook the occasional bad rinse job or missed tangle.

"Lean your head forward," she said. "Let me look back here by your neck. Good. Now tip it that way so I can see your ear... okay... and the other way... good. No bugs yet! I'll just–"

Her fingers, taming curls and parting the hair to expose his pink skin, found a hard bump. R.J. jerked and uttered a brief yelp, and squirmed out of her grasp.

"Did that hurt? Oh, sweetie, Mommy's so sorry! You've got a big lump on your head and Mommy didn't realize it. I thought your owies were all better."

"I'm okay," he said again, hands once more raised protectively.

"R.J., I need to see."

"No."

"Let Mommy see your head."

"Hunh-unh."

"I won't touch."

He gave her the dubious scowl he always gave the pediatrician upon being told that an injection would be 'a little pinch.'

"I'll just move your hair out of the way so I can look," she said, and crossed her heart. "Promise."

Grudgingly, he held still. She parted the curls again, and bit back an alarmed exclamation.

Thoughts whirled and spun through mind: How late was the urgent-care open? Would she have to take him to the emergency room? Who could she get to come sit with Megan, or would she have to lug the baby along as well?

Somehow, she kept her voice steady. "R.J., what's this on your head?"

"I dunno."

"Does it hurt?"

"It itches."

"Do you have other itchy places like that?"

He nodded, and pointed to a spot a few inches over. Melinda raked more curls out of the way until she saw the source. Another one. Another… what?

Ticks? Were they ticks of some kind? Enormous bloated dark-brown ticks clinging to his scalp?

Scabs? Swollen goose-egg lumps covered with crusty scabs of dried blood?

"Are these the only ones?" She heard the words come out, heard them still in that steady, nice, normal concerned-but-not-hysterical mothering tone. "Or do you have other places that itch like that? What about your feet?"

"My feets don't *itch*," he said, like she was being stupid. "Just my head."

"How long has your head been itchy?"

R.J. shrugged. "I dunno."

Melinda looked again. Not touching, because she'd promised. Just looking. Looking at reddish, irritated skin around the base of two lumps roughly the size and shape of thimbles, poking up from the top of R.J.'s scalp. A fine layer of velvety rust-colored stuff that made her think of flocked wallpaper covered the lumps, except where R.J. had scratched it away flecks and flakes. Underneath, she could see a shiny brownish-blackish substance that looked solid and hard, like bone or fingernail.

They look like antlers.

That was crazy, and she tried to reject it.

But they do.

Tiny, budding baby-antlers. Like those of a fawn.

"I know I said I wouldn't touch," she began.

He was halfway across the room like a shot, hurting feet or no hurting feet. "You promised!"

"I'm sorry, sweetie, but Mommy really does have to–"

To what? R.J. was sprouting horns. Horns!

"Okay," she said, holding up both hands to show she was harmless. "I won't touch."

He stayed where he was, watching her as she slid from the edge of the bed and slumped leaning against it.

Call someone? But who? She could just hear herself trying to talk coherently to a 911 operator, or medical hotline nurse. What would she say? What *could* she say? If she told anybody, sooner or later it was bound to get out. The reporters... God, what would the reporters do? Their lives had already been on display more than she'd ever wanted.

Horns. Those were *horns* growing from his head.

She didn't know why. She didn't know how. It made no sense.

Little boys just didn't suddenly start having horns grow out of their heads.

If people found out...

Would they take him away?

They would. Someone would. Doctors at first, wanting to study him. Scientists. What next? Ominous men-in-black from shady government agencies? Conspiracy freaks and alien abduction believers? Crackpot cultists who thought he was the Antichrist?

Melinda burst into tears.

R.J. stared at her, then joined in.

"Mommy?" he sniffled. "Do you still love me anymores?"

"Of course I do, sweetie," she said, trying to collect herself. "Mommy's just... Mommy's just trying to figure out what's going on. Why you have those... things... on your head."

"Are you mad at me?"

"No. No, R.J. I'm not mad. Can you come here and give Mommy a hug?"

He came to her, and she saw that while he wasn't limping or hobbling, he wasn't exactly walking normally either.

She drew him into her arms, suppressing a shudder because this was her son! *This is R.J., the same R.J.* He felt the same, he smelled the same.

So he had horns? So what?

"I'm sorry, Mommy."

"Don't be, sweetie. You didn't do anything wrong."

He snuggled into her lap and she held him, both of them there on the floor at the foot of his bed with toys and stuffed animals all around, and posters of animated characters on the walls. Melinda rocked her body back and forth, crooning low the way she did to comfort the kids when they weren't feeling well. She rested her cheek atop R.J.'s head and felt the twin nubs of those baby-horns through his hair.

"Do they hurt?" she asked after a while. "Can you feel them? Or are they like fingernails?"

"They're itchy," he said. "They hurted some before but only some. When they comed up."

"Like when Megan's getting a new tooth?"

R.J. nodded.

"I think the itchy will go away," Melinda said. "Do you remember when we saw those deer at the zoo? And they were rubbing their antlers on the tree trunks? The zookeeper said it was to scrape off the fuzzy stuff. I bet it's the same thing."

"Are they gonna be antlers?"

"I don't know, sweetie."

He was silent for several seconds, then asked, "What about my baseball hat?"

"Probably be kind of hard to wear a hat with antlers," she said.

"Yeah, I guess so."

They sat and hugged and rocked.

"Can I look at your feet?" she asked. It only dawned on her now that she hadn't seen him barefoot in several days. Always with shoes, or at least with socks, when before she used to have to remind him to put something on his feet before he went outside.

Not that he's been going outside much, either.

"Okay." He removed his shoes, then glanced warily up at her as he was about to pull off a sock.

"I won't be mad," she said.

His feet were... changed. Or maybe *changing* would be a better word. Instead of being five individual little pink jellybean-shaped digits per foot, his toes looked sort of crunched together with a deep cleft, up the center. Not webbed like a duck's, but... *melded? Fused?* The toenails had also fused, and were longer and thicker... plated, almost... curling under.

"See?" R.J. extended his legs, bare feet sticking out.

"Hooves," Melinda said softly. "They're turning into cloven hooves."

"What's that mean?"

"You know how horsies have hooves, right? Well, some animals, like deer and goats, have hooves that are split in the middle."

"Oh." He studied his feet.

She didn't know what else to say. What else was there to say?

R.J. asked, "Am I gonna hafta live in the zoo?"

"No!" She squeezed him tight.

"They aren't gonna put me in a cage or maybe in the circus?"

"I won't let them."

Hearing him give voice to some of her own fears only made her wonder how in the world she'd be able to keep the promise she'd just made. *What am I supposed to do, confine him to the house forever?* But she couldn't very well take him out in public with horns and hooves! To the mall, to the park, to the grocery store... let alone the doctor's office for regular checkups... Kinder-Club and school would certainly be out of the question!

"I'm kinda scared, Mommy."

"I know, sweetie. I am, too."

"I wish Daddy was here."

"So do I. Oh, I wish that so much."

"How come the skylops had to go and kill Daddy?"

She went still, almost holding her breath. The children who'd come out of Cornucopia two weeks after the cave-in had hardly said anything about what happened in there. They said it was dark, they said it was scary, they said they were hungry and only wanted to go home, and couldn't remember anything else.

"The skylops?" she asked, keeping her voice gentle. "What's that, R.J.?"

"Wasn't really a skylops," he said. "That's what Tiffy called him at first but he was really just a guy. Except he wasn't just a guy."

"What was he?"

His reply sounded like a name, but an unfamiliar one that she could only fumble with.

"Paul Nader?" she echoed.

"Uh-huh."

"And he's the one that…" She choked down a sob. "He's the one that hurt your daddy?"

"Uh-huh. Cut him and pushed him on the sharp rocks. Then he took me away to the stinky cave with the monster-faces and the yellow in the walls. They had all kinds of horns. Bunches and bunches. He took all of us there. He put handcuffs on our feets."

He trembled, and she stroked him, soothed him. "It's okay, sweetie."

"There was a pit," R.J. said. "With people in it. Dead people. Except the one girl. She wasn't dead yet when she went in the pit. The imps got her. And the skylops-guy, he had the seed things. I think they were seeds. Maybe they were eggs."

Seed things? Eggs? Imps?

R.J. snuggled against her, quiet for so long that she might have thought he'd fallen asleep, except that she could still feel the tension and trembling in his body. His *Bob the Builder* clock marked off two whole minutes before he spoke again.

"Mommy? You know the guy with no hair? The guy who worked at the caves?"

"The tour guide?" She couldn't remember his name. Dobbs or something.

"Uh-huh. He was there, too. He fighted with the skylops, but the skylops won. The skylops killed him. Like he killed Daddy. Stuck him with a big twisty horn."

Melinda had no idea what to say. "Paul Nader did that?"

He nodded. "Right before the seeds he gaved us."

"What seeds, R.J.? Like the ones we planted in the window boxes?"

"Not flower seeds. They were all white and round and stinky. I think maybe they were imp seeds. Or eggs. I dunno, Mommy, I dunno!"

"Shh." She patted his back. "It's okay. Just tell me the way you want to tell me."

"I can't 'member no more," he said. "Except Grant and Didi helped me climb, and carried me when I got tired."

"That was nice of them. What happened to the skylops?"

R.J. frowned thoughtfully. "I dunno, Mommy. I guess he's still down there in the caves. I guess."

CHAPTER 31
Spiral

"Mr. Yidori," Nolan said, leaning back in the leather chair and crossing his leg so that his sleek black wingtip rested on the opposing knee, "I can't do the job you're paying me to do when even *you* are holding out on me."

Thomas Yidori's marble-topped desk looked large enough to park a car on. Yidori's executive chair had the height advantage, and he also had the impressive backdrop of a floor-to-ceiling, wall-to-wall plate glass window at his back. On a clear day, Nolan was sure, the view would have been staggering. On a damp night like this one was, thick fog diffused the lights of San Francisco. Forty-three stories up, Yidori's office could have been floating on a cloud.

"Is this your way of telling me that you have made no progress?" Yidori gave a slight hoist to one thin brow, his lips pressing into a line. He had the steady eyes of a hawk, a full head of lush black hair dusted silver at the temples, and the outward serenity of a jade idol.

"It's my way of telling you that I have a few questions I need answered before I can go on," Nolan said.

"In other words, you've made no progress."

"Did I say that?"

"You have not yet found my daughter."

"And you're not exactly going out of your way to make it easier for me." He grinned. His *disarming* grin.

Yidori didn't disarm. "I am not in the habit of making things easier for people, Mr. Nolan."

"Well aware of that." He dropped the grin and put on a serious look. Focus and concentration. "I thought that in this case, you'd make an exception. We're not doing a business deal here, Mr. Yidori. This isn't about contracts, negotiations, politics. This is about Kimmy."

Yidori inclined his head. "Very true, Mr. Nolan. You'll have to forgive my guardedness. The privacy of my family is of the utmost importance to me."

"More important than their safety?"

Ding! Point for Nolan. He let himself swagger a little. Only a little. And on the inside, where Yidori wouldn't notice. Fun as this might be, he had to remember that it was no joking matter.

"What is it that you wish to know?" Yidori asked. He minutely adjusted his cuffs.

Nolan decided to take that as a sign of nervousness. Possibly even of capitulation. On their previous meetings, Yidori had been still as a stone.

"For starters," he said, "I'd like to know why you came to me."

"You were recommended by an associate," Yidori said. His tone suggested this associate might not be getting a thank-you gift basket for the recommendation.

"Nice to hear, but not quite my point. Why a private investigator at all? As your move of first resort, I mean. If you believed your daughter had run away from home, why not contact the police? If you had reasons to suspect a kidnapping, why not call in the FBI?"

"I did not want to involve the police. They move too slowly and are too bound by procedures. They would not assign much priority to the search."

Nolan gave a wry twist of his mouth. "I don't know about that."

"Why?" The other brow arched this time. "Because I am a wealthy man with many influential connections?"

"That's certainly part of it." Nolan tried not to show how he was impressed with that eyebrow trick. Most people could only do it with one or the other. Not both. They weren't... *ambi-eyebrow-dextrous.* "There's also the media attention."

A swift, pained look tightened Yidori's features. "Let us not forget that."

"After what happened at Cornucopia," Nolan said, aware that he poked at a sore spot and kind of getting a kick out of it, "your son and his girlfriend – excuse me, his *fiancée* – being lucky to make it out with their lives, your daughter missing and presumed dead but then miraculously reappearing two weeks later..."

"Yes, yes." Yidori made a get-on-with-it gesture.

"The news coverage, the magazine articles..."

"I assure you, Mr. Nolan, I know all too well about that. Which is a substantial factor in my desire to keep this new crisis quiet."

"What about your daughter's medical problems?"

Jab! Left hook out of nowhere! Yidori never saw that one coming!

"Medical problems?" He hooked a finger into his shirt collar, tugged at his tie, then regained his composure. "As I'm sure you know, Mr. Nolan, the doctors said that aside from a few scrapes, Kim cam through her ordeal in exceptionally good health."

"So, then..." Nolan did a minor wardrobe adjustment of his own, pinching the sharp crease on his slacks. "She was at the Bayview Clinic for some other reason? Something non-medical? After all, that was where she was the last time anyone saw her before she went missing."

He's reeling, ladies and gentlemen. He's on the ropes and the challenger is moving in for the TKO!

"My son has been seeing specialists at Bayview Clinic," Yidori said. He seemed to have realized what his hands were doing and brought them under control, laying them flat palms-down on the smooth marble.

"Reconstructive work, of course," Nolan said, nodding. "Putting his jaw back together. Fixing his teeth. I understand he's going to be on a liquid diet for quite a while, poor guy. I had my tonsils out when I was a kid and after about a week, I was plenty sick of Mom putting my food through the blender."

"We're not discussing Makoto, Mr. Nolan. Kimmy–"

"Wasn't visiting her brother at the hospital, Mr. Yidori. He was released two days before she disappeared. I know she wasn't there to pick up something he'd left behind, either. She had an appointment of her own."

"How do you know that? You have no business sticking your nose–"

"You hired me to snoop around," Nolan said, with a casual shrug that was anything but casual. "What was it you said? That you hired a P.I. because you wanted someone who wouldn't be 'bound by procedure'? I know your daughter was at the Bayview Clinic, and I know she was there to see Dr. Gaines, and I also know that Dr. Gaines is a cosmetic surgeon."

Yidori did not gape, but he did stare. Some of the color had drained from his face.

"Now, see, that's the part I don't get," Nolan went on. "Kim wasn't badly injured in the caves. I've seen pictures of her that were taken after. I saw her on the news. I've talked to people in Elk Lake, and I even talked to that reporter, the Schwartz woman, the one who was there when they came out. Everyone agrees that she wasn't disfigured in any way. So why did she have an appointment with a cosmetic surgeon? She's eleven years old, so we can rule out botox or boob jobs."

He's down! Yidori is down! The champ is kissing the canvas!

The office went pin-drop silent. Yidori braced his elbows on the table and massaged his temples and forehead. He rubbed his eyes. He pinched the bridge of his nose. When he met Nolan's gaze again, he looked haggard and tired, like he'd aged a decade and hadn't gotten a single good night's sleep the entire time.

"So, what's the matter with Kimmy?" Nolan asked, pressing it. "What was she doing there? Why did she run away? If I'm going to find her, I need to know. I understand your desire to protect your family's privacy. Having something like that splashed all over the newspapers and tabloids… but I'm on your side here. You hired me. I work for you now. If I'm going to earn the money you're paying me, I need to have the tools necessary to do my job. I can't find out where your daughter is if I don't know what's going on."

"Fair enough, Mr. Nolan. You make a very valid argument."

With a deep breath, exhaled in a long sigh, Yidori rose from his chair and turned to face the window. His pose was so classic that Nolan wondered if he rehearsed it. Shoulders squared, head high, hands clasped at the small of his back. Nolan could see a ghost of his reflection in the glass, against the dark fog-blanket and the diffused spangles of city lights.

"This is… very difficult," he said. "What I am about to tell you, I doubt you will believe. Not even Dr. Gaines believed it, until she saw for herself in… and even then she insisted on taking x-rays to rule out the possibility of a hoax. A hoax, Mr. Nolan. Do I seem the sort of man who would perpetuate a hoax, under these or any circumstances?"

"Not at all," Nolan said. "After what your family's been through? I'm sure it would have been the last thing on your mind."

On Thomas Yidori's mind, maybe… but Nolan also knew that the dust of that cave-in hadn't had a chance to settle before there were opportunists popping out of the woodwork, eager to get themselves a nice slice of the attention pie as well as an *a la mode* scoop of whatever financial results came with it. Some were victims or relatives of victims. Most weren't. Most only wanted to be able to put it behind them and move on with their lives.

"When we received word that Kim had survived," Yidori said, "we were overjoyed. We didn't care about being on television or any of that. We only cared that our daughter was alive, and we could bring her home."

Nolan nodded, figuring that if he could see Yidori's reflection, then Yidori could see his. He said nothing, though as Yidori continued to describe the first few days after Kim's return, he made the occasional encouraging noise and kept on with the nodding.

"She was fine at first," he said. "Withdrawn, yes, and shaken, but much her usual self. We had her see a therapist. He used the term 'flat affect,' are you familiar with that term, Mr. Nolan?"

Flat affect was psych-speak for zombie, but Nolan wasn't going to say so. "Non-reactive. Blunted. Indifferent. Apathetic."

"She began spending most of her time alone in her room," Yidori said. "Often with the lights out, because she claimed that the brightness hurt her eyes and gave her a headache. We became concerned. Then we noticed..."

His voice trailed off, and he took another deep breath.

"Noticed what?" Nolan asked.

"At first, we thought it was... a blemish, a pimple. Eleven seemed young to be getting acne, but, given the recent stress..."

"Sure. My sister used to break out like crazy right before finals."

"We bought her the usual washes and creams," Yidori said. "They had no effect. The spot grew larger. Day by day. It... swelled. The skin became furious red, inflamed. Kim said that it was tender, painful to the touch. And that it felt hard. Not filled with fluid, like a blister or boil would have been. Hard. Like a carbuncle. We made her an appointment with a dermatologist, but the night before she was to see him, the... growth, the lump... it split."

"It popped?" Nolan envisioned blood and pus and watery serum, and tried not to wrinkle his nose.

"No, Mr. Nolan. It split. The skin split. There was something underneath it. A conical extrusion of bone."

"Excuse me?"

"We canceled the appointment," Yidori said. "We didn't know what to do, were terrified of making the wrong move, of drawing attention. The last thing any of us wanted was more sensationalism. Can you imagine? We didn't want our daughter turned into the media equivalent of a sideshow freak!"

"Mr. Yidori, back up a couple steps. What, exactly, are we talking about here?"

Yidori turned from the window. "A horn, Mr. Nolan! A horn growing out of my daughter's forehead." Yidori brought his hand from behind his back, curled it into a loose fist with the index finger sticking straight out, and held it to the center of his forehead so that the outthrust finger pointed up at approximately a forty-five degree angle.

"A horn," Nolan said. "You mean like a... a... unicorn horn."

"It grew at a shocking rate," Yidori said. "In two days, it measured six inches from base to tip. It resembled ivory. Twisted into a spiral."

"A unicorn horn," Nolan said again.

"I am not making this up, Mr. Nolan. *That* is why my daughter was at the Bayview Clinic. She was going to Dr. Gaines to have that thing removed. Now do you understand why we went to such efforts to be secretive?"

"Yes." He also understood why Dr. Gaines had sounded so off-kilter during their phone conversations. She'd given him the usual spiel about confidentiality, but under it... "I understand. What happened next?"

"Next? Next, Kim vanished from the clinic. Since there have been no demands, I have to assume that she left on her own." Yidori dropped into his chair again. His shoulders were slumped, and he looked defeated. "She was reticent about the hospital, about the surgery, but we agreed that removing it was the only option. What else could we do? She couldn't go through life with a horn growing from her forehead. I don't know why she would have done this. I don't know where she could have gone. Something like that... it can't be hidden, Mr. Nolan."

"Could Dr. Gaines be involved in her disappearance? Wanting to study her or something?"

"Emily Gaines is a cosmetic surgeon, not a mad scientist."

Nolan studied him across the cool marble gleam of the desk. What Yidori was telling him was insane and impossible. *A girl with a unicorn horn?*

"Mr. Yidori, I'm having kind of a hard time with this. Not that I'm accusing you of lying or anything. But how could something like this happen?"

"It's only a private clinic, not a prison–"

"Not how she got out of Bayview. How she could grow a horn out of the middle of her head. That isn't..." He waffled between 'normal' and 'possible.'

Yidori spoke before he had to choose. "The cave. Something in there, something deep underground. It did something to her. Changed her. *Infected* her. I don't know. But in my heart, I am certain it's because of that damned cave."

"So how come it hasn't done anything to the other survivors?" Nolan asked.

Both eyebrows went up. "How do you know it hasn't?"

"*Touché.* Okay, then... let's say that Kimmy did leave the clinic of her own volition. If what you're telling me is true, she's kind of got to stand out in a crowd. You can't really hide something like that. So where is she? Where would she go?"

"I believe," Yidori said, "that I'm paying you to answer those questions."

Nolan resisted – barely – doing his Daffy Duck '*touché* number two!' impersonation.

He did some haggling with Yidori, hoping for a release of information that would give him permission to look at Kim's medical records. Particularly those x-rays Dr. Gaines had taken. He doubted they'd do him a hell of a lot of good in finding the girl, but he had to see for himself.

Later, after he'd left the office and taken the long elevator ride to the opulent lobby, after he'd tipped a wink to the night receptionist and gotten a glare from the security guard, after he'd trundled through the brass-and-glass revolving door and emerged into the cool mist, Nolan hailed a cab and had it take him to his favorite martini bar.

Most people, when they thought of a private investigator hanging out at a bar, would picture a seedy lowlife dive filled with cigarette smoke, or maybe a titty bar that was a front for a crime boss. Not someplace like this, upscale, trendy, modern.

But then, most people still heard the words 'private investigator' and thought trench coat and fedora, telephoto shots of cheating spouses through the blinds of no-tell motels, and getting pistol-whipped by muscle-bound thugs while tied to a chair in some abandoned warehouse.

"Ah, the good ol' days," Nolan muttered, removing his laptop from its case and setting it up on the little round table in his usual back corner booth.

He ordered a club sandwich to go with the first of what he expected to be three or four drinks, and munched on Cajun-seasoned dried chickpeas. While he sipped and snacked, he also surfed.

By the time his sandwich arrived, he had barely lowered the level of his second martini. His attention fixed on the laptop's screen, mesmerized. Inside him tingled building sense of having walked right into something big.

Did Yidori know any of this? He couldn't. He would have said so.

Did it connect?

It had to connect. Too much of a coincidence otherwise.

Nolan flipped open his cell phone. What with mellow jazz and lively bar chatter, he wasn't worried about being overheard from way back in his cozy corner.

"I've been doing some checking on the others," he said when Thomas Yidori answered. He talked fast, so he could get his say in before the barrage of questions and demands began. "It's not just Kim. Most of them are gone. Ran away, like she did. Or disappeared under weird circumstances. *Violent* circumstances."

He heard a few sharp intakes of breath from Yidori, a few blurted half-words Nolan steamrollered right over.

"The teenage girl who was on TV with her stepmother? Well, the stepmother's dead and the girl is missing. The boy who lost his mom and sis, and got taken in by mom's boyfriend? Boyfriend and *his* kid are both dead and the boy's long gone. Cops are looking at the kids themselves as suspects."

"Suspects?" Yidori did manage to get that entire word out.

"This is big," Nolan said. "Listen, I'm sending you an e-mail, links. Something definitely bizarre is going on with all of them. I'd bet my life on it."

Chapter 32
Earth Mother

They survived.

The brood-spawn-young-offspring.

She had formed them of her body. Shaped them, sheltered them, nurtured them, given them life.

These special ones. The six who went above, curled within their hosts as they had once curled within their protective shells. Hatched, bonded, growing and thriving.

Adapting.

As all of her kind had adapted so long ago.

This was a return. The beginnings of a reclamation. What had once been theirs would be theirs again.

Slowly. Gradually. In time.

There was an endlessness of time.

How many ages had passed since they were driven below the surface? She did not know. Ages enough that water had carved out new caverns from solid rock and adorned them with decorations made in increments, drip by drip.

Ages enough that the dust was finally washed from the skies, and the small furry creatures rose up to claim the world that had once belonged to her kind. When they had been many, and mighty, and strong.

Her sense of the broodlings was keen. They were always unsure at the start. Clumsy. Afraid. Alone. They cringed from the vast openness and harshly burning sun.

But they survived.

They matured, and gained control.

Her spawn were tenacious.

These ones would succeed.

Others had tried in the past. Tried, and failed. Not through any fault of their own, but through the fault of their human hosts' fellow creatures. Who had comprehended enough to fear. And enough to kill. And to make their myths, their lore.

Demons. Devils. Monsters. Dragons. Gargoyles.

Fauns. Satyrs. Manticores. Minotaurs.

Incubi. Succubi. Lamias. Fiends.

Giants in the earth. Titans. Cthonians.

Countless underworlds of cold blackness or gaseous heat.

Horns cut from heads, holes cut in skulls. To let out the evil spirits.

The club-footed, the hunch-backed, the deformed.

Bodies drowned. Bodies burned.

Rites and rituals. Exorcisms and sacrifices.

To some, she was a dark goddess. Worshiped, hated, dreaded, revered. Honored and placated. Beseeched and abhorred. They knew her by many names. None of which were true. All of which were true.

Until mankind had forgotten.

Until the subterranean passages and rivers shifted, until caverns became closed off by rockfall, earthquake, avalanche, glacier. Until tribes had moved on, abandoning or shunning their former homes.

Until reason had come, and science, and talk of her kind was cast aside as superstition.

Now and then, nonetheless, bold broodlings had ventured above. Their forays were short-lived. They were hunted and slaughtered, or driven far into the wilderness. Only legends persisted.

This time, these ones...

They would thrive.

Their hosts were young, healthy.

The bonding transference had taken place while the broodlings were still in their shells, freshly spawned and barely developed. They had hatched within. They had not been left weak and helpless to wriggle their way toward living flesh. They had not been forced to compete with each other. They had not needed to crawl in through some orifice or burrow through skin to find sustenance and safe haven.

Perhaps because of that, perhaps because each had hatched within the host, able to affix itself at once to the soft inner throat lining, all six had taken. Not a one had been rejected by the host's natural defenses.

She was well pleased with her brood.

And with the pollinator.

Her drone, her servant. Protector of the lair. Bringer of the hosts.

He tended them well during that initial change, as the broodlings sent their tiny questing hooked tendrils into the brain stem, along the nerves. When the incubation was nearly complete, he led them to the surface.

Now the next stage in their metamorphosis had begun.

By the time the swarm-spawn hatched, those six would be ready.

The hive-host screamed at her approach. A feeble scream, despairing, mindless, devoid of hope. Warm, milky fluid sloshed as the hive-host made a futile effort to lurch itself out of the pool.

"Cut the shit, Colin," the pollinator, once called Rory, said to the hive-host. "You're not going anywhere, so just quit it, cut it out, cut the shit."

Again, the hive-host screamed. It heaved and wallowed. The only parts of it that still seemed almost human were its hands – desperate clutching clusters of fingers waving from the quivering mass – and its head. The rest was a swollen, fecund sac that almost overflowed the shallow limestone depression.

Half-grown broodlings moved over it in a ceaseless rhythm of grooming. They nipped away pallid white patches of dead skin, and sealed the raw and weeping old wounds with plugs of jellied secretions. Pulsing waves of sound and vibration issued from them as they sought to give comfort to their unborn siblings.

The pallid mother-goddess crouched over the hive-host and pressed her seeding-horns against the thin, slime-coated outer membrane of its skin. She felt momentary resistance and then a piercing-through, a sinking into gelatinous warmth. The hive-host shuddered. A wailing cry of misery spilled from its still-human mouth.

Broodlings scurried up onto her, adoring and attentive and seeking to nurse although they were past that need. She let them.

Indulgent. Proud.

A gathering rush tightened, then flowed out of her in a surge. Each seeding-horn opened. Each ejected a stream of swarm-spawn. Tiny dark motes, swirling and dispersing, issued forth from her in a warm gush.

Swarm-spawn. Hundreds of them. Joining the thousands more already teeming inside the hive-host's body.

There, she knew, they would eat and grow and multiply. When they were near to hatching, she would have the pollinator take the hive-host to the surface.

The hugely bloated sac would burst. The swarms would be released.

And the six, her special offspring, would be there to guide them.

ABOUT THE AUTHOR

Christine Morgan works the overnight shift in a psychiatric facility and divides her writing time among many genres. A lifelong reader, she also writes, reviews, beta-reads, occasionally edits and dabbles in self-publishing. She has over a dozen novels in print and more due out soon. Her stories have appeared in several anthologies, been nominated for Origins Awards, and given Honorable Mention in two volumes of *Year's Best Fantasy and Horror.*

She's a wife, mom, and possible future crazy-cat-lady whose other interests include gaming, history, superheroes, crafts, and cheesy disaster movies.

http://christine-morgan.net/

www.ingramcontent.com/pod-product-compliance
Lightning Source LLC
Chambersburg PA
CBHW031249170626
46807CB00001B/51